Basket of Rain

Basket of Rain

To Jean

Read & Enjoy

Moya Goatley

Moya Goatley

EMILY PUBLICATIONS

Copyright © Moya Goatley 2000
First published in 2000 by Emily Publications
47 Dulwich Wood Avenue
London SE19 1HG
United Kingdom

Distributed by Gazelle Book Services, Falcon House
Queen Square, Lancaster LA1 1RN

British Library Cataloguing in Publication Data
A catalogue record for this book is available from the British
Library

ISBN 0-9539304-0-8

Typeset by Amolibros, Watchet, Somerset
This book production has been managed by Amolibros
Printed and bound by T J International Ltd, Padstow,
Cornwall

For Ma & Pa with much love

"Sometimes in life, you've got to dance like nobody's watching."

Guy Clark, American singer

Chapter One

If I choose to wear carpet slippers to church it is of no concern to anyone but myself and possibly my Maker. After eighty-nine years walking this earth the least I am entitled to is comfortable feet." Doris Roberts glared at her neighbour. "Thank you for calling anyway, Mrs Cronin."

"*Interfering busybody,*" she thought. "*Go and find a more suitable case for your do-gooding and leave me in peace. What is the wretched woman babbling on about now?*" Begrudging both the time and effort Doris forced herself to listen.

"…so I said to Harry, 'Harry,' I said, 'that Mrs Roberts needs looking to…all by herself in that big old house since her hubby…passed on. However does she manage?…going to church in slippers…it's not right,' I said. 'I'm not going to let another day go by. I'm going to pop in and see the old lady, have a bit of a natter. That'll do her good,' I said, 'buck her up a bit, nice bit of company'."

Doris fingered her hearing-aid. Sometimes people grew sparing with their attentions if they thought that you were very deaf. Mrs Cronin was made of sterner stuff.

"Nothing like a bit of a chat is there, dear?"

She raised her voice.

"I said, 'There's nothing like a bit of a chat, is there, dear?' Cheer you up a bit."

"*Go away,*" shouted Doris in her head. "*Dear God! What have I done to deserve such torture?*"

Aloud she said, "Now, if you would excuse me."

She made as if to stand but pain, with fiery fingers prodded her to reconsider. Reluctantly easing herself back, she tried to be resigned to the chirping of the falsely cheerful voice. Doris Roberts closed her eyes and a feeling of dread took hold of her. She was trapped by age and arthritis, trapped by this insensitive creature who was stealing her afternoon. Left to herself, who knew what she might be doing, reading perhaps; though to start a new book might require a leap of faith in the future. She may have been listening to music or writing a letter, watching a silly quiz on television, doing a crossword or just dreaming and remembering, sitting by the window enjoying the weak winter sunshine. She would rather do anything than be stuck here with this silly prattler.

She had rights, did she not? One heard of animal rights, lesbian rights, civil rights, any number of rights. What about an old woman's rights? Life was short. The life remaining was too short to waste. How many afternoons could reasonably be left to her? It was a question she had pondered from time to time, calmly, philosophically, never shying away from the inevitability of death. Now the thought made her breath catch in her throat. Her heart seemed to skip a beat then raced uncomfortably. She felt cheated. Why should she have to put up with this annoyance? Surely at this stage of her life there was some element of choice.

Slowly panic and anger gave way to a new resolve. "*My life is still in my own hands. I have spent a great deal of my time being thoughtful and polite, pleasing others. At least this fool has made me realise that I do not have the time any more. I am going to have things my own way from now on.*

"*If you were a fly I would swat you,*" she thought with venom. Her eyes flew open. She felt strangely exhilarated.

"I should like you to go now," she said firmly.

There was scarcely a pause before her neighbour plunged into another torrent of words.

"Oh! It's no trouble. Now, don't you worry. I have all the time in the world."

"I do not," said Doris.

"Yes, well I was saying dear, you must get so lonely. I dare say it's hard for your son and daughter to look after you. People lead such busy lives nowadays, not that I blame them but there's no time for the elderly and the infirm. Loneliness can become a habit so don't forget I'm just on the doorstep. You only have to call, just call and I'll be there to help. Mind you I never have a moment to myself. You know what they say—'If you want something done ask a busy person'."

Mrs Cronin laughed without mirth.

Doris stiffened. "*Hard for my son and daughter to look after me indeed! I am neither a pet nor a lunatic. Oh! What is she saying?*"

"Harry says I do too much but I say it doesn't cost anything to be cheerful and show a bit of sympathy, take people's minds off their problems, eh! Harry worries about me, oh!—but you don't want to hear my…Do you get a lot of pain with your hip, dear? Have you…?"

"*Pain I can come to terms with,*" Doris thought.

She answered, "Mrs Cronin, thank you for coming. I am quite sure your husband is right. My family is in constant touch and I am not lonely. I shall not need your help in the future. Please go now."

"Just you remember what I said, dear," said Mrs Cronin, taking not the slightest offence at the old woman's curt tone. "I'll just pull the door closed after me so you don't have to move."

With her departure, the room seemed to grow chill and dark. The silence was not comforting.

"*If only I could move,*" Doris thought.

Mrs Cronin's visit had somehow brought her life into sharp focus. Just a few hours before she would have said that she was content enough, seeing few, keeping herself apart, not questioning the direction her life was taking. Indeed what direction could it take, save towards the grave? Now she was seeing her life in a different light and she did not like what she saw. She was old, alone and in pain, helpless. What use was she to anyone? Had she not over-stayed her welcome? Frank, her husband, was dead. Her children's children had children. All of them led full, busy lives. They loved her, of course they did, but they did not need her. They had asked her to live with them but she had preferred her independence. She had lived her life, let others get on with theirs.

Slowly the afternoon light died as Mrs Roberts sat on battling against an alien self-pity.

"*Must pull myself together. Damn the woman.*"

She felt lost, as if a fog had descended obliterating her path…or…or was it that the path ended here in loneliness and fear?

"Oh God," she begged, "don't let me think such thoughts!" God, was it fair to call on Him? In all honesty, had she not always used Him as a sort of spiritual Insurance Policy, a Divine Stopgap in times of trouble? What premiums had she ever paid? Did she have the right? Had she ever had the right?

"Frank," she whispered. "Frank, help me."

"Come on, old girl, do buck up your ideas. Plenty worse off than you."

Doris could almost hear the scornful words.

"Easy for you," she retorted, "no 'mortal coil' and all that. Don't be so bloody patronising."

"That's better," said her dead husband cheerfully, "have a bit of spirit. Fight back."

Doris fought. Slowly the small hard core of her earlier resolve revived itself and gained in strength.

As if awaking from a dream she became aware of her physical discomfort and slowly raised her hand to wipe away unaccustomed tears.

Her immediate problem now was getting out of the chair. Her limbs were stiff from sitting too long in the one position. Gripping the arm-rests, Doris attempted to heave herself up but her hands would not support her weight.

4

Again and again she tried. Whimpering with the effort she did not at first hear the diffident voice. "D'ya know yer door was open?" The old woman was startled.

"Who are you?" she asked sharply. "Never mind. Come in. Come in. Put on the light."

"Can I 'elp?"

Doris took a deep breath, swallowed her pride and said firmly, "Yes."

With infinite patience the girl helped the old woman to the bathroom and found a cardigan to wrap around her trembling shoulders then gently rubbed the cold hands back to life. Together they went into the kitchen where Doris slowly and painfully made tea. She felt grateful that the girl seemed to understand that she had to do this for herself. She had to keep active. One of life's ironies was that, when young, though full of energy, you spent an unconscionable amount of time lazing about but, once old and you could do with a rest, you had to keep moving for fear of seizing up.

Back in the now warm sitting-room the girl explained that she had come as part of the community care project being run from the school. She and her classmates had to find an elderly person who would appreciate a regular visit and perhaps a bit of a helping hand.

"I was scared when the door was open and you was all in the dark," she said.

"Could not even close the door properly," muttered Doris. "Stupid woman." She shook her head.

"I would not appreciate a regular visit. I do not need help." She tried to soften her tone. "No, child. I do not want to be an experiment. I do not need anyone coming in."

She was grateful, she said, for the help she had received but she was weary.

"You go and find someone else," she said in a kindlier tone. A thought struck her. "How did you choose me?"

The girl laughed. "Just live up the street, innit? See ya

at yer window all the time. Don't ya make me?"

"Oh! Bless me. Child, I can't tell one of you from the other."

The girl stood up.

"I'll be off then," she said in a steely voice.

Doris felt puzzled. Something icy had dispelled the burgeoning warmth between them. What had happened? She had expected the girl to try harder. Would it really be such a bad idea to have a regular visit? It might be interesting to observe the younger generation at close range. Almost for the first time, she studied her visitor and suddenly she understood. "Oh wait!" she cried, flushing slightly. "How could you think I meant?…oh Lord! I can't tell one of you apart because you are all so young, not because you're black."

The two stared at one another. It seemed a long time before the girl nodded and said, "D'ya wan' me to come then?"

Doris paused. "Shall we try it for a while? Only you, mind. Don't go telling everyone that I need help because I don't. I have a family of my own."

The girl nodded without comment.

"You know," said Doris reflectively, "I like this street now. It used to be rather quiet and dull. Now there is a bit more life to it. What with the fruit shop opening up and all you young people coming and going these days somehow there seems to be a lot more colour about the place."

They caught each other's eye and giggled. Doris felt a bit light-headed.

"You must forgive me. I have quite forgotten my manners. Tell me, child, I still do not know your name."

"Me real name Rita but dey call me Ritzy, Ritzy Johnson."

Doris smiled. "It suits you. Good afternoon, Ritzy Johnson."

Chapter Two

Doris lay in her warm morning bed with her eyes closed. She felt at peace with herself. Yesterday, unexpectedly, she had come to a turning point in her life.

"*Good for the brain to have a shake up every now and then,*" she thought. "*Drifting, that is what I was doing, just drifting, queuing at God's door.*"

The old woman opened her eyes and turned to face the window where wind-lashed rain battered itself against the panes and ran diagonally across the glass.

"*I will not be going out in my slippers today,*" she smiled to herself. "*What a day to start a new life! But, a new life I am going to have.*"

Old and arthritic she might be and no stranger to pain, but she had enviable advantages. She had her children's love, few money worries and, above all, an active brain.

"*I need an interest. That girl Ritzy seems to be a nice child despite butchering the English language. I think I did the right thing in letting her come to see me so long as she understands that I have no wish to be peered at by a lot of strangers. Let her classmates find their own old person for themselves.*"

"Oh! Who is that? Mrs Evans?" She reached for her hearing-aid.

"Well, who else would it be, might I ask?" said Mrs Evans entering the bedroom. Her smile swiftly became a frown.

"Still in bed. That's not like you. Not feeling well today?"

"I am feeling very well indeed," replied Doris. "Do take off those wet clothes. Shall I make you a cup of tea?"

"My goodness! We are feeling energetic today. I'm supposed to be your help, not the other way around."

The woman laughed as she removed her headscarf and shook her damp hair free.

"Believe me, you're in the best place. You just stay there if you're happy. You look comfortable enough."

Doris shook her head.

"No, I must get up. I have come to a decision and I have plans to make. I am going to please myself from now on."

"Going to be a lady of leisure then, eh?" asked Mrs Evans, bustling about the already spotless room.

"No indeed. I do not mean that at all. I'll have enough rest in my grave. I am going to take more of an interest in things. My brain has been somewhat absent of late. Yesterday, a child, well, a young girl really, came to see me as part of a school initiative. I did not recognise her yet she lives in this street."

"You want to be careful who you let into your home, love."

"I certainly will," said Doris dryly. "Interfering busybodies, do-gooders and bores will definitely be excluded."

Mrs Evans helped Doris out of bed.

"I'll just go and sort out your breakfast while you dress if you think you can manage. I'm glad you seem brighter. Do-gooders, whoever could you mean? You wouldn't be talking about Mrs Cronin by any chance would you? She means well, poor soul. I don't think her marriage is very happy."

Doris grunted non-committally. From the kitchen, slightly off-key singing vied with a different tune on the radio. The conflict was curiously comforting.

"I am doing all right, Frank," said Doris softly as she made her way to the bathroom.

The morning passed swiftly and happily. Mrs Evans dusted and chattered. Doris listened with only half an ear. Her mind was racing. Mrs Cronin had been right in one respect at least. The house was big, much too big for one old woman. Since turning the ground floor into a self-contained flat, the rooms upstairs lay empty. They were frequently inspected and aired but they were a source of concern. Their waste often distressed Doris. One heard so much about homelessness these days. Well, she would talk to her daughter about it again. Could there really be any harm in giving someone a home?

"Your family rung yet?" asked Mrs Evans.

"No, not yet. Have you time for a small sherry before you go?"

"Bless your life, no. I've got to do my old gentleman. Miserable bugger he is, if you'll pardon my French."

As soon as she heard the door click shut Doris began to prepare vegetables. She prided herself in cooking a proper midday meal. It was a slow business but it gave her satisfaction. Then she poured herself a gin and tonic. She and Frank had regularly taken what they called their "pre-prandium libation" during the years of his retirement and now she kept up the routine. It was the time of day when she generally felt at her best. The daily ritual was now perhaps the clearest echo of life as it had been before his death.

While her lunch cooked she sipped her gin and spoke to Frank. Shortly after he had died, when the pain of her loss was almost physical, Doris searched desperately for some connection with him. Panic gripped her when she could not even bring his face to mind. He seemed to have gone completely from her. One day she had switched on the radio, unable to concentrate, just letting human speech fill the silence. Gradually it was borne in upon her that it was a personal problem phone-in.

"My dad's passed away," wept a youthful voice, "I know it sounds silly but I can't find him no more and I wanted to tell him tons of things."

"Write him a letter," said the advisor crisply. "Get out a piece of paper and just write him a letter."

"*Stuff and nonsense,*" thought Doris. Nevertheless she reached for her notepaper and did just that. For weeks she wrote whatever came into her head of good or bad or inconsequential, the myriad, random things which make up a life. One day Frank was there. She could feel his presence in the room. The fact that he seemed to be disagreeing with her did not detract from the relief she felt. From then on her letters took on a lighter, more bantering tone. When arthritis made writing too painful, she had got into the habit of setting aside a short time to talk to him.

Deep in her thoughts, she did not at first hear the telephone. When at last she lifted the receiver, it was to be greeted by the impatient voice of her daughter.

"Where were you, Mother? I was worried."

"Good afternoon, Joyce," Doris replied calmly. "I'm not so swift as I once was."

"How are you today, Mother? You're not going out in this dreadful weather are you?" The tone was abrupt.

"No, dear, I am not going out." Doris was patient, wondering why her daughter apparently equated old age with idiocy.

"Good. Robert's suffering dreadfully with his back and I think I may be coming down with a chill so we may not be able to get up to see you this weekend."

"That's all right, love," said Doris equably.

"Well, we are both getting on, you know, Mother."

"I said it's all right, darling. Listen Joyce, I was thinking about the rooms upstairs. Could we not...?"

Her daughter drew in a sharp breath.

"No, Mother, not another word. It's far too dangerous. Don't you read the newspapers?...all the dreadful things that happen? Now please put it out of your mind."

"Yes, dear," said Doris submissively and after a few more exchanges hung up.

"*Oh! Dear! Joyce by name but there is nothing joyful about that woman. Poor girl, she's always had the world on her shoulders.*

I'll just have to talk to Gareth, see what he has to say about it."

Once lunch was over and cleared away, the old woman sat by the window. Rain continued to pour down. Water streamed along the gutters, splashed the hurrying feet of passers-by, shapeless and anonymous beneath raincoats and umbrellas. Groups of young children on their way home from school gleefully stamped in the puddles while their harassed mothers chivvied them along. Small boys stood over the gratings, giggling while the water bubbled over their wellington boots. Mr Panano from the grocery shop opposite shooed them away, and they ran off, shouting with laughter. Doris smiled at the sheer joy on their faces.

She watched them out of sight then turned her attention to a cryptic crossword. After a few moments, she gave up. Today she could not concentrate. Restless, she wanted to start her new life. There must be something even someone of her years could do to fill the days that were yesterday revealed to be empty. Doris shook her head to rid herself of the negative thought. *"Never could abide whinging."* Still, life with Frank had been full and active. She smiled ruefully, remembering times when she would have welcomed a brief respite from involvement in her husband's varied interests and enthusiasms.

There had always been another journey, at home or abroad, a visit to yet another historical site, ancient monument or relative (both ancient and modern); a concert or lecture to attend, Grand Prix to be followed, research to be undertaken into the latest subject to engage their curiosity and imagination.

Doris shifted impatiently in her chair. Where could she start to recapture the verve and vivacity of those days? One had learned to anticipate the frisson of never knowing if an evening would end in blood-raising argument or helpless laughter.

A solitary figure caught her attention, head bent low, shoulders hunched almost sideways in a vain effort to avoid the downpour. It was a miserable day to be out...and yet…and yet! Would it not be exhilarating to feel the rain on your face? Would not the struggle make you feel alive?

"Dear God, if I ever get to heaven may I please have a little spot where it rains just every now and then? Dear God, let me not live or die without contrasts."

Good, the older children were beginning to put in an appearance. Duffel-coated girls talked animatedly to baseball-capped boys who seemed oblivious to the deluge through which they walked. Doris followed their progress, feeling unaccountably anxious. Just as they were passing her window one of the girls threw back her hood in a gesture that clearly said, "Now d'ya make me?" and grinned up at the old woman. Doris waved. She relaxed. This was what she had been waiting for. In a little while she would do a few jobs. There was work to be done. First, she must get out some of her old French language books. It crossed her mind that she might be able to find someone in need of a bit of tuition. Her French was not bad; at least she had few difficulties understanding the French output on the World Service. Good idea that! *"Doris Roberts, you are a genius."*

A knock sounded at the door. With difficulty she got up from the chair and went to answer it.

"You all right, Mrs Roberts? You need me?" asked the breathless woman on the doorstep. It took Doris a moment to recognise her visitor.

"Mrs Panano, what can I do for you? Come in, do not stand in the rain."

The woman stepped into the hall.

"I run when I see you wave. I think you need help."

"I was waving to my friend. I don't need your help, thank you," said Doris and immediately regretted the coldness of her tone. This was no way to behave. Independence was one thing, rudeness quite another.

"I am sorry," she added. "I'm getting to be a crotchety old woman."

Her neighbour laughed. "It's the weather. I'm glad you're all right. We like to keep eye on you, you know!"

"No, I didn't know," murmured Doris, genuinely surprised.

She stood at the door watching Mrs Panano running back across the road to the grocery shop.

"*So kind, and all this time I had no idea they knew me at all.*"

She shook her head in wonder.

"*Where have I been? I feel that I have been asleep for a long, long time. Frank, was I always so blind?*"

Gareth rang that evening.

"Mother, what's this I hear about you wanting to take in lodgers," he said without preamble.

"*Joyce has wasted no time,*" thought Doris.

"Well, it does bother me, Gareth, as you know. It seems so selfish. I was not very kind to Joyce this afternoon. She said she had a chill and I'm afraid I did not pay her much attention." She smiled ruefully. "I realise I should not have mentioned the flat to her."

"Mum, you know Joyce, she worries about the grass growing because she's not in direct control."

"*At least Gareth is prepared to listen,*" thought Doris as she replaced the receiver.

Chapter Three

January battled its wet and windy way through to February. Doris had so much to keep her occupied that she was not too distressed to be confined to the house. Gareth, as promised, came down to London to discuss his mother's plans for the future. He persuaded her to abandon thoughts of filling the upstairs rooms, at least for the moment.

"After all, Mum, you never know when any one of the family may want to descend on you to see the bright lights."

Her son nearly lost the argument at that point.

"Hmm," grunted Doris. It was not a family habit "to descend" unannounced and in any case all but one of the great-grandchildren were below the age of twelve and therefore most unlikely to take such an initiative. Their parents and grandparents never seemed to have a moment to indulge in whims.

Keeping such thoughts to herself, she agreed to wait until she had given the whole thing a great deal more thought. To an extent she appreciated and understood the reasons for her family's objections. It was not as if she needed the money and it would entail too much worry and responsibility, for them as well as for her. Perhaps they were right...perhaps.

Gareth was quite encouraging about the tuition idea.

"Why don't you ask that girl, Ritzy, is it? Didn't you say she was taking GCSEs? If she's not taking French herself, maybe one of her friends..." He bent over and kissed his mother on the forehead. "Keep the old brain box in trim eh! Good luck with the new career."

When he had gone Doris sat in a sort of glow. The words "new career" buzzed around in her head.

"*Ridiculous, absolutely ridiculous,*" she told herself, failing utterly to suppress a giggle.

"*Frank, what a lark! Eighty-nine and a new career.*"

Preparations had to be made. She read French novels, ordered a French language magazine from the newsagents and brushed up on her grammar. Most days one or more of the family rang to chat and to find out how she was getting on. Sometimes Doris found herself frantically wondering who was on the other end of the line when a voice said "Hello Gran" or the words that gave a special thrill, "Hi! Great-grandma."

Ritzy visited regularly. She was a bright, articulate girl who amused greatly with tales of school and her large family. A lot of the talk was incomprehensible, spattered as it was with talk of CDs, the net, DVDs, e-mail, PCs and other technical-sounding terms. All were spoken in a curious mix of the accents of the West Indies and South London. Doris sometimes stopped listening to the meaning to relish the flow of the words.

"I'll ax 'round 'bout the French," said Ritzy; "maybe closer to exams there'll be a few sweatin'. Don't suppose they could pay though, maybe 'elp ya out a bit eh!"

"Now, Mother, don't do anything silly," said Joyce, "like advertising in a shop window or in a newspaper. You never know who you might attract.

"*That sounds a good idea,*" thought Doris.

"No, dear," she said obediently. "Joyce, love, I am only going to offer a few hours of French conversation a week. There is absolutely no need for you to worry. You know I have done something of the sort in the past."

"Oh! Mother, you're not going to resurrect that old story, are you? When people don't understand, it can be so embarrassing. If you're in need of companionship why don't you go to the club attached to your church? So much safer for you."

"Joyce," said Doris with asperity, "swapping ailments over sticky buns and weak tea with a lot of old folks is not my idea of fun and no, I can't guarantee that I will not be an embarrassment to you."

She sighed as she put down the phone. Poor Joyce, so caring, so careful and so exasperating. Revive the old tale indeed! Why should she not tell people that she had taught conversational French before? Nothing very remarkable in that, except that it was in Paris, in a brothel, at the behest of a Scottish lady who had said it would be good for 'her girrrls'. Doris smiled at the memory. Well, how was she, as a young girl newly arrived, to know that there was anything untoward in the arrangement? How could she, a well-brought-up young lady, be aware that the shabby, gentile, rather dusty house she visited of an afternoon was "known" in some exclusive circles or that the primly dressed girls, who habitually looked a little tired, were not as carefully shielded from life's little oddities as she herself was? One is so accepting when one is young.

"Now, what's on the agenda for today?" Doris spoke aloud. It somehow made her feel more purposeful. "Now let me…Oh! Lord. No. Not today! I couldn't stand it."

Out of the corner of her eye she caught sight of Mrs Cronin making for her front door. She let her head drop forward, feigning sleep. It might work. Anything was worth trying to avoid a woman who made you aware of every unacknowledged wisp of fear and every nuance of ignored pain.

"*If I was as bad as she makes me feel I should be quite happy to go to my grave,*" Doris thought.

Nothing seemed to deter Mrs Cronin from her mission to befriend the elderly woman, neither polite requests, subterfuge nor plain speaking had any discernible effect. Even calculated rudeness drew only a sympathetic pat, the words "It must be so difficult and painful for you, dear" and a promise to return soon.

"*Dear God,*" Doris prayed with eyes shut tight, "*please find that woman another purpose in life soon.*"

The doorbell sounded persistently. With a sigh its owner hobbled to meet her fate. Well, she could not play dead all afternoon, could she?

"I saw you at your window, snoozing, and I thought to myself, I thought a doze is all very well but a person needs a bit of company. Then you'll sleep better tonight eh! Aren't I right, dear?"

Doris waved her in, pointing her stick towards the sitting room. Her visitor placed a chair opposite hers in the window and there they sat, practically kneecap to kneecap.

"*Please God, I am so sorry if I am using You…but…!*"

"Did I tell you I had a visit from my son recently?" asked Doris, feeling suddenly inspired. Perhaps if she talked a lot it might temporarily stanch the mind-numbing flow. Mrs Cronin looked surprised to be given voluntarily this scrap of information. Her mouth flew open but before she could utter a sound Doris plunged on.

"So good of him to come in this dreadful weather all the way down from Suffolk. He and Rose, that's his wife, you know, have just moved to a smaller house. Of course having so much to do, settling in and so forth, Rose could not come with him this time. Such a shame! Her name is really Rosaria, Irish girl, a really pretty name do you not think? She is a grandmother of course but I still think of her as a girl." Doris came to a breathless halt.

"Did you mind?" asked Mrs Cronin solicitously.

"Mind!…mind her being a grandmother!" said Doris in some surprise.

Her companion's face flushed slightly. "No, dear. I mean your son marrying a—" she lowered her voice "—an Irish girl."

Doris stared, puzzled. "Why on earth should I mind?"

"Well, you know, the fighting, all that shooting and the bombing and all…and—" Mrs Cronin emphasised each syllable: "a diff-er-ent re-lig-ion…Ro…man Cath-o-lics."

Doris felt an overwhelming urge to laugh. She covered her mouth with a trembling hand. "We're all…children of God," she managed, willing her face to match the piety of her words.

She must remember to tell this to Rose. Dear, delightful Rose.

"Mrs Roberts."

Doris started at the sound of her name.

"I am so sorry," she murmured. "I was miles away."

Mrs Cronin looked apologetic. "Are you all right, dear? I hope I didn't upset you…you know….bringing back painful memories and all…you must have had such worries. I think you're very brave."

She shook her head and stood up, smiled sadly and left.

Doris sat and watched Mrs Cronin cross the road to the shop. The small, huddled figure looked somehow …defeated was the word that sprang to mind. She shuddered, a lump rising unexpectedly to her throat.

"*Poor woman, poor, silly woman.*"

"No," she said emphatically "I will not be brought down."

She took a few deep breaths.

Gradually her clenched hands relaxed.

"*Now, how should one word an advertisement on a postcard?*"

She switched off her hearing-aid so as not to be disturbed and set to work.

Chapter Four

The wet days dried out and the wind all but died. Doris ventured out to the library and to the church but the leaden grey skies seemed to press down on her and the deepening cold chilled her bones.

"I had better be careful until the weather improves," she mused. *"If I catch something they will never let me alone. Heaven forbid. Let's just keep the activity mental."*

For the next few days she allowed herself to be pampered a bit more than usual by the willing Mrs Evans. She read a lot, prayed a little and welcomed few. Appropriately, the vicar called in that period. He was a young man whose joy in his religion was apparent. He spoke in a pleasantly familiar way about his Maker, as if God had just popped out of the room and would be back any second to sort out the odd problem that may have cropped up in the meantime.

Doris respected him for his hard work and dedication but mostly she was grateful for his lightness of spirit. Neither of them could understand why some people treated God with stuffy solemnity when it was perfectly obvious that He had a sense of humour.

"Come in, Andrew, how nice of you to call."

The man entered quickly, grinning hugely and rubbing his hands together. "Doris, have you a cup of tea on the go? It's freezing out there."

Doris could not help but smile back. "Of course I have," she said warmly.

The vicar sat at the kitchen table, chatting desultorily while his hostess made and poured tea. Gratefully he cradled his steaming mug in both hands. "Ah that's better. How are you coping with this cold, Doris?"

Doris slowly raised the tea to her lips and took a tentative sip before answering carefully. With Andrew, there was no social fudging of truth. "Physically I am coping, but…I don't quite know how to put this succinctly." She replaced her cup in its saucer.

"Take your time," said Andrew encouragingly, "we have all the time in the world."

Doris smiled to herself. Did the "we" refer to Andrew and God or Andrew and herself? "Very well," she said. "I feel as if life has played a trick on me rather."

Andrew finished his tea in a single gulp and reached forward to cover Doris's hand with his. "Go on," he urged gently.

She smiled at the kind, eager face. "I thought I had reached an age when I was settled, settled in my beliefs and the pattern of my life, no more upheavals, just a gentle drift from now on. I thought I could watch the play from the wings." Doris paused, searching Andrew's face for understanding. She went on, "But I find I am a player after all."

A silence fell between them, the old woman and the young man giving strength to one another.

Doris was pleased that her hand was still held in the broad, capable hand of the vicar. Andrew knew the value of touch. Few people seem to realise that one of the sadnesses of widowhood or indeed old age was that seldom were you touched in affection any more.

Andrew spoke, quietly teasing. "Big role is it, Doris?"

Doris returned his smile, but answered seriously. "No, Andrew, it is small, quite small, but it seems to be demanding, sometimes more demanding than I think I can cope with, and that is…that is what concerns me. I've been asking for a lot of help lately and I'm not awfully sure it's fair. I am not sure that I have the right, or that I give anything back."

Andrew looked relieved. "Do you think I could have some more tea please?"

Doris withdrew her hand. "Oh, of course, what am I thinking about? Would you like a biscuit, or perhaps a slice of cake? I sometimes wonder whether you eat properly."

"Oh no, just the tea will be fine." Andrew watched her closely as she pushed the replenished mug towards him. "Tell me, Doris, if I don't come to see you for a very long time and then I suddenly turn up on your doorstep asking for your help, will you turn your back on me?"

Doris looked shocked. "Of course I wouldn't," she said stoutly, "you know you're always welcome."

A huge grin spread over Andrew's face. "Well," he cried gleefully, "I daresay God is pretty much the same, big enough to take a fair few knocks and snubs. Does that answer you, Doris?"

Before she could reply the doorbell pealed.

"I'll answer it," said Andrew, bounding out of his chair. He returned with Ritzy. "Doris, I'll leave you in these capable hands," he said, buttoning his coat and putting on his gloves. "Give me a ring if you have any worries. I'm never there of course, or at least it seems like that, but the message will get through. You know I've got an answering machine. I often think it's a bit like praying when you use one of those things. You have to have great faith that everything's working and you sometimes have to wait a long time for an answer." He bent and kissed Doris. "God bless you both," he said. "Ritzy, remember me to your grandmother."

"Help yourself," said Doris pointing to the teapot.

"Thanks but I can't stop, Mrs Roberts. Only came in 'cos I didn't see ya at yer window. But you're all right, innit? Check ya later, OK."

"OK," said Doris.

She hummed to herself as she cleared away the few tea things. Andrew's visit had done more for her than all the pills in a chemist shop. "*How thoughtful of Ritzy to pop in like that.*" The doorbell sounded again. One of them must have forgotten something.

Opening the door Doris found herself clasped to her daughter's tweed-clad bosom. She had a brief impression of warmth and cleanliness. Almost immediately, she was wrapped in her son-in-law's firm embrace. His arms felt strong, his body solid. For the briefest of moments, Doris felt tempted to cling to this dependable rock. Then she was welcoming them inside. "Joyce, Robert, what a lovely, lovely surprise. Now what about something to eat? What about a drink?"

"Mother, do stop fussing." Joyce was smiling, her voice warmer than on the telephone. "Let's sit down and chat for a while, then I'll make the tea."

She made sure her mother was comfortable before joining her husband on the settee.

"Did you have a nice drive up?" Doris asked, longing to know the reason for this visit, but from weary experience knew that first must come the travel-detail ritual. With controlled impatience she waited while her daughter recited the route that they had taken from Canterbury, their reasons for taking that route, how many miles they had got to the gallon this time, how long the journey had taken.

"You got here safely anyway, that's the main thing," Doris broke in, lest they should feel encouraged to give more in-depth information. "Now tell me, what made you decide to come."

"Half-term," said Robert, taking his pipe from his pocket.

"*Good,*" thought Doris, "*they're not going to dash away.*"

"I'd forgotten about that," she said. "I believe Ritzy's school is on holiday next week."

"We're glad you found a nice young friend," said Joyce primly. "She sounds delightful when you talk about her on the phone, but..."

Doris smiled. "I had a feeling there was going to be a but."

"...but," her daughter continued, "we thought we ought to come up and see for ourselves just how well you are."

"Sorry, Joyce."

"Snow," said Robert, plunging his hands into pocket after pocket.

Doris did not tell him that there were matches on the mantelpiece, he knew that already. This searching was another ritual. He would interject a word, possibly two into the conversation, allowing his wife to expand on his themes before retrieving the matches and settling down contentedly with his pipe. Doris ignored him.

"Robert believes we are going to have snow before the day is out, so we thought we'd best come before driving becomes impossible. You know it's not been unknown to be snowed in where we live. Certainly the sky looks very heavy."

"I am sorry for the drivers, but I hope it comes," said Doris. "I love to watch the children."

"Chair," said Robert, standing up, patting his clothing.

"Mother, I almost forgot." Joyce looked cross with herself. "How could I forget the most important thing? We've brought you a present."

"That's nice," said Doris doubtfully. "Are you going to tell me what it is, or should I guess?"

Her daughter frowned. "It's not exciting, Mother, but—"

"—practical," finished Robert, at last putting his pipe in his mouth and reaching for the matches.

"We think you'll find it very useful," said Joyce. "I'll just go out to the car and get it right now."

Doris and her son-in-law waited in companionable silence, each in their own way enjoying the pipe smoking.

"Here you are." Joyce returned with a sturdy-looking leather cushion.

Doris thought it looked a bit hard. She felt disappointed. What dull presents are given to the elderly! "Thank you very much indeed," she said politely, eyeing her new possession with scant enthusiasm.

Her daughter laughed. "You don't understand, Mother, here, let's get you up and—"

"—demonstrate," said Robert.

Doris found her present unexpectedly comfortable. Now Joyce looked like a child with a secret. Doris looked at her daughter in wonder. She was indeed a different person in the presence of this monosyllabic Robert, positively girlish.

"Mother, see this." Joyce guided her mother's hand to a knob on the side of the cushion. "Now pull that out and see what happens." She stepped back and watched her mother fumble a little at first, then succeed in pulling out the knob.

To Doris's immense surprise, she found herself being pushed gently to her feet.

"What do you think, Mother? You said you had difficulty getting out of the chair."

Doris sat down with the help of the cushion and stood up again. "Trust you two to get just the right thing. I really am grateful. I believe I heard about them on that Radio 4 programme. I never...I never thought to have one."

"Good show," said Robert, puffing contentedly.

"Oh, they've been out for years," said Joyce, bending swiftly to kiss her mother before making her way to the kitchen.

The tea made and served, the three sat and chatted. Doris regaled her visitors with mildly exaggerated tales of the awful Mrs Cronin and the extensive Johnson family.

Joyce and Robert brought her up-to-date with their gossip.

She was kept pretty well informed with frequent phone calls and letters, but there were times when she had discreetly to inquire who had changed jobs, who had passed an examination, who'd had the flu, the measles, the chicken pox. She began to feel a bit bewildered now, while Joyce talked of her son, daughter, grandchild, her brother Gareth's three sons and their wives, who between them had so far produced five great-grandchildren for Doris. She thought, "*I'll have to sort it all out tonight when I go to bed.*"

"Come on, old lady," said Robert, patting his wife's knee. "Time to go."

"Old lady indeed, just because I'm turned sixty-five," Joyce protested, not looking at all displeased.

Doris noted with amusement that her daughter actually blushed. "It's survivable," she smiled, "Now, I'll come and see you off. No, no, no." She waved away their protests and offers of help. "I have got no excuse now, now I have my wonderful new toy."

That evening Doris lay in bed too tired for sleep, allowing her mind to drift pleasurably. Perhaps tomorrow her advertisement would bear fruit. All things considered maybe it was just as well nobody had called today. Joyce would not have approved; time enough to face the music when she had made definite arrangements. Besides, what was there to worry about? Did she not have kind neighbours and friends to "keep eye" on her, as Mrs Panano had said? That should put her daughter's mind at rest. Had she thanked them properly for the cushion? It would certainly make life a lot easier. But Joyce was quite right, it was aesthetically lacking.

Doris sighed and turned her face to the window. Through partially drawn curtains she watched the first tentative flakes of the promised snow quietly fall to the earth. A few settled on the winter-stark branches of the tree outside her window. As if emboldened by this precarious success, the gentle invasion continued, increased and spread until the whole street lay in its silent thrall. It had been such a satisfactory day, and now it was drawing to a hushed and hopeful close. Doris gazed at the snow and, soothed at last, fell asleep.

Chapter Five

"My knees are so stiff I doubt I'll get up again ever."

"Self-inflicted wounds," snorted Mrs Evans, hurriedly taking off her coat.

Doris grinned sheepishly and winced.

"Showing off you new contraption, that's what did it. Been at it for days now you have," grumbled the woman, "but you never learn." She shook her head. "It's a wonder you didn't charge admission to watch you bounce up and down. I'll tell you this for sure, you are going to move today because I'm going to change the sheets on your bed. I can't stay around here all day. This afternoon I'm going to take my grandson and an old tin tray and we are going to slide down the slope in the park and pretend we're at one of those fancy ski resorts in Switzerland. I haven't got time to fuss around a foolish old woman with no more sense than a sparrow." While she uttered this speech, she helped Doris out of bed with a gentleness that belied her tone.

Once she had left, Doris felt restless and dissatisfied. The Christmas-card freshness of the snow had lasted but a brief while. Wheels and boots had wrecked its beauty. It had been shovelled from road and pavement and it lay dirty and discarded in the gutters.

"*Maybe I am a foolish old woman,*" thought Doris, "*but I would love to see the children playing on the slope. I should certainly love to see Mrs Evans there.*" The thought made her smile. She tapped her chin thoughtfully. "*I wonder.*" The phone rang and she answered absently. Yes, she said, she would be at home the following evening, but to make sure she answered would he please knock three times, pause, then knock twice. She replaced the receiver a little annoyed with herself. She should at least have asked the name of the young man who wanted to study French.

The rest of the morning dragged interminably. For once, Doris did not cook lunch but prepared a sandwich and instant soup. She ate them, peering anxiously up and down the road. Now that the children were on holiday, they could be anywhere. *"Please God make Ritzy come home for her lunch,"* prayed Doris. *"I must find out if they have a telephone."* At that moment, her own telephone rang. "That will be lovely," she said. "You come any time you like." She said goodbye and straightaway forgot which member of the family had rung her. *"Please come, Ritzy, please. Oh there she is."* She rapped on the window with her stick.

Startled by the apparent urgency of the command, the girl ran to the door. "What's up, Mrs Roberts, d'ya need 'elp?"

"No, no, Ritzy, well yes." Doris laughed, panting a little, "Wait until I get my breath."

Three-quarters of an hour later, the pair sat waiting for a knock at the door. "Car for Roberts," said the man standing on the doorstep. "Where to, Mrs?" asked the driver, once Doris and Ritzy were sitting in the back of his cab.

"Oh, just drive around," said Doris airily.

Ritzy giggled.

"You've got to have a destination," grumbled the driver.

"I don't see why; back here will be the ultimate destination, of course, but in the mean time would you please drive out of this road?"

"Humour me, give us a clue."

"Mrs Roberts wants to see the snow," explained Ritzy.

"Blimey, I don't half get 'em," muttered the man under his breath throwing the car into gear with a marked lack of sensitivity. Doris drew in a sharp breath. *"Terrible way to treat a gearbox; no feeling, no mechanical sympathy. I bet he rasps the handbrake too."*

They drove down roads no different from the one that they had left. Somehow, even the snow on trees and roofs looked grey and forlorn. Doris shook her head sadly.

"Why don't we go to Crystal Palace Park?" asked Ritzy. "Some of me mates was goin' to hang out there."

Doris instructed the driver. She looked swiftly at her companion "It's good of you to give up your afternoon like this," she said.

"Don' be soft." The girl waved away the compliment.

The cab turned into the carpark.

"This is more like it," said Doris, gazing delightedly at broad expanses of unbesmirched whiteness carpeting the ground, the trees bearing their glinting winter burden with ease. In the distance, children ran about, bright splashes of colour darting back and forth. On the calm clear still air, their shrieks and laughter carried easily to the watchers in the car.

"'Spec' me mates is on the bigger slopes round there."

"Come on, Ritzy, let's go."

"It's a long walk. Ya sure ya'll be alrigh'?"

"Oh course I shall," Doris retorted impatiently, getting out with the help of the driver. "We shan't be long," she said to him.

She could not have said a truer word. It took just three steps to prove that her stout sensible shoes were most unsuitable for ice and snow. She slipped and would have fallen but Ritzy swiftly caught her. She steadied herself, panting a little as pain jolted through her, then, leaning heavily on her friend, returned to the cab.

Doris sat very still, staring steadfastly at the tranquil scene through a blur of tears. A warm hand gently squeezed hers. She tried to smile. "I'm a stupid old woman, I wanted to feel it…I wanted to feel the snow." Her tears spilled over and coursed down her cheeks. "I've just remembered," she said irrelevantly. "It was Rose who rang me. Rose is coming down to London."

The driver started the car, this time slotting in the gear with fluidity. "It's only yer shoes," said Ritzy. "What ya wan' is boots."

On reaching home, Ritzy ran to the open front door, whilst Doris paid off the driver. He refused the tip she offered him.

"I'm sorry…you didn't…sorry," he mumbled.

Mrs Cronin appeared out of the blue. "I saw you go off with the black girl," she whispered. "I was worried, you know you only have to give me a shout, and…"

"Your have to speak up," said Doris loudly and wickedly. "It's my hearing that's impaired, not my eyesight."

Mrs Cronin looked flustered, darted a quick look at Ritzy and scuttled away.

Later that evening Doris spoke to her daughter-in-law. "I'm sorry I was a bit distant with you this morning, love."

Rose laughed. "Distant is it? You were practically non-existent, you were so far away. I was going to ring you back and then I thought wouldn't it be awfully cruel if you were somewhere nice."

"I was certainly miles away," said Doris, hurriedly biting back an explanation.

It was too soon to laugh at the childish disappointment of the afternoon.

"I expect you're like the rest of us, bemused by the weather. I go out in so many clothes, I look like Michelin man. Ah, but how can you complain when it is so beautiful and you can come home to a warm house? Oh Ma, I must tell you. Up here, you can see the occasional bit of bright yellow gorse peeping out from beneath a fairly heavy blanket of snow. You know, it makes you feel like a child, discovering that a tiny piece of pretty wrapping paper has been torn away to reveal a tantalising glimpse of a beautiful present."

"Rose, it's a joy to listen to you," said Doris, seeing vividly the small splash of warm gold against the cold stark white of the snow. Laughter rippled down the telephone wires.

"Ah now, it is poor you must be for entertainment down there. Listen Ma, we must arrange for you to come up here when we're settled." Rose laughed again. "The weather I mean, not us. We'll keep a bed for you amidst the chaos. Moving to a smaller house has in no way stemmed the constant flow of humans and animals. The only difference now is that people lie around in sleeping bags rather than beds."

"I'll practise stepping over things," said Doris, feeling her spirits rise.

"Haven't you had enough practice over the years, Ma Roberts? Talking of practising, I've heard all about the new granny-aid. Is it wonderful? Gareth and I were only saying the other evening that you won't know yourself with great gadgets from now on."

"Why is that, Rose?"

There was a slight pause before her daughter-in-law answered in her rounded tones. "God forgive me, maybe I shouldn't say it, but now Joyce is officially an old lady she'll be into every aspect of this growing-old business. Well you know how thorough she is? By the time she reaches your age she'll be an expert. In the meantime, you'll reap the benefits of her research."

"You are a wicked girl, Rose." Doris smiled at this accurate assessment of her daughter. Only when she had hung up did she realise that she still did not know the reason for the earlier telephone call.

Television could not hold her attention, nor yet the play on Radio 4. Though cheered as ever by Rose, she still felt niggled about the failure of the afternoon's outing. Was she really getting so feeble that she could not even go out and face the elements? Was she to be wrapped in cotton wool for the rest of her life?

"Frank, I'm feeling old."

"Well you are old," said Frank maddeningly, "but the problem today was that you had the wrong equipment. You were never very good about things like that, Doris. That

30

girl Ritzy was right. You should have worn your boots."

"Don't be ridiculous," Doris snapped. How could her husband sound so smug? "I do not have any. I haven't worn boots for years. They must have been thrown out."

"Nevertheless," said Frank imperturbably, "you'll find them in the cupboard under the stairs. When did you ever throw anything out?"

Doris was scornful. "You could never even find your own things when you were alive."

"And you would never be told."

Ignoring him, his widow turned her attention back to the play. There was much grunting and groaning. The effort to make sense of it was too much. "Oh all right," she grumbled, "all right. I'll look."

Doris found the boots in the cupboard under the stairs. Old-fashioned they were, fleecy-lined with zips up the front. She picked them up and blew dust from them. Shaking her head in disbelief, she sat on the chair in the draughty hall, a boot in each hand. She looked from one to the other. Suddenly she was laughing. She laughed until the tears streamed down her face and her sides ached. "*Oh Frank, if anyone knew they would surely think I was mad. Would you not think that if I argued with myself that I would win, or put another way, I not only talk to the dead, but I argue with them and they win. You win. You always bloody did.*"

31

Chapter Six

Sometime in the night a fresh fall of snow had powdered the drab face of the road and restored its fairy tale appearance. Doris noticed first the sun reflected on the crystal-bright filigree of branches against the vivid blue of the sky. Next she saw the boots standing neatly facing her near the end of the bed. They were sensible, practical, warm-looking and ugly. Doris listened to the crunching feet of passers-by and looked at the boots. They represented freedom and a second chance. "*On that basis,*" thought Doris, "*they are simply quite beautiful.*"

Mrs Evans came and went. Ritzy somewhat bewilderingly came and went. She chatted unfathomably about clothes sizes and bus passes and woolly hats. Doris tried to say to her that she would be welcome to bring a friend along one day but the girl's mind was clearly elsewhere. Why were people acting so oddly? There had been something about Rose's conversation yesterday which she could not quite put her finger on. "*Imagination I suppose.*" She dismissed the idea from her mind. Telephone calls were answered with as much patience as she could muster. Then she was into her bedroom and into the boots. They dangled on the end of her legs and seemed to have been made for feet twice the size of hers. "You'll have a fine grip on the earth in those, love," said Frank. "Might even have to pay ground rent."

The doorbell pealed. The ancient zips refused to budge. "Oh drat the things," exclaimed Doris, tugging first one and then the other while the bell rang with unattractive insistence. There was nothing for it but to answer the door looking like Minnie Mouse.

"Oh ya've got boots, that's good innit," said Ritzy, taking Doris's arm and propelling her towards the sitting room.

"*The poor child has quite taken leave of her senses. What is all the excitement about?*"

"Jus' sit there a minute, Mrs Roberts. We've got a surprise for ya. Me brothers'll be along in a sec. I know ya said we wasn't to bring no one else, but I need 'em, see."

"But Ritzy, I..."

The girl was gone. Silence. A cold draught from the front door. A clang in the hall. A squeak as from machinery. Curious as Doris was she could not take her eyes from her footwear and raised her ankles to survey the boots. Why on earth had she bought them? Surely she had never found them attractive. It must be possible to combine comfort and good looks.

"Comfy are they?"

Doris looked up to see two enormous young black men looking down at her. They seemed as solid and immovable as rocks.

"Oh budge!" cried Ritzy, unceremoniously pushing them aside. "Ya take up such space."

The young men moved awkwardly.

"Do sit down," said Doris faintly.

"That's Nathan and that's Benoit," said Ritzy. "Ya do pronounce the 'T'. Mum read it in a book. This is Mrs Roberts. Mrs Roberts, I know ya said I wasn't to bring no strangers but I thought Nathan and Benoit would be all right, 'cos they're me brothers."

"Ritzy," Doris spoke with deliberation, "take a deep breath, give yourself some time and then tell me calmly what is happening."

"Sorry," said Ritzy, "only I thought it was a great idea, so we got the things together and Gran said it was all right. She don't hardly ever use it and the boys said they'd help."

"Rita," said one of the boys, "y'ain't makin' no sense, she don't get ya."

"OK," Ritzy sighed. "That one is Nathan, he's nearly eighteen, he's the eldest of us. The other one is Benoit, it is never shortened to Ben. He is my twin brother."

Doris glanced curiously at Benoit. She had never before heard Ritzy speak with such care. Benoit must be a special person. She smiled at the boys. "It is very nice to meet you," she said shaking hands with them in turn. They perched on the edge of the settee looking everywhere but at Doris.

"Dey yer records?" said Benoit, his eyes wide as he looked on the collection.

"I suppose they are," said Doris. "Frank, my husband, was very keen on Bix Biderbecke. You are very welcome to come and listen to them some day but for now perhaps you can explain."

Nathan cleared his throat and frowned.

"Oh Nathan, you're so slow," Ritzy interrupted. She slid to her knees and leaned her elbows on the arm of Doris's chair. "Look, Mrs Roberts, yer gear was all wrong yesterday. Yer ears was freezin' and yer legs was blue. We thought ya'd be all right if ya was all wrapped up. So look." She reached into a bag behind her. "We brought ya these." She placed a pair of bright purple tracksuit bottoms on Doris's lap. "'Ave a feel, Mrs Roberts, they're ever so thick and warm and they're all soft inside. They'll keep ya real cosy and ya can keep yer tights on underneath. It's good you found yer boots, innit?"

"Oh Frank told...I mean," said Doris swiftly, "I remembered where I put them, I was trying them on when you came because I was going to try to walk to the library but they seem a bit big, and I can't undo the zips."

Ritzy looked thoughtful. "Ya need t'ick socks. Benoit, you run home and grab a pair of socks, them Damart ones. Don't wake up, dad. He's on nights," she explained to Doris. "What kind of books d'ya like? Nathan'll get 'em for ya."

Nathan frowned. He had the look of a reluctant volunteer.

"Well, I quite like Dick Francis, but…"

Nathan looked relieved.

"Don't worry, he always has spare tokens. He only gets out one book at a time. He ain't no Stephen Hawkins," said Ritzy.

The young men departed. Doris fingered the vivid pants. "It's been years since I've worn trousers. I really don't think…"

Ritzy unzipped the boots. "Then it's years since ya've been comfortable. Come on, Mrs Roberts, let's get ya changed before the boys get back."

There was no arguing. Doris found herself being helped out of her skirt and into the purple pants. Ritzy said she hadn't brought the top because she knew that Mrs Roberts had plenty of warm cardigans. She was wearing a nice green one now, so that was all right.

"I brought ya some boots," said Ritzy, indicating the bag, "but it's best ya have yer own." She gazed at Doris. "Who's Frank?"

"Oh, my husband, he died late last year."

"Ya must miss him."

"I do," said Doris hesitantly.

"Never a cross word, eh?" said Ritzy and looked embarrassed.

Doris laughed. "Oh goodness, child, we rowed all the time." "*If I knew you better,*" thought Doris, "*I would tell you that we row now.*" "Ritzy, dear, I am still at a loss, why do we need your brothers and these clothes? I really wanted only to trot to the library and one old woman, no matter how feeble, does not need three of you to take her there."

"We're going to take ya to see the kids on the slope, like ya wanted, innit."

Doris felt a lump rise in her throat. "Oh that is sweet of you, but how? The car could not get close enough yesterday."

Ritzy darted from the room and returned pushing a wheelchair before her. "Yer carriage awaits, madam," she said with a flourish.

Doris froze and felt herself shrink back in her seat. "No," she whispered through lips grown suddenly dry. "No, I…I…I can't."

"It's all right," Ritzy reassured her. "It's safe, really it is, and it's dead clean, we all had a bash at it this morning. Still squeaks a bit, but it's all right really."

Doris swallowed hard. "I cannot go in it. I'm not ready."

Frank had been in a wheelchair, briefly, towards the end. "*Towards the end.*" Doris shuddered. To go out in a wheelchair was to surrender. It was too soon to make such a public statement. "I'm not ready," she whispered again.

"That's OK," said Ritzy cheerfully. "Yer coat was all wrong too. Looked all right but didn't do no good, so we brought you Benoit's new padded jacket. It'll be a bit big for yer. Mine was a bit grubby," she added, plunging her hand once more into the bag and producing a jacket with enough colours to rival a rainbow.

Doris was struck by the incongruity. No one wearing that garment could be thought to have finished with the world. It screamed life. Almost without realising it, she raised her arms and let Ritzy help her put it on. With difficulty, she found her voice. "I don't think I want to go in the wheelchair," she said, her eyes pleading with the girl to understand and not to be hurt. "Maybe I…"

"Oh ya'll be fine," said Ritzy, wrapping a Crystal Palace football scarf twice round Doris's neck and tucking the ends inside the jacket. "The boys are ever so strong, they'll look after ya." She stepped back to admire her handiwork.

Benoit came panting back with the socks. "Mum said we forgot this." With a face-splitting grin he produced a green, black and orange cap from his pocket.

Doris felt the first weak smile tug at the reluctant corners of her mouth.

"Go on, Doris," said Frank. "You'll look like a Christmas tree."

"*This is serious, Frank.*"

Ritzy sorted out Doris's footwear.

"It certainly is if you intend to turn your back on this opportunity, or are you getting so ancient you can't adapt to changed circumstances? You used to enjoy the odd challenge before you got so old."

"I'll go," said Doris vehemently, and rammed the cap firmly down over her ears.

Benoit flattened himself against the wall and, narrowing his eyes, peered with elaborate caution up and down the street. "Coast is clear," he hissed, and dramatically waved the others out.

Ritzy prodded him affectionately. "Idiot," she said.

"Wagons roll!" he whooped, pushing the wheelchair into the tiny front garden.

Doris, ignoring him, said that she would walk to the end of the road.

Nathan took charge of the chair and started off alone. The twins tucked Doris's hands into the crooks of their arms, and the three of them set out, Doris treading slowly and carefully on the treacherous pavement.

Ritzy watched every step while Benoit all but danced her down the road. Doris could feel his pent-up energy. She glanced ahead at Nathan whose gait looked most peculiar. His head moved from side to side at a tempo seemingly divorced from that of his feet. She had heard of people who marched to a different drum but had never thought to meet one personally. Then she noticed the wire emerging from beneath his cap and leading to his pocket. "*Oh poor boy,*" she thought. "How long has Nathan been deaf?" she asked.

Ritzy hooted with laughter. "Oh you are funny, Mrs Roberts. He's not deaf. He's got earphones. He's got his music."

Doris felt foolish. She should have realised.

"Nathan!" Ritzy gave an ear-piercing yell. Her brother didn't pause. "Oh he's so slow," she said, and yelled again.

"Shut up, Rita, you sound like a town-crier."

"I just wanted to know what he's playing."

"Dire Straits remix innit."

"I believe I have heard of that group," said Doris. "They've been around a long time, have they not? Who is that?" she asked when a pretty Indian woman nodded and smiled at her.

"She lives next door to ya."

Doris stopped walking. "Oh dear, I seem to have been going around with my eyes closed. I'm afraid I know very few of my neighbours anymore, not now a lot of the houses have been turned into flats. Of course, these are big places. It's right that they should be fully occupied."

"Let's not stop, Mrs Roberts, ya'll get cold," said Ritzy gently.

"Hang on a mo'," said Benoit. "I'll get the chariot." He ran after Nathan.

"OK?" Ritzy tucked a blanket round Doris's knees.

"Quite comfortable, thank you."

"Don't sound such a cold fish," said Frank.

"Keep yer hands inside, keep 'em nice and warm."

"I'm not sure how I'll take to wheelchair riding," said Doris with a nervous laugh.

"Well," said Benoit, "this ain't exactly the Ferrari of wheelchairs. See how it goes and by next week we can have it souped up for yer. What do you think of that...Mrs R?"

Doris had to laugh. A souped-up wheelchair indeed! Feeling warm and cosy in the unfamiliar clothes she settled back to enjoy herself. It was pleasant to be able to gaze about her at leisure without her attention being the prisoner of her feet. The air was clear and the sun shone. Ritzy and Benoit chattered and giggled while Nathan took his turn with the wheelchair and grunted occasionally.

Doris was pleased that they did not try to include her in their incomprehensible jargon. Their speech moved seamlessly between South London English and West Indian patois. It was pleasant just to listen to the sound and rhythm of their animated chatter.

"Ritzy?"

"Yes, Mrs Roberts."

"Ritzy, I've just had a thought. We can't possibly go all the way to Crystal Palace Park. It is much too far for you all to walk, let alone push this wheelchair. I can't think why it did not strike me before."

"Not to worry, we're going to take you by bus, I thought you knew. That's why I needed the boys."

Doris closed her eyes and gulped. "I can't possibly get on a bus. I can't remember the last time I was on a bus," she said in a voice that did not seem to belong to her. "I...I... could not get up the step."

Benoit placed his hand briefly on her shoulder. "We'll look after you, Mrs R. Ya'll be OK."

Doris believed him. Somehow he knew her fear. It seemed to her that he knew it but did not brush it aside as others would do.

At the bus-stop Doris stood while her companions folded the wheelchair. It was nice to stretch your legs.

Nathan and Benoit hoisted her effortlessly up the steps of the bus. She didn't even have to bend her knees.

"Blimey," said the driver, "I wish I'd worn my bleeding sunglasses. They'll never lose you in that outfit, love." He waited until she was safely seated. "Will that be cash, madam," he asked in deferential tones.

Doris was confused until she heard the laughter in his voice. "Oh I think my friends...I never...ever thought I would ride on a bus again," she confided.

He put his hand on his heart "I am deeply honoured that you've chosen mine. This is, of course, the free promotional tour." He winked at her and started the bus.

On Crystal Palace Parade everyone departed with smiling faces. The driver helped Benoit swing Doris off the bus. She thanked him for his kindness and he thanked her for brightening his life.

Ritzy was grinning ear to ear. "OK, Mrs Roberts?"

Seated once more in the wheelchair Doris nodded. "Very much OK, Ritzy. Come on, boys, let's go."

Chapter Seven

On wooden trays, tin trays, plastic bags, and all manner of improvised sleds, they hurtled down the icy slope, the excited happy children, the yelling teenagers, the toddler-clasping mums and dads. They sped down the slope in a blur of vibrant, singing colour, then trudged back up in their vivid reds and blues and pinks and greens.

Doris, watching from the pathway overlooking the slope, felt the cold air pinch her cheeks and nip her nose. It made no headway with her feet and hands. She sat in comfort and delighted in the scene before her. Breathless boys and girls with laughing faces shouted greetings to her attentive escorts. "Go on," she urged them, "I'm perfectly all right here. Besides, I should love to watch you enjoying yourselves with your friends, please." She reached out her hand and gently pushed at Nathan's arm. He gave a smile so fleeting that it could almost have been a trick of the light, and left.

Doris saw him join a group of young men who had made a steeper slide a little apart from the others.

A gaggle of giggling girls claimed Ritzy; they flitted about the wheelchair like gaudy butterflies and then they were off, slipping and sliding in a joyous welter of arms and legs.

"Don't touch the brake, Mrs R," Benoit warned before leaping over the edge of the path and executing a perfect glissade. His laughing eyes never left her shocked face. Only when he safely reached the bottom did she let out her breath. How on earth did that boy manage to stay on his feet like that? He was brilliant. Her gaze ranged over the noisy jostling crowd until she found Ritzy who was holding hands with a fair-haired young man. "*It could be a while before she remembers the old woman in the wheelchair,*" thought Doris. She spotted Nathan just as he regained the path and was preparing to thunder down again. Where was Benoit? She searched among the woolly caps and found him at last halfway up the slope. As soon as he saw that she was watching him, he pretended that he could not hold his balance. Feigning desperation, he clawed wildly at the slippery surface, failed to find a purchase and, spread-eagled, slipped backwards, looking like a cartoon cat. Suddenly he checked his progress and with mock relief showing on his face, hung there for a moment. Doris burst out laughing when he let go and somersaulted to the bottom.

She clapped her hands and waved, acknowledging the show put on for her as especial pleasure.

"Enjoying yourself, Granny?"

"Yes," said Doris, still gazing fondly at her new friend. Turning her head, she found herself staring into two mocking eyes. Her heart began to pound as the young man leaned towards her, resting his hands on the arms of the wheelchair.

"Like a push, Gran, a nice little ride towards the trees?"

Doris could feel his breath on her cheeks. She tried not to cringe from the menace in his voice and the unmistakable hatred on his face. "No thank you," she said steadily. She felt more puzzled than fearful. As if by magic, Benoit and Nathan appeared by her side. The young man released his hold on the chair.

"Your Granny looks a bit pale," he said with a scornful laugh.

"She see yer ugly face, man," said Benoit, panting a little.

"Please," Doris whispered, fearful that they might fight.

Nathan stepped forward. "Fuck off," he growled with a voice that seemed to come from the depths of the earth.

42

Doris looked at him in some surprise. It was the first time she had heard him speak. "*Not quite the words I would have chosen but most effective,*" she thought as her would-be tormentor skulked away.

"You don' wanna take no notice of Lester," said Benoit. "He's mad. He's only just learned his ancestors was slaves. He'll get over it," he added casually.

Doris looked sharply at him. For once he seemed to be entirely serious. She shuddered. Could hatred such as she had seen in those eyes be dispelled so quickly?

"Oh look," she cried, pointing to a toddler who was sailing down the bank, thickly clad legs clasped tightly about the neck of its parent. The baby was giggling helplessly, pummelling his father's head with glee. "*Please God, let this be what I remember of today.*"

"D'ya wanna go home, Mrs R?" asked Benoit. His brother bent down as if to take off the brake.

"Certainly not," said Doris. "We've been here no time at all. I doubt if I'll be bothered again, go on, go on." She waved them away. "*If I go home now,*" she thought, "*I'll feel as if I'm running away. I'll be diminished somehow. Five minutes by myself is all I need.*" "Go on, I mean it," she urged again. "The snow won't last all that long, don't waste it on my account. There is really no need."

Nathan raised his arm in half-salute, and strolled off.

"Tell you what," said Benoit, "hang on a minute." He ran after his brother and returned looking triumphant. "'Ere ya are!" he exclaimed. "Have a bash at these, make ya blend in with the crowd." He grinned and placed Nathan's earphones carefully over her hearing-aid and put the little CD player on her lap. "It will turn itself off, so don't worry, Mrs R. Enjoy."

Sound filled Doris's head. Benoit was gone before she could ask him to turn it down. Oh well! She shut her mind to the brisk rhythm and looked beyond the people at play to the trees clothed in their winter finery. Here and there a branch showed darkly naked against the snow. Slowly she became aware of a soft guitar playing in her head. It was a gentle tune, with gentle words. Never mind about the bad things some people do and say. Forget the tears and the fears, laughter will follow pain. The sun will dry out the rain, so why worry? The tune and the words seemed to fill the sky. Her eyes, unexpectedly moist, were drawn to its cloud-speckled azure, tinged with pink and mauve, then moved their focus to a nearby bush. Huge, iridescent drops of melted snow fell in tune with the lovely liquid, descending notes rippling in her ears. She sat very still after the music died, aware that this moment of beauty would live with her.

"Mrs Roberts?" Ritzy's voice seemed scarcely above a whisper. "I'm sorry ya was left on yer own."

Doris shook her head. "I had Dire Straits," she said lightly.

The girl's face brightened. "Nathan likes all the old groups."

"I enjoyed it. My dear, the whole day has been lovely."

"Not over yet. You ain't felt the snow and that's what ya wanted. Wait till the boys get back." Ritzy peered round impatiently. "Oh, where is that Nathan? He's always so slow. Oh, by the way, this is Derek." She gestured casually to the boy hovering behind her. Nathan and Benoit came back dragging a toboggan.

"Are you boys going to give me one last demonstration?"

"Mrs Roberts—" Ritzy sat on her heels by the chair and made a proposal. "We worked it all out. It'll be ever so safe. The boys will take ya down and Derek an' me will be at the bottom but it won't be necessary, really, 'cos we borrowed this 'cos it's got a brake, what ya think?"

Doris looked from the eager face of Ritzy to the obvious power and strength of her brothers'. "I think," she said slowly, "I think I'll do it." "*Frank, have I always had this reckless streak? Don't go away, I may be joining you soon.*"

On the toboggan, she felt safe and protected between Benoit and Nathan. She did not, however, feel comfortable. Pain threatened to cloud the excitement of anticipation. It

44

was put determinedly to one side. *"I know I'll suffer for this but I do not care."*

While they waited at the top of the bank for a signal from Ritzy, Doris stretched out and scooped up some snow, letting it ooze slowly through her fingers. It felt crisp and clean. She held it against her cheek, noticing as she did so that the screams and squeals had faded away. A hush had fallen as children and adults alike stopped their frolicking and turned to stare. "Good lord, they are staring at me." A path was cleared with people lining both sides.

"All right, Mrs R? Hang on then."

They were off. The toboggan streamed towards the trees. Doris felt fear, an ache in every bone and a wild exhilaration as they whipped through the air. The crowd gave a cheer when all too soon the ride came to an end.

"Oh look," called someone. "She's crying, is she all right?"

Ritzy came swiftly to her side, full of concern to see tears running down the old woman's cheeks. Doris could only shake her head. She felt herself being lifted off the toboggan and carried up the incline. At last she found her voice. "It was wonderful," she murmured. "Quite, quite wonderful."

Chapter Eight

Doris groaned when she heard the coded knock at the door. She had forgotten the appointment with the French student. "I am sorry that you had to wait," she sighed wearily, leading her visitor into the warm sitting room.

"Please don't concern yourself, Mrs Roberts," said the young man. "I'm well wrapped up against the inclement weather, as you can see."

"A very grand accent indeed," thought Doris, her interest aroused.

"As I said on the telephone Mrs Roberts, I should like to perfect my French."

"I am not sure I can offer you perfection," said Doris with a slight smile.

"I see." The man frowned. "What are your qualifications?"

"Might I know your name before we start this interview?" Doris suggested gently.

"Forgive me. My name is Raza Abolhasan." He had come to England from Iran to acquaint himself thoroughly with English custom and practice. He wished to improve his French before going to France, where he intended in the same manner to study the French people. He would then return to join his father's firm. He gave Doris to understand that it was a very large important firm.

"It seems that you have set yourself a daunting task, Mr Abolhasan," said Doris wondering if she would be considered a suitable specimen for examination. "How long has your father given you to get to know us?"

"My father has left it to my own discretion," he replied in French.

"*Good accent,*" thought Doris, "*and you know it.*" "That's very good," she remarked. "Let's talk for a while in French and see how we get on. Mr Abolhasan, please sit back and relax."

The young man smiled a faint smile. "Thank you."

Doris racked her brains to find something to say. She was tired and not at all sure that she wanted the company of this solemn pompous young man. She said the first thing that came into her head. "The unrest in your country must be upsetting for you?"

Raza Abolhasan looked puzzled. "Oh these things are inevitable, naturally one must expect a few deaths in a conflict," he shrugged. "I find the English most peculiar in that respect. They place such emphasis on the individual. If there is a plane crash, or something of the sort in a foreign land, they go berserk, and if one or two Britons are killed the papers are full of it. Yet wars in which thousands die are virtually unreported."

"Surely your country cares similarly for its own people," said Doris.

"In general yes. But if one or two die it's of consequence only to the immediate family." He switched back to English. "Tell me, Mrs Roberts, will you be able to help me? I had hoped to get expert tuition."

Doris hesitated. "I think I could help you achieve a certain fluency. I am not formally qualified to teach, but I have lived in Paris and I have a reasonable vocabulary." "*I might teach you one or two other things as well,*" Doris thought.

"Oh, I see," said Raza. "It may work. You see I only like to talk to people of interest, people of importance. I literally haven't the time for run-of-the-mill people. Is that the right phrase?"

"Are you absolutely sure you have the time now? I am honoured," Doris snapped.

47

The young man smiled graciously, sarcasm quite lost on him. "Oh yes," he said, "I came here intending to spend half an hour with you."

"Joyce, I'm sorry you were worried but I'm perfectly all right. I'm a little tired now but I'll tell you about my lovely day tomorrow. Goodnight and thank you for ringing, my dear." Doris put the phone back in its cradle. Well, perhaps not all about it. She smiled in remembered pleasure. On impulse she lifted the receiver again and dialled her son's number.

"Is anything the matter, Mum?"

Did Gareth's voice sound a little strained? "Everything's fine, love, I just suddenly thought I should like a word with Rose before I go to bed."

There was a slight pause. "Could I get her to ring you in the morning, Mum? She's just gone upstairs herself. Just a minute."

There was a click on the line.

Just as Doris was beginning to think she had been cut off, Rose's voice breathed warmly in her ear. "Isn't he awful," she asked, "giving me the star treatment when I only sneaked up here to preserve my schoolgirl complexion? Believe me I need all the beauty sleep I can get," she laughed.

Doris felt strangely relieved. "Rose, love, I am sorry I disturbed you. I expect that you're exhausted with the move and all, I know you are always on the go. I just wanted to share my marvellous day with you. Can you believe it? I went out in the snow, and I heard this lovely music and then...well, you will not believe that part of it. I do want to tell you all about it, but tomorrow when we're both rested. Oh, and there was this extraordinary Iranian boy."

"Ma, it sounds like one of those days you'd like to bottle. I'd love to hear about every second. Give me a ring tomorrow and you can pour it all out, every drop." With an airy laugh she was gone.

Doris carried the happy sound to sleep with her.

Chapter Nine

Good morning, Mrs Roberts. How are you? What can I do for you?"

"I'm fine, thank you," said Doris seating herself in the chair being held out for her.

"It's an attractive idea," said the doctor running a weary hand through his hair as he sat behind his desk. "But, generally speaking, people rarely come to tell me how well they feel. Surgeries usually run on the principal of no news being good news." He looked mournfully at the prescription pad in front of him.

"But I have come to say I feel perfectly well," said Doris unabashed. "It's just that I would like you to examine me so that I can tell my daughter in all honesty that I am fine."

Doctor MacIntyre cleared his throat and placed his hands together in a silent clap. "Now let's get this straight. You are feeling fine but for some reason your daughter won't believe you, so you want me to add the voice of authority. Now tell me, Mrs Roberts," he said shrewdly, "what is it that you don't want your relatives to find out?"

Doris coloured slightly. "Nothing," she protested. "Well, I am rather stiff and my knees…well, they are a bit sore."

"I see, and what brought this on?"

"I went tobogganing," said Doris placidly.

"You did what?" the doctor's head snapped up.

His patient composed her features.

"Say again." This time she had his full attention. "I may have misunderstood."

"I went tobogganing," she repeated. "You know…on a sled…you slide from the top…to the…bottom."

Her voiced trailed away when she saw Doctor MacIntyre's melancholy face break into a smile. The smile became a laugh.

"The devil you did!" he said, getting to his feet to begin the examination. "Ay, they're a bit tender," he mused. "And who led you into this mischief?"

When Doris mentioned the Johnson family, he nodded as if that explained everything. "Have you met their granny? It's a wonder the two of you didn't form a team, on your toboggan, start training for the Olympics."

"I had her wheelchair," said Doris.

The doctor resumed his seat, grinning broadly. "You seem to have got away with it this time, but I wouldn't make a habit of hurtling down hillsides. Now you can go home and tell your daughter that you did your doctor a power of good."

Chapter Ten

Doris did not return home straightaway but, with great care, made her way to the church. She sat at the back and let her thoughts drift as her eyes gradually became accustomed to the light shining dustily on the empty pews.

It was strange how her life had changed since the day that Mrs Cronin had left her front door open and Ritzy had walked in. Was it really a mere month since she had said "I like to keep myself to myself"? Well, that idea had gone by the board.

Doris let her eyes wander idly over the familiar stone, glass, wood, gold and mosaic of this building which was so much a part of her life. Down the years, it had known her joys and sorrows, her departures and her home-comings. Its walls had absorbed her angers, doubts, and her breath-catching moments of happiness. There had been other churches in other countries but this was the one to which she returned. She did not come regularly but treated it as an old friend, a dependable, patient friend whose doors were open in continuous welcome.

Many of her contemporaries were dead. Communication with those who remained was sporadic, as if all energies had to be spared for day-to-day survival. Andrew understood a little of the isolation and he tried to help, urging her to join in the activities of the elderly in the church hall. It was not enough to have in common with someone the fact that you were of similar age and alone.

"*And now, thanks to Ritzy, a new world is opening up for me,*" Doris thought. She wondered if Briony, the eldest of her great-grandchildren, was helping some other old person where she lived in Wales. I must write to her. Perhaps she liked Dire Straits too, but possibly not; had Ritzy not said that was "old" music?

Doris smiled to herself. What a lovely day yesterday had been. She was looking forward to recounting it to Rose. Joyce would be pleased that she had enjoyed herself but Rose would see the sparkling colours, hear the laughter of the children and the music, feel the snow and the sunshine.

A heavily clad figure shuffled into the church, and slid into the pew in front of Doris. She knew that this mobile bundle of clothing was Rodney, the local gentleman of the road. He turned around and smiled at her. "Very good vicar here, madam," he said in superior accents. "Keeps a nice warm church, always a pleasure to come here."

"Yes, it is comfortable," answered Doris, trying not to breathe in too deeply.

Rodney's face and hands looked clean enough, but if his clothes had been in contact with soap and water it had happened a long time ago. "I'm sorry, God, but I'll have to go." Doris closed her eyes. "I'm sorry I did not actually get around to praying."

"Madam."

"Yes, Rodney." She stared in fascination as he flicked at his filthy outer garment, before unfolding a napkin and laying it carefully on his lap. From his pocket, he produced a crumpled paper bag out of which he took some dainty sandwiches. Who had gone to the trouble of cutting those crust free triangles? With careful fingers, he laid them on the grubby napkin. "Madam," he said politely. "Would you do me the honour of sharing my luncheon?"

Doris replied with equal courtesy, "Thank you, no. I have already made other arrangements."

"In that case madam, if you will excuse me." With a

flourish he produced the *Financial Times* from his sleeve and, smoothing it out, began to read.

Doris stood up to leave. She had nearly gained the door when Rodney spoke in sonorous tones. "Bloody nuns," he said scornfully. "Sent me out the *Sun* to read."

Gratefully breathing in the sharp clean air, Doris rested, leaning her hand on the back of the stone bench. A few moments were needed to take in what had just happened in the church. Rodney had not just offered her lunch. He had in his gentlemanly manner forgiven her for a misjudgement she had made a long while before. He had been offended when she had taken pity and offered him money. Declining the gift, he had thanked her coldly for her kindness. Watching him walk away with icy dignity, the realisation had grown that it was foolish to suppose that this man was poor. Doris sighed contentedly. It was good to be forgiven. *"Perhaps one day those unfortunate nuns will expunge their guilt,"* she thought.

Piercing cold insisted that she return home. Several phone calls had to be made, then she wanted just to sit and enjoy the past few days in retrospect. Turning into her own road, she came face to face with Mrs Cronin. To her immense surprise, the woman shot her a scared look and muttered inaudibly from behind a hand raised swiftly to her face. Doris watched her scurry across the road regardless of oncoming traffic. Extraordinary.

"She is not being very cautious," said an Indian voice.

Doris turned to find herself in the company of the woman she now knew to be her neighbour. "I think I may have upset her," she said ruefully.

"Surely not," laughed the woman, straightaway making the idea seem absurd. "May I walk with you? Please take my arm."

Doris leaned on the woman's arm with great relief. Suddenly it seemed a long way to the house. The women exchanged names and views on the weather, as they slowly made their way along the slippery pavement. "You're very tired, I think," said Jyotsna Kumar. "Please come and have lunch with us. It's all right," she added gently; "we live in the lower flat."

"Mama, Mama, why are you so late, Mama?" The children dashed forward excitedly, then stopped short when they saw Doris and stood shyly with their heads bowed.

"Mrs Roberts, this is my son, Tariq, and my daughter, Sunanda. Children, what do you say to our guest?"

After a brief pause, the little boy shot out his hand to Doris. "You are welcome to our home," he said solemnly.

The little girl clung to her mother's sari and could not be persuaded to say a word.

"Run and tell Ayeisha that we've an extra person for lunch," said Jyotsna, giving her daughter a little push.

It was only then that Doris noticed the woman sitting cross-legged in the doorway leading to the kitchen. She smiled at her and received a cheerful, almost toothless grin in return. The woman nodded and smiled continuously while the children dragged her to her feet.

"Ayeisha doesn't speak English," said Jyotsna.

"That must be lonely for her," replied Doris.

Her hostess shrugged. "These people are very resilient—Please make yourself comfortable, Mrs Roberts. Please excuse me while I go to the kitchen for a moment."

Doris sat on a straight-backed chair. The children stared wide-eyed at her. The two of them had a hurried consultation. Finally the spokesman said, "Please to sit on the sofa, it is more comfortable and soft. Mama would wish it."

Having thanked him gravely and explained the difficulty of getting out of a low chair, she added, "I am not as agile as Ayeisha."

Sunanda giggled and hid her mouth behind her hand. There was another whispered conversation. "Please may we watch television. Now it is our very, very favourite programme."

Doris smiled at the urgency and politeness battling in their voices. She glanced at her watch. "Oh, that's one of

54

my favourites too, if it's all right with your mother, let's have it on."

Tariq ran to switch on the television, while his sister wriggled with delight. "All eyes to the television, please," she begged, giggling nervously at her own temerity.

Within a very few flickering moments, Doris's eyes were drooping and she began to doze. Much later she told Rose how embarrassed she had felt when she had at last awoken to find the children playing quietly before the blind eye of the television and their mother reading. "Oh but she was so sweet," said Doris. "She really made me feel at home. I was especially glad that the children had not missed their TV programme. Did I tell you, Rose, I slept a full hour?"

"How can you be surprised when you've been hopping on buses and going in for winter sports...and what happened next?"

"Oh she just smiled and brought me some soup, and generally made me feel that it was the most natural thing in the world to fall asleep in a stranger's home. We had a nice chat. Her husband, Javid, is here on a sort of exchange for a few years. He's a lecturer. Physics, I believe, like Robert. She was telling me that in India you are supposed to welcome the weary traveller and offer him hospitality. He might be a holy man or a God in disguise...so...you can't turn him away even if he stays for weeks."

"Did...you...tell her Ma?" asked Rose.

"What?"

"That you weren't holy."

"I did," said Doris easily, "but she still made me welcome. I also assured her that I'd leave as soon as I finished the soup."

"She must have looked relieved then."

"As relieved as I'll be when you get off this line." They laughed together.

"Have you told Joyce all about your adventures, Ma?"

"Not quite all. You know how she worries. I feel a bit sad sometimes that I can't share... Oh well, thank God I have you, Rose dear. I am afraid I just told her I was taken out in a wheelchair."

"You've done it now, Ma," said Rose. "Guess what you'll be getting for your birthday?"

"No I can't have that," laughed Doris, in mock horror; "it would be state of the art. What would Benoit say? He's going to soup up his granny's one for me."

Chapter Eleven

Concorde nosed elegantly across the brittle ice blue sky between clouds rubescent in the setting sun and Doris knew that spring was finally on the way. As yet, daffodils had failed to trumpet its arrival. The melting snow had left the earth naked and drab while bare-armed trees reached up to the sky like obedient children waiting to be dressed. The bitter wind howled its denial of warmth and ripped with malicious fingers everything in its path. It rattled the windows, drawing Doris towards them to make sure they were securely fastened. It was then that she heard the deep familiar rumble. Her heart beat faster as she looked up and there was the plane emerging from the clouds like a star stepping out of the wings. Craning her neck, she watched it out of sight. It was so beautiful, this piece of gleaming future in the here and now. A man-made miracle in the sky! Doris felt elated. Spring was definitely on the way, now it was light enough to see Concorde. From now on she would be able to see it every evening, watch and wait for it, then track its brief passage as she had been doing for the past few years.

She returned to her seat in front of the television. The news was over, the weather-forecast of little interest. Doris switched off with her newly acquired remote control, then twiddled the knobs on her portable radio until she found a Beethoven symphony. That would do. She closed her eyes, feeling like a survivor. As far as she was concerned, the winter was over and done with. Overall, it had been a good season.

The last few weeks have been enjoyable. Once the tobogganing story had leaked out Doris had been deluged with telephone calls. Nearly every member of the family had rung, some admiring, some incredulous, others muttering dire warnings. Feeling much cherished, she thanked them, reassured them, mollified them. It was not an easy task with Joyce. Doris pursed her lips at the memory. "Mother, how could you be so foolish? What were you thinking of? You could have broken your bones, killed yourself even. You let strangers into your home. Mother you have no conception of the evil of today. What do you know of this Iranian boy…or any of the others for that matter?"

The tirade had gone on and on. Doris had contained her impatience as best she could. "Joyce, please listen. I got references from the firm where the Iranian boy works, the others—I presume you mean the Johnsons, the Pananos, the Cronins, the Kumars—live in this street and are all kind, respectable people. As for the day in the snow, it was enormous fun. I cannot and I will not be shut away. I refuse to die in stages."

"Mother," her daughter had cried, "the trouble with you is that you love everybody. You just can't see…"

"Joyce!" Doris had spoken sharply. "I see the ugliness. I watch television and I read the newspapers. I know about the muggings, the rapes, the robberies, and the murders. There is litter in the streets and obscene messages on walls. Cruelty and fear are integral parts of life today. I know these things. I see these things. It is just that I do not choose to look for them. I have no intention of hiding, terrified behind my front door, waiting for the doubtful solace of the undertaker." It had been a difficult task, but Joyce had eventually been placated. "I am feeling on top of the world," Doris had ended emphatically, rubbing her knees and trying to keep the pain out of her voice.

The Beethoven chords crashed to a very satisfactory conclusion, giving Doris the impetus to get up and close

58

the curtains. It was quite dark outside now, and huddled figures hurried homeward. Steel shutters shielded the Pananos fruit and vegetables from sight. No chink of light or flash of colour escaped them. It looked grey and bleak out there.

Behind her in the room a lonely oboe played forlornly. Doris turned decisively and switched it off. Really, Mozart did have his dreary side. She knew the piece, knew it would perk up in a little while but she could not wait. Her thoughts drifted to Ritzy who was slowly introducing her entire family. Now, besides Nathan who grunted amiably at her...at least she supposed it to be amiable, and Benoit who all but stood on his head to make her laugh, Evra and Marcus had become occasional visitors. Even if they did not pop in, they made a point of looking up at the window and waving. Marcus was a solemn chatterbox, Evra, a little girl seemingly composed entirely of gleaming teeth and pigtails. *"I wonder when I'll meet their granny,"* Doris thought. *"Perhaps I ought to go and see her, thank her for the loan of the wheelchair. That's an idea. I get so many visitors now, if I'm not careful, I'll not get out at all."*

In the past few weeks, Jyotsna and the two children had dropped in once or twice. Tariq and Sunanda happily stared at the television, while their mother spoke softly to Doris. They seemed to have many very, very favourite programmes.

Raza Abolhasan came twice a week. He amused, enraged and charmed Doris. He paid her the first money she had earned in years; "And I do earn it," she said tartly to Rose. "Oh but I am so pleased with myself I feel like framing it."

"That's no good, Ma," replied Rose, "you should make your money work for you. Take my tip, use it as a bookmark."

Doris absentmindedly fingered her library book, smiling at the memory. *"Frank, our Rose is still making me laugh. Remember the first time Gareth brought her home to us. That would have been in the late 'forties early 'fifties. Goodness what a long time ago that seems. Joyce and Robert not long married. Were the twins born then...? Yes of course they must have been. Never have*

59

been very good on dates. Gareth newly qualified, full of enthusiasm, all set to astound a breathless world with the brilliance of his architectural designs. Rose, dear Rose came to tea, stayed to supper, so amusing and pretty we did not want to let her go. We were in fits of laughter and poor Gareth was furious because he had planned to take her to the pictures. It's funny. I can still see his glowering face. I must remember to ask him if he has forgiven us for that evening. When… " The sound of knocking broke into Doris's thoughts. She frowned. "*Who can that be? Raza doesn't come until tomorrow evening. I'm not expecting anyone. Double glazing or market research it will be, I expect.*" "Damn it," she muttered, peering through the spy hole in the door. "*Can't see a blessed thing. Well, a man I think. Even my best friends look grotesque through this blessed wretched contraption.*"

The doorbell rang, making her jump.

"Who is it?" she called crossly.

A voice answered but she could not hear. She asked again but it was no good. Opening the door on a chain afforded no greater view of the man but at least he could be heard.

"Harry Cronin, Mrs," he said. "The wife sent me."

Feeling somewhat surprised, Doris invited him inside. He perched on the edge of the settee nervously pinching the creases of his trousers. "Lily said she hadn't called to see you for a while." He nodded to himself. "She said you'd be worried."

"She is all right, is she not?" asked Doris. "I did see her the other day, but…"

"Said you'd be worried," Harry repeated. He looked glumly at his boots.

"I did wonder why she hadn't called," said Doris. There was silence. Was the man deaf? Perhaps she should speak louder. "I do hope she isn't ill," she said carefully.

The man shifted his feet slightly. "Said you was kind to her, said you'd be worried."

Doris waited and studied her visitor. It was obvious that nothing further was forthcoming, at least for the moment.

He sat awkwardly. His work-worn hands ceaselessly worried the material covering his knees. Clearly, he was a man not given to idle chatter. He was frowning, presumably at the effort of thinking of something to say. Doris looked at him curiously. It was difficult to believe that this was the man who apparently had opinions on every subject. How often had she groaned inwardly on hearing the words "My Harry says". "*Now I wish he would say something. Do they complement one another?*" she wondered. "*This taciturn man and his loquacious wife, or do they drive each other mad?*"

"Mr Cronin," she said gently. "I am not entirely sure why you are here."

The man looked ill-at-ease. He ran a finger under his collar and cleared his throat. "Uh um! Lily said you'd be lonely. Wanted me to come and keep you company."

"How very kind," murmured Doris.

She paused before asking if he would like a drink. He shook his head and they sat once more in silence. Doris's thoughts began to wander. It would be good to see Rose when she made her planned visit to London. Phone calls were all very well but they were no substitute for her warm living presence. It was the same with Joyce, so much softer face-to-face.

"She bother you?" Harry Cronin's voice was rough.

Doris looked at him, startled. "I beg your pardon."

"Lily, does she bother you?"

"No, no of course not," Doris protested, feeling uncomfortable with the lie. Where was this leading?

Harry looked at her directly for the first time. It was a look that did not expect to find what it sought, a look bewildered and frustrated. "She interferes," he said gruffly. "I tell her not to...but she interferes."

Doris was relieved when he lowered his eyes. The naked sadness in them was shocking. There was something here more than mere irritation with a wife's gossip and chatter. Feeling that this private man would hate any overt acknowledgement of his pain, she spoke briskly. "Mrs

Cronin, Lily is very good to take an interest in me. If you are going to be kind enough to sit with me for a while…shall we have the wireless?"

Without waiting for a reply, she switched on the radio. The music flooding into the room always made her think of spacious country houses and flower-dazzled English gardens.

"Vivaldi," said Harry after a while, his hands at last resting on his knees.

Doris felt perplexed by her visitor. He was a quiet man but one could feel an anger in him, a suppressed energy. Violence was too strong a word. One could not imagine how it might manifest itself—this energy. Watching him as he listened attentively she felt no apprehension.

"He was an orphan."

"I'm sorry, Mr Cronin."

"Vivaldi, he was in an orphanage."

"I had no idea," said Doris. "I'm afraid I selfishly take the pleasure these composers give me without learning a great deal about their backgrounds."

"The orphanage helped with his musical education," said Harry as if she had not spoken.

"I am grateful to them," said Doris.

Harry nodded solemnly, and his hand began very gently to beat time to the music. In the winter-warm cosy room, pictures of spring were conjured up. Primroses and crocuses gleamed yellowly beneath trees rich with buds and the promise of greenness. Birds, plump with self-importance, perched on branches and sang joyously in the clear air. Earthy smells rose from damp undergrowth.

"I remember being young, very vividly. It is strange to think I may never again walk through an awakening wood. Certainly I will never scramble on slippery rocks in a fast running stream, but music like this eases the loss."

Harry Cronin slowly shook his head as if sloughing off sleep. "Forests," he said and sighed. "With me, it's forests."

Doris looked at him expectantly but he did not elaborate. To her surprise, she found that she would like to know more about his forests. She had the feeling that he wanted to talk but a lifetime's reticence was not easily overcome. Reluctant to probe or intrude, she hesitated before speaking.

The music ended and a newsreader told of a strike, a motorway crash, a missing child found raped and murdered. Harry's hands formed fists. His mouth became a thin tense line. "Bastards," he whispered venomously. "Bastards."

Doris shivered and turned off the radio. Harsh reality had intervened and the moment to talk about forests and fantasies was lost. "I should like it if you could spare me the time to come and see me again, Mr Cronin," she said.

"Bastards" he muttered again, his thoughts still with the dead child. He stood up endeavouring to force his features into a smile. "I've got tapes," he said, blushing furiously. "I use them while I work at the carpentry."

"Tapes?" echoed Doris. "Oh! Music tapes, oh! Of course."

"Vivaldi, Mozart, Shostakovich," said Harry, and started to edge towards the door.

"Lovely," said Doris. "That would be very nice, Mr Cronin."

"If there's anything, you know...anything, good evening." He was gone in a flurry of embarrassment.

Chapter Twelve

O h Mother, I do worry about you," said Joyce. "You say that you trust him but he sounds so odd, I do wish you would take care whom you let into the house."

Doris gripped the telephone in exasperation. "Damn it all, Joyce, at my time of life I am not going to lie or shield you from my in-your-eyes incautious doings. I am trying to share an experience with you. The fact I can ring you proves that I am absolutely fine. Can you not just accept that? I enjoyed listening to Vivaldi with Harry Cronin because he knows how to listen…to music, at least. It was peculiar sharing an evening with him after years of seeing him go to and from his workshop. He's a carpenter you know. What is more I am looking forward to his next visit."

"All right Mother, don't upset yourself. I just wish you wouldn't get involved with people who seem unsuitable. Before…"

"Before," Doris interrupted, "before a few months ago I was well on my way to being a docile manageable old woman and I was lonely. I am sorry, Joyce, but it's true. Apart from the daily phone calls from all of you what did I have?— the occasional letter from a friend in an old people's home complaining and measuring Britain's decline by the falling standards of the puddings. Now each day is different and I thank God I agreed to let Ritzy visit me. For the first time in ages I am living." Her voice softened. "Since your father died…well I am feeling my way to being a complete person again. Try to be happy for me, darling."

There was a sharp intake of breath at the other end of the line. "I *am* happy for you, Mother," said Joyce in a tight voice. "I just can't be as flippant about life and your safety as Rosaria is."

Doris was taken aback at the bitterness in her daughter's voice. Suddenly she felt very old and weary. "Joyce, darling," she said, "I value your caring very much."

Chapter Thirteen

Doris was out of sorts. Mrs Evans' cheerfulness died in the withering atmosphere. She went about her work in silence until the bell rang. Peering out of the window she said, "It's the black girl. Shall we let her have a happy day or shall we ask her in?"

"Sarcasm does not become you," growled Doris scathingly. "Please answer the door, Mrs Evans."

"You know, Doris," said Frank, "there are times when you're a sour-faced old..."

"Come in, Ritzy," said Doris. "What can I do for you?"

"Nothing," said the girl brightly. "Yer'ip playing you up?"

"No, my hip is *not* playing me up as you put it. I do not know why people persist in thinking I have a bad hip. If you must know I ache all over and I'm stiff."

"You are that," muttered Mrs Evans.

Doris ignored her. "I am an old woman. What else can I expect? I don't know why people have to fuss."

"Someone's upset ya, innit," said Ritzy, propping herself down on the settee and peering shrewdly at Doris.

"Certainly not. I told you my hands are very arthritic today and my hearing-aid does not seem to be working very well."

"I should go now, love, if I were you," said Mrs Evans to Ritzy. "Neither good for man nor beast today, she isn't. Bad-tempered old besom." She glared at her employer.

"If you have quite finished, perhaps you would have the courtesy to allow my visitors to choose for themselves whether they stay or go, a choice which equally exists for you." Doris spoke frostily.

Mrs Evans picked up her coat and, putting it on, fiercely thrust the buttons through the buttonholes. "How is your grandmother, Ritzy? Now there's a person I call a real lady," she said and departed.

Ritzy grinned. "What's the matter, Mrs Roberts?"

"Absolutely nothing," snapped Doris.

"That's good," said her visitor sitting back, clearly intending to stay.

"*Why do you not go away?*" thought Doris. "*I'm not up to cheerfulness today.*"

Ritzy chattered on, seemingly unaware of her icy reception.

"What are you saying?" asked Doris querulously, fiddling with her hearing-aid.

"I said Benoit's really pissed off." Ritzy spoke without raising her voice.

"Benoit, why? I wish you would not use such expressions."

"Well, ya know the pop group."

Doris nodded. She did not remember having been told about a group but felt no inclination to admit it.

"Well," Ritzy continued, "remember I said they rehearsed at a friend's house? Well they can't no more. Neighbours was creatin', because it was doing their 'eads in, and they're really 'acked off, 'cause they were just gonna do their first gig."

"Gig?" echoed Doris.

"Yeah, bummer, innit? I mean they'll still do it but it's not the same. I mean, you need rehearsals don't ya, specially when ya're booked for yer first gig and ting? They're real wicked, straight. But it's so hard to get started. They worked all their spare time doing odd jobs to get money for the stack and gear and ting and...now they've fixed their first gig...they want to get it together."

"Ritzy, I have no idea what you're talking about. Please

67

try to speak with more clarity," Doris commanded imperiously.

"You're putting on your duchess act," said Frank.

Doris had understood perfectly but she wanted time to think. Her companion spoke again.

"They was kicked out. Wasn't no trouble or nothin', they was jus' too loud. Trunks, he's the drummer, his mum created. Said she couldn't stand it no more. Not the music, she was irie 'bout dat. She couldn't take the neighbours having a moan so she told the boys they'd have to pack it in."

Doris grunted.

"If you're going to jump, jump," said Frank.

"What are they called?" asked Doris

"Obsidian," said Ritzy. "It's Nathan see, he's into geology, you know...you know rocks and all...rock band...black rock...get it?" She giggled. "We had to look it up in the dictionary when he first said it but it sort of grows on you."

"Yes, yes," said Doris impatiently. "But why can't the boys rehearse at your place?"

"No room innit. 'Sides, Dad does shift work and so does Mum, and then there's Gran and the little kids...they go to bed ever so early. Same for the others."

"What about the church hall?"

"For goodness sake, Doris," said Frank, "she's an intelligent girl, she'll have thought of all of that."

"Costs innit," replied Ritzy. "Anyway, they could only have it once a fortnight. Always got Boys Brigade, guides and old people and ting."

Doris grunted. One phrase stuck in her mind. "They worked all their spare time to get money." That was quite untrue. They had spent many hours with her.

"Use the rooms upstairs. They're empty."

Ritzy's mouth dropped open. "D'ya mean it? I mean they really are heavy, Obsidian I mean, loud yeah."

"Yes of course I mean it. I said so, did I not? Now go away," said Doris sharply. "We shall have to discuss details some other time. There will have to be rules, responsibilities.

Go on, go on, child. You have achieved your objective, now leave me in peace."

Ritzy paused halfway to the door and dashed back to place a resounding kiss on Doris's startled cheek. She fled.

"You're a fortunate woman she didn't walk out," said Frank, "using that tone of voice to the poor girl. It's enough to give the elderly a bad name."

Doris closed her eyes and mentally hugged herself with delight. Doubts might come later but for now there was only pleasure. No longer would the upstairs rooms weigh on her conscience. It would be nice to have the young people coming and going. Joyce would just have to accept that she was still capable of making her own decisions.

"Cooey. I just thought I'd slip in when I saw the black girl come out, all right."

"Come in, Mrs Cronin." The words were spoken through gritted teeth. "*I will make an effort, I will,*" Doris told herself as the woman sat down, words already spilling out in a steady stream of varied mournfulness disguised as relentless cheer.

Trying to appear attentive, Doris caught references to "my Harry," National Health Service, the cost of living, terrible news reports, the weather. With a sense of relief, she heard the mention of religion. There might be a point of contact there. No, apparently the fear of God was lost to the country in general and to young people in particular. The two women sighed.

"I don't think that's entirely true," Doris suggested gently. "Look at the children from the comprehensive, giving up their spare time to visit the elderly. Andrew says they're a great help down at the church."

"I think you're too trusting," said Mrs Cronin. "I wouldn't have anything to do with them. You ought to be more careful. Old Mrs Tracey won't have them in her flat. She don't let no one in her flat."

"Good Lord!" said Doris. "Is she still alive? I thought she had died years ago, I never see her."

"No," said Mrs Cronin triumphantly. "You wouldn't. She don't let no one in her flat. She don't open her front door to nobody."

"I see," said Doris trying to maintain her patience. It might help if she were to change the subject. "It was very good of your husband to come and see me."

"Ever so sensitive is my Harry," said Mrs Cronin. "Gets ever so upset with the news. There was this murder, and this business in Africa. I tell him we've got enough to worry about in this country. After all it's only blacks killing blacks, isn't it?"

Doris closed her eyes and shuddered. *"Dear God, give me patience."*

Chapter Fourteen

Good grief," exclaimed Doris stepping back involuntarily from the apparition at her door.

Ritzy laughed. "It's all right, Mrs Roberts; she don't bite. This is Fiona, the brains of the outfit."

The brains of the outfit smiled at Doris. A tall girl, she towered above her companion, her height accentuated by blonde-, green- and purple-streaked hair, radiating stiffly from the crown of her head. Blonde circles gleamed disconcertingly behind her ears. The circle motif was continued on her cheeks with large dots drawn in brown. Lips and eyes were framed in deep purple. The overall effect was that of a leopard wearing an elaborate head-dress.

"Will you not come in?" Doris whispered, unable to take her eyes off the girl.

"Sit down, Mrs Roberts," said Ritzy giggling, "you've 'ad a shock. Gets most people like that."

Doris sat. "*What on earth have I let myself in for?*" she asked herself, trying in vain to peer at the face beneath the flamboyant makeup.

A black-gloved hand shot towards her. "My name is Fiona Warrender but they call me If."

"How do you do, If."

Ritzy laughed. "Sends out odd signals, don't she?"

"Go with the flow, kid," said If with silky command.

She was not quite sure what the words meant exactly but Doris found herself sitting a little straighter and paying attention to this extraordinary girl with the surprisingly soft cultured voice. Ritzy was right about the signals.

"I manage Obsidian, Mrs Roberts," said the girl. "I'm here to discuss terms."

"Terms?" echoed Doris, trying to remember why the name Warrender was so familiar.

"The rooms upstairs. We need them badly, but we are in no position to offer you money, so I'm here to work out a deal."

"*Warrender... Warrender. Of course, '...today Ambrose Warrender for the prosecution told the jury...*'" Doris had it now. This girl's father must be the lawyer who seemed never to be out of the news. Extraordinary.

"We're here to work out a deal, Mrs Roberts," the girl repeated with gentle insistence. "If you're still willing to let us use the rooms."

There was challenge in the tone if not in the words. Doris looked steadily at the weirdest person ever to step into her home. "Yes, of course I'm still willing. I see no reason why I should go back on my word."

If and Ritzy briefly exchanged glances.

"Come along," snapped Doris. "What is this deal you're talking about? I made no mention of money."

"We have to get things on a proper basis, Mrs Roberts," said If, flicking open a notebook and reading a list of the requirements, suggestions, commitments and promises that left her listener in a state of bewilderment. "You see, Mrs Roberts," she ended at last, "it's not so simple as just walking in and using your rooms. What do you think of the outline?"

The purple lips smiled and painted cheek-dots seemed to dance about the girl's questioning eyes.

Doris had the odd feeling that she had been listening to a foreign language she once knew.

"On the other hand," said If, "now you know what it involves you may want to back out. If that's the case, it would be a great help if we could just store our stuff until we find..."

"Shut up, If," Ritzy interrupted. She turned to Doris. "What she said basically was that we could pay ya a bit towards the electricity we'll be using, but the rest we'd have to make up doing odd jobs for ya, tings ya'd have to pay for, doing yer back garden, window-cleaning and ting. That's the bit where If spoke about negotiating an exchange of assets. She means yer rooms for our odd jobs. She's right about ya thinking about it, innit. Ya did say ya didn't want no one coming in. I mean ya like yer classical music and…"

"Ritzy dear, I also like meeting people with…" She glanced sideways at If. "…with whom I would not normally come into contact. It's far too easy to retreat to pleasures tried and true. My intention is to remain in complete control of the rooms upstairs. I told you the other day there would be rules and regulations. I too have given the question a lot of thought, and have been making lists."

Could Doris detect a slight flushing beneath If's garish makeup? It would not do any harm to let it be known that she was no fool.

With a great deal of giggling and lively discussion, arrangements were finally made. The members of Obsidian, Trunks, Benoit, Squirrel and Taps with If and Ritzy would be free to go upstairs every day after school and all day Saturday, but they would have to leave early on the evenings when Raza Abolhasan came for tuition. Anyone else would have to get special clearance.

"What about the wimp?" drawled If from her relaxed position on the floor.

"Shut up," said Ritzy without rancour, idly aiming a kick at the recumbent figure.

"What or who is the wimp?" asked Doris.

"Derek," said the girls in unison.

"I thought he was a very pleasant young man."

"Quite," said If in clipped tones.

This time Ritzy's kick was harder. "Is it all right if he comes too?" she asked.

Doris nodded. "I am feeling a bit tired now. I think we've covered all the points. Oh, there is just one thing. When you all come into the house I'd rather you did not come into my rooms unless I invite you. I will give the spare key to Benoit. Until I get to know the rest of the group I don't want anyone else to have it. You will have to sort out a code on the bell because I can't keep popping up and down. I expect you all to respect the few rules I have laid down." Her face grew grave. "Listen carefully. I will *not* tolerate anything to do with drugs. One mention, one hint and you're all out. No second chances. Please remember that while you are under my roof I consider you my responsibility."

Ritzy and If as far as one could tell looked equally serious. "It will be all right, Mrs Roberts," said Ritzy, "ya won't have no bother."

"You have our word." If squeezed Doris's hand painfully.

"You've done it now," said Frank, when the girls had left. "Joyce will be furious. Even Gareth may have a moment of alarm. It's bad enough you letting foreigners and black people into your home, just wait until they see If. Ho! Ho! what a laugh."

Doris shifted in her chair. "Don't go on, Frank, I know what I am doing."

"My dear girl, of course you do. You have unleashed an ineluctable force," said Frank gleefully. "I'm proud of you."

His widow began to laugh softy. "I am rather proud of myself."

Chapter Fifteen

Of course the way it will work out, Rose, is that they won't be in the house that much. They have to do odd jobs to pay for their instruments and they are going to do a bit for me. Apart from that, they're all studying for their exams. I just do not know how they find the time for everything. I think it will work out."

"Ever the optimist, Ma," said Rose.

"Is there any other way? Listen, love, I wish you could see If."

"Maybe I will," said Rose lightly. "I am coming down your way next Tuesday. I'll call in pretty early if that's OK with you."

"Marvellous. Oh lovely, oh I'll look forward to that. Come at the crack of dawn, we'll have a good old natter."

"Ma, we'll talk the hind leg off a donkey."

Doris laughed as she replaced the phone then chided herself for not asking why her daughter-in-law was coming down to London. *"Selfishness, pure selfishness, too busy with my own affairs, oh well!"* Restlessly she turned her attention to the weather, peering out of the window to see how her fellows were dealing with its effects. She must go out today.

During the last few days, the telephone had effectively tethered her to the house. Compared with her family's concern, the pop group moving in was a relatively quiet affair. Doris made the acquaintance of Trunks, Squirrel and Taps. Under If's careful stage management, they had been ushered in and out with remarkable brevity and had acted with a decorum surely foreign to their natures and ages. Ah well, doubtless there would be time enough to get to know the real nature of the owners of those preposterous names. There had been a few bangs and crashes when their equipment had arrived, but that was understandable.

Doris stood up. It was still cold outside with just a hint of watery sunshine. She would wear the coat that Ritzy had said "looked all right but didn't do no good". After a moment's hesitation she picked up her newly acquired lightweight adjustable stick. Might as well give it a go.

Just as she was leaving the house, the phone rang. Firmly closing the door, she ignored its summons and set off up the road to the Johnson house.

"Dahling, come in, 'bout time ya come see me," said the black woman. She held the door open wide and Doris stepped into a clean-smelling welcome warm hall. "Me son asleep," said Granny Johnson, pointing to the ceiling and making elaborate quietening gestures. She led her visitor into a fairy-tale room where every surface was covered with glass and silver and porcelain, which glinted, gleamed and sparkled.

Doris gasped. Never outside a department store had she seen so many ornaments in one room. Mrs Johnson laughed, a warm joyous explosion of a laugh. Doris looked anxiously at the ceiling. Ritzy's father must be a remarkably sound sleeper.

"Ya like all me treasures? I been collectin' dem for years. Take the weight off yer feet. Take a good look while I make us a cup of tea."

Doris eased herself into a chair and gazed in unfeigned admiration at the astonishing sight. She found even more remarkable the fact that there was not a speck of dust to be seen amongst the bric-a-brac.

"I have never seen anything like it," she said when her hostess returned pushing a trolley piled with tea things, cakes, biscuits and a bottle of rum.

"Ya like a drop in yer tea, dahling?" said Mrs Johnson unscrewing the cap.

"No thank you, it's a bit early for me," replied Doris.

Mrs Johnson laughed gleefully. She poured a generous amount into her own cup. "Me belly got no clock," she chortled.

Doris could not help but join in the laughter.

"What's your name, dahling, or do I call you Mrs Roberts like me girl Ritzy?"

"Doris, oh please call me Doris. I've been meaning to meet you for ages. Thank you for the wheelchair."

"Ya're welcome, Doris. Dey call me Rejoice."

"I beg your pardon."

"Rejoice, me name Rejoice. How could I be anything but happy with a name like me parents gave me? Thank the Lord." Her face grew serious. "Ya know the Lord? Ya got Jesus in your heart?" she asked with startling intensity.

"Yes…I…you…you have seen me at the church," Doris answered feebly, feeling faintly intimidated by her companion's uncompromising stare. She lifted her cup to her lips searching for something suitable to say.

Rejoice at last lowered her eyes and pushed a plate of biscuits towards her. "I seen ya dahling in that quiet place." Her face suddenly broke into a broad grin. "Sometime too quiet for me Jamaican soul."

"Ritzy told me you left Jamaica several years ago, do you miss it greatly?"

Rejoice snorted and her eyes narrowed. "Ya wan' talk sunshine and toto cakes or you wan' talk real talk?" she asked sharply.

"Real talk," said Doris calmly, and relaxed back in her chair.

The tea grew cold while they spread open the years that led to their meeting. "I joke ya early on girl, I do miss the sunshine and I'm goin' back dere to be buried on a warm hillside. Dis country too cold for me ol' bones."

Doris smiled. "Well I hope you will enjoy a bit of that

sun when you get to Jamaica. It seems hardly worth the fare otherwise."

The two women laughed and sat for a while in companionable silence. It was broken by a soft sigh. "Jamaica a dream, jus' a dream now." Rejoice spoke wistfully. Her face, bent towards her hands lying palms upward on her lap, took on an expression of sad surprise. It was if she could not understand why those hands were empty. "Just a dream," she repeated. "Dis me home, England me home, here I born me children. Here me husband buried. Dis me home."

Doris felt tears prick her eyes. She reached out and placed a hand gently in the hand of her new friend. They smiled at one another.

"De Lord alway send me someone," Rejoice whispered. She shook herself as if awakening from sleep. "The Lord alway been good to me," she said. "He alway dere. I tell ya 'bout me friend Mistress Parker, she and I friends long since Jamaica. Dey take her to hospital one day after she collapse. Soon as I hear the catastrophe I dash over dere and the nurses dey say to me dey say, "Ya've got to be quiet now, Mistress Parker, she die, she go peaceful now and it past visitin' time. Can you believe that? Me friend dyin', and dey say it past visitin' time."

Doris shook her head. Rejoice sighed. "I say to them, I say I come on the Lord's business and the Lord Jesus don' know no visitin' time. I go into that hospital ward and dere she lie all quiet and her eyes closed and she small, small like little child. De ward was warm but I cold, dere's no-one but death by me friend bed." The black woman shivered at the memory. "I try to be quiet like dey say but how can I let my friend die without tellin' Lord Jesus she comin'. Maybe He don' know she got friend down here. I take her cold hand and I call on the Lord Jesus. I say Lord Jesus, Rejoice here. I say it loud. Maybe someone else hear and they glad the Lord know no visitin' time. I say, 'Lord Jesus, me friend Mistress Parker, they say she die, please make her better.

She still got lots to do down here Lord.' I say, 'Lord Jesus she stay I happy, if she go I happy she with you.' "

Rejoice's face glowed and her voice rose even stronger. Doris winced as the hand clasping hers tightened, and her other hand was seized. "*I do not doubt God heard if she called out like that,*" she thought.

"You hear what I say?" shouted her companion.

Doris felt a oneness with the Lord's suspected deafness. Had her hands been free she would have adjusted her hearing-aid. She nodded.

"I pray and I pray for me friend, and the nurses they all fussin' 'round and they tellin' me to go like I a mad person. They want the ward neat but nature not neat, death not neat." Rejoice, shaking with remembered indignation released Doris's hands. She continued, "I go. I happy now. I know the Lord is with Mistress Parker. I feel He with her now."

"Did she recover?" Doris asked, feeling moved by the woman's obvious unshaken faith.

Rejoice laughed, her face shining with happiness. "Lord bless ya, she 'live now, livin' in Brixton. When I walk from the ward she open her eyes and she ax for a glass of Lucozade."

With difficulty, Doris managed to suppress a giggle. Jesus and Lucozade! An incongruous yet powerful combination. She cleared her throat. "I am glad your friend recovered. I think you must have been a great comfort to her."

"I jus' pray, that's all I done. Lord Jesus gave her de will. Lucozade gave her de energy."

Doris did not protest too strongly when Rejoice asked her to stay for lunch. She was enjoying herself immensely. The two women moved to the kitchen, ate bacon and eggs and talked non-stop.

If and the pop group featured large in the conversation. "I hear nothing bad 'bout that girl," said Rejoice fiercely, as if expecting a challenge.

"After the initial shock, I found her very likeable," Doris remarked.

"Don' talk to me 'bout shock," cried Rejoice. "The first day she come I sit in here all sleepy. Little Evra run in; 'Someone to see ya Granny,' she say, gigglin'. I open me eyes and nearly jump out me black skin. 'I'm If,' she say, and tells me all about looking for an old person to look after. 'I come every week,' she say business-like and she go before I can tink what to say." Rejoice's face softened "Now I thank the Lord she come. I'm not lonely, I got me children but If give me someting different."

Doris nodded vigorously. "That is exactly how I feel about Ritzy and her brothers. I think the young people of today are very caring."

Rejoice snorted. "Ya wouldn't know from the newspaper. Dey paint 'em all black."

"Are you sure you mean that?" Doris began to laugh.

Her companion looked puzzled at first, then her face broke into a huge grin. She gave her thigh a resounding slap. "I tink I jus' make a racist joke. Ah! It's a funny world." Rejoice stood up. "Now Doris, no argument ya hear me, girl?"

"Well just a little, mind, I don't usually drink rum." Doris lifted her glass. "Cheers," she said. "Thank you for a lovely day, I am so glad I came to see you." She took a sip and felt the liquid spread warmth through her entire body.

Rejoice laughed. "I'll drink a toast to ya, Doris Roberts," she said, holding her glass high. "Basket of rain, dahling. Basket of rain."

"What does that mean?" Doris asked.

"Lord love ya, we all got rain, we all got sorrows. May all yer sorrows last as long as rain in a basket."

The two women sipped their drink. "That is charming, I must remember that" Doris raised her glass. "Basket of rain, Rejoice. Basket of rain."

Chapter Sixteen

Doris scarcely noticed the cold as, leaning heavily on her stick she made her way home. She felt tired yet exhilarated. At last she had found someone with whom she could giggle without feeling she was betraying the solemnity seemingly expected of her advanced age.

Rejoice's toast lingered in her mind. "Basket of rain. Basket of rain. What does that remind me of? No matter, it will come to me. Basket of rain," she muttered to herself, taking pleasure in the words.

Unexpectedly pain gripped her knees with a cruelty that almost took her breath away. With difficulty she hobbled to lean against a garden wall. If she could just rest a moment, she would have the strength to reach her house. Gradually her breathing became easier and the excruciating pain faded to a dull ache.

"*Come on, Doris Roberts. You are all right now. Once more the rain has slipped through the basket.*" A wry smile hovered briefly on her lips. "Of course," she exclaimed loudly, much to the amusement of a passer-by. "Of course." She lowered her voice: "I remember now. It reminds me of that Dire Straits song, the one I heard that day in the snow, all about sunshine coming after rain. "Mmm," she smiled to herself. "Now we've got that straight let's see if my legs will carry me."

"Private conversation or can anyone join in?"

Doris, gingerly taking her first step, jumped.

"Sorry, Gran," said the young man with the spectacular cerise Mohican hairstyle and a stud in his nose. "Help yer?"

Without waiting for an answer, he tucked her free hand into the crook of his arm.

Wincing slightly, Doris took a deep breath and steadied herself.

"You look like you was trying to launch yourself off that wall, and give a running commentary," said her colourful Samaritan. "Where do you want to go, Gran?"

Doris indicated the direction with her stick, leaning gratefully on the denim-clad arm, "I'm very slow. I do not want to delay you, young man. I should be all right in a while."

"No sweat, Gran."

The unlikely couple made their way down the road, which was beginning to reawaken with after-school activity. Two boys ran past them towards Jyotsna and her two children who were just coming into view. They shouted and whooped, causing heads to turn angrily. Doris froze when she saw one of the boys bend down, pick up a stone and hurl it with frightening accuracy at the Indian woman. Doris saw her pause momentarily, before calmly raising her *dubhatti* to cover her face and then walk on without a backward glance.

"I'll get the rotten cowardly little sod," said Doris's helper, freeing his arm and thundering after the two boys.

Doris was left to struggle on alone. "Are you all right, my dear? Oh my goodness, you had better come inside at once," she said, on reaching Jyotsna and seeing blood trickle down the side of the woman's face.

"You get used to it," said Jyotsna, pulling the *dubhatti* further across her cheek to try to hide the sight from Tariq and Sunanda.

Doris looked at the wide-eyed worried faces of the children. "Come along," she said briskly, unlocking the door. "You two go and switch on the television. Come along, my dear, you and I'll go and make some tea."

In the kitchen, Doris gently wiped the blood from Jyotsna's face. "What do you mean you get used to it? Has this happened before?"

"This and the spitting, the ugly words and much, much worse."

"I am so very sorry," said Doris; "how can you be so patient?"

"I am not patient," said Jyotsna fiercely. "I said that I was used to it, not that I accepted it."

Doris was surprised by the intensity of the woman's anger. "You have had a shock, my dear. Let me pour you a cup of tea."

"No." The normally gentle tones were harsh. "The shock came the day the first stone was thrown; the day a man stopped my little girl in the street and called her a black bastard, the day I opened a parcel and read the card enclosed." Jyotsna lowered her eyes and her voice. "It said 'shit to shit'." She reached out her hand to Doris. "I am sorry I have brought ugliness to your home. I do not think you know about the hatred. I think you belong to the other part of England, the England that does not know, does not believe in hatred, the part that cannot believe, either through national pride or because in loving or at least tolerating, cannot grasp that everyone is not the same. The hatred exists, endemic, deep-seated, horrible…" Her voice trailed away. She closed her eyes. "I'm sorry, I did not mean to offend you…you see…"

"My dear, you are the one who has been hurt," said Doris, putting her biscuits on a plate. "Can you see to the tea while I take these into the children?"

In the sitting room, Tariq and Sunanda were sprawled on the floor, laughing uproariously at the cartoon antics on the television. "They did not hear me come in," said Doris on her return to the kitchen. "They will be fine for the moment." She sat down. "Ah, that's lovely, it seems an age since I last sat down."

The two sipped their drink until the silence was broken by Jyotsna. "I do not tell my husband about these incidents any more. He works in an environment where the prejudice is insidious, more civilised, the insults subtle, discrimination with a courteous face. He cannot believe that any of the acrimony is directed at him. Even when that…that loathsome parcel arrived he thought it was a mistake. Because we are here temporarily, people cannot possibly want us out. Mrs Roberts how are they supposed to know?"

Doris shook her head.

"How are they supposed to know?" Jyotsna repeated. "All they see is an Asian woman and her dark children and they think we are immigrants. I am glad we are not." She spread her hands flat on the table. "What can I say to my children when they ask, 'Why Mama, why is that person being nasty to us?' How can I explain to them about ignorance and hatred? I do not want them to know about such ugly things. I do not want them to grow up here. I'm sorry." Jyotsna spoke wearily. Her fingers began lightly to trace the cut on the side of her forehead.

"Is that very painful? Perhaps you should lie down for a while. I can get the children something to eat. I have been thinking, Jyotsna, should we not tell the police?" Doris asked in concern.

The Indian woman gave a soft mocking laugh, chilling to hear. She stood up and taking the cups to the sink began to wash them. She said, "There is nothing the police can do; even if they caught this boy they would soon be another one to take his place. It is better not to make a fuss." She dried the crockery and turned to lean against the sink. "My face will be quite well in a few days and by then too I hope Tariq and Sunanda will have forgotten." Her voice lost its bitter edge. "We shall go home now, Mrs Roberts, you have been very kind. I…"

Doris interrupted her. "Will you forget, Jyotsna? Will you be able to forget, put it into perspective? How long will you go on suspecting every smile, every running footstep? Try and give us another chance, not least for your own peace of mind. Think of that young man who raced after your attacker."

Jyotsna smiled weakly. "I understand what you're saying, I will try not to paint you all with the one brush. I really must be going now, Mrs Roberts. Thank you for listening and for being so patient. Please do not come to the door with us, you look weary."

Doris sat on in the fading afternoon light, feeling a mixture of sadness, anger and a profound sense of her own powerlessness. How many black or Asian woman were meekly suffering, not wanting to make a fuss? The stories Jyotsna had told her were not new but now she was personally involved. The morning had been joyous, but reality had made itself felt with its threatening unsettling presence. "*That is ridiculous,*" she thought. "*The time spent with Rejoice was just as real as the time spent with Jyotsna. Why should distress be more real than joy?*" In lethargy's grasp, she lingered on in the gathering gloom unable to reassure herself or shake off feelings of unease. In her mind's eye, she saw a pair of hate-filled eyes, the eyes of the boy who had menaced her in the snow.

She jumped when she heard footsteps in the hall.

"Mrs Roberts."

Doris sighed with relief when she heard the anxious voice. "I'm in the kitchen," she called. "Don't put the light on for the moment, love."

Ritzy was full of concern. "Borrowed Benoit's key 'cos we heard there'd been a bit of bother and ya was mixed up in it. Ya all right, innit?"

"Yes I am all right," said Doris. "I had a lovely time with your grandmother this morning."

"Yeah, but someting's up now, innit? Come on, why're ya sitting in the dark, eh?"

Doris told her about Jyotsna. "Then I started to think about that boy, the day you took me out in the wheelchair."

"Lester," said Ritzy. "Ya don' want to pay no mind to him, we don't hardly see him no more since he bunked off school. Anyway ya don' want to waste yer time tinkin' 'bout a prat like him." She moved to the light switch. "Come on, let's put the light on. Shall I warm up a tin of soup? Yer hands is purple, I can see 'em from here."

She did not wait for an answer but set about opening and searching cupboards. "Oxtail, ya bought it so ya must like it. I'll do ya oxtail."

She toasted great doorsteps of bread and set them on the table beside the steaming bowl of soup. Doris watched rivulets of butter melt into the hot golden toast and began to cry.

"Don' let the race ting get to ya, Mrs Roberts. Come on eat up while it's still hot."

Doris raised her spoon obediently and listened while Ritzy chatted about GCSEs, her family, Derek, the pop group. "Ya've got to get a good night's sleep, 'cos tomorrow's the big day. They're gonna start rehearsals tomorrow, innit. I hope it'll be all right."

"No reason why it should not be. I'm looking forward to it," said Doris making an effort to sound cheerful. "Oh Ritzy, dear, this has done me good."

Ritzy gave a squeal. "Nearly forgot, Benoit told me to remind ya about the Grand Prix on Sunday, going to watch it, are ya?"

"Yes I hope so, please thank him for me. You'd better go, love, I know you've got homework to do, and Ritzy."

"Yes, Mrs Roberts."

"Thank you."

Chapter Seventeen

Doris gave only half her attention to *Any Questions*. A ripple of laughter or applause occasionally aroused her from her reverie. Soon, however, the demands of her own questioning drew her away again. She turned off the radio and stood up to stare with unseeing eyes at the cold empty street outside her window. Since Ritzy's departure, she had spoken on the phone to her son and daughter. Brief and unsatisfactory calls they were, falsely cheerful, devoid of reassurance. Gareth seemed to be preoccupied. Rose was at a committee meeting, is that what he had said? Listening to his tone of voice, Doris had missed the actual words. Joyce wanted only to be told that all was well. Her mother tried to say what she wanted to hear. There was no point telling her about the laughter of the morning or the tears of the afternoon.

"*But I want to share everything,*" thought Doris wistfully. "*I don't just want to be what others think I am. Now I want to shut myself away from a world grown unfamiliar and unpleasant, but tomorrow I know, I hope to God, I will not feel like this. All through my life, I have bounced back. No doubt tomorrow I'll again see my way clear and once more welcome the unexpected.*" She moved restlessly about the room, hands absently touching familiar objects. "*Tonight I almost understand old Mrs Tracey locking herself away,*" she thought. "*Almost...almost. I feel like a stranger in a strange combative land and I cannot face the fray. The rules and the weapons are unknown to me. I want to retreat into my own cosy familiar world. I don't feel equipped to face the version of the world that revealed itself today."*

The window drew her once more and she gazed up and down the quiet frost-gripped street as if seeking a means of escape. A shadow detached itself from behind her garden gatepost and she drew in a sharp breath. "No," she breathed, "not tonight." Dropping the curtain, she limped to the front door.

"Mr Cronin," she called softly. "Harry."

The man came towards her, his boots ringing loudly on the garden path. Apparently embarrassed by the noise, he awkwardly walked the last few steps on his toes. "I didn't know, I wasn't sure, I mean I had to come. Mrs Roberts I have to tell…"

"No," Doris broke in firmly. "No, Mr Cronin, I am sorry, please don't be offended but not tonight, I can't tonight."

"But I…" the man looked deflated. "Mrs Roberts, I…"

"No." Doris closed her mind to his appeal. "Goodnight, Mr Cronin, please believe me, you will be very welcome some other evening. Forgive me." She leaned against the closed door listening to the reluctantly retreating footsteps fade into the sharp night. "Oh Frank, it may be selfish, but I need help myself tonight."

"I know love, I know. You can't be strong all the time. Go to bed now. You'll be your normal inquisitive, stroppy self in the morning."

Doris began to drag her stiff legs towards the bedroom. The tears she had been holding back escaped and ran unheeded down her cold cheeks. "I miss you so much, Frank, I need the warmth of your arms around me. I feel so alone." Her hand was on the door-knob when she began to cry in earnest. She entered the bedroom sobbing unrestrainedly. Removing only her shoes she crawled into bed and drew the blankets tight about her. Frank was silent. Shuddering still, Doris tried to pray.

Chapter Eighteen

With a jangled crash of chords, the rehearsal began. Doris automatically put up her hand to adjust her hearing-aid only to find that she was not wearing it. Until memory revived, she was slightly puzzled to find herself fully clothed beneath the bedclothes. Reluctantly, she opened her eyes to gaze with disbelieve at the bedside clock. It was almost midday. Mrs Evans must have come and gone and decided to leave her in peace. *"I haven't slept in this late in years,"* she thought. *"Do I feel rested!"* Like a tongue probing a troublesome tooth, she sought the pain of the previous night. Only a wistful sadness remained. Frank at last was laid to rest and she would not be hearing from him again.

"Doris Roberts you have jumped another hurdle," she told herself. *"Up you get. There is work to be done. You cannot save the world but you can help."* Her hand hovered over her hearing-aid. With a wry glance at the ceiling, she decided to forego its benefits while she had a shower and made tea and toast and read the morning mail.

Amongst the usual enticements of fabulous wealth was a letter from her eldest great-granddaughter. Briony, it seemed, quite liked Dire Straits but that was mainly because her dad was into them. She was more into Steps. Doris resolved to ask Ritzy about present-day music.

Warmly clad in tracksuit and jacket, she left her cacophonous house for the comparative quiet of the Saturday street. On her doorstep, she paused to look around and sniff the air. Damp earth and bare trees beneath thin ghostly sunshine held little hope but was there not a hint, the faintest smell of spring? Despite the lack of evidence, Doris decided that there was, and breathed in the chilly air with satisfaction.

Mrs Panano serving fruit outside the shop shouted across the road, "You all right, Mrs Roberts?"

Doris waved her stick and smiled. It was difficult to believe that this street going peacefully about its business had yesterday been a place of menace. She drew her scarf tightly about her neck and set off towards the church.

"Much more comfortable, this old wooden stick of mine."

"Talking to yourself again, Gran."

"Was I, dear? Oh dear." Doris looked up to see yesterday's helper grinning at her. His hair made her think of some exotic bird and yet Trevor looked curiously old-fashioned. Surely, that was the style in the 'seventies? "Oh I am so glad I have seen you. I wanted to…"

Mrs Cronin appeared out of the blue. "I was just going to call on you, Mrs Roberts, dear," she said, placing her hand possessively on Doris's arm.

The young man made a move to leave. "Please do not go, Trevor," said Doris.

"Good afternoon, Mrs Cronin, nice to see the sunshine, is it not?"

Mrs Cronin clutched her headscarf tightly about her face and looked doubtfully at the sky. "Yes, well, I won't hold you up now, take care won't you?" she said, casting meaningful glances at the young man while edging away. She managed to convey the impression that she was escaping with her life.

Doris smiled at her companion. "I wanted to thank you for helping yesterday. It was very thoughtful of you."

"No sweat, Gran," he said, shuffling his feet. "Sorry, I dumped you though."

"Did you catch up with the stone thrower?"

"No, I put the frighteners on his mate, though." The young man grinned, then looked embarrassed.

Doris gazed at him shrewdly. Some questions are best left unasked. Moving away, she said, "Oh! Another thing I wanted to say was, I think your hairstyle is quite splendid, a real work of art." She smiled to see a scarlet blush spread to the very roots of his creation. She fancied he looked pleased.

❦

"Jesus Saves" read the sign outside the church. Beneath it, some wit had added "With Barclays Bank". "You have to smile," said a cheerful voice.

Doris turned round. "Andrew, how nice. I was hoping to see you."

"And I you," said the vicar. "I was going to call on you later this afternoon, can you spare the time to come into the vicarage now?"

The two sat by the open fire drinking Guinness. Doris spoke of her experiences and feelings of the day before and how, finally, she had come to terms with Frank's death. "I thought I already had, you know," she said. "I used to convince myself that he was still making decisions, giving his approval, chiding me for leaving things undone, urging me not to be fainthearted. It was quite a revelation last night to discover that I had been doing it all by myself. That reminds me, if you see Rodney do you think you could ask him to call and see me? Now, Andrew, what was it you wanted to see me about?"

The vicar put down his glass and said carefully, "Actually it does tie up with what you have been saying. I wish you would consider joining us at the club."

Doris tutted impatiently. "Really, Andrew, not that again. I do not want to be labelled, classified, identified with or pushed into a group. I thought I had made that perfectly clear." She felt herself flush with annoyance. Did the man not understand a word that she had been saying?

"Yes," said Andrew calmly. "You made it quite plain." He shot her an amused glance. "I just think you might be just a tiny bit selfish."

Doris looked at him in astonishment. "What in God's name do you mean by that, Andrew Sedley?"

Andrew smiled. "In God's name," he said, "I think you may be wasting your talents. Let me explain." He shifted into a more comfortable position "You see, it seems to me that you have given old age and its attendant problems a lot of thought and you face some of those problems with humour and courage, in your own words jumping hurdles. It seems to me, Doris, that you could share a bit of that strength with others."

"You do talk the most utter nonsense," scolded Doris, finishing her drink and placing the empty glass firmly on the table. "Were you not listening when I told you about the tears I have shed, the silly niggly fears...?"

"Yes, but you face them. Doris, you have the ability to analyse and rationalise your fears. You don't shut yourself away and let life pass you by. Yesterday you witnessed violence. You were frightened, angered, saddened, yet today you are out on the streets. You are articulate and you could share that sort of spirit."

Doris fumbled for her stick in exasperation. She stood up and buttoning her jacket spoke angrily. "And the one fear I cannot conquer or quell is the terror, to me it is a terror, of being lost, pulled down, submerged. I want to cling on to my individuality as long as I can."

Andrew left his chair and took her reluctant hand. "That determination is exactly what we need, despite the fear, independence can be maintained. Don't you see, Doris, you can inspire others?" He spoke eagerly, his eyes alive with sincerity and hope.

Doris looked at him steadily. "You disappoint me, Andrew. You want to put me in a safe slot just like Joyce. Tuck the old girl in with the rest of the old folk. Flatter her a bit about her supposed usefulness and she will conform in no time at all." She moved to the door. "Andrew, I repeat, I haven't got the herd mentality. I never have had. I want to keep my fears to myself. If that is selfish so be it." Had Doris had the strength she would have slammed the door after her.

Breathing heavily, she stood on the garden path while behind her Andrew gently clicked the door shut. She was furious with her family, her friends, the vicar and herself. Her entire body longed to stomp away but she had to content herself with struggling rather painfully in the direction of the church. "Nobody understands me," she muttered. "They all want to fit me into their version of me, nobody knows me." She sat at the back of the church and shared her anger with her Maker. "Could you not help to make them understand, you are God after all? There is an awful lot of confusion down here, with a bit of effort I am sure you could sort something out. Nobody expects a miracle, just a bit of understanding."

Light from the stained glass windows cast multi-coloured pools of reflection on the intricate mosaic floor, illuminating particles of dust floating in each cold pale ray. Quietly a woman waged war against the dust that had already come to rest. She had an air of calm satisfaction as she worked deftly amongst the pews. Watching the woman's patient repetitive movements Doris gradually felt her anger seep away though Andrew's comment about selfishness still stung. "*Come on, Doris Roberts, where is your sense of humour? You sound like a teenager, 'nobody understands me'.*" The thought invited and secured a smile. "*Thank God,*" she thought.

Hunger prompted a move and Doris regretfully left the enveloping peace of the church for the doubtful delights of a nearby cafe. The proprietor seemed surprised to find a frail old lady in the midst of his noisy leather-clad clientele, and treated her with a deference more suited to precious porcelain. Doris resolutely closed her eyes to the seeming squalor. She was amused by and grateful for the attention and the steaming mug of tea pressed on her before she was given a chance to ask for anything. The assumption seemed to be that she was unwell. She warmed her hands on the hot mug while the man fussed around the table, ineffectively flicking away crumbs, needlessly moving the pepper and salt. "I am rather hungry," she said. "Is it too late to get something to eat?"

"Never too late, or too early, love. What do you fancy?"

Doris ordered and sipped her tea. It had been generously sugared, in case of shock, presumably. Her fellow customers were shouting to make themselves heard above raucous laughter and blaring pop music. They looked happy enough, even if they did sound as if they were quarrelling. A scuffle broke out at one table and the shouting grew louder and rougher. "Keep it down, lads," bawled the proprietor in a voice to render superfluous any artificial aid to hearing. He shot a look at Doris that clearly said she was a delicate responsibility. She smiled and shook her head and pointed to her ears to indicate that she could not hear properly and she was not offended. The words had not been directed at her; besides she had heard them all before. The drop in sound was brief and barely perceptible. "*Might as well ask the steam to stop steaming*," thought Doris looking at the streaming windows. She was enjoying watching the boisterous crowd of young men and women in their studded leather clothing. They seemed to belong to a different tribe from Ritzy, If and the other teenagers she was beginning to know.

The plate placed in front of her was piled high with enough food to satisfy the hunger pangs of a man engaged in hard physical labour. Doris felt a little daunted. Its presentation was less than attractive but it was piping hot and she did need something. With trepidation she cut off a piece of unidentified meat and cautiously put it in her mouth.

"Everything all right, love?"

She raised her eyes to find the cafe's owner peering anxiously at her. She swallowed. "Delicious ...it's...absolutely

94

delicious." She hoped the surprise in her voice was not offensive as she tackled the meal with considerable enthusiasm.

Replete at last, she went to the counter to pay a compliment and what seemed to her a ridiculously low figure. "Will you be all right, Mrs?" asked the owner solicitously. "Do you want one of the lads to see you home?"

Fleetingly, Doris saw herself clinging perilously on the back of a hurtling motorbike, a Harvey Davidson mayhap. She coughed to disguise a chuckle. "You are very kind. I've been looked after splendidly." After the damp clinging warmth of the café, sharp sunless cold came as a shock. "*I hope Rose wraps up warm when she comes down,*" Doris thought as she moved homeward as swiftly as she could.

Chapter Nineteen

Mother you don't know what you might get in a place like that with those awful people? said Joyce.

"Yes I do, dear," said her mother. "Good, plain food, well cooked, a warm atmosphere in an entertaining environment and all that reasonably priced. I may go there regularly from now on."

"Mother you're hopeless."

"*Not quite, Joyce, dear,*" thought Doris replacing the phone. "*Life looks like fun again. There is hope.*"

The doorbell rang. "Vicar said you wanted to see me, Madam. May I be of some assistance?"

"Good evening, Rodney. Please come in." Doris held the door open.

"Thank you, but no. I enter no one's house saving that of the Lord. He alone I find to be an undemanding, welcoming, albeit silent host."

Doris felt taken aback. "Well I would hate to go against your principles, but could you at least step into my hall while I fetch something? If you do not wish to share my heat I should like to keep it in for myself."

"I'll wait here," said Rodney firmly, and sat on the doorstep with his back to his would-be hostess.

Doris reluctantly pushed the door shut. She returned several minutes later pushing a shopping trolley. "If the mountain must come to Mohammed! This is the only way I could manage it," she said feeling rather pleased with herself. She was wearing boots, an extra cardigan and her jacket. The Crystal Palace scarf was wrapped round her neck.

"Please allow me," said Rodney, swiftly standing up and taking the trolley. From it he took two cushions and laid them carefully side by side on the doorstep. With elaborate care, he held Doris's arm whilst she lowered herself cautiously onto one of the cushions. Rodney sat beside her. "It's a little chilly this evening but quite pleasant, do you not think?"

Doris agreed and drew a light rug across their knees. They sat in silence and watched lights appear in windows, curtains being drawn, the occasional plane flash across the star-spattered sky. A young couple, quite oblivious to the watchers, stood beneath a street lamp and kissed. "One is given to believe that present day youth is blasé," said Rodney, "this selfish, couldn't care less society. Yet…" he stroked his unshaven face reflectively, "…yet they still fall in love."

"And thank God for it," said Doris briskly. "Would you like a drink, Rodney?" She reached out for the shopping trolley.

"Allow me," he said, producing a bottle of sherry and two glasses. He held the bottle to the light to read the label. "Good, good" he muttered and began to pour.

"You approve then?" asked Doris dryly, accepting the glass.

"Your very good health, Mrs Roberts," said her companion. "Yes, this is very fine."

"My son-in-law has good taste." They sipped their drink and shared a packet of water biscuits. Doris felt a little wary of offending her guest at this impromptu picnic. She longed to discover the practical details of his life but had to settle for his well-considered views on the EU, Hong Kong, the Middle East, East-West relations, the papacy. Closer to home they discussed the Irish question, genetic engineering, the royal family, the London Eye in the Sky, surrogate motherhood, nuclear fuel, law and order, education, the now and future role of the Millennium Dome. They politely but firmly disagreed on many points while they finished the bottle of sherry.

"Such a pleasant way to spend an evening," said Doris suddenly. "Stimulating conversation, excellent company. Rodney, the time has come, always leave the party while there is still some life in it. Would you please help me to my feet?"

"My pleasure and honour, dear lady," murmured Rodney, easing himself up from the doorstep and offering his arm. It reminded Doris why she had asked him to visit her.

"In that bag—" she pointed unsteadily to the shopping trolley. "Would you do me a favour and take those few clothes off my hands? They belonged to my husband. I can't imagine how I overlooked them when I cleared out his things." She was glad it was now dark and Rodney could not see the lie in her eyes. She could sense him stiffen and hesitate. "There's a suit and top coat, quite good quality I believe. The days are still extremely cold. I should like to think they were being worn by someone who would appreciate them. It really would help if you were to take them." She struggled to her feet feeling very stiff and not a little tired.

Rodney removed the clothes from the trolley, holding them out and examining them carefully in the light from the street. At last, satisfied with their suitability, he helped Doris lift the trolley into the hall and thank her graciously for the rewarding evening.

She was washing the glasses when the newly installed kitchen phone rang, making her jump. She picked up the receiver with care. "Don't hang up. You may hear something to your advantage," said a familiar voice.

"I may hear alarm bells and see flashing lights if I press the wrong thing on this newfangled contraption," said Doris. "Joyce's idea. Prin, how lovely to hear from you. Wait just a minute while I sit down." She dried her hands rapidly and eagerly picked up the phone again. "Now, Prionsias, it

98

has been an age since I heard from my favourite grandson." She drew in a sharp breath. "Oops! Should not have said that should I?" she giggled.

There was an answering laugh in her ear. "I do believe you are a bit squiffy, Grandmother."

"I have been drinking alfresco," said his grandmother with studied dignity. "What is the advantage of which you speak?"

"Well, are you ready to come out of hibernation?"

"Speak plain English, boy, what are you talking about?"

Prionsias answered in feigned surprise, "I just thought all old ladies were wrapped up in red flannel and tucked away for the winter. I wonder…"

Doris laughed at the absurd notion. "You are a clown, Prin Roberts. What did you wonder?"

"Whether you were ready to come out of moth balls." His voice lost its bantering tones. "Seriously, Gran, can you be ready to roll tomorrow morning? I'll come and pick you up. Eleven-thirty suit you?"

"Lovely, lovely, lovely," said Doris, wondering if a hangover might not be her fate in the morning. "In what shall we roll?" She was definitely feeling light-headed.

"Gran, go and get some beauty sleep," said Prin with amused concern. "I'll see you in the morning," he rang off.

"*I should not have said that, of course,*" mused Doris as she laid out her clothes for the morrow. "*But he always has been my favourite.*" She sat on the bed and slowly undid her cardigan buttons. Her thoughts were far away with a sad-eyed sickly baby lying in Rose's arms. Doris could remember that day as clearly as if it were yesterday, the day when Prionsias had come into their lives. Was it possible that since then over thirty years had gone by? She sighed and reached out for the alarm clock. Tomorrow was too important to risk oversleeping. That skinny child was now a handsome successful man. It would be a pleasure to go out in his company. "*Besides,*" thought Doris, "*I would go anywhere with a man who makes me laugh.*"

Chapter Twenty

Sunday morning sunshine, a Ferrari, red, shining, sleek, deceptively quiescent. "In which we roll," said Prionsias in a vain attempt at nonchalance. Fingers full of pride softly stroked the gleaming metal. "What do you think, Gran?" he asked. "Magnificent?"

Doris nodded. "It is beautiful. It looks alive, as if it might spring forward at any moment. Does the performance match the appearance?"

"Just wait till you hear her purr, Gran. Actually the engine is really quite special, a sort of grown-up version of the design that took Niki Lauda and Jody Scheckter to three world championships. You remember?"

"The Grand Prix is on television this afternoon. I'd like to see it but of course I can always watch the highlights tonight."

Doris walked to the rear of the car. "512 BB. A Boxer. Good grief, Prin, you must be doing well in your line of work."

"Nope," said her grandson, grinning cheerfully, "in hock up to my eyeballs, Barclays owns my socks."

Doris laughed. "You look as if you think it's worth it. Oh Prin, it really is gorgeous."

Prionsias opened the passenger door "Only problem is it's left-hand drive."

"The only problem," said Doris tersely, "is how do I lower myself into this glorified roller skate?"

Her grandson looked aghast. "Grandmother Roberts, I thought you had a soul. A roller skate, roller skate, you call the greatest car in the world a roller skate. Besides you've got no excuse, if you can get into a toboggan you can get into a Ferrari."

Doris was quite breathless by the time she had manoeuvred herself onto the magnolia leather upholstery. "Prin, I may never get out again," she gasped as he fastened her seatbelt.

"Sit here a bit while you get your breath back. I should have checked. Have you locked up OK?"

Doris nodded.

"Do you know why this is called a 512 BB?"

"5 litre, 12 cylinder, Boxer Berlinnetta," said Doris promptly, smiling at the surprise on Prin's face. "I learned a lot from your grandfather. He was a car man. Back in the 'thirties we used to go to Brooklands, you know." She stopped. It was not fair to talk about the past when Prionsias was itching to enthuse over the acquisition of his dreams. "Apart from that I don't know a great deal about it," she lied.

"Oh well," said Prin looking relieved, fastening his own seatbelt. "You know how it works don't you? The fuel goes in through four triple-choke Webber down-draught carburettors. Each engine bank has two cam shafts. To drive all those would cause a lot of noise, so Ferrari went away from chain driven cam shaft drive units to belt driven units, so, although it makes beautiful noises it doesn't clank or make a row like the other ones used to. This is a…"

"Prionsias."

"…so called mid-engine car. The drive…"

"Prionsias."

"…unit placed between the wheel base forward of the…"

"Prionsias."

"Yes, Gran."

"Drive the car."

Prin laughed and the engine roared into life. The car remained poised for several seconds then surged forward through the Sunday streets of South London to the A2.

Doris had fleeting glimpses of heads turned to stare. She watched the car's handsome reflection as they flashed past shuttered shop windows. "Does your brake work?" Prin teased, noting that his grandmother automatically pressed her right foot to the floor.

"It's funny," she said, "it must be five or six years now since I gave up driving but I still think as a driver. Sometimes when my mind is miles away I will find myself standing patiently by a red traffic light. I get some funny looks I can tell you."

"I can imagine. I thought we'd have a blast down the M2 then return in a more leisurely fashion via the Bull. How does that grab you?"

"It...grabs...me," she gasped with difficulty as the car seemed to leap beneath her and hurtled forward until hedges were a blur and trees appeared to stand mere inches apart. Sky, cloud and field merged into one muted blend of colour. Doris's heart beat a little faster and she gasped for breath. Cars on the inside lane appeared to crawl sedately while the Ferrari aimed unerringly for the horizon.

"Just over this hill and we'll really put her through her paces," yelled Prionsias, throwing his grandmother a swift smile.

She took a deep breath and realised with joy that it was not fear but excitement that gripped her. Relaxing, she uncurled her clenched hands and forced her eyes away from the road ahead to the speedometer. Not believing what she saw, she glanced sideways at Prin. His face was a picture of concentration and pure naked delight. The muscles of his thigh tensed as the accelerator was slowly and carefully pushed to the floor. Doris leaned back, the controlled roar of the engine in her ear. Beneath a spring-bright sun, the red, beautiful curves of the bonnet shimmered and sparkled as the insatiable Ferrari smoothly consumed the motorway miles. All conscious thoughts suspended, Doris gave herself completely to feelings of sheer exhilaration. There was no way of knowing how long it was before she noted with disappointment that they were slowing down and moving into the inside lane. She heard her grandson swear under his breath. "What is it, Prin?" she asked anxiously.

The engine still sounded sweet as Prionsias indicated and slid effortlessly into a lay-by and switched off. While applying the handbrake, he hissed the word "police" and an adjective that Doris chose not to hear. She had no time to exclaim over the apparent magic of the electrically controlled windows gliding downward before a shadow fell on her and the policeman began, "Good morning, madam. I thought I ought to warn…"

"Good afternoon, officer," said Doris brightly, "is it not a beautiful day for a ride in the country?"

The man looked bemused. "It is my duty to warn," he cleared his throat "uh um we um…I thought you were driving." He looked uncomfortable. "We were very concerned. Do you know what speed you were doing when you passed us, madam?"

"No idea whatsoever," said Doris with a beatific smile. "I am afraid I was just enjoying the sunshine. It is quite warm through the glass you know."

"Quite so, madam." The police officer turned his attention to Prin. "May I see your driving licence, sir?"

Prin had already extracted it from his wallet. He joined the policeman now standing at the rear of the car and handed it to him.

"It's not right is it, sir?" said the policeman, painstakingly perusing the document.

"No," murmured Prin with eyes downcast. "No, sir."

"No," said the policeman, walking around the car and peering from it at all angles. "Not right at all. Not right at all."

Doris smiled sweetly and waved at him, he shook his head sadly.

"Just not right to frighten an old lady." He squatted down to peer at the tyres. "Your grandmother, sir?" he asked.

Prin nodded, not trusting himself to speak.

The policeman stood up and patted the Ferrari's roof, smiling suddenly. "She's certainly a beauty, sir."

"My grandmother?" said Prin, incredulous.

"The car," said the policeman with lugubrious patience.

The two men stood together in mute admiration, blind to everything save the magnificent vehicle, deaf to the continuous roar of other cars thundering by. The policeman handed back the driving licence. "I've never booked one of these before," he said mournfully, "these Boxers. Seen a few, mind you," he said brightly. "Never seen the engine though."

The words hung in the air for a few seconds before Prin caught them. "Oh please let me show you." The rear bonnet rose to reveal a forest of carburettors, black crinkle casing and polished aluminium.

The policeman gave a low whistle of appreciation. "You—could eat your dinner off that if you had a mind to. What's she got, power I mean?"

"Nearly four hundred horse power with rejetted carbs and a modified exhaust system. Of course that way you can get through a lot of tyres. The originals were 225370 WKCRX by…"

"Prin," Doris called in a quavering voice.

"Just a moment, Gran."

"You'd best see to your grandmother," said the policeman. "Look after her, sir."

"The car?"

The policeman bent down to peer inside the car. Its occupant smiled gaily at him.

"Your grandmother. I wouldn't want to upset the old lady any further," he said, staring fixedly at Doris. "You can never replace your granny." He stood up. "If I were you I'd take her for a quiet cup of tea. As it happens your speed was not recorded, so I'll leave you with a word of caution. I expect you know the speed limit in this country. I should stick to it in future if I were you, sir. Might I suggest Brands Hatch with your type of driving."

Only when the police car had disappeared did Doris and Prin dare to look at one another. Laughter exploded from them in great loud guffaws, chests heaved, sides ached and tears tumbled down cheeks. "Not right to frighten an old lady," gasped Prin, leaning on the steering wheel and giving himself up to fresh paroxysms of mirth.

"She's certainly a beauty, sir," Doris mimicked and pressed her handkerchief hard against her streaming eyes. "Oh I would have loved to have seen his face when he thought I was driving."

At last, Prin leaned back. "Well Mrs Roberts, how do you feel about carrying on, or do you feel too delicate?"

"You can never replace your granny," said Doris and laughter broke out afresh. "That was wonderful, Prin, the ride I mean. I was completely caught up in the thrill of it. What amazed me is that, though I knew we were going tremendously fast there was no real awareness of speed. It seemed almost as if we were floating. When we had to slow down it was the end of a unique experience." Doris turned her head to look at her grandson. "Tell me, Prin, just how fast were we going?"

"159 miles per hour."

Chapter Twenty-one

I am glad to see that you are not intent on flouting every law of the land," said Doris, eyeing Prin's glass of orange juice while she gratefully sipped a gin and tonic.

"One can't be a fool all one's life, Grandmother," said Prin. "Not more than once a day anyway. Besides, I reckon I'm a marked man now. There won't be a policeman in the county who won't know me, well, the car anyway."

"I'll never forget today," said Doris. "I have had such fun." She chuckled at the memory. "Boney!" she exclaimed suddenly. Several heads turned and the noise in the pub dropped fractionally.

Prin choked on his drink. "Good grief, have you been reminiscing with Mum?"

"No, no. I have just remembered what we used to call you as a child, Why?"

Prin frowned. "No reason, but the other day, quite out of the blue she called me Boney. Nobody has done that since I was a very small boy. It seemed a bit uncanny, twice in one week."

Doris had a far-away look in her eye. "Do you remember why you had that nickname?"

Prin nodded vigorously. "Oh yes, very clearly," he groaned dramatically. "Oh boy, do I ever. I was always scared that people would find out what it was short for. Scarred me for life, that nickname." He laughed aloud. "It became increasingly difficult to say it was because I was skinny, talking of which, will a sandwich do you? I think it's a bit late for proper food. Another gin and tonic?"

"Yes please, ham with mustard and most certainly another gin." Doris watched her grandson tread his way through the chattering throng. Boney, Mum's little bonus, yes, she could imagine the embarrassment. *Still, it was apt at the time,"* she thought. *"That would have been…19…50…60? Well thereabouts anyway and…Rosaria and the children staying with Frank and me. Where was Gareth at that time? Odd how selective memory is…"*

She looked up. "Goodness, that was quick, Prin."

He grinned down at her. "Actually I've been standing here for ages trying to attract your attention. There you are, Gran, help yourself to mustard. Still flying round in the Ferrari were you?"

Doris placed her glass in the limited space on the table and balanced the plate of sandwiches on her lap. "You have to be dextrous to enjoy yourself nowadays," she said tartly. "No, I was thinking about the day your mother brought you home."

Prin took a hearty bite of his sandwich. "It must have been a shock."

Doris smiled to herself; he sounded like a small child asking for a repeat of a favourite tale. She sipped her drink.

"Well, yes it was, as you are perfectly aware."

"Yes but you tell it so very well."

"Mmm," Doris grunted. "Flatter as you may I'll not battle against this hubbub. This sandwich is very good by the way."

They ate and drank in their own oasis of silence amidst the clink and clatter of Sunday lunchtime hubbub. Laughter and smoke rose and lingered on the air. Weak sunlight lent a sparkle to the hanging glasses and explored the dark and twisted beams of the old pub. Beneath those beams, colourfully clad men and women, mostly young, chatted, giggled, listened and posed. *"Another tribe,"* thought Doris and reached for her stick.

"Fit?" Prin enquired.

She nodded. "That was lovely, thank you."

Out in the carpark the cold was sharp. Doris leaned on her grandson's arm. As she breathed deeply, the air felt cleansing to her throat. "Where is Elaine today? I'm sorry not to have asked before."

"With her parents," said Prin as they reached the car. After opening the door, he turned to face his grandmother. "She's gone to tell them about the baby. I dropped her off there before I came to take you out."

Doris allowed herself to be lowered into her seat before she was hit by the full implications of what he had said. "A baby?" she whispered. "Why did you not tell me before? Oh I can't tell you how delighted I am. Are you...are you happy, Prin?"

His face broke out into a huge grin. "What do you think? We're both ecstatic. I don't think either of us can quite believe it yet. We've waited such a long time."

Doris looked reflective. "So that is why you want to hear the old story. That is what today has all been about. Oh! This is the best news." She turned to face Prionsias and asked gently, "What about the Ferrari, will you be able to keep it?"

"Probably not," said Prin cheerfully. He flashed a quick smile. "But I will have had it, Gran, that's the main thing. You see I'll always be able to say that once I had a Ferrari, the best Ferrari ever built." He reached toward the ignition.

"Don't start it just yet," said Doris. "You really do want me to tell you about your arrival?"

The man beside her nodded, looking straight ahead, his face suddenly deeply serious.

Doris turned her head away, resisting the temptation to touch him, locked as he was in his own private world. Her eyes fixed on a motionless, budless tree. The thought flitted through her mind that it might be dead, that it might never stir to another spring. With a small smile, she began to speak in a low soothing voice. "In the ...'fifties...'sixties...I...I was never terribly good with dates,

108

Rose came to stay with Frank and me. Gareth was away on some project. Nigel would have been about two and little Aidan no more than two or three months old. It was summer and every day Rose would take them to the park. As I was doing a bit of tutoring then I seldom went with them. In any case, I liked to have a meal ready for everyone when they came home. One day Rose came back with a sad tale—well, rather more than a sad tale actually." Doris shot a swift glance at Prionsias sitting in a strangely tense waiting stillness. She continued. "She had met a young girl with a baby. The girl was no more than a child herself, a frail frightened little thing, Rose said. At first she did no more than smile shyly but gradually Rose drew her out. Well, you know Rose can talk an oyster open."

Prin gave a fleeting smile but said nothing.

"Every day we heard about this poor child. To be absolutely honest, Frank and I were concerned because Rose was so obviously worried about the girl's situation. For instance, the baby had to be carried all the time, no pram, you see. We thought she had enough on her plate with her own children. She used to take little bits and pieces of clothing with her to the park, but the girl refused pointblank to accept charity or come home to meet us but she would eat if Rose said it was a picnic." Doris laughed softly. "To this day I doubt if Nigel ever goes voluntarily on picnics. Day after day Rose met this girl and fed her. Prin, do you really want me to go on in such detail?"

Prionsias bent forward and the engine roared into life. Startled birds screeched and rose in a brief squall of feathers, black against the ice-hard sky then dropped to blend once more into the bare countryside.

"I am so sorry. I'm being frightfully selfish, Gran. I shouldn't keep you sitting there, especially, as you say, I know the story backwards."

They moved slowly across the deserted carpark, past the pub, now shuttered, silent, somehow secretive and uninviting. "You're not selfish, Prin. I understand the need to be told things again and again because deep down there is a doubt. Some things you have to know with every fibre of your being before you can accept them. It was only the other day when I finally knew that Frank was dead."

"And are you all right, Grandmother...truly?"

The car edged into the road and picked up speed.

"Yes," said Doris simply. Her gaze fell on bare ploughed fields, freshly groomed it seemed in herringbone pattern. In some the shadowed earth looked soft as sable, smoothed with the gentle hand. The ground had been raked, worked over, tended and left to nurture the delicate plants that would push their way strongly through the dark earth to the light. "When will your baby be born, Prin?"

"September."

Doris nodded "I'll change my will. You and Elaine are already mentioned of course."

Prin blushed and his grip tightened on the steering-wheel.

"Why should I differentiate between any of my grandchildren?" said Doris firmly. She let the question hang in the air before she asked, "What do you want to know, Prin?"

Her grandson relaxed and grinned. "Everything, everything you can think of."

"In that case you can buy me a cup of tea, I'm parched after that ham, quite salty I thought."

In a cottage that claimed to provide eighteenth-century food they toyed with twenty-first century artificially flavoured confectionery. "I hear you have your own resident pop group," said Prionsias. "What are they like?"

Doris placed her cup carefully on its saucer. "Dreadful, quite dreadful. Of course, they only moved in yesterday so perhaps I am not being fair. They are, however, extremely enthusiastic, determined, and hardworking and that counts for more than anything. I can put up with a few discordant notes I think. I used to feel so selfish having those empty rooms. Now I feel I am doing something useful. You of course might think they are wonderful." She paused. "Hot Metal, I think they said they were. There are so many expressions nowadays that I do not understand."

Prionsias laughed. "Heavy metal maybe, hot metal has got to do with printing. I hope it all works out."

"Things do on the whole." Doris raised her cup to her lips, staring keenly at her grandson. "It is not always immediately obvious but things generally work out for the best."

The open fire crackled and threw dancing shadows into the dimming room. They ordered more tea and asked the waitress to refrain from switching on the electric light until other customers should come in from the cold. Doris eased her stiff limbs into a more comfortable position and continued with her story. "One day Rose came home, extremely distressed and told us that the girl had begged her to take her baby. She was quite desperate and did not know where to turn. The poor child had been sent from Ireland in disgrace to stay with distant cousins who in turn had thrown their hands up in horror and had professed themselves equally appalled by her condition. They boarded her out with a woman who helped her through the birth and cared for her and the baby after a fashion. I think the woman did her best but I believe she was paid very little. This arrangement could not go on for long. The girl was given an ultimatum, give up the baby and she would be forgiven and allowed to go home, otherwise the two of them would be out in the street. The cousins just did not want to be bothered with the little country girl and her problems."

"Could she not have gone somewhere for help?" asked Prin. "I've never understood that…well I've never given it much thought to be honest, not until now."

Doris sighed. "She didn't dare. It had been drummed into her that she was wicked and she would harm her family if she drew attention to herself. They made her believe that she was evil and not fit to look after her own baby. From her point of view there was nowhere she could turn and she couldn't risk starving her baby."

"Poor cow," said Prin softly.

The room was now almost in darkness. From the hearth spread generous waves of warmth while fickle light picked out a cup here, a plate there, the soft drape of a tablecloth, the brightness of tears in an old woman's eye. "Yes," said Doris, "she was desperate. One week more they gave her in the lodgings, one week to decide her baby's future. After that, payment would cease and she would be on her own. What could she do? Nobody would employ such a wicked girl. Being such a sinner she could not turn to the church for help and besides she was terrified of the child going to an orphanage. Deep down she felt that exchanging her baby for salvation was wrong and she was sure that that is the way it would be. She wanted desperately to have some say, no matter how small, in what happened to him. She did not expect anything for herself but there was just a faint hope that the kind lady in the park whom she had grown to trust could help her baby. It was unbearable to think of him facing a totally unknown fate."

"Poor little cow," murmured Prin again.

Doris shifted in her chair. "I don't think any of us slept very well that night. We had talked ourselves hoarse thrashing the whole thing out. There was no avoiding the moral dilemma placed on our doorstep and we all had to face it. This was not a question of a quick helping hand, a bit of charity, a feeling of uplift and on to the next good deed. This was a lifetime commitment to two people. You see we could have taken in the baby, but the girl herself needed looking after. It was all just too much responsibility. Believe me, we thought of every possible solution but nothing seemed adequately to fill the bill. We were however all agreed that we could not turn our backs and say this is not our problem when very clearly it had become so." Doris lapsed into silence and stared into the fire.

"What did you decide?" asked Prin quietly.

His grandmother shook her head. "Nothing. We sent Rose off the next day to try and persuade the girl to come home with her so that we could discuss it and advise as best we could. To this day, I feel a little ashamed that I avoided the issue. I would like to think that I would have responded with total generosity but we shall never know."

Prionsias smiled. "I don't think there's any real doubt, Grandmother, do you?"

"I don't know, love. I honestly do not know."

"Everything all right?" The waitress popped her head around the door. "Just ring the bell if you need anything," she added, and swiftly withdrew.

"And everything is all right," said Doris softly, more to herself than the man listening intently to her every word. "Leaving the children with me next day, Rose went a little earlier than usual to the park. There was no sign of the girl, but as Rose neared to the bench where they usually met she could see that it was not empty."

Prin bent forward and appeared to be holding his breath.

"Feeling suddenly afraid she ran forward, and..." Doris briefly touched her grandson's hand. "...and there you were wrapped up like a parcel and with...a note addressed to Mrs Rosaria."

"A note?" Prin interrupted sharply. "I never heard about that before. What did it say, where is it, is it still around?"

"Your mother, your real mother said...well I remember it word for word...it said, 'Dear Rosaria, you have been very kind to me and I am very sorry but I don't know what else to do because they said I have to go home and leave my shame in England. In Ireland I was told that they were bad people in England and I don't want to give my baby away to people like that. You are a nice lady and you are very kind to your own children and I trust you to look after Prionsias because he is a very good baby and does not cry a lot. If your husband will not let you look after my little boy please find him a nice home with kind people, and please tell them to tell him that I loved him very much. I will pray for you and your family every day. God bless you.' " Doris sighed. "Such a long time ago and yet I remember every word. I read it and read it and read it, it was signed 'yours faithfully, Siobáin Horgan'."

Prin stood up to stand by the window and gaze at the darkening countryside. He said, "So Rose picked me up and took me home?"

"Well, not straight away. She said she had a feeling that she was being watched, so, holding you in her arms she sat and waited, hoping that the girl would change her mind. Finally, of course, she had to return home and eventually contact the police. Rose explained that she knew the mother and showed them the note. I suppose that if it happened nowadays you would have been taken into care but after some superficial enquiries, they said it was more in the nature of a private arrangement. They said they would keep the case open but I do not believe that anyone made any serious effort to trace your mother."

"So you decided to keep me?"

"Rose did. I don't think there was ever a doubt in her mind; from the very start you were her baby. It was almost uncanny the way the two of you took to one another."

"What about Dad?" asked Prionsias returning to the table and sitting down. "What did he say when he came back and found another one in the nest?"

Doris hesitated and chuckled softly. "He said that the last thing that he wanted was a scrawny, snotty-nosed Irish brat, that had he wanted another child he would have gone about it in the normal conventional way, that Rose was a lovely girl but it was a shame that she no longer had the sense she was born with, that she was quite, quite mad, that in future she would only be allowed out with an escort, that the rest of us were equally certifiable, that he doubted any of us had any sense to come in out of the rain, etc., etc., etc. The diatribe lasted quite a long time. He then went out, found himself a solicitor and adopted you.

Chapter Twenty-two

Gracefully, the Ferrari drew up outside the darkened house. A small knot of people standing outside it turned and gazed anxiously at the car.

"Why, all my friends!" Doris exclaimed. "Prin, dear, it looks like we shall not be able to talk anymore tonight but I will get you out that note."

Prin helped her undo her seatbelt while she waved to the watchers on the pavement. "Don't worry, Gran, you've already told me more than I knew before. After all these years, I can afford to wait a little longer for the rest. To be honest it makes me feel a bit disloyal to Mum."

"Yes, I can understand that."

Willing hands helped heave Doris to her feet. "We was only worried 'cos ya said ya was gonna watch the motor racin'. We didn' 'spec ya to be out so long," said Ritzy.

"Ya missed the Grand Prix," Benoit whispered, gazing in awe at the Boxer. He stretched out his hand then pulled it back as if reluctant to verify that the car was real. "She's…" Words failed Benoit.

"She certainly is a beauty, sir," said Prionsias, and his grandmother giggled as they made their way towards the front door.

Mrs Panano quietly took Doris's arm. "I come over when I see the young people many times come to your door. This is painful for you, yes?"

Doris smiled wryly. "Self-inflicted wounds I am afraid. I have only myself to blame, sitting on the doorstep like a teenager last evening. Well, I daresay a teenager would have better sense. Then haring about the countryside with my grandson."

While she spoke, she observed Harry Cronin edging away from the small group. Doris had noticed him standing in the shadows. "Please don't go, Mr Cronin," she called. "I should like you all to join me for a drink. It's so kind of you to concern yourselves about me. Mind you, I haven't got any sherry but there is bound to be a drop of something or other. Benoit, if you have your key with you can you open up and put on the lights and the fire please?"

"Don't worry, dear lady, I can see you are, how you say, fatigued," said Mr Panano. "We will arrange everything for you."

Prin sorted out drinks. Ritzy drew the curtains and fetched biscuits from the kitchen. "It seems that we are having a party," said Doris to no one in particular. Harry Cronin refused to budge from where he sat awkwardly on a chair by the door. "There is such a draught over there, do come over by the fire."

He shook his head seeming content enough to watch and to listen. The Johnsons told Prionsias about the group. He in turn gladly extolled the virtues of the Ferrari. The Pananos expressed their surprise that Doris should allow her rooms to be used for a pursuit as noisy as a pop group. "I always have this to fall back on." Doris spoke as if imparting a great secret, pointing to her hearing-aid and winking conspiratorially at Ritzy. The conversation turned again to cars. "I think you had better tell me the result of the Grand Prix, Benoit, I doubt I'll be able to stay awake."

"No fret, Mrs R. Taped, innit."

Doris was touched.

"Have you always been interested in car racing," asked Mrs Panano. "For me it is noise, noise, noise." She made a gesture of disgust. "I no like."

"Oh yes." A faraway look came into Doris's eye. "Frank, my husband, was keen. I became equally enthusiastic. In an odd way, now he has gone I find that I watch programmes on his behalf." She laughed suddenly. It was such a happy free sound that the others joined in.

"She's off," said Prin. "Go on Gran, let's have it."

"Well, fill up the glasses, draw close and I'll tell you about the olden days. Put out the lights, Kenneth and we shall tell ghost stories." The lights went out. "Ha! I didn't mean it literally," protested Doris. "I was quoting my mother, a great storyteller she was." Doris gazed into the fire. "My goodness, this takes me back. No, no, don't switch the lights on again. It's rather cosy this way, do you not think?"

There was murmured assent.

"It takes me back," Doris repeated. "It takes me back to Christmas time when I was a very small girl. My mother would draw the curtains, rake the fire and sit us down, my brothers and me. 'Now Kenneth,' she would say, 'put out the lights and we'll tell ghost stories.' My father would grumble about filling the children's heads with nonsense. Nevertheless, he always found a tale to make us shiver with delighted fright.

"We used to live by the sea in a very tall narrow house with rather more stairs than I would care to tackle nowadays. I slept near the top of the house, and in order to get to my bedroom I had to climb several flights. In those days, there were no lights on the landings. My mother would leave the kitchen door open but there was never enough light to guide me all the way. About halfway up, there was a room, a spare room that I dared seldom enter even in daytime. I would start to climb, determined that this time I would be brave but as I approached the room, the faint light from the kitchen served only to envelop me in shadows, large shadows of mysterious shapes that undulated and slid and drifted from the walls to hang coldly about my shoulders. It seemed to me that clammy hands were reaching out to draw me into that room. My heart thumped unbearably as my feet raced to escape those grasping, clinging hands. Gaining the haven of my bedroom I felt quite safe once more and filled with a sense of achievement. Yet again, I had survived nameless horrors. The nightly creaking of the old house worried me not a jot but entering that bedroom in broad daylight with sunlight streaming through the windows my body would grow icy cold. My heart would race but not as fast as my little legs which delivered me in record time to the cheerful safety of the kitchen." Doris paused, absent-mindedly rubbing the legs that worked now only by sheer effort of will.

"D'ya ever find out why the room scared ya?" asked Ritzy. She was sitting on the floor hugging her knees and gazing dreamily into the fire.

A strange sadness gripped Doris. "*How much of this child's life will I see? How much will I see of Prin's baby?*" She smiled fondly at her grandson and held out her glass to be refilled. The rest of the company waited in silence for her reply. There was a harmony in that warm peaceful room. This was a moment to command time to pause, a moment to hold and remember. With a pang of regret, Doris let the moment go and cast her mind back over the years to a room that had once been the focus of all her fear. "At first my parents said it was my imagination. Nobody else reacted to the room in quite the same way as I did. My brothers teased me unmercifully, tried all sorts of ways to lure me there. No matter how much I tried, I could never explain the nature of my fear. My mother did wonder if I had actually seen something but my father said it was just a phase I was going through." Doris chuckled. "What a useful phrase that is. Having gone through a lifetime of phases I daresay I am going through one now, as yet unnamed."

"Was it…d'ya stop being afraid, Mrs R?" Benoit gently prodded her back to her tale.

"What, my dear?" Doris looked vaguely at him.

"The room, Mrs R."

"Ah yes…yes I did stop being afraid, once I discovered the truth. You see we had a great-aunt, a wonderfully dotty old lady who used to descend on us from time to time surrounded by boxes and trunks. You would have thought that she had come to live out her remaining years in our house judging by the amount of luggage she brought with her. Looking back, it must have been a great strain for my parents but we children revelled in the novelty of her visits. From her appearance, dressed as she was in shapeless unrelieved black, her face alert and serious, you would expect a forbidding presence. Yet we knew, though I'll never be able to explain it, that she was smiling inside. We loved her but we were also in awe of her. We liked nothing better than to watch her take over and disrupt the entire household."

"And she slept in the spare room?" asked Prin.

Somebody made shushing noises. Doris looked a little puzzled. "What is it, can you hear something?"

"There's no one at the door," said Harry Cronin.

"Where was I?" asked Doris.

"Your great-aunt was disrupting the household."

"Ah yes, how well I remember those days, all a lifetime away, a different world. Do you know we had a maid? That would hardly sound politically correct now. We had a maid and a gardener and a daily woman. There were no bottles for the milk back then. The milkman would gill it out from the churns on the back of his horsedrawn cart. I do not think it is my imagination but it really did taste so much creamier and richer then. The maid would fetch a jug from the kitchen when the horses' hooves rang out in the street and she would run and get it filled. The milkman sometimes added an extra ladle of milk for the little un, that was me."

She shook her head as if doubting her memories. "Oh I am sorry," she said. "I'm going off at a tangent. No, the point is that when my great-aunt was around all routine went out of the window. 'Books,' she would say, 'books are the thing. Read a book and you have mother, father, friend, child; you are never alone, never alone. Laughter, tears, knowledge, adventure all there, all there, all there.' " Doris laughed. "I expect you have guessed that her trunks were filled with books; she never travelled without them and doled them out to friends and strangers alike. 'Have a book dear, it will do you good.' Our little maid used to live in dread because the aunt would sit her down and make her read a page or two. I can hear her now. 'Please, Mum, I have to do the vegetables.' In the end, we all took to carrying books with us, otherwise there was no peace. Mealtimes became moveable feasts. My poor harassed mother would come into the drawing room and very quietly tell us to wash our hands. The aunt would look shocked. 'Hannah, really, the children are reading. They are feeding their souls.' We loved it; even father had to wait for his dinner while we finished a chapter. Finally of course he put his foot down, banished the books, the trunks and the aunt from the drawing room. There was a perfectly suitable room upstairs he said. There had to be balance in our lives."

Doris looked triumphantly at the assembled company. "Bet you all thought I had forgotten the room, did you not?" she laughed. "At my age memory plays tricks and I know I repeat things but I get there in the end, mostly. Anyway, my brothers were deputed to help carry the books upstairs. They tried to make me join in and when I stepped back in horror, doubtless turning pale at the very thought, Great-aunt Madeleine wanted to know the reason. 'He's back then,' she whispered, when I tried to explain my feelings. 'I'd forgotten,' she said, visibly distressed. She sat down suddenly, looking from one of us to the other. 'I put it out of my mind, I never thought to tell you. Listen, my dears.' She then told us how she had once slept in the room years before when my grandmother lived in the house. She had woken up in the middle of the night to find a man bending over her. He was clutching at her wrist and imploring her to help him. So urgent were his pleas that she felt herself impelled to follow him. It was only when her hand touched the door-knob that she realised that she was alone. It took her several seconds to register the door was still closed though the man had disappeared. Understandably, she was more than a little perturbed but finally put it down to a bad dream. She was not keen to question why the door-knob was wet and why, when she jumped out of bed, her bare feet had found patches of damp on the bare polished boards."

Doris paused and looked with satisfaction at her attentive audience. The sharp intake of breath had been most gratifying. She waited until once more the room was deeply silent before continuing the tale in low mesmeric tones. "Great-aunt Madeleine lay in bed, sleeping fitfully, waking at times to the howling lashing storm raging outside. Though she wrapped the bedclothes tightly about her she could not get warm. Her hands seemed to resist all attempts to dry them. Perhaps it was only imagination but the moist touch of the door-knob was still on her fingers. The next day came news that three men had drowned in the night. One of them, after his marriage, had lived briefly in our house before his in-laws sold it to my grandparents. My great-aunt said that the vicar was inclined to be doubtful about her story but agreed to come along and bless the room. After that there had never been a disturbance, apparition, manifestation, whatever you care to call it, until I sensed something. Curiously, from the time I heard the story, I ceased to fear the room, but…" Doris paused when the telephone shrieked for attention "…but," she repeated, reaching for the receiver, "I always had to wipe my hands dry after touching that door-knob."

Smiling to herself she picked up the telephone and found herself reassuring Joyce that she was quite safe despite being absent all the day long. The lights were switched back on and her guests gathered up their coats and began to tiptoe away. While she placated her daughter, she waved and smiled her goodbyes and gestured to Prin and Mr Cronin to stay. "Give my love to Robert," she said brightly and replaced the phone with a sigh. "Prionsias, do not dare tell the rest of the family about our brush with the police—" she raised her eyes in exaggerated despair "—or they'll lock me away for sure. I certainly would never hear the end of it

121

from your Aunt Joyce. She was a trifle upset that I was out all day today. I really can't imagine why anyone would want to make a fuss. At my age you have to face the fact that death is inevitable. It could be said that I am living in bonus-time and it would be a sin to fritter it away by being careful. At least that is the way I see it."

Doris turned to Mr Cronin still sitting impassively by the door. He did not return her light-hearted smile. "Will you please excuse us for a moment, Mr Cronin, I'll not be long."

In the bedroom Doris took a letter from a box on her dressing table and silently handed it to her grandson. As he unfolded it, something fell out and fluttered to the floor. Prin bent and picked it up. He turned the ten-shilling note over and over in his hand. In a strangely controlled voice, he said, "I'd forgotten these, you tend to think money is always the same." His attempt to smile was unsuccessful. "My inheritance, I take it."

Doris nodded and watched him place the two notes carefully in his wallet. There was a tightness in her throat that made speech difficult. What could one say? This was a long-awaited yet dreaded moment. Now that Prin was to be a father the time was right. There was more to be told but that would have to wait.

"Thank you, Gran, thank you for everything."

Doris waited, enveloped in a breathless hug while her grandson recovered himself. "Right, that's it," he said breezily, pretending to shove her way. "Enough of this sentiment, I must be on my way." His voice dropped and he gestured towards the sitting room. "Will you be OK with him? He is a bit odd isn't he?"

"I have nothing to fear from Mr Cronin," said Doris. "Away with you. Give my love and congratulations to Elaine. I will phone her in the week. Take care, love. Watch the speed."

Feeling suddenly weary, Doris sat on her bed listening to the Ferrari's departing roar. "I'll be with you in a little while," she called but made no move. Decisions would soon have to be made. This business with Prin was so very delicate, her steps would have to be wary indeed. Perhaps she could ask Andrew's advice. Dare she? She would certainly have to apologise first. A deep sigh escaped her lips and she stood up to face the more immediate problem of Harry Cronin.

Chapter Twenty-three

Doris was greeted by the sweeping strings of plaintive violins. "I took the liberty," said Harry, pointing to the tape recorder. He shifted his feet. "Shostakovich," he said. "Hope you don't mind, using the machine I mean...Or Shostakovich?"

Doris shook her head. "Of course not, I am only too pleased. Do sit down Harry."

"I lead you astray last time," said Harry.

"Oh?" Doris waited.

"Yes, I looked it up." Harry fell silent.

"Oh." The pair sat in waiting stillness while the music sweetly surged. Doris felt confused. How had he lead her astray? This was not at all what she had expected to hear. "What did you look up?" she asked diffidently.

"In my composers' book, I looked up Vivaldi. He wasn't brought up in an orphanage, he used to work in 'em. A lot of famous musicians did in them days, attracted by the standards of musicianship."

"Oh."

"He had remarkably red hair."

"Oh."

The music soared to new heights. "Shostakovich," said Harry after several minutes.

"Yes."

"Very keen on football was Shostakovich," said Harry. There was a suggestion of a smile on his lugubrious face. "I have got that right." Violin bows swept over doleful strings, speaking more clearly than words of dreams unfulfilled, promises unkept.

"*Unfortunate choice,*" thought Doris.

"I hit her," said Harry.

"Ah." Doris quietly let out the breath she had been unaware of holding. The words had brought no surprise, no pleasure to find that she had guessed correctly what they would be. "I am ready to listen, she said.

Harry Cronin looked wildly about the room, then surprisingly sat back almost casually and began to speak. "She doesn't, she won't...listen I mean. My Lily, she won't listen, not to me, not to music, not to anyone. But ...and...there's no way, I've tried." Harry sighed heavily. "God knows I've tried." He glanced at Doris, then rapidly looked away. He pressed his hands together tensely and began again with increased urgency. "She talks...she talks all the time, she talks and talks but she says nothing, nothing...nothing to hold onto. She uses words like they was useless, picks 'em up and throws them away. I can't get near her for those words."

The bitter-sweet music, an exploration of near despair, had ended but seemed still to linger hauntingly on the air. Doris suppressed a shiver, momentarily feeling the conjured-up isolation and bleakness. "She's afraid, you see," said Harry. "Afraid of the silence, afraid of hearing..." He paused and added quickly, "just afraid." He was quiet.

Into the room came the faint hum of a passing car, a distant voice raised in farewell, the rattle of frost-stiffened branches against a window pane. "She said you were her friend, are you? Is that true?" Harry asked abruptly.

Doris blinked, startled by the aggressive questions. "Yes of course, yes," she faltered, then spoke more firmly. "Yes, she has been kind to me, if I...naturally I would like to help you both." She rose and turned over the cassette, hiding her face from Harry. She was not at all sure that he would find the truth there. By no stretch of the imagination would she call Lily Cronin "friend". Still, the poor woman did deserve some sympathy and understanding.

Doris returned to her seat, eyeing her visitor carefully. His whole body appeared to clench as if he was trying to hold something inside himself. "*Poor man,*" thought Doris, "*poor man, God help him. God help me.*" "Why did you hit her, Harry?" she asked quietly.

Harry gave a start and frowned. He raised his arms and then dropped them in a gesture of hopelessness. "I tried to talk to her. I wanted her to listen. She wouldn't listen to me. She just wouldn't listen." The distraught man shook his head. "Her voice went on and on, it wouldn't stop. It wouldn't stop." Harry's hands covered his ears as if even now he could still hear the maddening sound. "I even shouted to her but she kept on, and on. Then...then..." his voice sank to a whisper. "Then I hit her, I hit her with all my strength. Oh my God." The man's head fell forward and he began to sob, ugly, rasping, shuddering sobs that sent a shiver of unease down Doris's back.

Looking at her hands, she awaited the storm's abatement. At length Harry drew a handkerchief from his pocket and dabbed roughly at his eyes. "I'm sorry," he mumbled and mightily blew his nose.

"Why?" Doris hesitated. "Why does Lily not want to listen? What does she not want to hear?"

Harry squeezed his lips into a thin line and whispered something.

Doris leaned forward. "I'm sorry, I did not catch what you said."

Harry sighed wearily. He looked old and tired. "There was a baby. Poor Lily was ill nearly all the time she carried the child but she was happy, looking forward...we both...we wanted a family you see. There was a lot of love."

"What happened?"

"She died, the child. She died before she was born."

"Oh, I am so very sorry."

Harry smiled, a look of great tenderness softening

126

his face. "She was perfect you know. Tiny. Perfect. She looked as if she was asleep. I touched her, my daughter …before…before…" Harry faltered, grew silent.

A faint hiss from the gas fire was the only sound in a room that seemed to be holding its breath. What could one say? Expressions of sorrow seemed woefully inadequate, indeed inappropriate in the face of the man's unmistakable pride. Doris could only wonder at the resilience, the strength, the power and ability of the man to see the triumph beyond the sadness. Once, Harry Cronin had had a daughter and he had held her for the briefest of moments. Nothing could take that away from him. Nothing could mar the memory. "Harry." Doris bent forward and touched him on the arm. "Are you saying that Lily has never come to terms with the loss of her daughter? I know you can't replace one baby with another but could you not have tried for another baby?"

"I told you she shut me out, didn't I?" said Harry harshly and quietly. "She doesn't know."

Doris shivered. "What do you mean she doesn't know?"

"They told her it was dead and they took the baby away without her even seeing it. They said that was the best thing in these cases. They said it would only upset her if she knew what it was. Best to put it all behind us. They was wrong. What do you think, Mrs Roberts? They was wrong, wasn't they?"

"Yes Harry, I think they were."

"It was too late when I worked it out you see. It was like I had something and she didn't and I wanted her to have it. It was her right. I wanted her to know. I thought we could… Why couldn't we? We could have shared. It's all we have…it's…" Harry's words failed him. He shook his head and rubbed a weary hand over his face. "I'm sorry…I…you look tired." He stood up abruptly. "It was good of you to hear me out. Appreciate it." He spoke gruffly, suddenly embarrassed at revealing so much pain. He began to edge towards the door.

"Sit down for just a moment more please," said Doris firmly. "Thank you for the compliment of giving me your confidence. I would not presume to give you advice." A picture of Prin as a young baby flashed through her mind. Almost to herself she reflected, "Some secrets you have to be prepared to take to the grave." She brought herself back to the present. "On the practical side, how is Lily now? I did notice that she was hiding her face."

Harry looked relieved and alarmed at the same time. "Eh? Oh...oh she's all right. She didn't want to tell no-one about me. Loyal, see? Yes..." He nodded without taking his eyes from the floor. "She's all right now."

"Good," Doris spoke briskly. "You know I am always here if...well I would be most interested to see that book of composers of yours sometime." She stood up to escort her guest to the front door where they exchanged a few words in the pleasantly sharp air.

Doris stood and watched while Harry walked home along the quiet street. Was it her imagination or did his step seem just a little lighter? *Confession is notoriously good for the soul. I wasn't much help to him but I hope he is easier in his mind now. Poor lonely man. Poor lonely wife.*

The old woman feeling very tired indeed, shut and bolted the door and hobbled painfully to switch off lights and prepare for bed. "What a day," she muttered. "Can I really have crammed so much in?...and I forgot to tell Benoit...ah! it's odd the memories that flood back...about the car for four pounds, the one with the kitchen chairs. Oh well, there is time."

She sat on the edge of her bed to undo her clothing. Today had so much to do with babies, an unborn baby, a dead baby, a lost and found baby. *Dear Prin.* The soft chuckle took her by surprise until she realised that it was coming from her own throat. It grew in strength and volume until she was laughing aloud. "You can never replace your granny." Oh that poor policeman, if there were only some way to thank him for the entertainment he had provided.

Chapter Twenty-four

D ecided to come back to the world, have we?"

"Go away, Mrs Evans," croaked Doris from the depths of her bed. "Why are you here at the crack of dawn?"

An indignant grunt greeted this question. "Crack of dawn is it? When did you last see the dawn might I ask? Been overdoing it again I suppose. Stiff as a board now I daresay and you can't move a muscle. Am I right? It's a shame there is no correlation between old age and common sense."

Mrs Evans dusted and tidied with quite unnecessary vehemence. Doris tentatively wriggled a reluctant toe. Unsuccessfully hiding the resultant twinge, she murmured, "Go away and leave me alone."

Mrs Evans came and stood over the bed. "And what happens when you want the lavatory or when you want to eat or drink? Have you thought of that? No, of course you haven't. Not a thought in your head you haven't. Why you have to cram a week's activity into a single day I'll never know, unless you're gripped by an extreme anxiety to meet your Maker."

With a disgusted snort, the woman turned on her heel and left the room, closing the door none too gently. Within seconds, she was back. "I am going to collect the extra fruit you ordered for that pop group. Much appreciation you'll get for it. Take you for granted, they will. Walk all over you, them. End in tragedy it will, you mark my words."

Doris started with the slamming of the front door and groaned. That wretched woman was right, of course, not about the teenagers but about going to the lavatory. When you are old and immobile, albeit temporarily, it had perforce to be a planned operation. *"Don't be long,"* she prayed.

Drifting in and out of sleep, grasshopper-like, her mind touched briefly on her concerns. *"I will ask Rejoice's advice about Prin,"* she thought. *"I am so glad I met her, must remember to take that stick with me when I go along there. She will like that. Oh hell! It must be dreadful to feel permanently the way I feel today. Do hurry up, Mrs Evans."* Her thoughts drifted to Andrew. *"Must make my peace with him, he should have known better. Still, perhaps I should have listened at least to Rose. Something nice for her lunch. Damn, should have asked Mrs Evans, drat the woman, where is she?"* Doris forced her mind away from her present predicament but found it too painful to stay long with Lily and Harry Cronin. *"Such sad souls."* She thought of the pop group. The memory of their music was less than attractive. *"Just get on with it and leave me in peace."*

Without enthusiasm she opened an eye to gaze at the uninviting day outside her window and remembered with grudging relief that Raza would not becoming that evening. *"I can do without his pomposity and superiority."* To Joyce she pleaded silently, *"Do not contact me today. I haven't got the strength."*

Mrs Evans returned and, ignoring all pleas and protestations, got Doris out of bed and into the bathroom, supervised the ablutions, helped her to dress and set her down with tea, toast and a boiled egg. "I got some fruit, some tomatoes, mushrooms, and I got a nice bit of tender steak for your daughter-in-law. She'll like that. Always struck me as being a hearty sort of girl with a sensible appetite. I...it will be easy for you too. If you don't have to run in a marathon or go horse racing with the Queen Mother you should be able to get up a nice little meal."

Doris grunted. "Mrs Evans, you are absurd."

"Am I indeed? Am I the one exhausted today? Am I the one with about as much movement as a wooden doll and hoarse from talking?" She sat at the table and poured herself a cup of tea. Her voice softened. "I've told them all to keep away from you today. Well, I only told Mrs Cronin but it amounts to the same thing."

Doris felt a twinge of annoyance. "I wish you wouldn't do that, Mrs Evans, I may have been needed."

Mrs Evans replied calmly, "I never had you down for a hypocrite. You know fine well that you don't want to see anyone today."

"That includes you," snapped Doris. "I will thank you not to interfere again in my affairs."

"Suits me just fine," said Mrs Evans, rising from the table, whisking away the crockery and rapidly washing it at the sink. "I can think of more pleasant ways to spend my time. Truculent you are…very truculent." She left the room and returned buttoning up her coat. "Goodbye, Mrs Roberts."

"Goodbye Mrs Evans." "*Damn the woman,*" thought Doris, "*she's quite right. I don't want to see anyone. Dear God, don't let anyone come near me today.*"

A quiet day was spent dozing in her chair by the window. A few people waved from the street. The group let themselves in quietly and only muffled sounds came from above. For once the telephone remained silent. Towards evening, Concorde crossed a clear sky and Doris, good humour restored, watched its progress without distraction. She thanked the Lord. He had, without doubt, answered her prayer.

Chapter Twenty-five

Doris stood at the front door and sniffed the cool morning air. There was about it that curious indefinable smell of impending spring. "*A green smell*," she thought, "*definitely a green smell.*" The trees were still as bare as ever, the earth beneath them innocent of weed or flower and yet the world had imperceptibly loosened the stark grip of winter. Doris shook her head. "*It will be daffodils and bluebells next and indestructible daisies in the grass.*" She felt energy surge through her body, a strength to deal with whatever came her way.

"It's only a bill, love," said a voice, "don't raise you hopes."

Doris jumped. She had not noticed the postman approach. She laughed. "You can't do it. It is no good you trying to put me off today. It's a gorgeous day and that's that."

The man looked doubtfully at the sky and grinned. "NHS gives out happy pills now do they?"

Doris took the letter from him. "I am expecting my daughter-in-law, coming down from Suffolk."

"Look out for you all right, does she? That's what I like to hear. Take care, love."

With reluctance, Doris closed the door on the awakening day. Everything must be just right for Rose, everything ready so as not to lose a moment of the visit. Mrs Evans would pop in briefly just to make sure. Raza Abolhasan would not put in an appearance until well after

Rose had departed. Doris all but hugged herself in delight. The whole day would be hers, a whole day with the person she loved best in all the world. She had been shocked when the idea had first occurred to her that she could love someone more than her own flesh and blood. So deep in thought was she that she took several seconds to hear the doorbell.

"Ma, 'tis worse you're getting. I was looking through the window and I could see you dreaming. Where were you this time?"

Doris looked into the sparkling eyes of her daughter-in-law. "At one of the weddings I believe," she said. Then they were hugging and laughing.

Breaking free, Rose refused the inevitable offer of tea. "Just let me draw breath, Ma. I know you hate journey talk, but the traffic was desperate. We crawled to, over and after the Dartford crossing, bumper to bumper, inch by frustrating inch, can you imagine? God only knows where they come from at that hour of the morning, and to think they do it every day."

"Come on now, you simply must have a cup of tea. I've had the kettle boiling already."

"Ma, love, I must admit I'm parched. I can't, I've come down for this examination thing and they said I mustn't eat or drink. Isn't it awful? You know me and my cups of tea."

Doris's mind felt dull and slow. "Examination…" She echoed the word as if it had no meaning for her.

"A medical." Rose gave a self-deprecating laugh. "Didn't I tell you, Ma, I'm jumping on the bandwagon, isn't it all the fashion to have check-ups nowadays? Executive check-ups they call them if you please, can you believe it?"

Her mother-in-law looked shrewdly at her. Rose stood up and studied herself in the mirror. "Gareth signed us all up on the medical insurance thing and I thought I might as well get his money's worth. So I'm going to have a good going over, Harley Street if you don't mind. Sure wouldn't

I use any old excuse to come down to London and do a bit of shopping? Wasn't I always a great one for the style?" She turned to face Doris. "Do you think I have too much makeup on? I left in such a rush."

"My dear, as always you look quite lovely." Doris spoke warmly and swallowed her disappointment. "Will you have lunch in town?"

Rose gave a little cry and squeezed Doris's hand. "Oh I'm a terrible thoughtless woman, you've prepared something, haven't you? You have, of course you have, you always do. Look I tell you what, can we have a meal in the late afternoon? Would that be all right? Oh I could kick myself for letting you down."

"Rose, Rose," Doris interrupted, "save your breath. You come back here whenever you can and I'll be ready. It is only a bit of steak, nothing to make a fuss about."

"Great," said Rose. "I've got to fly. I'll bring back a drop of wine."

"Lovely. And Rose."

"Yes Ma."

"You will tell me everything."

Rose bent to pick up her handbag "Sure, won't the whole world know that Rosaria Roberts went all posh and paid a fortune in Harley Street?" She blew a hasty kiss and was gone, leaving Doris to ponder.

Without Rose's exuberance, the room felt empty, and the air a little chill. Half-memories of an unexplained telephone call teased her brain. "*If only I had listened properly. Am I right to feel so nervous, or is it that my nose has been put out of joint because Rose isn't stopping for lunch? Yes, that must be it. I'm just being foolish, should have known better. Surely Gareth would have told me had something been wrong. Yes of course he would.*"

Mrs Evans came and stayed longer than planned. Doris listened to a seemingly endless flow of grumbling, grateful for the distraction. Alone again, normally time-consuming tasks were completed with unwelcome rapidity. Doris wandered from room to room, looking with mounting displeasure at her tidy home. She stood at her kitchen window, absentmindedly chewing a piece of bread and butter, gradually becoming aware that her knees were aching and the food as attractive as soggy cardboard. In exasperation she opened the window and threw the bread to a hopeful bird. She limped back to the front room where, armed with a very large gin and tonic, she settled herself by the window.

Fighting restlessness, she tried to work up an interest in the Panano's customers. "You don't give a damn about them, Doris Roberts," she said aloud, "not when you have Rose on your mind. If you were younger and fitter you could have gone with her, and not have to face this intolerable waiting." "*If...if...foolish wasteful word.*"

Suddenly she was angry with herself. "*All this unproductive self-pity and you are the one Andrew wants to lecture to the old people. Much good would it do them.*" She felt a renewed twinge of annoyance with the vicar, then annoyance with the world in general. "*Why does somebody not ring?*"

"Why do you not ring somebody?" she answered herself. She was about to stand when she noticed Benoit trying to attract her attention by hopping on one foot while endeavouring fruitlessly to clutch at the other. "*Absurd boy!*" Doris, despite herself, smiled and felt her spirits rise. Eagerly she waved him to enter.

"Why the miserable face, Mrs R? Look like ya've lost the Grand Prix. Thought ya was 'aving a visitor today. What's up, what happen, couldn't come?"

"No, she has come but she couldn't stay. I got things mixed up. I'll see her later."

"Tings'll be cool, Mrs R. Time fly ya'll see. Every ting'll be irie."

Doris looked at the boy's eager face and sighed heavily. "That is just the trouble, Benoit, I have never known time to go so slowly. I am sitting here fretting over things I didn't even know worried me. I keep thinking about Mrs Tracey all on her own and shut away from everyone. I hear about the rumours of renewed trouble in Iran and I wonder what Raza will have to face. For all his pomposity, he is little more than a boy and a lonely one at that. There is Andrew too. I should like to get myself straight with him. I don't know how to make him understand I am not the person he thinks I am. I worry about you and Nathan and Ritzy. People say that the young have it easy nowadays but I know that's not true. It is just that the problems are different, if anything it is harder. Well, that's my way of thinking anyway. In many ways, ours was a more structured lifestyle. Life is so much easier when decisions are made for you. Then there's Prionsias, I don't know what to do about him."

"Mrs Roberts, Mrs Roberts!" Benoit placed his hands on her shoulders and looked down into her distracted eyes. "This sound like a tea with two sugars job; you just sit down, I known for my wicked tea."

"I am sorry...I..."

"Sit," Benoit said peremptorily, interrupting Doris and pushing her gently into her chair.

Seconds later she heard kitchen activity and only moments later it seemed he was back with two steaming mugs. "I didn't know you drank tea. There's Coke in the fridge."

"Never no mind 'bout me, talk me de tale."

Benoit was easy to talk to. Doris stopped asking herself why she was confiding so easily in a seventeen-year-old boy. He listened well. He understood. She did not have to explain whys and wherefores. A smile, a nod, a raising of an eyebrow said more than words that she was right to be concerned about this, daft to worry about that. "What do you worry about, Benoit?" she asked.

"Oh, usual innit, world peace, savin' de whale, rain forests." Her visitor grinned at her and suddenly seemed to find his hands of enormous interest, examining them minutely and muttering something.

"Sorry, Benoit, I did not quite hear you."

136

"I wan' to write."

Doris felt surprised "What do you want to write?"

"Books, poetry."

"How wonderful."

"D'ya tink so? I thought ya'd laugh."

"Why should I?" Doris sounded indignant. "It's an admirable ambition. What sort of poetry do you write? You do write I take it. It is not just an airy-fairy dream that someday you will put pen to paper."

Benoit smiled at her. "Ya hear of Benjamin Zeffaniah."

"I have heard him, occasionally on Radio 4 I believe. Are you saying that that is your style?"

"Kinda. I'd like it to be. He makes words…" the young man made a gesture of helplessness with his hands.

"…dance," said Doris. "I know what you mean. The words have legs and they dance in your head and when you hear them there's a thrill of recognition as if…"

"…as if dey yer own all along." Benoit finished the sentence for her. He leaned forward speaking earnestly. "I wan' to be able to do that, get my words into people's heads. Make dem smile, cry, make dem feel someting, make dem tink."

"Might I hear or read something you have written?"

Benoit looked both pleased and terrified. "Yeah, ya sure?"

"I am sure," said Doris.

They beamed at one another. He bounded from his chair and ran to the kitchen, returning with a can of Coke in his hand. He opened it, and tilting his head back, poured it down his throat. "Tell ya what, I'll get a few bits and I'll bring back the Grand Prix tape and set it up for ya, OK?" Without waiting for a reply he was gone.

The powerful snarling machines had the necessary mesmeric effect on Doris as they hurtled in colour-blurred procession around the circuit. As ever on the first day of the new season, she had difficulty matching driver to car, car to constructor. Only the Ferraris in their distinctive red was she able to identify immediately. It was pleasing to see that new British lad doing so well. *"He will make a name for himself that one,"* she thought. *"He has the nerve and the flair."*

While the victor sprayed the crowd with champagne, the video turned itself off unexpectedly. Doris blinked, and suddenly too tired to move dozed before the flickering screen. She awoke to a delicate perfume and unmistakable sounds of tea preparation. Without opening her eyes she smiled contentedly, Rose was back.

"I let myself in, Ma, hope you don't mind, only I could see through the window you were dead to the world. Did you have a lovely sleep?"

Doris looked into Rose's eyes "Of course I don't mind; I know you all have keys in case I fall down and die all shut away like poor Mrs Tracey."

Rose drew a sharp breath and concentrated on laying down the cup of tea she was holding. "You don't like a lot of milk do you, Ma?" she asked.

Doris eyed her with mild surprise. "No, love, that looks just right. What was that expression you used to use?"

"Strong enough to trot a mouse across." Rose smiled and sat back in the armchair. "That was my mother," she said, leaning her head back and closing her eyes. "She could never stand anything wishy-washy as she called it, and that went for people as well. I remember the first time Gareth and I had a right ding-dong battle in front of her, all vituperative looks and lacerating words. You heard us once or twice yourself. During the brief lull in the invective she stood up. 'Well thanks be to God for that,' she says. 'I was afraid you'd married a real plaster, a lump of a man. He'll do,' and she marched out leaving the two of us with our mouths hanging open." Rose sighed. "I was thinking of going over there, Ireland I mean. Go and see my old mother before I'm much older." Her voice trailed away as she drifted into sleep.

Doris prayed that no one would come to disturb the peaceful moment. Rose's face in repose looked tired and yes, her makeup was a little heavier than usual. Obviously, sleep was what she needed after her early start but nevertheless her mother-in-law was impatient to hear how the day had gone. What had happened in Harley Street? There was so much she wanted to discuss.

Rose had a knack of going directly to the heart of the problem. What would she make of Harry and Lily Cronin? What advice would she give about Andrew? Out of the corner of her eye, Doris caught a movement and she swiftly turned her head towards the window. For a split second her breath caught painfully in her throat. "Frank," she whispered. No, it was impossible. Her heart pounded. The man in the street doffed his hat with a studied air of solemn courtesy. Doris released her breath with a sound that was half sob half laughter. It had been difficult to recognise Rodney, a new smart Rodney in her husband's clothes. She raised her hand in brief acknowledgement and watched him walk away leaving her shaken and a little in dread. There had been a moment when she had believed that Frank was alive and standing outside her window. She had even been about to stand up and go to him. Could this confusion of reality and imagination be a portent of things to come? Was it a forewarning, a small indication of future senility or just an isolated incident, a mistake that anyone, any age might have made? After all, Frank's clothes had fitted Rodney perfectly. Doris consoled herself that because of her earlier disappointment she was tired, vulnerable, over-sensitive and more than a little fanciful. With a grunt of self-disgust she rose and made her way to the kitchen.

"Ma, I have a great idea. Why I didn't think of it before I'll never know. Why don't you come up and stay with us for a few days?"

"I can't imagine anything nicer," said Doris. They had eaten the steak and, now pleasantly relaxed, lingered with the wine. "But what about Raza? I can't just go off and leave him."

"No problem," said Rose, "he'll have two teachers for the price of one. We'll treat him to grand conversation, entertain him with real culture, the Gaelic variety. I'll stay the night and off we go in the morning. I'll ring Gareth right now."

Chapter Twenty-six

O f course," said Rose, smoothly changing gear, "we can't offer you Concorde but the GR10s race in pairs across the sky, making quite a satisfactory sound." She was driving with more than usual care, threading her way through the thunderous workaday traffic on the A12.

Doris shot her a sideways glance. There was a tension in her daughter-in-law that had not been there the previous evening. Superficially all was well, but underneath…what?

It was a cold morning, the sun, pale and distant, offered only illusory warmth. A blue haze rose from fields dusted with faintest green as new plants pushed resolutely through the winter's iron-hard earth. "You won't know it in a few months," said Rose, following Doris's gaze. "You come over the hill and on both sides of you stretch the fields of rape aglow with glorious colour, as if the sun itself had fallen and was shining from a million blossoms."

"It's rather fine now, Rose."

"A stark beauty. Well, if there was any sense to me I'd have thought of you coming up here earlier. I'm only consoled because it apparently didn't strike Gareth either and it's so obvious. We don't see enough of you."

Doris watched the speeding countryside and tried to listen to the small nagging voice inside her head. The illusive message seemed to be important. She shook her head; no, it was no good, there was no grasping it.

Rose caught the movement from the side of her eye and grimaced. "Sorry, Ma, I've been rabbiting on, I know it's hard to take. You should just hear the boys on the subject."

"To tell you the truth I wasn't listening. I was wondering if we could go shopping while I am up with you."

"Of course. Forgotten something, Ma, or are you having a feminine urge?"

Doris smiled a bit sheepishly. "I want to buy myself a jogging suit, maybe two. I've been living in the bottoms Ritzy gave me. You wouldn't believe the comfort. When I think of the struggle I have to get into tights, especially when my hands are particularly arthritic. One can't help but feel sorry for the blue-ankled elderly women one sees standing at the bus stop. I want to rush out and tell them of my discovery. I do not see why they should not be added to the grannies' uniform, camel-hair coat, Marks and Spencers' hat.

"Do M & S do hats?" asked Rose absently.

"Don't be pedantic?" snapped Doris. "You know what I mean."

Rose negotiated a roundabout. "Maybe we could set you up with a pair of trainers to complete the sporting image. Come to think of it maybe it's not a bad idea. It would save you wearing out your slippers in both senses of the word."

The next few days were a joy. Gareth, after welcoming his mother seemed inordinately preoccupied with his own affairs and left the two women to chatter to their hearts' content. They bought the fleecy tracksuits, tops zipped for ease of dressing and giggled a great deal over the purchase of the trainers. "You'll be off to the marathon in those, Ma."

"Do you think Lily Cronin will approve?" asked Doris, lifting her feet and surveying with great satisfaction the Velcro-fastened footwear. "Rose I will not know myself with the comfort." She grew reflective. "You know, love, for years and years I've been saying life is too short, a phrase uttered without a great deal of thought. Now for me at least at my age it is completely true. Even if I live to a hundred, eleven years is just a drop in the ocean when one is glad to be alive. The point is I intend to be selfish, have things my own way from now on. What do you say to that?"

"I'd say," Rose replied, "it was a good idea, but without hope of fulfilment. You'd make a bad fist of it, you haven't the practice. Come on, let's get you home and have a cup of tea, you have me worn out."

❧

"You know you are always welcome with us, Mother," said Joyce with heavy emphasis.

Doris sighed. "Of course I do," she said briskly. *"Damn it,"* she thought, *"why should I explain or apologise for visiting my son. Oh Joyce, why do you have to turn everything into a competition?"* Aloud she said, "I'm looking forward to my visit to you and Robert after my birthday." To her own ears the words sounded stilted and insincere. She made a face as she replaced the phone. When would she get it right, this prickly relationship with her daughter? Gratefully accepting a gin and tonic from Rose, she resolved to put all such insuperable conundrums from her mind.

"Tell me about the Johnsons, Ma," said Rose, sitting comfortably opposite her mother-in-law by the fireside.

Doris smiled. "What can I tell you that we've not already spoken about on the phone?"

"Oh I can't bear to miss a detail of all those new people. Wasn't it great with Raza the other night? Poor lad, didn't know what hit him with the two of us trying to get him to crack a smile."

"He is a very old young person." Doris gazed appreciatively at the sparkling bubbles rising in the glass, colliding with and bursting upon, teasing and tickling a floating slice of lime. "The Johnsons are rather like that, effervescent, full of life. No." She shook her head. "No, I'm wrong.

Nathan is not like the others, he is lugubrious, torpid, hidden, I have no idea what sort of thoughts he has. I just can't fathom him at all.

"What are the parents like?"

"I have never met them, hard-working, God-fearing people, shift-workers, Granny is fun, would like one to think she is very fierce and there is no doubt that she's tough. One had to be, to survive, to bring up one's children in a largely hostile environment."

"You mean the 'no Blacks nor Irish need apply' syndrome?" said Rose.

"Quite."

Both women looked into the fire, silent, thoughtful. "It is funny, you know, Rose, there are odd sorts of balances in life. I would love to be able to observe my own grandchildren growing up in the rather weird exciting place this world has become, but of course I can't, except by phone and letter because of distance. Now out of the blue I have been given this other family to view and perhaps in a small way to be a part of, at least on the periphery. I can learn from Rejoice's energy. She is heavily involved in the church. She has her own cronies who visit each other's houses and put the world to rights over tea liberally laced with rum. The fact that they are nearly all in wheelchairs or on zimmers seems not to matter a jot to them."

Rose grinned at her mother-in-law. "And you of course are as quiet and timid as a church mouse."

"There's ambition in that home," said Doris, ignoring her, "and I think it stems from her. They are all heading for university, I'm quite sure. Well, perhaps not Nathan. I can see Ritzy as a doctor or perhaps a scientist. Benoit will read literature. I wonder if…" She left the sentence unfinished. "What of the new baby, what of Prin's child? I was so happy when he told me."

"I was wondering," said Rose speaking slowly and carefully and not looking at her mother-in-law. "Did I do the right thing all those years ago?"

Doris bit back the instant reassuring words that flew to her lips and waited.

"You see, Ma, I'm not sure I wasn't being selfish. It's something I've been going over and over in my mind. Maybe I should have made more an effort to find Si…Siobáin." Rose stuttered over the name as if reluctant to say it, as if the name, once uttered, had a power over the occupants of the room. "Sure, it couldn't have been all that difficult to trace her. Did we really make enough of an effort? We knew she came from Kerry. I am sure she even told me the village but I must have blocked it out. How could I do that, Ma? How could I forget something so important as that? I must have wanted not to remember. I must have wanted to keep that baby for myself. I've been battling with that idea for quite a while. But now…" She shook her head as if to shake the thought away. "Ever since Prin told me that Elaine was expecting I haven't been able to get over the feeling that I deprived that poor girl all these years and deprived Prin of his true mother. Doesn't everyone have a right to know who they have belonging to them? I did block everything out. I only ever told Prionsias he was adopted, I never even told him her name."

"I did," said Doris, quietly. "I know it was difficult for you." Her heart thumped uncomfortably, fingers tightened round her glass as she tried not to convey her anxiety. The reaction to her words was neither hurt nor anger.

Rose gave a nod, a slight barely perceptible inclination of the head. She stood and walked restlessly about the room. Suddenly she turned and faced her mother-in-law. "I'm going to find her," she said.

"Oh no, Rose, no, you must not!" The words sprang from Doris before she had a chance to stop them. Her hand rose and fell helpless onto her lap. It was plain to see that words and gestures of protest were futile.

Her daughter-in-law's eyes looked steadily into hers. "No, Ma," she said firmly. "You're wrong, I must find her."

Chapter Twenty-seven

Gareth proved Doris's ally. If Rose had to go, well of course she must...but should she not wait until after Easter, until the weather improved, until after his mother's birthday, until her mother could digest the news of her arrival, until the whole family could be told in case they dropped in, until he Gareth could get some time off to accompany her, until she had a proper plan, until...until...

Doris was quite impressed with her son's inventiveness, she was sure that she would be unable to think of so many reasonable reasons why her daughter-in-law should not go to Ireland yet.

Rose protested vehemently, then suddenly she was serene again. She smiled. "I couldn't go before the birthday, could I?"

The sudden change of heart took Doris by surprise. She did not see what difference her birthday should make but she sighed with relief and chose not to question a benevolent fate.

Chapter Twenty-eight

"It was lovely to be away and now it is lovely to be back," said Doris, shamelessly cutting through Lily Cronin's long list of complaints. Ignoring references to loud pop music and the youth of today, she pointed to her ear and shook her head. "Batteries!" she shouted and made her escape.

Happily the key turned in the lock at the first attempt and she gained the cool of the hall, blissfully shutting out the petulant, complaining voice. Standing for a moment to catch her breath she looked round. Yes it was nice to be back.

Mrs Evans had dusted and polished and laid her mail neatly on the hall table. There were a few flowers lying loose beside the letters. They were fresh and exuded a faint sweet smell that mingled pleasantly with that of the polish. For a moment, Doris had a sense of loss. Frank would sometimes leave flowers on that very table, seek her out, demanding tea or an argument or a kiss. Later, she would find the forgotten blooms, drooping slightly but their message clearly alive. She sighed. Had she been a bit too hasty to close the door so firmly on Frank? What would he say now? "*Enough, enough,* "Doris admonished herself. "*Let's deal with the here and now. First the flowers in a vase while the kettle is boiling, then the mail, a short rest, a bite to eat before Raza's ever-punctual knock.*"

Chores completed, Doris sat watching at the window wondering if anyone other than Mrs Cronin knew she was back. It would be nice to catch up with the news. It was odd to think such a very short while ago she had shut herself away, had been loathe to admit anyone to her home, let alone into her life. Now she was eagerly looking down the road hoping to catch a glimpse of a familiar face. The house seemed very quiet. It might have been more fun to return on a day when the band was practising.

"You are contrary, Doris Roberts. First you want absolute peace and quiet, then you want none."

Doris sighed. "Hello, Frank; on the whole I'm quite pleased to have you back. I suppose I need you to chivvy me along."

"Better the devil you know, eh?"

Doris grunted.

There was a knock at the door. "Double glazing, market research, or religion?" asked Doris.

"None of those," replied the woman with a tired smile and a resigned air. "I'm a social worker, Hope Jordan." She produced an identity card. "May I come in, Mrs Roberts?"

"Am I obliged to let you in?" demanded Doris in her haughtiest tones.

"No."

"In that case you may enter." Doris opened the door for her visitor. "*Might as well hear her out,*" she thought. "*One must not always reject the book with the dull cover.*"

"Patronising," whispered Frank

"Do sit down."

A laconic movement of the wrist suggested that time was limited but nevertheless would be graciously shared.

"How may I help you, Mrs Jordan?"

"There has been some concern," said the woman, enunciating carefully. "I mean we were worried."

"Indeed?" Doris raised a quizzical eyebrow.

Mrs Jordan shifted in her chair and waited.

"*Who are we,*" thought Doris, "*who has been worried?*" She was longing to ask but the curiosity would not have set well with the look of disinterested politeness she was cultivating.

Mrs Jordan cleared her throat "I believe you've been away for a while."

"A few delightful days with my daughter-in-law," murmured Doris. "*How curious,*" she reflected, "*that I should have said with my daughter-in-law, not with my son.*"

"Pay attention, woman," said Frank. "This could be important."

"Oh you have family."

"Yes, of course." Doris tried a look of amused surprise. "Am I to understand that you were worried that I may not have had a family?"

"Yes, no, I mean your neighbours were concerned that you may not have been aware that your house was being used in your absence. They…"

"All my neighbours," Doris interrupted, "or just one? Am I right in assuming that the complaint or maybe complaints covered pop music, teenagers, or specifically black teenagers."

"Mrs Roberts it wasn't a complaint, though there was mention of loud music. We've a duty to look into all cases where the elderly may be at risk."

"*Cases…at risk.*" Doris's hand tightened on the arm-rest of her chair as she struggled to keep her temper. "Steady on, old girl," said Frank.

"At risk, what do you mean at risk? To save time, energy and further worry, let me you inform you of the precise situation. Under normal circumstances I would be at a loss to see why I should share my business with strangers, however well intentioned they may be. I assume that you are here because you accepted what was told to you in good faith…and what have you been told I wonder?"

"Oh do pause for breath and give the poor woman a chance," said Frank.

Doris frowned, ignoring her erstwhile husband. "I wonder what exactly you have been told. Could it be you were told that I was an old woman at the mercy of ruthless young people, some of them rather weirdly attired and some of them, oh horror of horrors, black youngsters who had conned, was that the word, who had conned their way into my home and are now no doubt using it, abusing it and using me for purposes other than respectable?"

"Mrs Roberts…"

Doris silenced her visitor with a soul-shrivelling stare; "Mrs Jordan, do I strike you as being the sort of person who is easily frightened, intimidated or gulled?"

"No," said the woman quietly, a small smile touching her lips. "Nor am I, Mrs Roberts."

"You've met your match, my girl," said Frank.

"Good," said Doris, "that means neither one of us has any problems."

The telephone rang three times while the two women drank tea. Ritzy called in briefly to welcome Doris home. Others waved a greeting through the window. "You see, Mrs Jordan, I am rarely left alone for long," Doris said. "Perhaps next time you come you had better make an appointment."

"I will do that, Mrs Roberts," said the social worker. "It was good to have met you."

"*It has been a truce, nothing more,*" thought Doris watching her visitor's car drive smoothly away from the kerb. She shivered, unable to dispel a feeling of unease. "*You are absurd, Doris Roberts,*" she told herself, "*why should she not come to see you again? She is really quite a pleasant woman.*"

"Oh do buck up," said Frank. "Tell yourself the truth. It's not the messenger you dislike but the message. You can't bear to think that you might need her or someone like her. God forbid that Doris Roberts should need a public guardian angel."

"I am not sure that I need a private one either," his widow retorted.

Frank was silent.

Chapter Twenty-nine

Doris was pleased with herself. There seemed to be a rhythm to her life that had not previously been there. After Frank had died she had closed in on herself, excluding everything that was different and strange. At her age what need did she have of the new? Experience had been hers aplenty and now it was time to rest and just be. She sighed with relief that that was no longer her attitude. Now each day was newly welcomed. Now she wanted to understand the world that had changed when her back was turned. On request Briony had sent her a tape of a brilliant group, Salmon Blue Traffic. Doris played it several times very loudly until Mrs Evans swore that her threat to resign was quite genuine, should the terrible caterwauling continue.

"If you have to have such rubbish, I can't imagine why you don't listen through those newfangled fancy earphones of yours, I really don't."

"Oh I couldn't do that," replied Doris. "They're for my own music."

Without regret she parcelled up the tape and enclosed with it a note to her great-granddaughter thanking her for the interesting opportunity of sharing her musical taste. "Well, at least I have had a go and now I can truthfully say that that style of music is not for me. Maybe if I had persevered..." Mrs Evans glared her to silence.

Her thoughts turned to Raza, a sad young man, pompous and aloof. She could not dispel the feeling that she had failed him. His French was good. He worked very hard and was an excellent pupil but there was no joy in him. By contrast, his contemporaries seemed to have mastered the balancing act of duty and fun. Doris had tried to interest Raza in her friends' activities but he greeted her efforts with an icy reminder that he came to her house to learn and not to socialise. There was no place for play in his life. Poor Raza. Even the exuberant Benoit wilted before his disdainful stare.

By and large, the arrangement with the pop group worked very well. They completed tasks allotted to them by the organised and organising If. The garden was kept tidy. Nathan did the heavy work, seemingly without complaint. He never smiled, rarely spoke, uttering a grunt only when it seemed that a vocal contribution was absolutely necessary.

Doris was no nearer getting to know Taps, Squirrel and Trunks. Under If's strict eye they kept their distance. Their enforced reticence was surely contrary to their natures. Derek too, was a bit of a mystery who hovered palely in Ritzy's shadow.

Benoit was without a doubt her favourite. His task in life was to play the clown, to keep everyone cheerful and happy. It was a task that he performed supremely well, yet of all of them, to Doris's mind at least, he was the most serious, the most dedicated, the most thoughtful. Doris said as much to his grandmother when she met her after church.

"Dey're all good children in der own fashion," said Rejoice firmly and wheeled herself away.

"Don't worry."

Doris turned to find the vicar smiling at her. "I am so tactless, I do hope I didn't offend her. I owe you an apology, I'm so sorry I lost my temper with you. I'm even sorrier I left saying it for so long, at my age a foolish risk."

"Forgiven, forgotten, I'm glad you're here today. We need your help, but first of all how was your trip, did you have a pleasant time?"

Standing amidst people streaming from church and quite oblivious to them, Doris told Andrew about Prin's desire to trace his natural parents now that he was about to be a father himself and about Rose's sudden urge to find Prin's mother. She had had no plans to confide her fears and now they were blurted out she stood as if bewildered by her surroundings. "I can't let her go to Ireland," she said. "I'll lose her." Her voice trailed to a whisper and her hand made a feeble fending motion.

"Have you asked her?" demanded a strident voice.

Andrew put a firm hand on Doris's arm. "Don't distress yourself. We'll talk this through, but for now…" he turned to the woman striding purposefully towards them.

"Have you asked her?" she repeated.

"No," said Andrew quietly "not yet."

"I'd say time was of the essence," said the woman.

"I'll bid you both good day," said Doris, feeling discomfited.

"No, no," said the woman, "I'm talking to you."

Doris obediently stood still. However one might wish to, one argued with Mrs Wilmacott as little as possible. It was known to be a time-consuming energy-wasting exercise and Doris felt she had little of either to expend.

"What can I do for you, Mrs Wilmacott?" she asked wearily, knowing the woman never paid any attention to you unless you could be of some use to her. She was a person who got things done.

"Mrs Tracey, we're very worried about her. Doesn't answer her door, never seems to see the light of day. Approach has been made, no response, like you doesn't attend the old people's club."

Doris suppressed the urge to say, "It's not compulsory, is it?" and moved from one protesting hip to the other.

Mrs Wilmacott looked annoyed, Andrew anxious. "Not the point," snapped the woman as if reading Doris's mind. "Not the point that the milkman apparently shops for her and collects her pension. Should be seeing the doctor,

153

check-ups, that sort of thing, not healthy, shut away. Want you to make approach, might listen, same age, won't heed me," she snapped, the idea of being ignored obviously incomprehensible to her. "Nor Andrew," she added in a tone that said that this was more understandable.

"Do you think we should interfere?" said Doris. "After all, if the milkman sees her and she buys food, well I don't…"

Mrs Wilmacott interrupted. "That's the whole point, he doesn't see her, it's all done with notes, most unsatisfactory."

"I still don't…"

"Doris," said Andrew quietly, "you may be able to help. Mrs Tracey used to come to church, I've been around there myself and I can't help feeling that something is badly wrong. Neither the police nor the social workers can do anything while she is apparently caring for herself. We need to reassure ourselves that all is indeed well and if you could persuade her to open the door and…a glimpse of her would go a long way to providing that reassurance. As our friend here says, perhaps you being of similar age could get to see her. She won't even answer any of us when we knock."

"Caring society," barked Mrs Wilmacott. "Can't let her rot, must act, not savages."

Doris, smarting from the woman's tone, wanted to say something pithy about independence and rights to privacy and freedom from unwarranted interference but pain gripped her leg causing her to gasp with the sudden fierce cruelty of it. "Right," she said when she had recovered breath, "I'll go and see her."

Chapter Thirty

Doris had a tussle with her conscience and emerged from the fray and from her home in a bad mood. She had spent a troubled and sleepless night worrying about Prin and Rose, berating Frank for his uncustomary silence, chiding herself for her easy capitulation to Mrs Wilmacott. Her hips ached, her head hurt, her hands were cold and, as she walked reluctantly to Mrs Tracey's house, large raindrops plopped dolefully on the pavement. *"Why me, why should I be the one to go? The world is full of people longing to interfere in other people's lives. Not me, so why am I chosen for mission impossible? I should have told that woman, I suppose I was so glad not to be the focus of attention."*

"Hi, Mrs Roberts." Doris glared unseeing at her punk friend and marched on.

The rain fell more insistently. Her pain intensified and she wanted to scream at the whole world. *"All right, Doris Roberts, pull yourself together and get on with it."* She steadied herself against the door post. *"Get a grip on yourself."*

Mrs Tracey lived in a middle-floor flat of a converted Victorian house. The front door was perpetually open, there being no one to take the responsibility of the long-lost key. The hall open to the elements was littered with tricycles, bicycles and prams in various stages of disrepair and ruin. They belonged to the occupants of the bottom and top flats and the ex-occupants of those flats. They belonged apparently where they lay in dust and rust-collecting disarray. Empty crisp and sweet packets lay in corners discarded by wind and careless uncaring people.

As Doris stepped inside the door, a musty smell assailed her nostrils. It was a smell that, like an unseen fog, swirled and clung about her and damply became a very part of her clothing. She quelled the urge to turn away before it become a part of herself. She opened her mouth the better to save her nose from the cloying ugliness of it. When she reached Mrs Tracey's landing, she was panting from her exertions. She stood in the gloom, listening to her own hurried breath and the faint thumping rhythm of the top flat's radio. She hesitated before knocking and put her ear to the shabby, scratched door. There was not a sound. Lifting the knocker she found that it was stiff from disuse and had to be pushed forcibly back into place. The resultant noise was muffled and ineffective. She paused. Should she try again or was there a faint shuffling sound? She waited. Her breath was slower now, her anger dissipated. She was in control of herself, all external thoughts banished. She concentrated purely on the job in hand. With resolution, she raised the knocker again.

This time surely there was a sound from within. Again, Doris pressed her ears to the door, straining to listen. All was still, so still that she fancied she heard the thumping of her own heart. Suddenly with shock she felt rather than heard soft breathing from behind the door. "Mrs Tracey," she called, "Mrs Tracey, it's me, Doris Roberts. I have come to see you." Silence, waiting. "Mrs Tracey, please. Can you hear me?" Silence. Surely there was someone there. Surely Doris had not imagined the proximity of another human being. She tried again, this time banging on the door with her ring. "Please, Mrs Tracey, are you all right? Can you hear me."

This time she was answered with a hoarse whisper.

"Is that you, Mrs Tracey? I am so glad. I could not hear what you said, will you not let me visit you for a while?"

"Go away."

"Oh please, I do not mean to intrude but we are all quite concerned for you."

"Go away." The voice didn't rise above a whisper but it was harsh, tremulous and terror-filled.

A cold dread washed over its listener. "Please, Mrs Tracey, please try to understand. I am Doris Roberts, you must remember, I have lived in this street for years. I only want to help you."

"For Christ's sake go away, leave me alone."

The words were mere grotesque sobs rasped out with such vehemence that the sounds were barely human. "Please." Doris stopped. She stood irresolutely on the damp, dreary landing. What could she do? She wanted to break down the door and comfort the poor frightened creature behind it. Helplessly she cast about for words but what words could penetrate the fear-fogged mind of her neighbour. The letterbox slowly opened and a crumpled newspaper page fluttered to the floor. With great difficulty, Doris picked it up. *"Damn! I haven't got my reading glasses."*

She hobbled to the window and smoothed the creases in the paper. There was no need to worry about the lack of spectacles. In bold letters the headline proclaimed: "The bruised and battered face of 90 year old Mrs Ivy Pending after her ordeal at the hands of heartless muggers." Beneath the words was a photograph of a woman with horrific facial injuries. That was all there was on the front page of the local newspaper, just that one story. It was dated more than a year before. Doris swallowed hard. So that was why Mrs Tracey was so afraid. She had nurtured this fear for so long a while, and every week doubtless more free newspapers popped through her letterbox with similar stories. The world must seem filled with thieves, muggers and molesters.

Doris felt shaken with anger. No, the newspapers were not wrong to show the important consequences of crime but surely there was a way of getting it across that these events, terrible as they were, were relatively rare and that indeed was why they made the front page. Surely it was possible to tell also of the hundreds of thousands of elderly people who live safe, secure, peaceful lives.

"I want it back, give it back to me."

Doris folded the grubby yellowed paper and slowly fed it into the letterbox, talking all the time as soothingly as she could. She felt the paper being pulled from her grasp and the lid fell into place with finality.

Footsteps inside the flat shuffled away.

"Watcher."

Doris started. She had not heard anyone climbing the stairs.

"I didn't know you lived here, Trevor," she said, unaware that tears coursed down her cheeks.

Her punk friend gazed down at her. "D'you want a cup of tea?"

"I couldn't do anything, I could not make her understand."

"Won't take long to put the kettle on. She's batty, ain't no helpin' her."

"Maybe if you…"

Wordlessly Trevor pointed at his head.

"Yes I see. If she looked out of her peephole you'd scare her to death." A faint smiled lifted the corners of Doris's mouth. "Yes, I would like a cup of tea but I am not sure I can manage the stairs. I feel…" Her voice trailed off. Trevor caught her as she swayed and carefully lowered her to sit on the stairs.

"Won't be a mo'."

Doris was vaguely aware that he had bounded off. "*Helpless, helpless, useless.*" The old woman softly beat her clenched fist against the dingy threadbare carpet covering the stair on which she was sitting. She leaned her head against the wall behind which a poor woman lived in constant terror. What could she do? What could anyone do, the doctor, the health visitor, the police, the vicar, the social workers, neighbours, all of them as helpless as she, Doris, restrained as they were variously by the law, reluctance to interfere, cowardice? If it was thought that Mrs Tracey was dead then they could break in, smash down the door, remove the body, problem solved. An idea came to Doris. Could she not get one or two of the boys to break down the door, then she could comfort Mrs Tracey face-to-face and show her that a fear-free life was possible for the elderly. There was no need to live dreading every knock and noise. "It would not be fair," said Doris, "it wouldn't be fair to the boys, not their responsibility. Oh damn, what the hell can I do?" In agitation she tried to rise. *Sheer vanity to think I could help, can't even help myself. I'm stuck again, well and truly stuck.*

"Mum said you was to come up, she told me off for leaving you here."

"My dear young man, if I did and could go up, you and your good mother would have me for life because I can't budge an inch."

"Won't have to talk to yourself, then." Trevor blushed. "Sorry."

Doris glared, then suddenly she started to laugh "All right lad, here, give me a hand."

"He and his mother carried me up to their flat," Doris told Rose later. "They were so kind. The mother had cranked the gas fire up to tropical level. She brought me tea thick with sugar and massaged my knees. I slept, despite the radio which they keep on all the while for the budgie who apparently shares a musical taste with Briony. It seemed rude to switch off my hearing-aid. Trevor ran round and borrowed Mrs Johnson's wheelchair and that's how I got home."

"Are you all right now, Ma?"

"Rose, that's the wrong question. The concern should be for Mrs Tracey. It is terrible to think of her living in squalor and fear. There are people who care but we are all powerless, totally powerless." Doris's voice dropped to a whisper. "I failed."

"Get some sleep, Ma, you're just weary. You'll feel better tomorrow."

As she slowly replaced the receiver it occurred to Doris that Rose sounded mighty weary herself. There was something wrong. Yet again she had been prattling about her own concerns and deaf to whatever was troubling Rose. Maybe Mrs Evans was right, maybe she was selfish. Again, she lifted the phone. The dialling tone was a bleak and lonely sound. Had she really expected Rose still to be there, waiting to tell all?

Chapter Thirty-one

Mrs Evans was even more scathing than usual. "Upset, I should think you would be upset, thinking you could help, getting yourself into a state. Sheer selfishness I call it, trying to help others when you need help yourself. Do you give a thought to the people who worry about you? Of course you don't. Mind you, that Wilmacott woman wants shooting. Use anyone she will, then take all the credit. Not that I can see what credit there is in disturbing a poor bewildered old woman."

Doris winced, hearing again the muted whimpers of fear from Mrs Tracey. "What would you do?" she challenged weakly.

"Break down the door, worry about the consequences later, if you're all that concerned. Scoop up the old lady, put her in a nice overheated home with a lot of gaga old folks and all you do-gooders will be satisfied."

"That is unfair," Doris protested.

"Is it? You'd take kindly to someone making your decisions for you, would you?"

The question hung in the air. "*It isn't at all the same thing,*" Doris thought but she did not have the words. How could she explain when she had withdrawn into herself after Frank's death, it was not because she had felt fear. It was because she felt safe. It was safe to be all alone. She was sufficient unto herself, free from the demands and dependencies of others, free from emotional obligations. Equally, it had been her decision to return to the world. A delicate shudder ran through her body. Back then, while she had believed herself impregnable behind her shell, even then had there been a Mrs Jordan planning to break down her defences, waiting to pounce and whisk her away to a pre-death death-like existence? Joyce would have been the first in line. "You know it's for your own good, Mother." Which of her family would have come to her aid? None. They would all believe they were helping. Rose, maybe Rose would stand up for her right to make her own decisions.

"My God, woman, you are becoming weak. You do like wallowing in a bit of drama."

"Shut up," said Doris to Frank.

"Oh very nice," said Mrs Evans. "It's ruder you're becoming. I have a choice, you know. I don't have to spend my time in such disagreeable company."

"I wasn't talking to you," said Doris frowning.

"Someone else here then, is there?" Mrs Evans snorted.

The sound was somehow comforting. The older woman began silently to cry. "Oh damn it all to hell," she said angrily, wiping away the tears with the back of her hand.

Mrs Evans looked relieved.

"I seem to be doing this a great deal lately," said Doris. "I will not spend the rest of my days in tears, never did see the use of it, weakness. Still," she fixed Mrs Evans with a fierce eye, "for all that you might protest there is a great deal in life that is unfair, we are all one step behind. As a child, you follow what the adults say. Just when you have worked out all the rules you are moved onto the next stage, young adulthood. Guess what? The rules have changed. You've got to move on. You can't stay here. Parenthood! Well, you just about get the hang of that when you wake up one day and the children...they have gone. You are just beginning to think that you have half an idea on how to do the job but there is no more time to practise, time is up. Marriage! Oh you can't pass that knowledge on to your grandchildren because it is obsolete. The world has changed. Marriage, post-children, starts to be quite pleasant.

You have smoothed some rough corners and made the compromises and then your partner dies."

Mrs Evans sighed and suddenly sat down heavily. "You'll not be consoled today will you?" she said dully. "So I'll just go home and not waste my time."

Her actions did not match her words and the two women stayed still, each locked in their own gloomy thoughts.

Rain dripped disconsolately from darkened skies onto strangers on the street outside. Through the double-glazing, cars and motorbikes sounded muffled and distant. As if in a dream, they came and went with seeming funereal slowness. Seconds slowly seeped away.

"You must be hungry," said Doris unexpectedly, "shall I make you something?"

Mrs Evans shook her head, more to emerge from the trance in which she had sunk than to deny her hunger. She sat further back in her armchair and spoke in a voice that was barely above a whisper. "Thirty-seven years I had with my Joss, with scarcely a day apart, then he had to go and die all alone. It was hard. I didn't want to leave him in that hospital bed. He was no age but I knew I wouldn't see him again. 'He'll be in good hands, Mrs Evans,' they said, 'you get yourself a good night's sleep. He'll want you with him when he opens his eyes.' Why could I not stay with him, I could have dozed in a chair? I couldn't find the words to argue. A fighter, me a fighter all my life and I couldn't find the words. Silent I was in the face of their plausibility. It all sounded so reasonable and they the experts after all. In my heart I knew they were wrong. I was a stranger, an intruder in their territory, powerless in the face of their professional kindness and unspoken insistence. My boys added their voices. 'Best go home, Mam, Dad's in safe hands.' Thirty-seven years and I knew in my bones I wouldn't see him again, yet meekly walked away, too feeble to say what was in my heart."

Doris closed her eyes as Mrs Evans relived the endless walk down dimly lit, hushed, polished corridors to a solitary life and found herself in another hospital by Frank's bedside. "He's quite comfortable, Mrs Roberts," the doctor was saying, "he's in very little pain. We can control the pain but there isn't anything further we can do for him. I am sorry.". "Thank you, doctor," Doris had said, unsurprised. She had nursed Frank at home before bowing to pressure to let the NHS take over. While there was a chance of a miracle she had been happy enough to sit with him every day in the hospital but now... "I'll be making arrangements to take him home then..." The young doctor had stared in disbelief. "I am sorry, excuse me," but Doris was holding her husband's hand; "I am taking you home, Frank," she whispered and had been rewarded with a slight pressure from the pale fingers.

"I am taking you home, Frank," she said aloud and opening her eyes felt vaguely puzzled that Mrs Evans was sitting with her in the dull afternoon. "They were all against me, but I brought him home and it was harder than anything I have ever attempted in my life—knowing that he was dying, wanting to make a good experience of it, yet, oh how strong is the power of hope. How incongruous that we should have to fight against hope to make the best of the present fleeting moment. I had to keep reminding myself that I had brought Frank home to die. They said he was comfortable in hospital, with me he was just at home, at ease. Dying is a lonely business best not undertaken in the presence of strangers, if it can be helped." She lapsed into silence, back now with Frank, after, on her insistence, seeming armies of nurses, helpers and family had departed and the only sound to be heard was her husband's laboured breathing.

"I've often thought I should have made more of a stand," said Mrs Evans.

"I had made myself a bit of supper," said Doris. "You know, life goes on, stiff upper lip, that sort of thing."

"A bit of cheese it was I had, stuck in my throat it did," said Mrs Evans, "but you know how it is. You say to yourself

I'll just eat this then I'll ring the hospital, don't want to bother them so soon after leaving. They'll get on to me quick enough if anything's amiss."

"I thought to myself these are Frank's last moments, to hell with carrying on as normal. The present normality is Frank is dying and I should be with him."

"The phone rang. 'Oh I'm fine, son,' I said, 'just had a sandwich, no need to worry about me.' That bloody cheese was choking me. I wanted to scream. I wanted my sons to scream but we were so civilised we let the moment go by."

Doris spoke softly. "I washed Frank and made him comfortable then I got into bed and lay beside him and held him in my arms."

"I got the call in the morning, very kind, but not family, 'didn't want to disturb your sleep, Mrs Evans, but your husband has passed away peacefully in the night.' What sleep?" Mrs Evans laughed mirthlessly.

"All night I held him in my arms, talking, remembering. I was fiercely jealous of that time with him. Part of me said that I was selfish, that somehow the children should be involved. I had promised to ring should anything happen but I could not bear to pick up the phone and say in words what I knew in my heart."

"By the time I got to the hospital he was no longer my Josh—just his body, clean and remote and officially dead. I had a new status."

"Sometime in the night I dozed off and when I awoke Frank was trying to talk. Luckily I had left in my hearing-aid because I had to bend close to his lips to hear. He was saying the children's names over and over again."

"I don't know if Josh opened his eyes again."

Doris sighed. "At first I was mortified but then I realised he was not in the present, he was calling to them as the children they were. 'It's all right, Frank,' I said, 'they are safely in bed, fast asleep'. 'Of course, my dear,' he said. A little while later I heard the death rattle and he was gone from me. He was dead."

Chapter Thirty-two

Y ou were our last chance," trilled Mrs Wilmacott, pouncing on Doris in the street.

"No, I was not," said Doris firmly, "I was just another option. From what I read in the papers the world is full of experts on the human condition, I suggest you consult one or several of those. I have my own problems." She was pleased to see that the other woman looked taken aback. Let her think that Doris was selfish, she seemed in any case to be the sort of person who decided what you were thinking.

Mrs Tracey was indeed one of the problems on Doris's mind but Mrs Wilmacott would be the last to know that.

"Well, I expect you did your best," the words were grudging, and Doris felt a sudden uplift of her spirits. To earn the disapproval of some was to gain a badge of honour. No doubt the woman meant well. Oh what a damning with faint praise was that. "Good day to you, Mrs Wilmacott," she said in her best retort-stifling voice and moved away as swiftly as she could.

She was off to suggest to Andrew that he write to Mrs Tracey. Perhaps she would take note of concerns expressed with care and sensitivity. She had after all been driven to her present state by the written word. Doris also wanted to discuss with Andrew her own personal concerns. It would help to get things clear in her mind. "*Poor man,*" she thought, "*to be the recipient of so much woe and worry.*"

Old Reverend Hardwick, Andrew's predecessor came to mind. Now there was kindness itself, noted throughout the parish for his patience and wisdom. If ever you have a problem, people would say, you only have to go and sit with him for half an hour and you came away positive of a solution. Oh, he was a man of few words. It was uncanny the way that he always knew just what one should do. Doris had been amongst those who knew that the Reverend Hardwick was never overburdened with the tribulations of his flock because he was deaf as a post, scorned the use of a hearing-aid and had years before learnt that his role in life was to assume an air of thoughtfulness and to nod sagely from time to time as each troubled soul worked out his own salvation in the peace and tranquillity of the vicarage. His was a wonderfully comforting presence.

Deep in thought, Doris arrived at that very door and rang the bell. Someone had stuck a sign on the post saying "Prepare to meet thy God". As she bent forward to read the small print beneath, she heard a chuckle behind her.

"Don't strain your eyes, Doris, it says 'evening dress optional'." Andrew waved a packet in the air. "I've just been down to the shop to get something to remove the glue. I really must do it now before it becomes a fixture. Do you mind sitting in the hall and talking to me while I work away, unless you need my undivided attention of course."

Doris shook her head. "No, not at all. Shall I make us a cup of tea?"

"Great stuff," said Andrew, taking off his coat and pushing open the door. "New discovery…instant tea…watch out, it's a bit strong…alongside the bread bin."

His visitor looked at him with distaste. "I'll give it a go," she said doubtfully.

"That's the spirit."

She hummed as she waited for the kettle to boil, feeling at home in the kitchen, grateful for the young man's casual acceptance of her. Then she was seated on the hall chair, mug of tea steaming beside her on the table and Andrew was nodding sagely from time to time in between grunts of effort as he scraped off the paper and listened to Doris's tale. She had no idea how she had got started. She only knew that her fears about Rosaria and Prionsias had come tumbling out along with the secret she had kept for over thirty years, and what a relief that was. Andrew, wise man that he was, refrained from giving advice.

Having successfully removed all trace of the poster with a bucket of soapy water and a sponge, he worked assiduously on the door and its surrounds until Doris noticed with amusement that he was wiping over the letterbox for the third time.

"Did you ever meet Reverend Hardwick?"

"No, there was a temporary man here before me. Why?"

"Oh, I was just noting some similarities."

"Oh."

"I'll explain sometime. Andrew, thank you for listening. I'll be off now."

"Not staying for the Seniors' tea? You could have a sandwich here if you wanted to wait."

Doris narrowed her eyes and glared at the vicar.

Chapter Thirty-three

It slowly dawned on Doris that she was hungry. Home seemed a long trudge, besides she could do with a bit of company. Why not go to the cafe? Which of her friends might be able to join her? Ritzy and all her crowd were at school. Raza, with great dedication and totally without humour, would be absorbing business practice. Jyotsna was at a High Commission "do". Lily—well please God the woman was busy. It was Trevor's day for signing on. Rejoice would doubtless be getting ready for the afternoon jollities at the vicarage.

Just as she was telling herself that, pleasant though it might be to get to know them better, not one of them could provide her with good adversarial debate, she spotted Rodney sitting on the bench by the bus stop. Easing herself down beside him she asked, "Rodney, does your reluctance to go in doors include restaurants or is it just private houses you dislike entering?"

Her companion lowered his newspaper and looked thoughtful. "I have on occasions been in such establishments," he said.

"Oh good," said Doris. "In that case how about a good meal and an argument?"

"That sounds like a perfectly splendid notion to me," replied Rodney, and folded the newspaper carefully.

Arm in arm they strolled to the ever-steamy cafe. Seated comfortably with huge unordered mugs of tea in front of them they studied the menu. "The last time I was here I had a sort of stew. I don't actually know what it was."

"Ginger," said Rodney. "He adds a sensation of ginger, brings out the warmth. Nice touch that."

"It is a bit chilly today," said Doris, "but I fancy …something…a little different."

"Might I suggest a warming addition to your tea, a judicious libation?" Rodney slid his hand across the table and slowly opened his palm to reveal a miniature brandy.

Doris giggled and emptied the bottle into both their cups. "You might indeed," she said. "We can pretend we are sipping aperitifs while we study our choices. Perhaps not," she added looking up as a shadow loomed over the table.

"You've got to order and pay at the counter when you've made you mind up," said the man, not looking at either of them.

They ordered burgers and added large dollops of ketchup and laughed when the extra onions they had requested fell onto their plates from the overfilled buns. Doris was feeling skittish and silly and immensely pleased with herself.

"What do you want to argue about?" asked Rodney.

Doris noticed how neat his movements were as he wiped his mouth carefully after every bite. It felt strange to see another man so at ease in Frank's clothes. "Oh I don't care, politics, Iran, crime, Islam, anything to make me feel alive. At my age it is a great temptation to sit back and let everything happen around you, the sort of attitude that says 'it's all down to the younger people now, nothing to do with us', no responsibility, no opinions, I do not want to fall into that trap."

Rodney smiled. "An odd concept that, Doris Roberts without convictions. Is this the same Mrs Roberts who against good family advice has opened her home to a musical group? I use the term lightly."

"What do you mean good family advice? I didn't think you would side with…"

Rodney ignored the interruption. "At a time when every other person of a similar age won't even open their front door to the wild rampaging young, or so newspapers would have us believe."

"It's nonsense, Rodney, you know it's nonsense. I am not denying that terrible things happen. No, that's too evasive. People do terrible things. Some young people do terrible things, but take a look around you, what do you see? Teenagers engaged in all sorts of activities, going to school, being involved in sport, forming rock bands, working part-time, looking after younger siblings, and some of them...oh...the radicalness of it, some of them have joined a school scheme to care for the elderly. I am not blind. I'm not demented. I see what is happening around me."

"Er! Mrs Roberts, do you think, how shall I put it?— perhaps it is a case of not, I beg your pardon, soiling your own doorstep. Could it not be that old people elsewhere are fair game?"

Doris felt her face flush. "So you say that they are all the same, that somehow a whole generation has been born evil, all equally capable of horrendous violence and dissembling. Common sense tells me that that can't be true. The faults of the few have been heaped upon the shoulders of the many who live ordinary blameless lives, odd, unfathomable maybe to our eyes, but blameless nonetheless."

Rodney thoughtfully dipped a chip in the tomato sauce on his plate. "So you, Doris Roberts, you alone live in a charmed oasis where there is no fear because everyone means well, no fear, because basic human nature is good."

Doris shook her head. "Of course I do not. Do I not live in the same world as everyone else? What I object to is the vilification of the young. The young of today are no different from any other age. The trappings, the problems are different, that is all. All in all, I think they rise to their challenges superbly well. They have pressures that I could not begin to think of bearing." Doris banged her mug on the table with intentional vehemence.

Rodney chewed another chip. "Excuses, excuses. My parents neglected me, they don't understand me, they didn't buy me designer trainers." He put his hand to his forehead in mock despair. "Oh the pressure, the pressure."

Doris felt anger rise in her throat like a small sharp object depriving her of breath. She was angry with Rodney and annoyed with herself for not remaining calm and collected. "*So much for reasoned debate,*" she thought. Damn it all, this was not the argument she had in mind. She snorted with exasperation. "Must we condemn everyone? Must we be so suspicious of motive that we close our minds, our doors, and our hearts and shut ourselves away from the potentially worthwhile, live in a vacuum to be safe?"

Rodney carefully wiped his plate with a piece of bun while Doris leaned forward talking earnestly. "My blood boils to think of all the lost opportunities. If we turn aside, if we ignore them then we only have ourselves to blame if the young turn to crime. It can be only that we haven't taught them to be responsible. Because people have access to more information than has ever been possible in the world before it doesn't mean that they avail themselves of it. It's not in the air, we do not absorb it automatically, by osmosis. There is more information but it seems to me there is an unconscionable level of ignorance. The young have to be guided just as they always have had to be but we are a throw-away society and we are in danger of throwing away our most precious asset, the young."

Doris picked up her mug. "I learned a long time ago that you can't save the whole world, only the idealistic young and the very foolish think they can. You can however help one or two, and with any luck they in their turn will…Well, in my case it is not even an organised thought. It is neither foolish nor altruistic. I had space. They needed space. That is it. An incidental benefit to me, is that it helps to keep me, however tenuously, in the twentieth century. Oh! And it keeps the rooms aired. What I can do against the wrongdoers is limited. I can't chase the stone-throwers like Trevor did that day. I can't fight them off if they choose to mug me. I am old and I am frail and I could not defend myself. They could rob me of my possessions and to be honest I would not mourn too much but they could never rob me of my basic belief in goodness."

"Mrs Roberts." Rodney put his hand gently on her sleeve trying to attract her attention. "Doris." She hadn't noticed that her voice had risen, nor that the hubbub around them had died away, even the music from the jukebox was less raucous.

Doris continued to speak, her hand fiercely gripping her now cold mug of tea. "You say that I feel no fear. I do. Like anyone else I jump at shadows and make unfair judgements about people based on appearance and my heart thumps because I too read the newspapers and watch television. What I will not do is show that fear. I am too ashamed of it. You hear a lot about rights nowadays; well, I have earned the right to live life as I choose, I will not let anyone intimidate me. If I allow myself to be dictated to by thugs I let myself down and I lessen the chances of other vulnerable people living independent lives. It is a risk but all of life is a risk. The question one has to ask is, is it worth it to me? The answer I have come up with is yes. I will not live behind doors and windows bolted and barred. I will not connive at my own gaoling. I will not be a prisoner, I will be free."

Doris was flushed and a little breathless, suddenly aware of the silence. Someone clapped and others joined in shouting with good humour, "You tell 'em, love. Go for it, Gran."

Slowly the cafe returned to normal. Doris bent forward and whispered to Rodney "I'm rather embarrassed."

Her companioned smiled. "No need, my dear lady. You have your fellow-diners' approbation. In today's parlance I believe you would call that your mission statement, though…"

"Not that," said Doris. "I meant every word. No, the reason for my embarrassment is that I am stuck. I can't open my hand."

The old man shuffled to his feet and began rhythmically to massage his friend's hand from wrist to where the fingers curled round the mug handle. His touch was gentle but sure. "For all that you yearn for freedom I'd say you'd be unwise to join me on the road just yet."

Doris smiled ruefully. "What we want and what we get...always a gap." Gradually her grip loosened and she was able to let go of the mug. "Give me a moment," she said, "while I work on the knees."

Chapter Thirty-four

"Oh Lord," said Mrs Evans after a glance at her employer's face, "what are we in for today? You've got that look in your eye."

"I haven't got the time for chit-chat. I have a number of commissions for you," said Doris briskly. "I have telephone calls to make and I do not want to be disturbed. I should like you to air and check all the rooms upstairs. I have no doubt the youngsters do their best but I should like to be reassured as to…"

"I've got legs too," grumbled Mrs Evans.

"I should like to be reassured that all is well," said Doris firmly. "A report is needed—no more. If remedial work is needed I'll make sure it is carried out."

"Do I doubt it," Mrs Evans muttered, sitting heavily and beginning slowly to change her shoes.

"Give the poor woman a chance to get her coat off," said Frank.

"Today I take it is a conquering-the-world day as opposed to a save-the-world day."

"Perhaps you should take a duster up there with you," suggested Doris. "Save you running up and down."

Mrs Evans sourly waved a shoe in the air. "Why don't I just nip up with the paint brush as well, brighten up the place a bit, then in my spare moments I could knock up a simple but delicious snack to help give those teenagers the energy for the caterwauling and banging and crashing they call music nowadays."

"That will not be necessary," said Doris frostily.

She had awoken with an urge to do. There had been enough shilly-shallying. What was the point of worrying when all she had to do was to pick up the phone and ask a direct question instead of going all around the houses? Doris resolved to ring Rose, ask her directly if there was something amiss other than her concerns about Prionsias. She would telephone Briony's parents and ask if they might spare their daughter for a few days during the Easter holidays, suggest that the child bring some of her tapes with her.

It crossed her mind that she may have been too swift to dismiss Salmon Blue Traffic. "Several generations behind I am," said Doris aloud.

Mrs Evans surveyed her slippered feet. "And there I was thinking that we were in a positive frame of mind, surely you mean several generations ahead?"

"What?" Doris tutted impatiently. "*When will the woman stir herself?*" There was so much to be done. For a start she must ring the mail-order company and ask them to collect the gadgets Joyce had arranged to be sent to her. Maybe when she was several years older she might find a use for them.

Rejoice must be contacted. If they put their heads together, they might come up with a solution on the subject of Mrs Tracey. In any case, she would leave a note for the milkman asking him to call. She would do that right now while waiting for the snail-slow Mrs Evans to move.

"Did you say your family were coming up for your birthday?"

Doris heard the suggestion with a mixture of surprise and annoyance. "You know perfectly well I haven't mentioned my birthday, or my family. I can't imagine why anyone would give it much thought. I have had eighty-nine of them already. It is not as if it is a landmark."

"Just asking," said Mrs Evans mildly, and left the room carrying a basket of cleaning materials.

"*It could be a landmark,*" thought Doris grimly, "*this could be the year when I lose everything.*"

"You always did have the flair for melodrama," said Frank.

His widow, completing the note to the milkman, frowned. Was Frank right? Was she being melodramatic. Rosaria herself had been the one to mention the birthday, saying that she would put her trip to Ireland on hold until after it. At the time, there had seemed a reasonable breathing space but now the day was approaching rapidly. "Oh damn and blast it all to hell," said Doris and threw down her pen.

Time-wasting worry strangled coherent thought. "*I'll never get anything done at this rate.*"

"I forgot the air freshener," said Mrs Evans. "I'll put that outside for you." She deftly took the note from Doris's hand and left the room again without further comment.

Soon afterwards, Doris heard windows and doors being flung open upstairs. The sound of activity restored her good humour and resolve. Her hand reached for the phone.

The morning was not entirely a success. Prin's wife Elaine was happy that Doris was happy about the baby but could she please be excused because she was going to be sick.

Nobody was available at the Johnson household. This was established after a confused conversation with a man who could not seem to grasp who Doris was but nevertheless would pass the message on to both of the Mrs Johnsons.

A strange milkman knocked, a disgruntled man who told Doris that he had just taken over the round, his predecessor having gone on to a new career, that he would appreciate advance notice of any order change and that his name was Mr Edwards. His potential customer took an instant dislike to him and resolved to get her milk in future from the Pananos across the road. She never could abide a man who emphasised his title. In the circumstances, Doris felt disinclined to broach the subject of Mrs Tracey.

She fared no better with the mail-order company. She was told by a well-rehearsed sing-song voice that only the person who placed the order could cancel it. When Doris tried to explain that she really did not want the goods the same words were spoken with maddening politeness at a slightly higher pitch and she was advised to have a pleasant day.

The telephone was returned to its cradle none too gently. Doris felt that had she been able to kick the offending boxes now cluttering the hall she would be all the better for it. She did not want a gadget for pulling up tights, nor yet an intruder alarm, nor a gismo to prevent her door being opened more than twelve inches, a thingamajig for this, a thingamabob for that.

Robert said Joyce was out. He could not or would not understand what his mother-in-law was saying. He was pleased that the goods had arrived safely. "No price too high for peace of mind," he said. Briony was monosyllabic, the word "cool" was repeated a number of times and Doris was left to wonder whether this was a positive or a negative response.

To her surprise, Doris got straight through to Rose.

"Ma, didn't I tell you'd be inundated with doodle-daddles and all manner of contraptions?"

"Rose, if I kept all those things I would have remote controls for this and remote controls for that, my whole day taken up with pressing buttons…"

"Lights working and blinking at you."

"Timers whirling and…"

"Whirligigs that clunk and click…"

The morning's frustrations were blown away in gales of laughter. "Have I got anything on my mind?" Rose exclaimed after Doris had asked her question. "You don't know the half of it. Haven't I got a million things going on as ever? Poor Gareth is worn out from me. Haven't you noticed that he's scarcely got the energy to lift the phone to find out how you are? On his behalf I apologise."

Doris half-listened to the animated chatter peppered with colourful idioms, interspersed with gleeful laughter.

She was fully aware that she was being charmed and diverted. It was such a pleasing sensation what was there to do but bask in the glow? No wonder Gareth was so in love with this woman who lifted your spirits and made you feel warm and protected.

"Terrible temper she has," said Frank, "and not afraid to show it."

"Ma Roberts!" Doris was suddenly aware that Rose was trying to attract her attention. "Ma, where are you? You're going away from me."

"Rose, forgive an old woman. Oddly enough I was thinking that Benoit has your quality of…how shall I put it, making the world feel upbeat. Is that the word I am looking for?"

"God only knows but it sounds good to me. I must tell Gareth, he says I'd have the skin off him with words, I have such a terrible temper on me."

"Funny you should say that, Frank…" Doris coughed and abandoned her sentence.

"Ma, listen, have you anything in mind for your birthday?"

Doris felt her heart beat a little faster. "No, well not the actual day, Joyce and Robert are coming up sometime to take me back to their place but we haven't settled on a date yet. As I said, I hoped that maybe Briony could stay for a few days if I am not considered too old to look after her. The thought crossed my mind that I might have Ritzy and Benoit in to tea. I have grown so fond of them as you know, or there's Rejoice. Oh…I…I don't know—as you would say, 'Ah sure, isn't every day a holiday for me?'"

"Was that a Cork or Dublin accent, Ma?" asked Rose. "Listen, we'll be in touch soon." She was gone and Doris to her surprise found that her mind was at ease. There was something to be told but Rosaria would tell it in her own good time. Rosaria would make everything all right.

Chapter Thirty-five

Like a long-hoped-for but unpredictable friend tapping you on the shoulder, spring had sprung its annual golden surprise. It seemed to Doris that yesterday the earth was heavy and bare, the grass mangled and sodden, wept on by naked dripping trees, yet today a pale sun shone on daffodils swaying in a gently teasing breeze. The grass beneath richly budded branches were softly green. "When did it happen?" asked Doris in wonder. "I would have sworn that everything was dead yesterday."

"You won't have long to admire it if you don't close the window. You'll have us both on stretchers," said Mrs Evans darkly. "Mind you, the fresh air beats the smoke those youngsters breath up there."

Doris turned in alarm. "Not…"

"No, not drugs," Mrs Evans was quick to reassure. "They're good enough kids I suppose but I wouldn't want them to know I said so. Beats me why they want to look so peculiar, mind you, pierced this and that, makes me shudder it does, it does really and there's the hair. Oh that black girl looks pretty enough—all those rags like we used to wear as children, only in bed mind you, to make ringlets. We'd die before letting anyone see us like that."

Doris smiled. "We had curling tongs—no occasion complete without the smell of singed hair. Trevor is the one I don't understand. I thought that Mohicans had gone out years ago. He is hardly a lad of the 'noughties or whatever they call the year 2000. And then there is

If, all those dyed bits and what about the elaborate makeup?"

The two women standing by the window companionably shook their heads. "Clever girl," said Doris. "Oddly enough she popped in to see me the other day and I barely recognised her. You get quite used to them looking weird. The hair on the top of her head, you know the bit she spikes, it falls smoothly over the dyed bits so you would never know. Saves her getting into trouble at school I expect, smart girl."

In silence, they stood feeling the warmth of the spring sunshine through the glass, enjoying the newness and the colour of the small front garden, aware but not focusing on the street beyond. "I hear them, you know," said Doris sitting and waving Mrs Evans into the opposite chair.

"Who?"

"The pop group, Obsidian, Taps, Trunks, Squirrel, the Johnsons."

"What do you mean you hear them?"

"The swearing. When they are going upstairs, they swear like troopers. It is as if they are in competition for the highest number of repetitions. Of course if I put my head out the door it's like turning off a tap, butter wouldn't melt."

Mrs Evans looked curiously at the woman. "Doesn't it upset you, the swearing I mean?"

Doris thought for a moment. "No, it is not directed at me. It's a habit with them, a sort of camouflage, not to stand out from the crowd. I go out just to remind them that I am here. You get to be invisible when you reach my age, you know, and when you are perceived to be deaf you are doubly absent." She chuckled "Can be an advantage sometimes, I know them all a little more than they think I do."

"And you trust them," said Mrs Evans.

"Of course. I dislike the alternative. No, if I am upset about the swearing it is because it demonstrates a paucity of vocabulary, a lack of awareness of the richness and diversity of the English language and a lack of imagination."

"Mmm, if I stubbed my toe I doubt I'd look for the most appropriate word," said Mrs Evans. "What do you think of that Derek?"

Doris caught sight of Lily Cronin peering suspiciously at the fruit in front of the Pananos' shop. "In all truth I do not know what to make of him, there is something shadowy about him, I just can't put my finger on it. Still, Ritzy seems to like him. Why?"

Before she could reply Mrs Evans gave a little squeal. "Here comes Mrs Cronin; shall I tell her you're not well? Ruin your lovely quiet day, she will."

"Certainly not," Doris snapped, annoyed to hear her own thoughts voiced so precisely. "She is a good woman, and she means well. I should hate to think she was being excluded falsely."

"Oh she means well, all right," said Mrs Evans tartly as she rose to answer the doorbell.

Doris failed to meet her eyes.

"Harry said you were to listen to Classic FM," said Lily Cronin, without preamble. "Some dirge or other as I call them. I like a good musical myself."

"*So do I,*" thought Doris. "*They're not mutually exclusive and I might get to like Blue Salmon Traffic or is it...er...Traffic Salmon? Ah well, must remember to ask Briony.*" She forced herself to pay attention. Odd that her mind should drift off whenever her neighbour called.

"I'll be away then," said Mrs Evans.

Doris looked at her with regret. It would have been pleasant just to sit and chat in the unaccustomed sunlight.

"Have you seen the price of fruit and veg over in that shop?" asked her visitor. "I don't know how they've got the nerve, I really don't, daylight robbery. Of course, you couldn't get a bit of English fruit, oh no, that would be too much to ask. Still, I bought you a few bits. I said to Harry, I said, 'I don't suppose any of those going in or out of that house ever think to give that old lady something, something a bit tasty, something to cheer her up.' " She placed a brown paper bag on a nearby table and sat down, pulling her chair close to Doris. "I see those black youngsters and God knows who going in and out and I think to myself I think, 'well, if that Mrs Roberts doesn't keep an eye to herself, then we'll just have to do it for her.' Then there's that old tramp, all cleaned up he is now. Where did he get those clothes I'd like to know? People always said he had money. That social worker didn't do any good as far as I could see. They're not interested. None of them are interested. Different story if you are a foreigner but they haven't got the time for the elderly these days, won't have you in the hospitals either. They figure you're going to die anyway. I was only saying to Harry the other night what chance do people like Mrs Roberts have and Mrs Tracey when they're all alone and lonely with no one to take care of them? They're at the mercy of...you don't know who's a mugger nowadays, or a murderer." Lily Cronin shuddered delicately, smiling all the while. "Anyway dear, I thought to myself and I said to my Harry I'll pop in from time to time, make you feel safe, make you feel that someone's looking out for you. Now, I know you don't want to be a burden but you mustn't worry, dear. I for one know my duty and it's no sacrifice to spend a little time with someone needy. It will be a weight off your family's mind too. You can't rely on anybody nowadays but you just remember I'm always here to do my little bit. Now Harry says I mustn't stay too long and wear you out." She laughed. "The men, they haven't got a clue have they dear?—don't realise us girls like a bit of a natter. Keeps us cheerful doesn't it? Now please promise me you'll be careful, we don't want you to end up a statistic, do we, dear? That chap with the hair is another one I wouldn't trust. I'll be off now, I'll see you soon." Lily Cronin stood, smiled sympathetically and left.

Doris slowly exhaled the long breath she had been holding.

Chapter Thirty-six

Doris found herself galvanised into life by Lily's diatribe or perhaps it was the effects of spring. Whatever the cause, she was full of energy. She was not alone and lonely. She wanted to dance. She giggled at the thought of whirling round to the music of Obsidian. Benoit would be her partner; he would sweep her off her feet and make her laugh and teach her whatever steps they did nowadays. She felt light-hearted and liberated, far from the pathetic figure she must present to Lily Cronin.

"Ya sound happy!"

"Ah Ritzy, dear, come in. Is it not a gorgeous day? Yes I am happy, I'm a very fortunate woman and I feel like a party."

"Cool," said Ritzy.

"*Ah ha,*" thought Doris, "*a positive response.*"

"When's it going to be, Mrs R?"

"Bless you, child, I only said I felt like a party not that I was going to have one. My party days are long gone."

"Go on, yer birthday soon, innit?"

Doris laughed. "Isn't there anyone who doesn't know about my birthday? No, love, I am in a silly mood imagining…well, you could do me a service if you will. Actually now that I think about it you can't, because you are not old enough for the off-licence. Perhaps Nathan would be so kind as to get me a couple bottles of sherry, the one favoured by my friend Rodney, Mr Thompsett. Things like that are too heavy for Mrs Evans. I don't want to burden her. Do you think Nathan would mind?"

"Course he'll go for ya. Anything else ya want? Benoit's coming along later to set up the video for the Grand Prix. Who are ya goin' to 'ave to yer party then?"

"Ritzy, I am not."

"I know, I know, ya was just imagining but who would ya have anyway?"

"Very well, let's play this game of make-believe. As it is an imaginary event I take it we can include anyone within the entire world?"

"Oh yeah, alive, dead, whatever. Anyone ya want."

"Right, well I can see I'll have to think carefully about this once-in-a-lifetime opportunity. Let's go into the kitchen, I'll put the kettle on."

The walk between the two rooms seemed swifter than usual, limbs more supple, joints practically pain-free. Doris filled and switched on the kettle, leaving Ritzy to complete the operation while she put her mind to the guest list. "First of all I'll have my entire family of course, Joyce and Robert and their lot, Gareth, Rosaria and their gang."

"Hang on a mo', Mrs R. What sort of party are we talking about, a day-time thing like a tea party or an evenin' bash, or sort of 'appenin' that people can pop in when they're ready and stay as long as they like?"

"The latter definitely and it has got to be somewhere spacious so we can have dancing."

"Ya gonna have a disco or what?"

"Good Lord, no," exclaimed Doris. "We shall have the real thing."

Ritzy looked doubtful. "What sort of band?"

"Obsidian, of course."

They both giggled. "So dat's their second gig sorted. Ya're not going to invite Mrs Cronin, then?"

"Certainly I'll invite Mrs Cronin."

Doris and Ritzy looked at one another and chorused, "She means well."

"We shall also have an orchestra to play musical airs and light classics. Harry Cronin can be in charge of all that.

Now, let's see." Drawing an ideal guest list was very thirsty business and the kettle did sterling work. "Queen Elizabeth the First would receive an invitation as would Enid Blyton, Thomas the Apostle, the aunt with the book collection and we shall ask her to read favourite passages," said Doris, "like they do on *With Great Pleasure* on Radio 4. Oh, and we must have Frank."

"About bloody time," said Frank.

His widow ignored him. "My friend, Hilda, she'll come. You'll like her, Ritzy, loved to pose philosophical questions. Before you knew it you were discussing Darwin, apes and man and all that, and debating nature versus nurture. 'How do you suppose the world would have turned if John Kennedy had not died that day in Dallas?' she would say and we'd be off re-writing history." Doris sighed. "I miss those conversations."

"Well, ya can have one at the party," said Ritzy.

Doris stiffened momentarily, then relaxed. "Of course I can. Cardinal Basil Hume would put in an appearance as would John Major and Sue Macgregor, that nice presenter on Radio 4. Jilly Cooper would come, I haven't read her books yet but she seems such a jolly sort of woman, and Dick Francis, good research. Dire Straits, Judy Garland, Kiri de Kanawa along with Obsidian would provide the musical entertainment. I simply must have Stephen Fry…and Oscar Wilde would be a definite."

"What about the catering?" asked Ritzy. "We've got to feed dem all."

"The man from the café," said Doris. "I don't know his name and we can have…Jamie Oliver to help him out. Now, what about you, who are you going to have, there is plenty of space?"

Ritzy picked up a biscuit. "Not my party; come on, who else ya gonna have?"

The girl sitting nonchalantly, swinging her legs from the kitchen stool, looked completely at home and giving every appearance of enjoyment. It was beguiling, as Rose would say 'an afternoon to bottle'.

"Do you think we should have Ainsley Harriet as well? I don't think two chefs are enough for the food."

"Yeah sure. And ya'll have to organise some drink."

"Oh yes," continued Doris, "we shall have to have real ale for Morse; he can discuss classical music with Harry Cronin. Richard Griffiths is another man I should love to talk to, actor on television, has kind eyes. We shall fly Alistair Cooke over from America, oh and Maya Angelou. We shall get her to recite some of her poetry, wonderful voice…and, talking about voices, Richard Burton, we must have Richard Burton. Tony Hawks the writer…I like his mind, makes me laugh and of course Benjamin Zeffaniah."

Ritzy jumped off the stool to answer the doorbell. "Now ya're really tinkin', ya've got one more, then I'll have to go," she shouted as she ran to the door.

Benoit and the taciturn Nathan returned with her. After a few pleasantries the brothers left again to perform their tasks.

"One more Mrs R, then I'm off," said Ritzy grinning from the doorway.

"Patricia Routledge," said Doris, "splendid actress, comedic and serious, a lovely person, I am sure we should get on."

"Rightio," said Ritzy as she gave the old woman a swift kiss and ran laughing from the room.

"Good choice," said Frank. "Should be quite a do."

"Shsss, Frank, I'm still thinking."

Doris's head was buzzing. Memories came flooding back, memories of her childhood, the war years, memories of friends and people she thought she had long forgotten. That evening she watched Concorde grace the sky and felt her spirits soar with it.

That night childhood friends danced into her dreams and holding hands with her played games and skipped in the sunshine.

Chapter Thirty-seven

W hy don't you get your hair done?" said Mrs Evans.

"What is wrong with my hair?"

"I thought that child was coming from Wales."

"What has that got to do with my hair?" Doris demanded suspiciously.

"You don't want her to think she's visiting the wicked witch of the west, do you?"

Doris was stung. Her hand rose to touch her head. "What are you talking about?" she said, puzzlement and anger in her voice. Peering at Mrs Evans, she thought she saw a look of satisfaction flit across her face before it resumed a studied bland air. "My hair is perfectly neat and tidy."

"Exactly." Mrs Evans vigorously liberated the dust from the top of a cabinet. It hovered in the morning sunlight, a glinting multi-coloured challenge.

Doris gazed at it in silence, red, green, gold, silver, blue, movement imperceptible yet the colours changed, mingled, divided until a cloud hid the sun and the magic disappeared.

"Haven't had your hair done since the funeral, you haven't," said Mrs Evans.

"I wash it in the shower, it's fine."

"When did you last settle for plain and tidy, with an emphasis on plain?"

"Mrs Evans I have no wish to continue this conversation. I find it rude and intrusive."

With great energy, the feather duster sought further

prizes. No picture frame escaped attention, no surface was left untouched.

Doris was exasperated. "Do you have to do that now? You usually work in another room or wait until I am out."

Mrs Evans sat down. "Look I have to say something—which of your friends or family is going to tell you you're beginning to have that...that old woman look about you?"

"But I am an old woman, how else should I look?"

"With a bit of style. You were always fond of a bit of style. Now you have that anonymous look. Your Mr Roberts would hardly recognise you with your tidy hair and scrubbed cheeks. When did you last put on a touch of lipstick, bit of colour to your face? I don't suppose you'll like me for it but I had to say. You used to be quite a pretty woman, some would say even a little vain."

"Stuff and nonsense, I don't know why I'm listening to you. What truck have I got with lipstick and hair-dos? I am an eighty-nine-year-old woman and I just want to be left alone."

Mrs Evans rose and began to gather up her cleaning materials. "Just a moment." Doris stayed her with a raised hand. "Why are you saying all this to me? Why are you saying all this to me now?"

"Because now you are stronger."

"Because now I am stronger," Doris muttered to the empty room. "What the hell does that mean?" Anger battered words and phrases back and forth in her brain, *"Straight hair, lipstick, makeup, old woman, anonymous, strong...strong enough to take insults. How dare the woman refer to Frank."* She, Doris looked perfectly all right, she knew she did. She looked perfectly respectable. She had only to look in the mirror and the matter would be settled. *"Huh!"* Why should she rise to such bait, ridiculous, utter nonsense? More important things to think about, plain, anonymous, old...

Doris had been dimly aware of the doors opening and clicking shut as Mrs Evans departed. Now a new sound was slowly being borne in on her consciousness. A bell was ringing with shrill insistence, a continuous piercing intrusion. Furious, Doris switched off her hearing-aid and struggled to her feet. Though mercifully muffled, the persistent clamour drew her to the front door. "What on earth do you think you are doing?" she demanded, puffing slightly from the effort of dragging open a reluctant door.

The pink-faced woman mouthed something at Doris and pointed at the doorbell.

"What do you want? Speak up, speak up, and for God's sake stop that infernal din."

The stranger appeared to speak and gesticulate exaggeratedly. She pointed to the bell and mimed pushing and pulling. Her hand pressed against her ear as if to ward off sound. Then she bent to take something from the bag at her feet. The woman was clearly mad. Doris thought of closing the door and abandoning her to her silent gesturing but the bell buzzed on and a little knot of people now stood by the gate. They too were staring and pointing at the pantomime. They appeared to be deciding to join the mad woman on the doorstep. Silent gesticulations! Doris suddenly remembered her hearing-aid and switched it back on, flinching at the result. She gave an involuntary gasp. The woman on the doorstep produced tweezers from her bag and with them disengaged the stuck bell. The silence was as shocking as the noise had been. For a few seconds everyone stood in frozen tableau, the people at the gate, the visitor, the old woman.

Doris was the first to recover. "Come in," she said and stood aside.

The young woman gained some composure. She picked up her bag and the folder she had propped up against it. From it she extracted an identity card and started to introduce herself.

Doris impatiently waved it away. "Come in, come in for heaven's sake, I can't stand here all day."

The woman hesitated.

"Now," said Doris at her most commanding.

Pamela Bridges was her name, the visitor said and she had come in connection with the Health Survey of England. Doris should have received a letter about it a few days previously. She had but was in no mood to acquiesce to anything.

"And what would this letter have told me? What is it all about? How did you get my name? How did you get my address? Why can you not just get my medical records from my doctors? Why do you want to interview me? Why should I give you my time? Is it compulsory?"

"Courting popularity again, are you, Doris?" said Frank.

Before they went any further, Ms Bridges suggested that Doris should look at her identity card. Her tone was courteous and firm. She would of course leave a copy of the letter but in the meantime she would briefly explain what the survey was about. "I'm sorry about the bell," she said.

Doris grunted and took the ID and only half-listened to her barked questions being answered with brevity and clarity. She was already perfectly aware of the contents of the advance letter. It was necessary to interview a cross-section of the population to assess present and future demands on the NHS. Names were not known in advance, the addresses being chosen from the Post Office small users' address file. The majority of people found it to be a pleasant and interesting experience.

"She's good," said Frank.

"And this is market research?" said Doris. Did she detect the barest hint of distaste on Pamela Bridges' face as she answered? No, it was social research and she worked for a Social Research Institute. She pointed to the name on the ID card.

Doris grunted again and handed it back. "Well I don't want to do it," she said.

"You don't have to make up you mind right now," said the visitor. "I'll leave a copy of the letter with you and I'll pop back in a day or two and we can have a chat about it and you can decide." She smiled, "I'll use your door knocker next time, shall I?"

Though Doris would not admit it, not even to herself at the moment, it was the "you" that did the trick. Had the would-be interviewer used the patronising "we" she would have been, as Prionsias would have said, "slung out on her ear".

Doris rose. "I am very strong," she said incongruously; "you can put that in your survey."

Pamela Bridges had the wisdom to smile and quickly depart.

"Joyce will be pleased that you may be getting sensible at last," said Frank. "You were quite right to say no."

Doris walked to the mirror. She saw nothing different from any other day, hair unadorned, skin clean, a perfectly respectable older woman, well, old woman, sensible. She smiled as she was reminded of her grandmother's oft-repeated words. "Pinch your cheeks dear and try and look intelligent." Well she had better get on. She must get hold of Rodney, then there was the door to get unstuck and the wretched bell to be fixed. The food for the child should be planned and organised. There were a million things that ought to be done and then perhaps she might pop across the road and ask Mrs Panano where she got her hair done. It always looked so shiny. The personal touch might be better than looking in Yellow Pages.

Chapter Thirty-eight

"Guess what, Gran?"

"I can't imagine, Trevor, so you had best tell me." Doris smiled at the excitement in voice and face. A small boy at Christmas could not have expressed such delight. "I've gotta job."

"Have you?" Doris mentally kicked herself for her inability to hide her surprise. "That is wonderful. Look I must hear all about it but we can't stand here in the street. Do you have time for coffee?"

"No dosh." Trevor blushed.

"No do… Oh my treat, we shall celebrate."

Arm in arm, they walked to the cafe, greeting and being greeted by friends and neighbours. Sunlit springtime smiles. Trevor was either used to the occasional stare or odd look, or totally indifferent. Doris revelled in the attention. It felt good being accompanied by such an exotic young man.

Lily Cronin approached. "Your hair looks lovely, dear, makes you look ten years younger," she said before scuttling away.

Doris was surprised and pleased and a little ashamed at having initially tensed when the solicitous hand had been stretched out towards her.

Before they reached the café, Rodney hove into view. "I need to speak to him," said Doris. "Would you be a love and stop him before he disappears?"

"You sure?" asked Trevor and pointed to his hair.

Doris leant on her stick. "Oh go on with you, the world is a good deal more tolerant and understanding than you give it credit for."

Her companion looked doubtful and ran off.

The three of them sat with steaming mugs of coffee. "Rodney, I should like to speak to you presently but my friend Trevor has news of great moment to impart to us."

Doris and Rodney looked expectantly at Trevor. "I've got a job."

"Yes?"

"I'm going to work in the garden centre, starting next Monday."

"Oh Trevor how marvellous, well done, lad, and what about...?" Doris indicated the Mohican hairdo.

"No it's OK, geezer's OK. Said he didn't have no problem. Reckon I'll look a bit of prat in the uniform though."

Doris had a sudden vision of Trevor as a giant blossom with Mohawk hairdo dyed green to match the uniform, and giggled. The men laughed with her. "I think you'll fit in splendidly," said Doris. "I can't tell you how pleased I am for you, your mother must be so proud of you," she said.

Trevor tried to appear nonchalant. "Oh you know."

"What will you actually be doing?" Rodney asked.

"Carting stuff 'round, working with the plants if I'm lucky." Trevor's voice grew husky with the disbelief of his good luck. "And they have courses, so I can carry on the stuff I was learning at the Wild Plant Centre."

For the second time that day Doris felt ashamed. "You mean you really are interested in plants."

"Oh yeah, always got me hands dirty, me, I'll do you some hanging baskets if you like, when..."

"I'll be happy to pay you," said Doris.

"More coffee, people?" The cafe owner shouted from behind the counter. Three empty mugs were raised in the air.

"I believe you wanted to see me, dear lady," said Rodney. "How can I be of service?"

"Ah yes, well it concerns both of you." She thanked the coffee pourer. "It appears to be no secret that I am to have a birthday soon." She waved her hand in a dismissive gesture "I can't imagine why anyone should want to fuss. It is only ninety but so many people asked me what I was going to do it got me thinking. No invitations, nothing formal but I thought I would just let my friends know that I'll be 'at home' if they want to pop in and have a beverage of their choice. I hope you will both join me." Doris looked from one to the other. "It is warm enough to have the garden furniture out and I have stocked up on your preferred sherry." She smiled at Rodney. He nodded. "Trevor, perhaps your mother would like to come along. Right, gentlemen, I have to fly, I am being interviewed this afternoon and I have so many phone calls to make."

She paid for a further round of coffees for Rodney and Trevor and left them discussing the window boxes outside the bank.

On the way home, she met Benoit and her heart gave a little leap as it often did when she saw his warm open smile. "Hi, how ya doin', Mrs R?"

One had to return the smile. "I'm doing fine, very fine indeed." Even had Doris all the troubles in the world, the reply would still have been the same.

In her quiet moments, sitting by the window, she had often tried to analyse what was special about Benoit. It was an evanescent quality that he possessed. Joy emanated from him. How could you define something as tenuous and intangible as a spark, yet solid as flesh? All she knew was that there was a bond between them. He made her happy.

"D'ya watch the Grand Prix?"

"Rather. What excitement, that pit-stop with the seconds ticking away at the corner of the screen, nerve-racking. I could feel my heart thumping, all that time wasted…"

"Hey, what 'bout that overtaking, really thought he'd screwed it up."

"Nearly touched on that bend."

"D'ya see that puff of smoke?"

"Thought he had had it then…"

"…But he 'ad it sussed real well and just shot through. Woo…oo…" Benoit whooped and punched the air.

Doris laughed. "Our boy for world champion?"

"No sweat, on his way today, José. Eh! Mrs R, reckon the rap?"

There were times when Doris did not completely understand the language used by her younger friends. One day she must ask for a glossary but not now. If she did not hurry she would be late for the interview. This would be the third visit from the Research Institute woman and she had no wish to let her down and "give the elderly a bad name", as Frank would put it.

"Must go, Benoit. I'll be late for my interview."

"Hang on a mo." Before she could say anything to stop him, he had loped away with muscled grace. "Gran don't need it today," he said when he returned with his grandmother's wheelchair. With what seemed like breakneck speed, they got to the house just as Pamela Bridges was locking her car. All three smiled.

"My grandson will carry those bags for you," said Doris, rising from the chair. She was rewarded with a giggle from Benoit and a quick veiled look of surprise from her visitor.

"Pass the word, Benoit," Doris called as she opened the front door.

Chapter Thirty-nine

Briony's mother said both she and her daughter would come up to London if that was all right. "That," said Doris, "would be wonderful."

Joyce did not think it was a good idea to have open house, especially as she did not think that either she or Robert could come up. They were looking forward to Doris's planned visit and would probably celebrate the birthday then. Elaine said that she was feeling a lot better. Prionsias and she might very well pop up to see Doris; good idea while she could still fit in the car. However, it might not be on the actual day. Prionsias said that he had put out feelers in Ireland but the name Horgan was pretty common over there. He said they were both busy but he and Elaine would try and see her soon. Gareth said that he was pleased it was working out so well with the kids upstairs, perhaps Doris could come up, and visit him and Rose again. It was very tiring going down to London.

Rose said, "Great to hear from you, Ma, I've been dying for a chat with you."

"Gareth said coming to London tires you out."

Rose's silvery laugh was like balm. "He's ramaishing. Don't take a bit of notice of him. Now tell me what's been happening. Oh, did Prin tell you he's made some contacts in Ireland?"

Doris's heart was beating fast. "Yes dear, do you think it wise, you know after all these years, disturbing…?"

"Ma, I know you feel like that, don't worry, they'll be

discreet inquiries. We wouldn't want to upset anyone, it's just for our own knowing. Sure she might have died by now or gone to America. Anyway, what happened with this interview you were doing? Sounds very grand being interviewed. Was there any money in it?"

It was with great difficulty that Doris turned her thoughts to Pamela Bridges and the pleasant hour she had spent with her. "Rose, it was fascinating, all done on computer, a laptop, never seen one before."

"And what was she like?"

"Such a nice woman, Rose. I'll write to the company. It is not a job I had given much thought to before, going round to people's homes and interviewing them. You would be good at something like that, Rose."

Rose laughed. "Because I'm nosy, you mean."

"Absolutely not. I mean you get on so well with people and believe me you would need to have the patience of a saint if they were all as obnoxious as I was to begin with. Oh I was in such a bad mood that day. She was telling me that the research goes on all the time, month after month, seeing people of all ages, even children as young as two.

"Talking about children I loved the photos of Nigel's children that you sent me. Isn't little Katie gorgeous? They're all gorgeous, all the grandchildren."

"I hear Briony's to descend on you. I should turn off the hearing-aid and buy ear plugs if I were you, unless you are deeply into...what's that other group she keeps on about..."

"Salmon Blue Traffic."

"I had a feeling you'd know the name. You'll get on like a house on fire. Listen, were you really horrible to the woman with the laptop?"

Doris paused; was Rosaria changing the subject? She dismissed the thought. Was she now to become suspicious as well as horrid? "Oh I was horrid," she said, "doing my duchess act as Frank says, said." "*Whoops!*" Doris found herself talking rapidly after that slip, now was not the time.

Rose was a good listener, and she heard that not only had Pamela Bridges brought the laptop but also scales and a stadiometer to measure weight and height. "So not only do I have to have the compassion of Mother Theresa, I have to be as strong as an ox. I'm not so sure that I'll apply for that job, Ma."

Doris brought the conversation round to the "at home" idea. "I should love you to come and meet all the people I've been telling you about."

"Sure, don't I know them already, with the great word pictures you create."

"You mean I talk too much," said Doris.

Rose ignored the interjection. "Can't I see the astonishing If and Ritzy's smile? I can almost hear Nathan grunt and the laughter of Rejoice. Oddly enough, the one I'd like to meet is the pale and elusive Derek. Ma, we've been talking for hours and I really must go now, we'll see what we can do about the birthday."

Doris watched Concorde slice through the sharp evening air and pondered. "We'll see what we can do." It did not sound too promising. Thinking back, she could not recall any great enthusiasm for her suggestion, nothing more than polite interest. Well it was to be hoped that one or two people could come and meet Briony. At the moment it seemed that there was only one person almost sure to come, a nice woman with a forgiving nature, Pamela Bridges.

Chapter Forty

"Now let me get this straight," said Mrs Evans; "you've invited Briony and her mum to stay for a few days, right? Right. So I suppose I'm the one who has to sort out the room for them upstairs, bedlinen, towels, that sort of thing."

"If you would be so kind."

"You have also, as far as I can gather, invited the world and his wife to celebrate a birthday that you said you had no interest in. 'I can't imagine why anyone would want to fuss,' that's what you said."

"You do exaggerate."

"The world and his wife," Mrs Evans emphasised, "and I suppose I'm doing the catering for that little shindig as well."

"Nonsense," said Doris placidly. "I have just asked a few friends in for a drink, that's all. Though if you did help me to lay out a few nibbles I would be grateful."

"A few people, hah!" Mrs Evan's raised her eyes to heaven. "A few nibbles, one drink, spread the word you said."

"I doubt if many will turn up. They all lead such busy lives and the birthday is nothing to fuss about."

"Not turn up—free booze, free food! Of course they'll come and they'll stay and you'll be stiff and tired out. Now I hear you have another one in tow. Collect people you do and not always the right sort. That's the trouble with you, you love everyone."

For the first time, Doris's composure was ruffled. "I do not," she protested. "There are some people I positively hate."

"Name one."

Doris failed the challenge. The two women then set about planning a shopping list in which Coca Cola featured heavily. Briony should be a happy girl.

After Mrs Evan's departure, still grumbling, Doris fell into a reverie; it would be so good to see Briony and Valerie, her mother. Letters passed between them, phone calls were made but nothing could compare with holding the people you loved in your arms. The last time the family had gathered together had been for Frank's funeral; it would be so good to see Briony without tears in her eyes. Not that the funeral had been unrelieved gloom. Doris smiled to herself. Poor Joyce had been so embarrassed. The church softly lit, hushed, expectant, Doris sat with her family in the front pew. Frank was not there, neither was he with her and she searched her heart to find him. Friends and neighbours were filing past the family, shaking hands, murmuring words of sympathy before taking their seats.

Doris went through the motions, her mind half-registered the whispered words of condolence, the questions, the awkward phrases.

"Sorry for your loss."

"It's always a shock, no matter what the age."

"Did he suffer much?"

"They can do wonders now."

"She'll need looking after now."

This last stirred Doris and then her hand was grasped. Lily Cronin's tragedy-filled face was inches from hers. In doom-laden tones she had asked, "Oh poor Mrs Roberts, what happened?"

"He died." The words shot out, flat, loud, startling those nearby into silence, shocking Doris herself. Gareth feebly suppressed a giggle and from Joyce there had been a sharp intake of breath.

Sombre organ music quietly drew the congregation together to focus on Frank's farewell. As if from a distance, Doris heard the service begin with a hymn. She did not recognise it as one for which Frank had any particular affection. She heard the vicar who was standing in for the absent Andrew begin to speak. Her mind felt in a fog. This was all wrong. She was in the wrong place. Something must be done. "Excuse me," she said softly. "Excuse me." She spoke more loudly and stood up. "Excuse me, but who are you talking about?"

The vicar stuttered to a halt in front of a congregation holding its breath.

"Mother, it's all right, Mother," Joyce whispered. "Do sit down, dear, this is a strain for all of us."

Doris shook off her daughter's restraining hand. "Who are you talking about?" she repeated.

The vicar recovered himself. "Mrs Roberts, please don't distress yourself, we are…God is with you in your sorrow over the loss of your husband."

Doris stood very erect. "I am not distressing myself. You are distressing me." She turned to Joyce who was tugging her sleeve "I will speak," she said. "I have the right." Her voice grew stronger. "Funerals are opportunities to mourn and to celebrate collectively the life that has ended. This is our one chance for all of us to share our feelings. Those who can express them will speak for the rest of us. I don't recognise the man you are talking about. I came here today…we, our family and friends came here today to say goodbye to Frank, to bid farewell to a real flesh-and-blood man, not the person you were describing. He was a stranger and I found myself vaguely sad that he died. It dawned on me that we were not mourning the man I had loved and sometimes hated for over sixty years and who had died in my arms." She had felt Gareth's hand on her arm and it was not in restraint but in encouragement. She turned slightly to face him: "You all have memories of Frank and I should like to share in them. I want to hear his name spoken, not in subdued tones but proudly. He was my friend, husband, a father, grandfather and I can tell you, to his immense joy, great-grandfather. He had friends, drinking companions and people who tolerated him. Frank loved to be sociable but he also loved his books and his jazz, his plants and fresh air and there were some television programmes that were not entirely derided. Frank was both arrogant and amazingly tolerant. He loved a good argument. He made me laugh. He was a real person. He had a vast amount of knowledge and was not over modest in flaunting it. He was a man, a bloody awkward one at times, irritating, infuriating and I loved him."

Chapter Forty-one

"Did you ask that bloke you teach?" Ritzy asked.

"Raza Abolhasan, yes, but he told me he did not have time for social interaction. All this in excellent French of course. He made me feel quite frivolous. I'm afraid I have failed with that young man," Doris smiled ruefully.

"It's a nice day for it anyway, stopped raining, people won't be dripping everywhere."

"Ritzy, love, I think I am in for a quiet day but I should like it if you could find the time to come back later to meet Briony. She and her mother have gone shopping."

"Ah! that's a shame."

"No, no, I am very happy, I have had lots of lovely cards and a few phone calls even though it is so early. By the way, why are you here so soon? I had thought that I would get changed before people started arriving, if indeed they do."

Ritzy had come, she said, to suggest that Doris, when changed into her finery might like to visit Rejoice while she and Mrs Evans brightened the place up a bit.

Doris was going to protest about not wanting a fuss but If's "go with the flow" popped into her head. "OK," she said and Ritzy grinned ear to ear.

She had also come with a birthday present, a bit of a party outfit. Doris held the gaily-wrapped package on her lap. "Talking about parties, I should like to send out a few more invitations."

"Yeah?"

"I have been giving it some thought. I should like to cheer up that girl Katie in *Brookside*, the one who never seems to smile and then there's poor Jill Archer on the radio, she could do with a break."

"Go on."

"Just five more if I may, then I think we'll close the lists."

"Righto."

"Thora Hird and Marilyn Monroe, I absolutely must have Marilyn Monroe—oh! and I must have Alan Bennett, John McCarthy and finally Stephanie Cole."

"I'll see to it straight away," said Ritzy and with a laugh she was gone.

Doris slowly opened her present. The colour of the cardigan defied accurate description. To say that it was pink was miserably inadequate. It dazzled. It glowed. It danced. It screamed. For the first time in her life, Doris felt the need to wear shades. Stroking the soft wool, she mused. Now what was she to wear? Somehow a discreet paisley dress no longer fitted the bill. "Face it, old girl," said Frank. "You have nothing that quite fits the bill."

"Mother, you can't." She heard the words as clearly as if Joyce was there. Having decided she certainly could, she got up to look through her wardrobe.

"Grey skirt," said Frank. "Don't fight it."

"Ritzy, do you think I should visit your grandmother? I know I am not expecting many people but some may come and I should hate not to be there to greet them."

"No we'll get ya back on time, ya ready then? D'ya wanna wear that skirt? Never mind. Lipstick looks pretty. Oh ya've got shoes with heels."

"The Queen Mother does and she's older than me," said Doris, "and she has a bad leg."

Ritzy had ordered a taxi she said because on the way to her grandmother's she had something to collect from the church hall.

"I can walk," said Doris.

"Not in those shoes, ya can't," said Ritzy. "'Sides, it's yer birthday, we thought ya'd like to see all the spring flowers in the gardens as we go by."

"Oh what a lovely idea," said Doris, and was in the car before she reluctantly let a disturbing thought creep into her mind. Was she being hi-jacked? Was it possible that Ritzy would be so treacherous as to lure her to a Seniors' afternoon? Even now, were old men and women awaiting her arrival? Andrew had said he could not come to the house today because he had to be at the hall. Doris stared out of the partly opened window and did not see the swaying daffodils, the narcissi, the freshly leafed trees, nor smell the blossom on the scented air. Panic rose like bile to her throat. She was not ready for con-senescence with her peers, the sticky bun brigade. It was difficult to breathe. Mrs Tracey must feel like this.

"Ya alrigh', Mrs R?" Ritzy looked anxious.

"I was wondering if I should call on Mrs Tracey. I don't like giving up on her."

"Not today, eh!"

The fluttering of Doris's heart subsided. She smiled. "You are right, I must concentrate on pleasant things today. I am so looking forward to you meeting Briony, and she is dying to meet the members of a real band. I hope you can all come around before she goes home."

Ritzy thought it could be arranged.

Chapter Forty- two

Doris declared herself quite happy to chat with the taxi driver while she waited for Ritzy outside the church hall. Her birthday was not quite as she had imagined but it was pleasant, apart from the earlier brief frisson of fear. She knew Ritzy was lying when the girl came running out to ask her inside. Doris did not hear the pretext, she was busy steeling herself. "*I'll go through with it,*" she thought, "*and I will keep smiling.*"

"Surprise." The word erupted in an explosion of sound. Faces, smiles, balloons, streamers blurred in a confusion of movement and colour. Doris felt herself being drawn into the throng to stand beneath a multi-hued banner. Bewildered, with a fixed smile she cast her eyes around for a familiar face, but nothing made sense. 'Happy Birthday' was being sung and the voices reached the rafters but could not seem to penetrate her brain. Her hand was being tugged urgently.

"Gan, Gan it's me, Gan Gan." That did it. A pet name like that was fine in private when a small child could not pronounce great-grandma, but in public! Doris turned to face Briony. "Deceitful child," she said. "Your great-grandmother is not best pleased." She fixed the grinning child with a steely gaze. It was a relief to stop smiling for a moment. Somebody brought a chair but Doris did not wish to sit but to move amongst the people she now recognised as family and friends, liars everyone of them.

Andrew motioned the hall to silence. "You will be pleased to hear that I'll be brief. We're here today to celebrate the birthday of our dear friend, Doris Roberts. Our task, you will agree, is to make sure that Doris has the happiest day we can give her. I feel sure she will start enjoying herself as soon as she has forgiven us for our small deceptions and knowing her generous nature it won't take too long. I won't embarrass her by saying too much, but Doris has a gift for friendship and we are all beneficiaries of that gift. Those of you who have drinks please raise your glasses and drink a toast to a lady of our time. God bless you all, happy birthday, dear friend."

Doris nodded to him across the hall, grateful that his words had given her time to recover. Her heart had returned to its normal beat and the smile to her face. Briony took charge, guiding Doris through a forest of outstretched hands, barely giving her time to embrace one undreamed of guest before rushing her on to greet another. It was breathtaking and exciting: Valerie and Briony, Patrick, his wife and their children, Joyce's daughter, Esther, and her boys. Doris wanted to hug them all and question, question, question, marvel at their being there. All she could do was to allow her hands to be grasped, her flushed cheeks to be kissed while she murmured half-sentences and disconnected words.

An arm went round her and she was crushed in a bear hug. "Great cardi, Gran, you are a true beacon in a dark world."

"Prin, how marvellous, and Elaine, you look beautiful."

"Naw," said Prin, "the beauty is outside."

Elaine thumped her husband. "You'll have to have another ride in it before it goes," she said to Doris who was dragged away before she could reply.

"Has nobody given you a drink yet?" asked Mrs Evans. "I watched you being pushed all around this hall like a football, bouncing here and there and everywhere. Come by here and sit, and let them all come to you. If we put your chair near the food, they can kill two birds with the one stone."

"Thank you." Doris eased herself down and gratefully accepted a drink. For a moment she was overwhelmed. There were so many people. How was she to talk to them all, how to cope with such a diverse crowd?

Andrew appeared at her side. "They're all perfectly happy, Doris," he said, apparently reading her thoughts. "Look at them, your family getting together; isn't it lovely to see the children running around, playing with Jyotsna's children, and Mrs Evan's grandchildren? Look at the good Mrs Evans helping Ritzy serve that delicious-looking food. If is marshalling her troops, I understand the band is going to play for you later. Mrs Wilmacott is splendidly shepherding the Seniors."

Doris dutifully waved to the old people seated in one corner.

"The Lunch Club and the Seniors kindly agreed to share the hall with you today," said Andrew. "Not that they needed any persuading—many of them have known you over the years and are only too pleased to wish you well on your special day."

Doris gave him a sidelong glance; even here he was trying to promote his propaganda. She forgave him. She was calmer now that everything was not happening all at once. There was time to observe; the music seemed quieter, movement less frenetic.

Ritzy brought her a plate of food and squatted down beside her. "All right? When ya've finished that everyone wants to talk to ya, will that be OK?"

Doris was suddenly overcome with a rush of love for this child and, had it not been for the plate in her hand, would have flung her arms around her. She could not talk for the lump in her throat and could not see for the tears in her eyes.

"Well, you really are in a state," said Frank. "Pull yourself together, woman; the least you could do is try and look happy."

Doris felt like a queen sitting on her throne to receive her guests. She noted with amusement that her minders,

Mrs Wilmacott and If, were regulating the flow of people wanting to have a few words with her. Benoit gave her a bone-crunching hug on behalf of the band who were setting up their equipment on the stage. The members of the lunch club filed past her and expressed a wish that she join them. Guiltily crossing her fingers, she said she would love to. They said it made a pleasant change from staring at four walls and her guilt evaporated.

"We hope you're having a lovely birthday, Mrs Roberts." Jyotsna in a stunning sari bowed slightly.

"Oh yes, indeed, where are the children? They all seem to have disappeared and only a few moments ago they were fluttering around my feet like spinning tops."

"Behind the stage is a small room beside the kitchen and the young children are laid out on cushions and blankets on the floor having an afternoon nap. It's like a dormitory back there."

"And the older children?"

"There is a storeroom with a television and they and Sunanda and Tariq are watching a 'very very favourite programme'." Both women finished the sentence in unison and laughed.

"I take it you helped with this lavish fare," Doris said.

"Because there are samosas and bhayjis?"

Jyotsna raised an eyebrow and smiled. "Actually, Mrs Cronin supplied those; I made the apple pies."

In between shaking hands and acknowledging the growing mound of gifts, Doris watched the changing pattern within the hall. The music had changed from jazz to the Beatles. No one seemed to take any notice as people, some of whom she could swear she had never seen in her life before, flitted from group to group. Others remained deep in conversation oblivious to the sounds and movement around them. The apparently ravenously hungry, with plates piled high, sat on chairs lining the walls. There were also the nervous prodders of food, with forks tentatively pushing at morsels as if expecting life to leap forth.

"Mrs Roberts, there's a day-bed ready for you around the back if you want a bit of a lie down." Now it was If bending over Doris.

"I'm so impressed the way you seem to have thought of everything. Certainly I'll have to get up presently, otherwise I'll be stuck but come and sit by me and tell me who everyone is."

"Right, who don't you...?"

"If," Doris exclaimed, "your hair—I can't imagine why I did not notice it before." If turned away. "Oh I see, it is just one side, may I touch?"

"Sure, what do you think, Mrs Roberts?"

Doris smiled, stroking the sleek head. "It's lovely, I thought it would feel hard somehow. That bright blue really suits you."

If looked pleased. "Right, now, who don't you know. Let's see, security at the door is Derek's cousin, you know, Ritzy's boyfriend, he'll be along later...and...there's..."

Was security necessary, Doris wondered?

"Oh yeah, gatecrashers and all," said If casually. "Anyway," she continued with her briefing, "there is..."

Scanning the faces, Doris frowned. It must be her imagination. Should she mention it to If? No, she was being silly, the lad on the door looked solid enough. Obsidian obviously trusted him. Looking around again, there was no sign of the young man she thought she had seen.

Prin appeared at her side. "Could you do with a rest, Gran? I understand that more people are coming along later."

"Oh Prionsias, dear, lend me your arm—I need a stretch before I seize up. Maybe we could sneak outside and have a peep at the car. Please excuse us, If. Let's see how Benoit's security guard is getting on. Do you think we need a pass to get by the one on the door?"

The flower-scented air was good to breathe. Prin and Doris strolled along the street talking desultorily and avoided the subject uppermost in their minds. It was great seeing his brothers, Prin said; they were all going to visit Rose and Gareth the following day. It was arranged that they would spend tonight at a hotel. Reaching the car, they joined the small knot of people admiring it and the security guard who was keeping them at bay.

"It'll have to go," said Prin. "Never get a baby seat in the back."

"You will make a splendid father," said Doris. "Could we manage a ride sometime?"

"You bet, Gran." Prin squeezed her hand. "I know you are uneasy about me looking for my mother but Mum is OK about it. Well, actually she seems quite keen herself. I can't help thinking that everyone knows more than…"

"We shall talk, Prin. I'll do what I can. I'm so glad you have mentioned it."

Chapter Forty-three

$\mathbf{A}$ wave of sound hit Doris and Prin as they re-entered the hall. "*They are still rehearsing*," thought Doris. "They're good," said Prin.

Doris felt shame-faced. She glanced around while adjusting her hearing-aid. Everybody seemed to be shouting at the tops of their voices, to counteract the rock music, she supposed. For the first time she noticed that apart from garlands and balloons decorating the walls, there were pictures and posters that somehow did not seem to belong to the church hall.

Ritzy came and threaded her arm through Doris's. "Ya've spotted dem then?" she said. "Only two we couldn't get but we got all the rest."

"Ritzy, what are you talking about, dear?"

"Come on." They went and Doris gazed at the portrait of Queen Elizabeth the First and moved onto Marilyn Monroe, Princess Diana, then a pop group. "Who are they?"

"Dire Straits." Ritzy appeared to be suppressing a giggle. On they moved to Cardinal Basil Hume and Patricia Routledge.

"That woman has got such expressive features," said Doris. Her eyes moved on to rest on the face of her friend Hilda. "Oh!" Her free hand flew to her mouth; her head turned to take in the other photographs and she found herself smiling at Frank. "Oh Ritzy, I have just realised."

"You said you wanted all those people at your party," said a familiar voice.

"Rose."

"Happy birthday Ma, great party."

"Rose, is it true? Gareth, how wonderful."

Ritzy ran off to get drinks while Doris hugged her son and daughter-in-law.

"This is beyond words, I just can't tell you what it means to have you all here. You will be able to meet all my friends, well quite a number of them but I am sure you're already well acquainted with the guest list. I can't get over the organisation that went into all of this. Aidan, Prin and Nigel are here, you know."

Gareth smiled and took his mother by the arm. "Come and sit down, Mother; you'll be worn out."

"We'll take some photos," said Rose. "Won't it be wonderful, Ma, you can dangle the youngest great-grandchild on your knee. Silly word, dangle, always thought it sounded dangerous. What's wrong, Ma?"

"Just being greedy; wishing Joyce could be here." A thought struck her: "Unless she is lying as well as the rest of you." Those around her looked blank.

Doris was back in her chair. The toddlers had woken to various degrees of cheerfulness and the odd furious scream competed with songs from the shows that had replaced the ear-shattering efforts of Obsidian. Cameras flashed, food continued to be eaten, drinks drunk, and If's troops moved around the hall with large black plastic bags to remove the detritus.

"Do you know all these people?" Rose sounded impressed.

"Some only by sight because the do had to be shared with the daily bookings," said Doris, scanning the room for those of interest to point out to Rose. Her heart thumped uncomfortably. This time she was not mistaken. Lester, the young man who had frightened her in the snow was definitely in the room. She shuddered. Just then Derek, the pale and elusive Derek as she thought of him, came to wish her a happy birthday and distracted her.

"Who's that?" asked Rose.

"I'll tell you when I have found out, dear," said Doris, somewhat cryptically. "Suffice it to say he is Derek, Ritzy's boyfriend. I...haven't got a handle on him yet."

People came and went, some only being able to stay for a few minutes. One of those was Doctor McIntyre. "I was hoping my visit would coincide with your pop group playing. I've heard so much about them. This seems a bit tame for you."

Gilbert and Sullivan was now playing jollily in the background. "Mind the knees, Doris, go easy with the dancing later on," was his parting shot.

Mrs Evans returned after "doing" her old gentleman. "Has anyone actually given you something to eat?" she demanded. "You looked flushed, which is an achievement against that cardigan. Is anyone controlling this mob? Those children are running wild, your great-grandchildren included."

Doris looked to see something amiss but all she could observe were children and toddlers chasing each other and hiding behind the legs of, on this day, the tolerant, and squealing with glee. Little Katie, determined to crawl, was constantly being scooped up by fearful, adoring adults. "Yes, I have had something to eat but I could do with stirring myself and having a look at the gorgeous spread and if it's at all possible I should love a cup of tea." Mrs Evans helped Doris to her feet.

"There's an old tramp round the back, wants you to go out, wouldn't go away," said one of If's helpers. He looked doubtful.

"Oh that will be my friend, Rodney," said Doris. "Let's take him out some food."

"Let's not," said Mrs Evans. "He's very choosy. I'll take him out some tea."

Doris and Rodney sat side by side on the bench at the back of the church hall. The late afternoon spring sun picked out leaves and flowers and stones to reflect its gentle light.

"Would you like something to eat, Rodney?"

The old man coughed delicately. Doris noticed that the cuffs of the white shirt protruded over raw pink-scrubbed hands. His hair when he doffed his hat was plastered to his head. She felt touched, not doubting that he had made these efforts with his appearance for her.

"Thank you no, dear lady," he said. "I understand that the cafe proprietor is to make his contribution later and I should like to partake a little then if I may."

"Really, who on earth arranged that? I don't even know his name."

Rodney coughed again and waved a deprecatory hand.

"I take it you won't say no to a cup of tea," said Mrs Evans, carrying two steaming mugs.

"I am indebted to you," said Rodney, accepting one of them.

Doris and companion sipped in silence for a while. As if from a great distance, music, chatter and laughter could be heard. She sighed. It was peaceful here by this sunny wall, no matter that they shared the space with the dustbins, and the growing number of plastic sacks, and the church cat sprawled in a pool of sunlight between two sparsely leafed straggly trees.

"Please accept my very best wishes for your birthday. I would hate to deprive you of time spent with your delightful family, knowing that this is a rare treat."

"Oh what was that?" The music inside the hall had stopped and the noise level rose and changed in character.

"Oh good, ya' alrigh' out here?" said Ritzy, putting her head around the door. "All sorted, dick'eads tryin' to gatecrash is all." She was gone.

The music started up again, light classics. "I was saying," Rodney continued, "that this must be a rare treat having all your family together under one roof. I came with…" He rummaged in his pocket and withdrew a piece of paper, "…this little gift."

Doris unfolded a lottery ticket. Before she could express her surprise and thanks Rose appeared with a tired Katie on her arms. Introductions were made.

"Stay where you are," she said as Rodney made a move to go. "This little one is out on her feet, but she won't lie down, so we thought that this might be the perfect opportunity for you to have a lovely cuddle. Let's see if she'll go to you." Katie wriggled then lay contentedly in Doris's arms. The two gazed into each other's eyes. "Gorgeous," said Rose and took a photograph. "Let's get one of you too, Mr Thompsett," she said, and clicked again and was gone. Katie's eyes drooped.

Doris turned over the lottery ticket in her hand. "Rodney," she said softly, "what shall I do with this if I win?" They smiled at one another.

"Invest in the future," he replied.

Doris folded the ticket and placed it in the hand of the sleeping child.

Chapter Forty-four

Mother, you can't."

Doris smiled. Good impersonation she thought and turned to admonish her daughter-in-law. Joyce was standing there with Robert, gazing at her mother with a mixture of excitement and embarrassment. "That cardigan," she said, putting out her hand to touch it as if she did not believe her own eyes. "It's...it's...so..."

"...bright and vibrant and helps to identify me as the cause of all this fuss." Doris opened her arms. "Come and give your old mother a hug. Now my day is complete, now that you're here."

Robert patted his pockets. "Present in car," he said.

Drinks were brought. Doris looked around to see who she should introduce to her daughter and son-in-law. Perhaps when they met her friends they would be less worried. She heard a sharp intake of breath and followed Joyce's gaze. "Who is that?" the younger woman gasped. "People like that shouldn't be allowed to come in here; isn't there anyone in charge, this is a private party."

"Oh, that's Trevor, and the girl he's talking to, the one with the blue hair, that's If, one of the organisers."

Joyce looked puzzled. "But Mother, when you described him, when you said his hair was quite spectacular, I imagined well...I'm not sure what I imagined. It must be nine inches high."

"*Nine and a half to be exact,*" thought Doris. Trevor had proudly told her so the other day. She was quite pleased to see Mr and Mrs Cronin come towards her. They came arm in arm, she looking shy and he dignified. They were a couple. Doris felt as if she was seeing them in a new light. She smiled warmly. "How lovely to see you," she said and meant it.

"I've brought some tapes," said Harry. "Nothing too heavy. Strauss waltzes. I thought perhaps at the heel of the evening." He blushed.

Evra and Marcus pushed Rejoice's wheelchair to rest squarely in front of Doris. "How are ya, girl?" she shouted. "Bet ya never got no surprise like today and I bet ya never got no rum in your tea neither." She laughed her booming, all-embracing laugh. Those within earshot stopped whatever they were doing and smiled as people do when they are caught up in a mood but don't know what has been said.

Gradually the whole hall quietened down, except for Dire Straits coming from the speakers. "Where's yer glass, girl? We gotta drink a toast." Someone gave glasses to the two women and Rejoice poured a generous amount into each of them. "What will be the toast, Doris girl?" she demanded.

Doris whispered, "Basket of rain."

"Ya've got it, girl." The old woman in the wheelchair slapped her knee enthusiastically.

Doris winced.

"Ya've got it good, basket of rain it is." She spun the chair to face the hall, narrowly missing Doris's feet and causing several drinks to spill as people jumped out of her way. "Listen!" She turned the volume up. "We're going to drink a toast to me friend Mistress Roberts, the toast is a Jamaican saying 'basket of rain'. Means we all got troubles but they don't last no more than rain in a basket, thank the Lord. Right ya all got that, you drink that with me friend Doris? Basket of rain."

Andrew, returning from driving some of the elderly to their homes was almost pushed back through the door by the sheer volume of sound as the crowd shouted in one voice, "Basket of rain."

In a blessed lull, the family had a chance to talk together while the hall was being rearranged for the final hours of the party. Chairs were lined up by the walls. Empty dishes were replenished, empty wine bottles replaced. Doris wandered around with Rose to see the rest of the pictures. "Ritzy said that there were two missing but there is another, Frank's brother, Reg, and I'm sorry about neglecting him."

"But Ma, you were just playing a game of make-believe." Rose put her arm around her mother-in-law and listened.

"When Frank was dying he asked me about Reg, had I heard from him recently, was he all right? He was worried about him. As you know, he'd died about a fortnight before. I lied to Frank, I told him Reg was fine and I have felt guilty ever since. I don't know if I eased his concern or did he sense the reality and feel betrayed? Do you think one is justified in withholding the truth for what we may think are the kindest of reasons? Is one ever right to keep secrets from one, possibly to the detriment of the other?" Doris fancied that the arm about her shoulders had tensed slightly. "I am sorry, love, that is all a bit heavy for a day like today. I must remember to ask Ritzy who the two missing are."

"No," said Rose, "it's days like today make you question your motives on all sorts of issues. It wouldn't be life if we didn't have moral dilemmas. Gareth and I were discussing…"

Harry Cronin apologetically interrupted their earnest talk. "One of the lads up on the stage said he'd show me how to work the sound system for when I play my tapes, and I don't know which one it is, I don't want to…"

"Ah, now, let's see," said Doris. "Benoit can't really be mistaken, he is always smiling, Nathan, well I can't see him managing a whole sentence. That leaves Taps, Squirrel or Trunks and I can never quite work out which is which but I think the one with the most body piercing is the one in charge of the equipment. Look there he is crossing the stage now." Harry trundled off looking brave.

Someone came along and said that the band was going to play again. It would be the only chance for their mums and dads to hear them play a real gig as they never went to clubs. Was it all right with Doris? The gracious answer was "yes". Doris thought it would be nice to meet Ritzy's hardworking parents at last.

Rodney sent word to say that the sherry was delicious, chilled to perfection and that he had enjoyed quite a lot of the music.

Doris summoned Andrew to her side. "I should like to say a few words before too many people have to leave. Could you attract attention for me please?"

"We'll use the microphone—can you manage the stairs?"

Whether she could or could not, Nathan and Benoit carried her up on to the stage. Andrew passed the microphone to Doris and she began hesitantly, "At a time like this only clichés will do. My heart is too full to look for apposite phrases and clever words. A plain 'thank you' is all I can manage. To say I am overwhelmed by your generosity and care is the simple truth. I should also like to say that you are all experts in the art of deception and after such duplicity I'll hesitate to believe another word uttered by any one of you."

Above the general laughter there could be heard from the back of the hall the shrieks and screams of the children racing round finally before they were whisked away to bed. "I will have so many memories to remind me of today but the one I think will typify this lovely day is that which is happening now, those children playing so happily together. The sound of their giggles I'll be able to replay it in my mind for many a long year—well, let's not get too ambitious, for many a long day. On the other hand, I'll never forget…no…I'll not go down that road or we shall be here until you regret…you will all have your own memories and

I can only hope they will be as rich and happy as mine will be. Thank you and God bless you."

Doris was carried back to her chair to a rousing "For she's a jolly good fellow". Goodbyes were said and kisses exchanged with the departing. Fresh people were greeted before everyone was blasted into silence by the startling opening chords of Obsidian. There was nothing to do but listen. Doris thought that she detected a pattern, and then wondered if it had not been wishful thinking. "They're good." Prin mouthed the words. Doris nodded.

"Excellent!" Briony shouted in her ear.

The Strauss waltzes played quietly, there were fewer people in the hall now, and conversations were no longer being carried out at full voice. Mrs Evans helped Doris to a small portion of the cafe casserole. Together they watched Rose and Gareth take to the floor, to be followed by Joyce and Robert and then Lily and Harry Cronin.

"That's nice," said Mrs Evans.

"Why?" asked Doris.

"Why is it nice that they are dancing?"

"Why all this today, why all this for me?"

Mrs Evans thought in silence then: "It's not yet a year since your Frank died and it makes people think. A person has regrets, they say to themselves, 'if only I'd said this, done that but now it's too late'. Today was perhaps a way of focusing on someone who is still here. It's a saying you have, isn't it? 'I do not want flowers when I am dead. If you want to give me flowers give them now.' Maybe that's what today is, flowers. Or maybe I'm talking a lot of crap, as the youngsters say today." She stood up to go. "You keep saying your birthday's not special but it is special because you're special." She bent and kissed Doris. "And I'll hate myself for saying that," she said and fled.

"I won't breathe it to a soul," said Doris to her retreating back.

"Talking to yourself," said an unfamiliar voice.

She looked up. "Pamela, I am so pleased you could come."

222

"Sorry I'm so late," said Pamela Bridges, "the last interview took longer than I thought. You're not dancing yourself?"

"Yes she is," said Benoit and pulled Doris to her feet. They danced to Strauss somehow and in his strong arms she was once more lithe and lissom and her heart sang and she would never be able to say how much she was in love with life.

Chapter Forty-five

Living in the well-ordered and comfortable cocoon that was Joyce and Robert's home was a pleasant restorative experience. In her own home, Joyce was more relaxed. Tempting delicate food was prepared and laid before Doris. Little outings were planned with precision, thoughtfully timed to minimise fatigue. Carefully chosen guests came for morning coffee, all cultured people of taste and sensitivity whose conversation neither irked nor challenged.

Peace prevailed in the immaculate house. Doris allowed herself to be pampered and cosseted and generally went along with Joyce's need for her to be the perfect acquiescent old lady, at least for the duration of the visit.

The two women enjoyed quiet talks and afternoons listening to Radio 4 plays, sometimes in the company of Robert and pipe.

The party was hardly mentioned, almost as if to do so would shatter the tranquillity.

"Mother, I understand that you are fascinated by...shall we say...unusual people, and it blinds you to reality. What worries Robert and me is that you have no control. It seems to us that anyone, any doubtful character could just walk into your home and...and...drugs, anything could be going on, smoking, fire."

Joyce held Doris's hand and peered earnestly into her face. "You are at the mercy of the naïve trust you place in unsavoury characters who leech onto you."

With heroic restraint, Doris kept quiet.

"According to you they're all blameless. You have this knack of accepting people just as they are or they appear to be and they take advantage of that. Anyone can see that they're all after something."

"*Me too,*" thought Doris.

"Go easy on her, Doris, let her unburden herself," said Frank and his widow inwardly sighed.

Joyce's voice grew more intense. "They want to suck you dry, Mother, I'm not being heartless, and I know that there are terrible problems, homelessness, racism, injustice."

"*Intolerance,*" thought Doris.

"But I don't see why you have to be the one to resolve them. I'm not saying…that you…" Joyce appeared to be searching for an apt word, "…your friends don't seem to be genuinely fond of you but it all seems so unnecessary that you should put yourself out so at your age. Surely you have done your bit already helping Rose with Prionsias."

Doris felt herself tighten inside as Joyce continued. "Do you know there was a social worker at your party, obviously keeping an eye on someone there."

"Oh Hope Jordan, nice woman."

"You know her?"

"Oh course, dear, she keeps an eye on me."

"What!" Joyce looked appalled. "We're not the sort of family that has social workers. Why wasn't I told? I would have made it crystal clear to her…she does know that you have a family? Mother this is so shaming." A thought seemed to strike her. "Are they watching someone else through you, one of those misfits, is that what it is?"

"Joyce dear, they are not detectives. In my case, I do not believe it is an official arrangement, not any longer. I think it is splendid that the old folk are being looked after."

"Well you've certainly changed your tune," said Frank. "What happened to 'I do not need a public guardian angel?' "

Joyce said, "You didn't notice because you were surrounded but a dreadful-looking man tried to get in with his awful scruffy dog. Imagine trying to gatecrash with that smelly mongrel on a piece of string, anything for a free meal I suppose. He kept saying he had a magazine for you, for your birthday, nonsense of course. I sent him away."

Doris said very quietly, "I'm sorry you did that. That was Paul, he is making something of himself selling the *Big Issue*. Good magazine, I like the poetry. I like Paul, he has such a lovely smile, has his pitch outside the cafe."

"I'm sorry, Mother, but how was I to know? When we arrived somebody else was being thrown out, a black lad."

"Lester," said Doris.

"Another friend, I suppose."

"No, of course not." They both smiled.

Joyce said, "Mother, I won't bring up the subject again while you are here, I wish, we wish that you would move, that area is just not what it used to be. Please try to understand, we just want you to be safe. I wish with all my heart that my mother wasn't content to live in a danger zone. What would Daddy say, he would be so worried."

Doris bit her lip. "Go on," said Frank, "tell her what I'd say."

"Joyce darling, I wish with all my heart I could ease your concern. I honestly believe Frank would say 'have fun, Doris'. You see love, I am the one with the life and I can't live the short time left by somebody else's standards."

Joyce gave a sigh. "Mother I love you, but I don't understand."

Doris felt sad.

Chapter Forty-six

Doris lay in the dark and admitted to herself how delicious it was to be where she was. She queried whether delicious was the right word and decided it was precisely what she felt. Joyce's spare room was tastefully and comfortably furnished. It was warm, no hardship when one had to rise in the night. Two bookcases contained a good selection of books. The bedside radio was pre-set to her favourite stations and there was also a collection of audiotapes should insomnia strike. A slight night breeze gentled its way through half-opened curtains and barely touched her cheek. It brought with it faint countryside smells. Out there all seemed silent until, listening very carefully, you could hear the stirrings and rustlings of plants and animals. In another few hours, the first rays of the sun would tentatively explore the sleeping earth. Birds would begin their busy day with a song.

"Your getting quite lyrical," said Frank

"Oh, hello, love," said Doris, her hand reaching out beside her on the bed. "*I am still doing it, I still forget you are not there, I miss you.*" A low steady snoring reached her from Robert's and Joyce's room. She smiled. Life goes on. She lay, too sweetly tired to take out her hearing-aid and too full of memories to sleep. The party had been wonderful, would feed her thoughts for a long time to come. It was like a film playing in her head...faces, smiles, colour, laughter and Joyce's anxiety that said "I love you". "Living in a danger zone"; she liked that. She would go home soon and make lots of phone calls and chatter and giggle and share the excitement of that day. She wriggled into a more comfortable position and thought how seductive was her present situation. In the morning Joyce would bring her tea exactly how she liked it, then help her to sit up and would switch on the radio. Doris would half-listen to the *Today Programme* and half-listen to the sounds of an efficient household getting ready for the pleasant day ahead. That day would be planned down to the last crumb eaten. "*I need never lift a finger ever again,*" she thought and drifted off to sleep.

Should they visit Canterbury Cathedral or drive to Whitstable to buy fresh fish was the question being debated when the telephone rang. While Robert went to answer it, Doris and Joyce sat in companionable silence gazing across the fields. Earlier in the morning, it had rained and now rainbow-coloured droplets on the window-panes reflected the sun's fire. A damp earthy green smell, fresh and inviting, wafted through the window. "Maybe just a stroll round the village might be nice," said Doris. "If it goes on like this we shall be able to sit outside in that sheltered corner and…"

"What's wrong?" Joyce rose as Robert returned to the kitchen. "What's wrong, tell me. Is it one of the children?"

"No my dear, nothing to worry about." Robert put a soothing hand on his wife's arm. Neither woman believed him and they waited in a kitchen grown suddenly drear. "I think it may rain again," said Robert "so perhaps the cathedral might be a better idea."

The hand he reached out to grasp the coffee-pot was not steady. Joyce stayed it and poured coffee for the three of them. "I think you should tell us what's wrong, Robert," she said.

Doris sat very still, hands resting on her lap, knowing that should her son-in-law unburden himself he would first search for the right form of words. An eternity passed before he cleared his throat and told Doris simply that her friend Rodney Thompsett had been found dead.

"What happened?"

Robert looked at Joyce as if for guidance. "I don't believe they have any details yet."

Doris felt that her brain was working very slowly. "They, details, who was that on the phone?"

"That was Andrew; you had mentioned that you would go home tomorrow and he felt you should be told before you got back to London."

"That man's got no sense. Why would he want to upset us with news like that, why could it not have waited? You must stay," said Joyce.

Doris searched her son-in-law's grave face. "There is more, is there not, Robert?"

He nodded, his mouth thin, white-rimmed.

"How can it be worse, the poor man is dead," said Joyce.

"Tell me please, Robert."

"Doris, I am sorry, I wish I could spare you too, my dear." He turned with a grim smile to Joyce, who looked startled.

"Doris, it is best you hear it first from...It seems that Rodney died in a fire."

Doris did not take her eyes from Robert's face and thought, "*How curious that after all these years he should call me by my Christian name.*" "In a fire." Her voice was flat. "He died in a fire." She looked puzzled. "*Rodney was in a building.*" A little hope glimmered in her eyes. "You must be mistaken. He would never spend any time indoors, an hour or so in a cafe or in the church but that is all, he would never sleep in a building."

"It was outdoors, Doris."

"Then how?"

"They think it was murder."

The alien word hung in the air. It had no part in their lives. Murder, cruel and harsh, there was no grasping it. The ugliness filled the room. Doris believed she might faint. A strangled sob rasped in her dry throat and left her gasping for breath. She waved away the two would-be helpers. She had misheard, the mind did that to you sometimes. You had read something in a book and lo! you were putting it into the mouths of anyone who spoke to you. Any minute now she would hear Robert say, "Are you all right, mother-in-law? Don't look so worried, you must have misunderstood something I said?"

"Have a sip of water, Mother."

Joyce held a glass to her mother's lips. Gradually Doris's breathing returned to normal. "Thank you Joyce. Robert, forgive me, I need to be sure. Did you say that Rodney died in a fire outdoors and the police believe he was murdered?"

"Yes."

"Oh my poor friend Rodney, oh the poor man," Doris wept. Her world had turned black.

Chapter Forty-seven

I must go back immediately."

"What! No, Mother, you can't. What can you hope to achieve? You can send flowers, we can pop into Canterbury and send them Interflora."

"I never send flowers to the dead, Joyce, you know that, and yes there is something I can do, I can bury him."

The three had sat on in the kitchen trying to make sense of Rodney's death and now Doris was quite clear about what she had to do. Of course, she would have to find out how. There would be a post-mortem she supposed and a police investigation. Would she be allowed to claim the body? Andrew would guide her in all of this. Having made the decision, a great lassitude weighed down her lead-like limbs and, barely able to keep her eyes open, she allowed Joyce to help her to an armchair in the front room and cover her with a blanket. She overheard Joyce say, "How can you encourage her to get involved in something so nasty? He was just a tramp, nothing to do with us. The only connection, and it did give me a turn when I saw him outside, was that he wore Father's clothes."

A long time later she heard Robert reply, "We can't stop her being involved you know. Best to let her go, love."

Robert drove Doris back to London, leaving Joyce with the task of ringing the family so that her mother would not have the pain of telling the sad tale every time one of them rang. During the journey, Doris was grateful for Robert's taciturnity. Her thoughts were focused on Rodney as she remembered him, offering to share his lunch in the church, doffing his hat as he walked by her window, sitting on her steps arguing about the Irish question, sampling Frank's sherry, eating in the noisy, steaming cafe. She was beginning to realise how much she had depended on him being a part of her life. Had she given him "flowers"? She hoped so. She closed her eyes but the tears squeezed out. Behind her eyelids, she clearly saw Rodney's grave smile.

Robert took his hand from the wheel and patted her arm awkwardly. Doris gave up the struggle and wept for Rodney and Frank and Siobáin and Rose and the sad misfits who had thought so little of human life that they had poured petrol over the sleeping man and had set alight to him.

Robert made tea while Andrew held Doris's hand as tight as he dared, as he told her that what had been left of Rodney's body had been dressed only in undergarments. The police believed the motive had been robbery. They would want to interview her because they were trying to trace everybody who had had recent contact with him. Robert, sounding remarkably like his wife, asked if that was strictly necessary. Was it necessary to give his mother-in-law all these gruesome details? "I have to know," said Doris "I would rather it came from an accurate source. Andrew, thank you for that. I dare say there are all sorts of rumours abounding. Now let's talk of more pleasant matters."

Doris papered over her raw grief with chatter while inwardly reflecting on the oddity of life, that it was the bereaved who frequently doled out the consolation. Robert would go home and tell Joyce that he had left her mother in good spirits. Andrew would leave feeling reassured.

"Please thank the Luncheon Club and the seniors for me, it was nice of them to let their peace be shattered like that."

"You could thank them yourself, Doris."

"Uhm." Doris tried to sound positive, as if she would indeed consider talking to all of those old people.

Andrew looked sceptical. He knew her too well.

"Good idea," said Robert.

"*It is a dreadful idea,*" Doris thought. Now was not the time to be told that the world was a dreadful place, nor to be reminded that she was old, alone, and vulnerable. It would take too much energy to explain that only one of those statements was true. She was old. The world was dreadful only in part. She shivered.

Both men observed the involuntary movement and declared that she must be tired and that they had better go if she was quite sure she could manage by herself. "I'll be perfectly fine and thank you both. Take care on the roads, Robert, and love to Joyce and…Andrew, perhaps you could find a few moments for me tomorrow."

"Of course."

The men kissed her and left. Doris sat at the window and watched them go their separate ways exchanging a word in the street.

"You don't have to be so strong," said Frank.

"I do," she retorted. "I have to think about it, about him and face the full horror of it. I can't do that while people are mouthing platitudes and foolish fears."

"A bit harsh, don't you think, old girl?"

"Maybe, yes I suppose I am being selfish but one of the consequences of this sort of terrible tragedy is that it brings out the 'nobody's safe nowadays' syndrome and people like me are subsumed into an anonymous mass of old people earmarked for double protection. My life would not be my own."

"Doris, there are no people like you."

Chapter Forty-eight

The days that followed were quite active. When she was not answering the telephone or the front door, Doris was writing thank-you notes for her birthday presents. Most of her callers wanted to enthuse about the party, unaware of their hostess's connection with the brutal murder being reported in the local newspapers. The detective who came to interview her was courteous, earnest, at great pains to appear to treat her correctly. Doris found him infuriating and felt guilty about such pettiness. "But Rose, he could get a prize for the number of times he called me 'madam'. He called Rodney 'the old man', and that annoyed me as well. The tone, even the words were polite but he grated somehow. Then he called me Doris as if we had been to school together. Finally, every time he said Doris, I said 'Mrs Roberts' and it worked. I did the same for Rodney and he became Mr Thompsett, I felt I had given him a bit of dignity."

"That's not what's worrying you, Ma, is it? Since when have you been a fan of formality?"

Doris paused and sighed. "You always were perceptive, love. You are right of course. There are images in my mind that I can't dispel. I now know rather more than I care to about post-mortems and inquests. I can't get it out of my mind but, oh Rose I…I can't…it's…it is too horrible."

"What is it Ma? Don't keep it bottled up."

"Though it was the fire that killed Rodney, he had also suffered a stab wound and that's why he could not get away.

His clothes were stolen along with his few possessions. What kind of heartless person would take the shirt from someone's back? It makes me so angry. There is this picture in my mind of Rodney and all I can see is his face and one bare white shoulder and he looks such a poor old man, so vulnerable, so frightened. I can't bear to think of his terror. Rose, he was such a gentleman." The two women were silent until Doris whispered, "They were Frank's clothes; that makes it worse somehow, as if it was my responsibility."

"Ma, I've had the party pictures developed. The one with the two of you and the child is lovely, I'll send it to you to replace the one in your head."

Doris wept.

Mrs Evans grumbled magnificently with every ring and knock and Doris felt immensely grateful to her.

"No point in telling those children not to come round bothering you, I suppose."

"No point at all. They still need to rehearse, why should I stop them? Changing my lifestyle is not going to bring Rodney back."

Police enquiries were continuing and the body would not be released until all formalities had been completed. Apart from the investigating officer's problems with nomenclature, Doris was very impressed with the efforts of the police. Everyone who had even a tenuous connection with Rodney was interviewed.

"Gareth," said Doris, "if he turned out to be a long-lost royal he could not have had more attention. I was so afraid that he would have been sidelined because he may have been considered outside society."

"Are they getting anywhere, tracing any family I mean? I don't suppose they'll get the killer."

"Not a soul. It is sad not to have somebody, is it not? Mind you, I would have been surprised had anybody come forward. Rodney seemed complete unto himself. It is sad though."

"He's got you, Mum. Did I hear right that you are going to take over the funeral arrangements when the time comes?"

"Yes, it is the least I can do."

"Good for you. Let us know if you need any help, I expect Andrew has everything in hand."

"He has been wonderful. It can't have been easy identifying the body, poor man. He said that Rodney's face was practically unscathed and somehow that was disturbing, I mean, what does that mean?"

"Mum have you watched the last Grand Prix?"

Doris was taken aback, then a smile could be heard in her voice.

"I get your point, Gareth, I *am* trying not to dwell on the horror, and, yes, Benoit watched the Grand Prix with me."

Outside there was rain, rain that seemed to linger in the air and cling to hair and skin, covering cars and buildings and roads with a film of moisture. It was a silent rain that seeped and crept into places already damp and dank. It seemed the world would never be dry again. To go outside would be to invite it to insinuate itself into your very bones.

Doris stayed indoors listening to Bach, Mozart and Brahms and immersing herself in books she had long meant to read, and mourning her lost friend.

Visitors who came dripped despite leaving umbrellas and raincoats in the hall. They chattered brightly and left Doris feeling that she had no clear idea of what had been said. Had she imagined that Ritzy had told her a long tale and called Derek a "lousy sod"? She must bestir herself and find out what the pale boyfriend had done. It must be important for Ritzy to use such uncharacteristic language in front of her.

The old woman dreaded the advent of Lily Cronin, expecting a smug "I told you so" regarding the state of the world.

"They got him," she said without preamble.

Doris's heart leapt; it was difficult to breath. "Rodney's killer?" she said in a strangled voice.

"No, no." Lily waved her hand dismissively. "The man who slaughtered that poor child after having his way with her."

"What child? What man?" Doris was puzzled then remembered the news bulletin all those weeks before.

"It's just been on the news," said Lily. "They should bring back hanging, though that's too good for those animals. My Harry said he'd string them up himself." She smiled cheerfully at Doris, who somehow got through the following few minutes without telling her visitor precisely what she thought of her blundering insensitivity. She exhaled slowly when the front door finally clicked shut.

Needing to be up and doing Doris decided to sort out old newspapers and magazines for recycling and found the copy of the *Big Issue* that had lain there since her birthday party. She sat in the chair by the window with the unopened magazine on her lap and thought about the vendor who had given it to her as a present. She could hear Joyce saying, "But Mother, knowing you, you've probably paid for it ten times over." No point in protesting that money was not point. *"And I haven't even thanked you for it, Paul...I shall, I shall."*

As she peered wistfully at the unceasing drizzle, Doris noticed Mrs Panano signalling to her from the shop doorway across the road and, resolving to pull herself together, she waved to her to come over.

"How are you, dear?"

"Rather disconsolate," said Doris truthfully.

"It is so sad for you, I think. Come, we'll sit and you can tell me all about it, yes?"

And Doris did. "Everyone is focusing on the sensation surrounding the death, the fire, the stabbing, the robbery, the investigation, the person who did it, but not the death itself. Hardly anyone seems to care that a good man has died. He was a good man and I miss him."

"He was your age, yes?"

"We were almost of an age."

"And you miss the arguments," Mrs Panano interrupted.

Doris looked at her in surprise. The woman understood. "How did…?"

"Pierro, my husband, he and Mr Thompsett would have a, how you say, 'right go' at the back door. If anyone heard they would think there was bad blood, but they talked about this and that, back and to, to and back. He had such words that I never heard but I loved to hear the sound, do you understand? While I worked at the back of my shop sometimes I'd shout 'Why do I do all the work? Why I do everything?' but they no hear me. Not him, not my husband, they were, how you say, running the world."

"I had no idea."

Mrs Panano laughed. "Where you think he got his fine cardboard boxes to sleep, eh?"

"I did not think." Realisation dawned on Doris. "Oh you are the one who cut the crusts from his sandwiches."

"That's right, very very fussy, but I liked him."

Doris felt a lifting of her spirits, joyous to be able to celebrate Rodney as a person with likes and dislikes and idiosyncrasies, a human being and not a pitiful victim with nothing to mark his life but his horrific death.

"Now," said Mrs Panano, "what else you got in your head?" She sounded as if she could comfortably deal with whatever problem might arise and had energy and sensible sympathy to spare.

Doris looked into the wide honest eyes and told of her fears for Rose and Gareth. Something was wrong, but she had no idea what it was.

"If there is something not right, they will tell you when they are ready. Maybe they don't want you to be upset. Maybe it is nothing."

"But I would want to help, I am not a child to be shielded."

"Everything has a time for itself, you'll see. It will be all right. Come, have you eaten? No one can be cheerful without food."

Doris shook her head. Her friend waved to the shop opposite and went to open the door for her husband encumbered by something that steamed beneath a tea-towel, a bottle of wine under one arm, a hamper dangling from the other. Like everyone else who came, he dripped. His large frame seemed to fill the room. He was awkward and friendly all at once. Smiling warmly at Doris he deposited his burdens on the nearest available surface and backed out indicating that he had to hurry back to his business.

Doris found herself being bustled into the kitchen and sat at the table. Piping hot lasagne in an earthenware dish emerged from beneath its covering. Knife and fork were produced, rich red wine was poured. From the hamper was brought a salad of delicate leaves soon to glisten with olive oil. Olives, fat and succulent, lay on a little dish begging to be bitten.

"Eat, eat," urged Mrs Panano, pouring a glass of wine for herself and reaching out a hand to change stations on the radio: a tune so jollily compelling that one was forced to smile burst into the solemn kitchen.

Doris, surprised by hunger, ate the delicious meal and the warmth and light of Mediterranean sunshine was in the kitchen. Mrs Panano poured olive oil onto a plate and mopped it up with bread still warm from the hamper and brought life to the tales she told of her family and her beloved Italy.

Chapter Forty-nine

Doris awoke and lay without opening her eyes and felt the warmth of the tentative sun play on her eyelids. She delayed with joyous anticipation her first glimpse of what would surely be a rare blue sky. Last evening she had resolved to go out regardless of the weather. There were element-cheating garments and footwear a-plenty. There had been enough shilly-shallying and self-pity; she must go and see Paul and apologise to him. The whereabouts of his squat was unknown to her. It struck her that there were quite a few things she did not know about her friends, the ability to accept people as they were, as Joyce called it. Maybe she should ask more questions.

"I thought you were going to stir yourself," said Frank.

"I am," said Doris with equanimity. "At my age I'm entitled to a quiet moment of reflection."

Frank grunted. "I might have said replacement activity but I see precious little activity."

"Damn and blast it, why should I not just lie and take my ease?"

"No reason," said a chastened voice.

Doris's eyes flew open and she found herself being peered at by a pink-faced Mrs Evans. She smiled. "You thought I was dead, you did, did you not?"

"No of course not."

"Yes you did, I could see it in your eyes." Doris chuckled. "Not yet. I can't go yet, too much to do."

With help, she rose and readied herself for the day. "If

you're going out and not actually contemplating suicide I should put on two of everything, it's bitter," said Mrs Evans.

In the hall mirror, Doris looked at the reflection of her wide-brimmed hat with distaste.

"It'll do," said Mrs Evans, holding open the front door. "You're letting in the cold."

"It will have to, I can't manage a walking stick and an umbrella."

The sun proved an impostor; there was no warmth in its luring rays touching branch and building, bare hands and cheeks. Doris found her gloves, waved her stick in the direction of the Pananos' and walked towards the cafe. She intended to go to the police station but not just yet awhile. There would have been no shortage of helpers had she wished but somehow felt that she should go alone.

"Fortification first," she said and looked around to see if anyone had heard. No one seemed to give the old woman in the hideous hat a second glance. Satisfied, she walked on glistening blossom-reflecting pavements. Though tempted she dare not look up from the treacherously puddled ground. At length she reached the comparative safety of a line of shops where the paving stones were more visible and evenly laid.

Easter seemed to feature heavily in the shop windows. Had she missed it? How could she lose track of time like this? Should she go to Woolworths to get Easter Eggs for the children? Her brain felt fuddled and refused to grasp a coherent thought. She stood in everyone's path and wondered if she should go home.

"I don't know what I'm doing here," she said.

"Me neither," said a familiar voice. "We should be baskin' in sunshine and sippin' someting long and cool."

Relief flooded over Doris as Benoit bent to plant kisses on her cheeks. The momentary touch of his lips was warm and welcome. She felt a rush of love for this boy who brought laughter with him like a separate entity.

"I thought you would be at school," she said and giggled for no reason whatsoever. She had the absurd feeling that, were she not encumbered by the stick, she would skip down the high street hand in hand with Benoit.

"Still alive, old girl," said Frank.

"Great hat," said Benoit grinning down at her.

"That does it," said Doris and recklessly pulled it off. She tried unsuccessfully to hide the resultant pain that shot up her arm. Half-laughing, half-crying, she leant on her stick and waited for the agony to subside to a dull throb.

Benoit looked anxious but had the common sense not to engage her in conversation until she had again caught her breath. "OK?" he was smiling again.

She nodded.

"You're brave," said Jim the cafe proprietor, glancing at his customer's dishevelled hair.

"Just foolish," said Doris, "and discombobulated."

"That's a new one," said Jim, raising an amused eyebrow and producing the usual steaming mugs. "Brings a touch of class to the place, don't she?" he said winking at Benoit.

"I haven't come to eat," said Doris "so I'll pay for the tea. I am off to see my detective, see if there is any news."

"Don't suppose they'll catch the bastards," said Jim gloomily.

"Ya'll be all right on yer own, yeah?" said Benoit.

Doris noted the reluctance in his voice. "Of course," she said, "off you go. Say hello to Ritzy, won't you?"

Doris sighed as she watched his tall athletic figure amble out of sight.

Jim pulled out a chair and sat with his sole customer in silence. They stared with unseeing eyes towards the door. There was no need for words. It was sufficient to the moment to feel the warmth and just be. Doris moved her head slightly to take in Jim's profile. He owned a cafe that catered for bikers, tramps and the odd old woman. That was all she knew about him. Did one need to know anything when one felt implicit trust? His strong face was lined and tired and yet he had the look of a man who knew where he was in the world.

"Do you have someone?" asked Doris.

"Steve and I have been together for about five years now. We look out for one another."

"Good," said Doris simply.

Chapter Fifty

Doris was enthralled by the police station. Having gone through fortress-like fortifications, she had found herself in a room at once startlingly up-to-date and curiously homely. Computers, coffee cups, telephones, printers, pictures of victims on the walls, pictures of loved ones on desks, plants as paperweights, overflowing rubbish bins, rows of police hats, handcuffs and keys, it was like any incident room she had seen on television and none of them—different, warmer.

Doris forced her eyes away from the mordant face of Rodney to a teenager grinning from a plastic frame. There was an air of quiet urgency but the young policewoman busily talking on the telephone took time to smile at the visitor. "Would you like a cup of tea?" asked the detective.

Doris had meant to say no, had meant to depart as swiftly as possible but her curiosity was stirred. She might never have such an opportunity again. She accepted and spent a fascinating hour marvelling at modern communications, learning about police procedures. As for Rodney, all enquiries regarding next of kin were completed. As far as could be ascertained he had never been listed as a missing person, at least not in the name of Thompsett. They suspected he had assumed that name. Thompsett Street was where he frequently slept before moving to the convent grounds. Perhaps it was the street he had first slept on when he moved into the area.

"He was a good laugh," said the young policewoman. "He used to stop me on the way to work of a morning, always said something to make me smile. First off, I thought he was begging and I ignored him but I suppose something made me listen. 'Have you ever heard of anyone being "mayed" when people are always dismayed?' I was halfway into the building before I cottoned on. After that, he always said something to make me smile or think about. Don't worry, we'll get those B——s if it's the last thing we do."

Looking at the fiercely resolute face before her, Doris did not doubt it.

"We are doing our best," said the detective, "we respected him." He went on to say that the body could now be released and funeral arrangements made.

"You have been very kind," said Doris. "Now, what can we do about Mrs Tracey?"

She left the station with "her" detective's promise to look into things. *"Ridiculous situation,"* thought Doris, firmly putting Rodney to the back of her mind. *"I should be able to do something myself, the poor woman could be dead while we all 'look into it'. Everyone is so politically correct nowadays, too bloody scared to take action."*

"You'll hurt yourself if you stomp about like that," said Frank.

"Should you not be in heaven or somewhere by now?" asked Doris. "If you have to be around could you not do something useful? Go and haunt Mrs Tracey, get her to open the door."

"Sorry old girl, I can only get into your head."

"Useless!" snorted Doris aloud, to the amusement of several passers-by.

Chapter Fifty-one

Andrew would officiate at the funeral service. Joyce disapproved but said that she and Robert would come. Gareth and Rose would round up as many of the family as possible. Prin would come down with Elaine. She was not so prone to sickness now.

Mrs Cronin pursed her lips and said the state should take care of such things but she and Harry would be there. She was a Christian after all.

The detective and the young policewoman would attend. Mrs Evans grumbled but said she would help with the catering.

"We'll give Rodney a great send-off, Ma," said Rose.

Doris felt an odd mixture of sadness and anticipation. The funeral would at least bring together some of the people she most loved. Rose sounded her old self, perhaps the worry was all in Doris's imagination. Anyway she would see her soon and judge for herself.

"I am just being selfish," she said to Joyce and immediately regretted this hostage to fortune.

"Well, Mother, you do worry us."

"*Thank God for that*," thought Doris. "*I can still make waves.*"

In the days before the cremation, she gave the problem of Mrs Tracey a lot of thought. The boys and girls were sent at intervals to knock on the door. The boys came back shrugging, there was no answer. The girls came back and said the place stank. Andrew himself went and pushed a personal note and church literature through the letterbox. Later Trevor found the small bundle of papers on the stairs with the words "go away" scrawled on it. Trevor said his mum spent a fortune on disinfectant.

Doris tried to contact Mrs Wilmacott but her interests seemed to be focused elsewhere. "*An unkind person,*" thought Doris, "*would think she only embraced winnable causes.*" The police said their hands were tied, there was no law against being a recluse. The social services dutifully knocked on Mrs Tracey's door. They could only suggest they said; if people chose to live in discomfort it really was their decision.

"What about the smell?" asked Doris. "Is it not a health hazard?" Were there not such people as health inspectors, did they not care?

Were Trevor and his mum who lived above Mrs Tracey and the Bangladeshi family who lived beneath her not in danger of goodness knows what, Doris asked her friends and neighbours, several council departments and many obscure-sounding bodies she found in *Yellow Pages*, anyone who would listen and a great number who would not. Her anger grew as she heard the phrases "don't like to interfere", "not my business", "they should do something about it".

Doris herself went round again but found that this time she could not manage the stairs. She called on the Bangladeshi family.

"Very good neighbour," said the smiling nodding woman, "very quiet."

Raging with frustration, Doris returned home to find the band members awaiting her. Puzzled she ushered them into her sitting-room. Normally they let themselves in and went straight upstairs. "Sit down, sit down," she snapped impatiently. They all seemed so big and immovable, towering over her like that and just as powerless as herself. There was Nathan, was he for her or against her, how could she decide? Benoit, yes yes he was her favourite but why did he have to grin so? Why did Derek have to look shiftier than ever? Why did Ritzy have to look so concerned and If (stupid affectation) so very bossy. Why do all their characteristics have to be so exaggerated?

"And why do you have to be so very irritable?" said Frank.

"Sit down," repeated Doris and then felt foolish to see they were perched about the room looking hugely uncomfortable. "Well," said Doris peremptorily, "what do you want?"

If looked at the others before clearing her throat and Doris grew more impatient.

"Well, speak up, girl."

Frank tutted.

"We wonder if we could, well…would it be all right if we came to the funeral?"

If's voice sounded uncertain while the others looked like they would rather be elsewhere.

"It's a cremation," Doris snapped, "not a funeral."

If wilted before the withering stare.

"Stop intimidating that girl," said Frank.

"Well we were wondering…" If whispered.

"Yes, yes, you said that. I haven't got all day."

"Could we come to the cremation?"

"You needed a delegation to ask me that?"

"Doris," exclaimed Frank, "you really are the limit."

Ritzy looked hurt. "We just wanted to help, he was OK," she said looking to the others for support. They gave a collective grunt and shifted awkwardly.

"Indeed?" Doris was at her most scornful. "It is a bit late do you not think?"

There was a sharp intake of breath ignored by the irate woman whose voice now shook with vehemence "Rodney is dead, it is the living who need help. If you had any thoughts in your silly heads beyond your own selfish concerns you would do something about Mrs Tracey."

"That's not fair," someone protested.

"But no, you have your pop music and makeup, drugs I dare say and God knows what. You do not help. What has happened, does youth not want to change the world

248

anymore, the world that we made such a mess of?" Doris was only vaguely aware of uncomprehending shocked faces before her, only vaguely aware of the throbbing in her hip. Impervious to stuttered protests, her diatribe continued unabated. "As you constantly remind us, we made a great mess. We fought misguided wars for sheer perversity apparently. We nurtured our pointless prejudices, inflicted our mind-numbing and narrowing ideas of religion, honour, sacrifice and such like on a world powerless to resist our unswerving dogmatism. That is what you think is it not?—that we ruined chances of creating a world where everyone can live in peace and harmony. If the world was yours things would be so much better but you bleat and you blame and you complain and make excuses. It is always someone else's responsibility. You have the youth, the energy, what are you doing with them? Take a drug and shut out the world. Where is your fire? Docility is the province of the elderly.

"You have inherited a world where an old man can be burnt to death for the few shillings in his pocket, or maybe just for fun, where a child can be used and discarded like so much dross, where an innocent woman can be stoned in the street for the crime of having a different coloured skin, a world where a poor old woman is so terrorised by brutal images that she eschews all human contact and that world is here in civilised London."

Doris looked fiercely from face to face with burning unseeing eyes. Her mind's eye was not blind and could not look away from Rodney's white shoulder or the blood trickling down Jyotsna's face, nor could her ears shut out Mrs Tracey's desperate croak.

"What do we do when we see these things on television? We change channels because we are bored, barbarity has become common place. 'It is sad about the refugees, this tragedy, that tragedy,' we say 'but what can you do?' and we shrug off the responsibility and say 'they' should do something. I know about the drugs, the van on the corner that might as well have a sign on the side Hash for Cash.

249

This is your protest, this is your rebellion? Well, I'll tell you a secret. The world is yours. What are you going to do with it? Do you know what the worst crime is? It is *not* failing. It is *not* messing things up. The worst crime is not even trying."

It was a long time before Doris heard the silence, the silence that emanated from the rooms upstairs and seeped through the ceiling and, almost like a physical presence hung heavy on her ears. She sat still in the darkening room while her brain struggled to understand the silence. "Frank," she said softly and the name echoed in the empty room. Street-lights cast shadows eerily swaying on the walls. Doris could not bring herself to move. Why was it so silent? Slowly she realised why there was an absence of sound. She shivered. It was a practice night but the band was not practising. They had left. She was alone.

Chapter Fifty-two

"Can't you turn that down a bit?" said Mrs Evans. "You can't possibly be enjoying that caterwauling and it's driving me mad."

Doris ignored her and tried to make sense of the discordance on Radio 3, tried to hear an obscure melody or recognise a hidden rhythm. There was nothing. The cacophony came across the airwaves, disjointed, recondite. It was 'Emperor's clothes' type of music thought Doris, someone at the BBC must be afraid to acknowledge it as pretentious nonsense.

"I never thought I'd hear myself saying this," shouted Mrs Evans, "but what those kids upstairs play is music compared to that fiddle-faddle. Well I can't stand it anymore, I'm off." She paused in the doorway. "By the look of you I'd say you're having one of those shut-out-the-world days. I don't suppose there'll be a potato peeled in this house today, so I cut up one of those pork pies you seem to like and done you a bit of salad, it's in the kitchen."

Doris stared out of the window. Daffodils stood faded and seer where once their golden heads trumpeted the spring. The grass lay damp and draggled and speckled with tattered white flowerlets torn by a capricious wind from the viburnum bush. It had flowered briefly, for no more than a fortnight, now gone before Doris had had much chance to smell its strong sweet scent. It would be such a long, long wait until it bloomed again. It seemed such an age since she had sat in this same empty room, cold and trapped by arthritis when Ritzy had come into her life. Difficult to believe that it was only a few months but oh, the changes that had been wrought! How her life had been changed and enriched in that time, from simple existence in solitude she had lived again, really lived, had allowed her heart to open and embrace others. Was that living over now that she had spoken those harsh and admonitory words? She could not recollect what the young people had said. She only knew that they had gone and she felt lonelier than she ever had before.

"It's up to you now, old girl," said Frank softly, "you pull up the drawbridge and retreat where no one can hurt you or you can find the strength to walk across it and be the Doris I've always respected."

"Respect has to be earned," said Doris and turned off the radio.

For days, Doris set about her tasks with a lingering sense of sadness, not only for Rodney whose farewell was planned, but for friendships gone awry. Time and again her hand hovered over the telephone, or she stood irresolute in the hall, her coat half on, but she could neither make a call nor leave the house. Shying away from soothing words, she did not share her loss, for loss it must be when none of the young crowd came near her. Not even a glimpse did she have of any one of them as she anxiously scanned the street. Only Raza came for his regular lesson but he had never been one of the crowd and brought no solace. She smiled grimly to herself. She might as well be the teenager, heart racing with every ring of the doorbell or phone. Her callers found her subdued but did not comment, putting it down no doubt to Rodney's forthcoming cremation.

"You're not planning anything elaborate now, are you, Mother?" said Joyce.

"No, dear," said Doris wearily and set herself the mental exercise of imagining what might constitute "elaborate". Six, no, sod the expense, twelve black-plumed black horses would pull a black-draped carriage on which rested the coffin, richly carved and highly ornamented. Police outriders would escort the stately procession that followed; both Catholic and Church of England bishops, silkily berobed and solemn-faced would walk with their black-clad clergy and white-gowned choirs. Community leaders of ethnic minorities would be represented. In pristine uniforms, police, high-ranking and lowly, would march to the measured beat of a lonely drummer. The slow relentless sound would urge the children to keep pace as they, straight backed and proud, trod streets uniquely forbidden to everyday traffic. Dressed in their Sunday best shopkeepers and business people, closed for the day to show respect, would follow, as too would neighbours and friends, young and old, and strangers drawn to the unusual spectacle would join in and follow. Perhaps there would be a Rolls Royce or two, each containing a sorrowful minor Royal.

Should the murmuring of the crowd obscure the lonely drum beat, perhaps there should be a brass band or a military band or why not a walking jazz band, why not all three? She would have to rethink the order.

"Mother, are you there?"

The irritable voice brought Doris reluctantly back from the funeral procession that was picking up its heels beneath brightening skies and turning into a joyous celebration. "We could have a street party," she said.

"Oh Mother!"

Doris thought, "Why *does she have to sound quite so exasperated?*" She felt cold and heavy with remembered sadness. If only she could confide in her daughter, say, "I lashed out, made unforgivable accusations, now my young friends have gone." Joyce would say, "Good, that's one worry off my mind, you were never wise to let them in in the first place."

"Are you being quite fair?" said Frank. "That girl is worried about you, she does care."

"Mother, what is the matter? I don't believe you've heard a word I've said."

"I am sorry, love." Doris took a deep breath. "I am rather upset."

"You always take on too much, and we have to pick up the pieces. All those hangers-on you have around you aren't worth a light, they're only looking out for themselves but of course you have to see the so-called good in everyone and you're completely taken in. We can't imagine how you got involved with the murder of an old tramp and now taking on his burial. It's so sordid. You're the one who needs looking after at your age."

Doris was stung. "At my age I should be gratefully ensconced in an old people's home, all tucked away nice and neat. I may be ready to die but in the meantime I am not ready to give up living, there is a distinction and I wish you could see it."

The telephone receiver was replaced with exaggerated care in its cradle.

"Damn, damn!" Doris's fist banged on the arm of her chair, to think that I was going to tell her how angry I was with myself for spoiling things with my hangers-on. Tears of frustration dampened her lashes.

"Excuse me," said Frank, "am I missing something? Aren't you the one who cares so much about other people? Aren't you supposed to be concerned for Rose—there's something you can't quite put your finger on—nervous for Prin and Elaine and the new baby and all that that could imply? Aren't you suppose to be worried about that isolationist, Raza Abolhasan, not to mention the odd famine and civil war dotted around the globe? Yet all I can see is self-pity. Poor Doris Roberts, poor helpless old woman."

"*All right, all right I'll go and sort everything out,*" Doris screamed inwardly and surprising herself hurled an epithet at Frank that she would never have uttered aloud.

Chapter Fifty-four

T he Lord is very forgiving," said Andrew.

"*That's fine,*" thought Doris, "*but I am not entirely sure that it is the Lord whom I have offended.*"

They were all busy studying said Rejoice, but she'd be happy to send little Evra or Marcus around to Doris if she wanted a bit of company. Evra was very good at helping to wind wool, she added. Senorita Fiona was very, very busy, said the Portuguese maid, would Doris like to speak to Mrs Warrender? Derek's mother had no idea where he might be, never did have, only ever saw him with his head in the fridge.

Doris abandoned the phone calls and gave her mind to Rodney's farewell. Mrs Evans was prevailed upon to climb the stairs. The rooms above should be made ready for occupancy should any visitors want to sleep up there in sleeping bags. Giving every impression that the words were being torn from her reluctant lips, she said that on the whole the rooms were fine, quite tidy when all was said and done, unnatural really when you thought it was those teenagers who had been using them all these months.

"You should get your hair done," she said suddenly, "you should go to that Sean you're always raving about, he'll fit you in."

Doris grunted, her mind upstairs in the empty echoing rooms, her ears straining to hear again the rasping raucous sounds that had caused her much irritation and prompted removal of her hearing-aid.

"You should get your hair done," said Rose when she rang. "You'll feel like a different woman and look gorgeous when we come down to see you."

Doris laughed for the first time in a long while. "My dear girl, I haven't looked gorgeous for many a long year."

"Yes, pop along," said Sean. "We'll fit you in."

Doris closed her eyes to the haggard, lined old woman who stared at her from the cruelly lit mirror. Sean's hands worked through her wet hair, shaping, moving, experimenting. Gradually the movements became circular, the touch firmer. Strong confident fingers massaged the nape of her neck and upwards to smooth and soothe her temples. When the fingers reached the bare skin of her forehead, she felt exhilarated. The strength of the fingertips paid no deference to her age and perceived fragility. She exulted in the unexpected feeling of life flowing through her.

"*Touch is so important, sometimes, Frank...*" The thought made her eyes fly open and brought a faint flush to her cheeks. Sean was grinning at her in the mirror.

"I felt you needed that," he said.

"I feel wonderful," said Doris simply.

Chapter Fifty-five

Just popped over to make sure you were all right before the...ordeal," said Lily Cronin breathless on the doorstep.

"She's...we're fine," said Joyce firmly. "Thank..."

"What a commotion, did any of you get any sleep at all?" said Lily, now in the hall.

"Yes it was rather disruptive, we're..."

"Will you be fit enough to go?" Lily addressed Doris from the front room's doorway.

By the time a cautious reply had been uttered, she was seated in an armchair and peering from face to face for confirmation. "What a commotion!" she repeated. "I didn't get a wink of sleep, with flashing lights and sirens and all."

"It was a bit disruptive." Robert echoed his wife, rising to offer his chair. The gesture was brushed aside impatiently.

Joyce frowned. "Mrs Cronin, we're just preparing to go to the cremation; of course we should be pleased to offer you refreshment when we return."

"Disruptive!" exclaimed Lily. "Didn't you hear the fire engines, the ambulances, the police cars?"

"Well, if you will excuse..."

"Joyce..." said Doris and shook her head. Why fight the inevitable? "What time are the cars coming?"

"Don't worry, Mum, they'll be here in plenty of time," said Gareth.

"I wouldn't intrude," said Mrs Cronin "only it's not really personal grief, is it?"

Doris pondered on why people addressed questions they thought were being asked. She watched the darting eyes of Lily Cronin and marvelled at her inability to discern the lack of welcome.

"I lost count of all the emergency vehicles. Goodness knows how many were injured with the ambulances and all."

"No more than one ambulance surely," said Robert, "and two police cars."

"There was a fire engine of course," said Gareth.

"Mrs Cronin," said Rose on entering the room. "Will you take a cup of coffee? And you could tell us all about it, we're all having one before we go."

All eyes turned towards her, all except one pair said, "How could you?"

"Last night," said Lily Cronin her voice trembling with triumph, "I heard it was an IRA gunman with a bomb."

"Ah, belt-and-braces chap," said Robert softly.

Lily ignored him. "Imagine! A bomb factory underneath our noses. You can't be too careful, me and my Harry are always careful, we never let no one in. We could have all been murdered in our beds. It just goes to show that you can never trust anyone." She looked directly at Rose.

"Was that two sugars or three," said Rose, smiling sweetly, "or under the circumstances would you prefer to help yourself?"

Lily looked faintly puzzled.

"Now there's a thought," said Gareth, "a gun and a bomb, which hand would you use for which do you suppose, what would you say, Rose?"

"Wouldn't it depend on whether you were left-handed or right-handed?"

"Ah that may be so," said Gareth, "but you'd also need to know if you were going to lob the bomb or plant it."

"A matter of priority surely," said Doris. "Frankly I think he would be ill-advised to carry both."

"He should put the bomb in his pocket," said Gareth.

"Ah, that only brings us back to the original question."

"Which pocket?" cried all but Joyce and Lily.

The latter sipped her unsugared coffee and looked mystified while the room erupted with laughter. Shortly afterwards Prin and Elaine arrived at the same time as the hired cars. Greetings were exchanged. Hustle and bustle. Who was going in which car? The pregnant Elaine was hurriedly kissed, no time now, proper hugs later. "Coats on," said Doris, "draughty places, crematoria,"—"*makes you shiver, think of your own mortality. Good that Elaine is going, sense of continuity, one out one in. Must concentrate on Rodney, must think of Rodney beyond this day. Weather fine, cold but fine. Blossoms on the trees, lovely day, how many more? Will the Johnsons come or any of the young? Just think about Rodney, this is his day.*"

Doris gazed from the car at streets no different from any other day, busy, traffic and people filled. No head turned to look at the mourners as they drove past. There were no dignitaries to stare at, no children, no drummer, no bands, just life going on, a life of which Rodney had once been a part. With surprise she felt Joyce's hand seek and squeeze hers. The pressure was so light and swift it could almost have been imagined. Doris knew it was real and smiled.

Chapter Fifty-six

The murmuring in the chapel was not of Rodney but of the disturbance of the night before. Rumours abounded. It was a fire at the convent someone said. No, no, it was definitely a drugs raid. Someone had had a heart attack. No, it was much more catastrophic than that, why else would there be fire engines and police cars as well as the ambulance? The Lily Cronin theory was repeated, it was definitely the IRA right in their midst, just when that sort of thing was supposed to have been all over. A yardie revenge killing was cited as were attempted murders, burglaries, foreign spies, smuggling clamp-downs. kidnapping, child abductions, illegal immigrant raids. Somebody said Rodney's killer had been arrested and the chatterers grew silent.

Doris was surprised by the number who crowded into the few pews or stood at the back of the room. The space was ill-lit rather than with the aimed-for subdued lighting. Some faces faded in lingering shadow while others stood out in stark relief. Doris found the effect disconcerting. She was reminded of a tale that she had heard of a film director who came early to a cremation. He had found the lighting to be not to his liking. Being alone, he started to experiment with switches, when to his horror the coffin began to glide inexorably through the curtains.

As she had been at Frank's funeral, she was seated at the front between Joyce and Gareth. The memory caused her throat to tighten. Closing her eyes, she tried to imagine Frank pushing his way into the pew and saying, "Sorry I'm late, old thing." She smiled ruefully, then jumped when a hand squeezed her shoulder, her eyes flew open.

"Our prayers have been answered," Andrew whispered and grinning turned immediately to talk to someone else.

"*Which prayers?*" thought Doris. "*The cure for cancer, no more starvation in the world, peace in our time for all time?*"

"That's my girl," said Frank. "I was afraid you were getting sentimental."

"Good news?" boomed Mrs Wilmacott, leaning precariously over Gareth.

Doris said yes because it seemed easier. The face that had been inches from hers withdrew, satisfied. Before many more bars of Strauss were played, her detective, very smartly turned out she observed, shook her by the hand. With gravity, he said, "It seems that you got your wish." Then to her astonishment he winked.

"What was that all about?" whispered Gareth, but before his mother could say "not a clue" the service had begun.

A crematorium official began a well-meaning, catch-all introduction as if by rote and Doris's mind began to drift. Rodney would be remembered, not perhaps by all in the congregation (did one still call it a congregation in a non-denominational establishment? How odd not to know after living on this earth all these years!), but he would pop into the minds of most. It would happen at odd times, the memory triggered by a sound, or sight, a word, a figure of speech. Suddenly he would be there. A man who had been...what?—a man with the courage to reject what was unnecessary to him, to live as he chose or a man unwilling, incapable of accepting the responsibility of conventional life?—a man who, though standing back from society, nonetheless had strong opinions about it and was not afraid to argue vociferously, making no concessions to age or apparent fragility; a man who had, almost without them knowing it, touched people's lives. Each person who had grown to like or respect him would recall their own particular aspect of him.

Doris, grateful that he never shied away from disagreeing with her, prayed that he would not be remembered solely for the gruesome manner of his death. At this moment, gazing at his simple unadorned coffin, it was hard not to feel anger at the mindless futility of it. There was too the guilt, the query in the mind. What if he had never been given Frank's clothes? If...

"Mum." Gareth caught her attention. "Did you want to say a few words?"

Patient hands guided her to a small lectern and she turned to face the assembled friends and neighbours of Rodney Thompsett. She looked around and without exception they were her friends too. Some, like the policeman and policewoman were newly acquired but friends nonetheless. "It strikes me," she said, "this could be my own funeral." Joyce's intake of breath could be heard clearly amongst others' gasps. "A few more members of family, maybe," continued Doris, "and one or two friends of Frank's who were not on their last legs, or perhaps would be, there is always someone at a funeral who makes you think 'is it worth their going home?'" There were a few suppressed giggles, a few uncertain expressions. "To those of you who are wondering that about me, the answer is emphatically 'yes'." There was a broad grin from Prin to his grandmother. "Yes, because every life is worth living, especially one that has been enriched by family and dear friends, including one as characterful as Rodney here. No one had the right to take his life and I am here to express my anger as well as my sorrow. Whoever committed that unspeakable act deserves no peace and will, I hope and pray, be tracked down and dealt with by the law. He, she, they have taken from all of us." Doris's gaze swept the room and her heart gave a lurch to see Ritzy and Derek and Benoit at the back. Maybe some of the others were there as well. She caught her breath, then continued: "He was a part of our community whether we or even he acknowledged it, not easy to get to know, a man apparently with no past, nothing with which one could identify. Nevertheless, one gradually learnt to recognise and admire the spirit beneath the outward appearance—no point in mincing words, a shambling, rag-bag of a man. Without imposing, he became part of our lives. Despite his lifestyle, he was fastidious, though apparently lacking in a sense of smell." She smiled. "He could be bloody awkward at times, downright obstreperous, a worthy adversary in debate. He was awkward both to us personally and to society and I am so sad that he has gone, I am sad that his family, I am sure there must be one, may never know that he was appreciated for his courtesy and wit and gentility. The cruellest theft is that of choice, and he was robbed of all choice to stay, to go, to say goodbye." She paused to look from one pair of eyes to another. Her face softened as her misted eyes caught those of Joyce and Rosaria. "It's left to us to say goodbye, God bless you Rodney, I will miss you."

"A blessing in disguise really."

"The murder!"

"No, no, last night, skin and bone she was, poor soul. I went with her, you know."

"Oh," said Doris, uncomprehending.

The woman who looked vaguely familiar moved away. There was no time to ask. She was seated in the pew as one holding court while fellow mourners bade her goodbye.

"Lovely peroration," said Andrew, "must fly. Herbert Lane's funeral. You didn't know him, did you?"

Without awaiting an answer, he was gone. Others came and went, but not those whom she sought.

"The young crowd came and went very quickly," said Rose as if reading her mind. "Are you all right, Ma? That was a nice speech."

Doris who could not recollect what she had said just smiled. "Let's go home and have some champagne," she said, resolutely getting to her feet. "There is life to be lived."

Chapter Fifty-seven

It had started with a 999 call. The caller had been precise, informative, and anonymous. Smoke was pouring from the middle floor of No 7 Gerards Road where an elderly woman lived. The old woman was likely to be infirm and in need of medical help. Fire officers had indeed found a great deal of smoke and thought it prudent to evacuate the occupants of the top and bottom flats before tackling the resolutely locked middle door. With paramedics standing by, they had broken it down. Inside they had found a barely human, pitiful whimpering shell of a woman, curled up in terror on the floor, but no fire.

"Did you know where any of the members of Obsidian were last night?" asked the detective, departing from the story.

Doris was surprised. Her mind had been trying to grasp the fact that last night Mrs Tracey had been rescued and was now safe in hospital. "In their beds I should say, why?"

"Oh I just thought I'd ask." Evasively. "I dare say their families will say they were all in bed too, or playing scrabble with young siblings or doing homework."

Doris was puzzled. "I...do not quite..."

"I won't keep you from your family. If you think of anything..." The detective said his goodbyes and left.

"What on earth could I think of?" said Doris relating the conversation to the assembly. "I feel as if I am being accused of something."

"Don't be paranoid, Mother," said Joyce ."Won't you have a cup of tea?"

"It will be something those young people have got up to, you mark my words," said Lily Cronin.

Doris glared at her and ignored Joyce. "Have none of you done anything about the champagne while I was hearing the news? We've got to celebrate Elaine and Prin's happy news? Come along, do I have to do everything myself?"

Toasts were drunk to Rodney, to the future, to the baby, to Doris. "God bless us, everyone," she said waving her glass in farewell to Mrs Panano and Jim and sundry others who had come to pay their respects after the cremation.

A reluctant Lily Cronin followed them, promising to return if she could be of slightest help.

"The sad thing is she means it," said Doris with a slight shudder.

"That's most unkind, you know she's a great comfort to you," said Rose and laughed.

The rest of the family joined in for no reason other than it was such a joyous and infectious sound. Her mother-in-law felt light-hearted and light-headed. "It's so lovely to have you all here," she said. "Robert, my glass is empty."

"Steady, old girl," said Frank. "Don't overdo it."

"I'd forgotten about you," said Doris.

"Had you, dear?" said Robert mildly.

"Perhaps you should have a lie down Mother," said Joyce.

"Don't try to explain," said Frank, "they'll lock you up."

Robert poured more champagne.

"What did he say, Gran, your detective? By the way, what is his name?" asked Prin.

"I do not know his name, I've left it too late and now I am embarrassed to ask," Doris giggled. "He said there was oodles of smoke but no trace of a fire and did I know where Obsidian was. Some of them were there this morning of course, but they disappeared afterwards."

"I bet I know what happened," said Prin, "why they wanted to know where the group was last night."

"I think I know too," said Elaine, "smoke, no fire, what a hoax!"

"Oh I see!" said Gareth

"But why the hell should they want to do that, and why there, was it sheer vandalism or what?"

"What are you all talking about?" asked Doris. "What vandalism?"

"Well, who'd be most likely to have access to a smoke machine than the members of a rock band."

"You mean it was a pointless, mindless prank, all that commotion in the middle of the night?" Joyce looked appalled.

"But why scare an old woman like that?"

"Maybe she wasn't the target."

"And what about the other flats, they had to be evacuated."

"That's what the young people are today, thoughtless. All those people involved, the fire brigade, the police, the ambulance people."

"Do you mean they aimed the smoke, could actually direct it at that particular door?"

"Does anyone know how Mrs Tracey is now? That woman in the crematorium said something about some poor old soul being all skin and bone, it must have been her."

The chatter burst around Doris's head, like so many unsettling bees. "*Can it be true? Will smoke canisters (must find out about those), be found? Why should suspicion fall on the one band I happen to know? Whoever has done it, why concentrate their efforts on that particular house, no, that particular flat? Why did...?*" Doris argued with herself. It could not possibly be as they said: "*There must be some other explanation.*" Several people today seemed to think she knew something. While the speculation continued around her, realisation dawned. How had she challenged them, what were the words she had spoken with such scorn? "*If you had any thoughts in your heads beyond your own selfish concerns you would do something about Mrs Tracey."* "Oh my God," she said aloud. "It wasn't pointless, it was all my fault."

For a moment there was silence, then, "It's all been too much for you, Mother, now you really should lie down."

Doris bristled, glared at her caring daughter, then docilely acquiesced; she needed to think.

Chapter Fifty-eight

Doris awoke to the faint murmur of voices and lay very still. Through half-closed eyes she looked towards the window where her daughter and daughter-in-law stood quietly talking. Though the words could not be heard, the tones were gentle and far from the usual brittle exchanges. In the fading light, she could not clearly see their faces but she had the impression that they were serious. With a pang she realised that they looked aged, no longer the girls she always thought them to be. Doris closed her eyes for a moment and when she opened them again the women seemed to be in agreement and Joyce had placed a conciliatory hand on Rose's arm.

The old woman felt puzzled but pleased to see a closeness she had longed for. For a moment there was silence, then a question clearly reached the listener's ears: "—And when will you go to Ireland, Rose?"

Doris gave an involuntary cry and both women turned anxiously towards her. Her heart was thumping uncomfortably and she couldn't catch her breath, speech was impossible. Her hand fluttered in the air as she tried to wave away their concern.

"Mother," said Joyce. "Rose is going to stay with you for a few days."

"But…"

"It's all arranged, first you then I'm off to see the Mammy," said Rose in an exaggerated Irish accent. A bright smile lit up her face. Doris could only try to quell the fear that threatened to overwhelm her. Slowly her breathing returned to normal. She became aware of her hand plucking nervously at the bedclothes and made an effort to still it, praying that they would not press her for the reason for her distress. On that score, there was no need for worry.

"It's all been too much for you," said Joyce in her more usual disapproving tone.

"I expect you are right, dear," said her mother and was greeted with a suspicious look.

"*Ah that's better,*" thought Doris.

"What shall you do, old girl?" asked Frank.

"*I made a promise, I never thought…I have always said that you have to be prepared to take some secrets to the grave but now with the baby coming there's a hunger in Prin's eyes and there is something about Rose that…oh my God I don't know what to do and I am worried about those young people, the band. Will they get into trouble? Oh I am so tired.*"

When Joyce returned with a cup of tea, she found her mother sleeping peacefully.

Chapter Fifty-nine

T here's a lot to be done," thought Doris. "*Must make sure Mrs Tracey is OK after her ordeal. Then there are the teenagers, I'll go directly to their homes and not budge until I speak to them. They can't avoid me forever. I will find out if they were involved the other night...um...and I'll stand up for them if necessary. I have been much too wishy-washy up till now.*" She sighed. "*I'll have to think what to do with Rodney's ashes, and then of course there's Rose...well, if she is to go to Ireland and learn everything, so be it. Before she goes I'll just have to make sure that these few days she is staying with me will the best time we will have spent together.*"

There was a light tap on the door and Rose entered. "I brought you a cup of tea. God, Ma, judging by the face on you, you'll achieve whatever you have a mind to, you look fierce determined." She sat on the side of the bed and grinned. "What have you got planned for us to do?"

Doris sat up. "Lovely cup of tea," she said, thinking how nice it was not to be asked how she was. "I was just thinking...we're going to have the best time ever."

"Don't we always?" Rose laughed and Doris felt every worry she ever had melt away.

It would hardly be jolly, pointed out Doris, visiting Mrs Tracey. Would Rose mind? Of course not, she was quite looking forward to it in fact, after all she had heard.

Before they could step forth anywhere the front doorbell peeled and Rose invited Ritzy and If inside. They perched awkwardly on the edges of their seats and spoke stiffly. They hoped she was well. They hadn't meant to cause offence by asking to go to the cremation. They had meant only to offer support. Rodney had been generous about their playing at the party, they had attended in the end because a funeral was more of a public event, more public than a wedding, say. They would like her to know that they, inclusive of the whole gang—even Taps, had adhered strictly to the conditions she had laid down regarding the use of the rooms upstairs. They were not drug-takers, though they had of course tried them, everybody did, but never in her house. It was no big deal.

It was a long speech delivered with great earnestness by both girls, turn and turn about. The older women sat and listened without interruption. Doris felt a mixture of emotions, pleased and relieved that they had come, respect for the courage this showed, longing for things to be normal between them again, and a strong desire to throw her arms around them. Most of all she wanted to see them smile.

"I am sorry I misjudged you," she said quietly. The words to her own ears sounded cold.

Ritzy and If stood to go. "We'll arrange to come and collect our stuff and…"

"If…that's all right?" said Ritzy.

"I never said you should not use the rooms!" Doris cried, shocked.

The girls looked at one another. This was a part of the visit they had not rehearsed.

"How about a drink?" asked Rose jumping up. "Sit still, the pair of ye, we've got loads of Coke in, haven't we, Ma?"

"We have," said Doris, not taking her eyes from her erstwhile friends. "I wanted some to clean those old pennies I found. I thought I would save them for the new baby."

All three gaped at this apparent non-sequitur.

Rose left the room and the two girls sat again.

"You leave them to soak overnight," said Doris, determined to fill the silence, "and in the morning they look all bright and shiny as if they have never been used. Great stuff, Coke. Mind you, I wouldn't touch a drop of it."

A ghost of a smile appeared on each girl's face as Rose returned with brimming glasses. "How is your grandmother, Ritzy?" asked Rose and then kept up a steady stream of questions that drew monosyllabic answers and covert glances at Doris who sat in silence.

"You've been talking your head off for eighty-odd years," said Frank. "Can't you make them a bit welcome?"

"I hope you'll all resume your visits," she said, interrupting Rose in mid-sentence.

"Oh very graceful," said Frank.

"Thank you," said Ritzy and If in unison.

"You will come back? said Doris.

"Do you think they'll come back?" she asked Rose after the front door had closed.

Rose laughed. "Of course they will."

"How can you be so sure? I am afraid I only made things worse."

"You made it sound like a royal command. They're really in awe of you, you know."

"Really?" Doris did not feel displeased in the least.

"Do you still want to visit Mrs Tracey?"

"Of course, I would have loved to have asked those two if they knew anything but I don't think it would have been wise. Listen, why do we not pop into Jim's and have some lunch, they are bound to have all the news in there? Did you notice he brought his Steve with him to the crematorium? He was not at all what I had imagined."

"How did you get to be so liberal, Ma? There's not a blush in you."

"I got old, Rose and kept my eyes open. My dear girl, there is enough misery in this world without being judgmental of one's fellow man. Come on, suddenly I am starving."

Chapter Sixty

Are you a relative?" asked the nurse.

"Yes," said Doris firmly. "I have been very worried about her."

"Right, well...a visit might help. Mrs Tracey isn't ...um...communicating. I would ask you however not to stay too long. We've put her in a side ward because she is rather distressed. I'll pop along in a little while."

Doris and Rose drew deep breaths and entered the bare soundless room. They exchanged glances. At first, the bed appeared empty; no movement disturbed the bedclothes. As they approached they heard a gasp, a soft intake of breath and discerned a small figure huddled beneath the white cheerless blankets. The head seemed to be trying to push itself into the pillow in an effort to escape. In a hollow-cheeked face, terror-filled eyes darted frantically hither and yon. One exposed skeletal hand moved slightly, the lips were stretched white against the pale gums in a silent scream. "Mrs Tracey," said Doris gently and the figure on the bed uttered a faint animal-like sob. "Rose, love, would you wait outside? You are a stranger to her and if I am alone she may just bring me to mind, God help us. God help her. I wish I could remember her first name, it might help."

"It'll be on the chart," said Rose, turning at once to the bed-end. "Madeleine," she said. "I'll wait outside."

Swiftly she reached forward and kissed Doris and left. "Madeleine." Gently was the name uttered as Doris drew up a chair and sat by the bed. She waited a little while then tried again. "Madeleine, I am Doris Roberts, do you not remember me? You are quite safe now, Madeleine, you are quite safe now, all is well." On and on she spoke the soothing words but still the restless eyes moved unseeingly about the room.

The visitor felt helpless. There must be a way to bring comfort to this tormented soul. If only she could reach out and touch the wasted hand with the warmth of her own and enfold the frail body in the security of her arms but any movement induced more fear. Words remained the only possible way to breech the seemingly unbridgeable gap. In low tones, Doris told Mrs Tracey where she was and tried to identify the sounds that came faintly through the heavy door. The nurses and doctors would be passing purposefully up and down the shiny-floored corridor, there would be patients being greeted, patients bidding farewell, porters pushing trolleys, files and X-rays being carried to and from labs, volunteers taking books, magazines and small comforts from ward to ward, visitors making inquiries, hustle and bustle, love and care.

Here in an oasis of calm, one could rest and recover and rejoice in the golden fingers of sunlight that freely passed through the slatted blind on the upper window and danced on the bedcover and painted the walls with needed colour.

Beyond the window across the road from the hospital was the park alive with buds and flowers and trees, glorious and green. Squirrels scurried hither and thither, pausing from time to time to sit on hind legs and bite some treasure held delicately in forepaws. Birds and butterflies, seemingly aimless, touched bush and grass and sky. Glimmering through the luxuriantly leafed trees was the quiet water of a small lake. Adults and tiny children could be seen by the water's edge. One adventurous toddler was breaking away from its parents' grasp and hurtling on fat unsteady legs towards the welcoming water. The chase was on, the baby laughed at the game. The mother's body betrayed her anxiety, she appeared to shout as she ran.

Doris, as she described the scene to Mrs Tracey, was too distant to hear the words, but it must surely be the child's name repeated again and again. Doris paused in her narrative as a thought struck her. In such a situation you made it short. Was that a way through? What would Madeleine have been called as a young child? Mad, Maddy, Della, Delia, Adele: she tried them all, muttering each name softly, repeatedly. There was no response.

The nurse popped her head around the door and, hearing the quiet murmuring, departed. Maddy, Della, Madge, what else could there be? Was she a Madeleine or a Madelyn, Lena, Lin…Lin…Linnie, Doris mused aloud? With a sigh she glanced at the tiny figure on the bed, imagining a child lying there, a little girl being lulled to sleep, and that child's name was what? "Linnie," she whispered, "my little Linnie, go to sleep now Linnie and when you wake everything will be all right." Was it her imagination or had Mrs Tracey's mouth relaxed, had the eyes slowed down their constant motion. "*Wishing makes it so,*" thought Doris but continued with her mantra. Falling herself into a sort of trance, she was unaware that Rose had come to stand beside her. "Sleep well, my little Linnie, sleep well, you're safe now, Linnie."

"Ma, Ma, look."

Doris heard Rose and returned to herself. Madeleine Tracey's eyes and mouth were closed and her hand was still. Madeleine Tracey was asleep.

Chapter Sixty-one

Could you not sleep either, love?" Doris looked up as Rose entered the kitchen at three in the morning. "I've made a pot of tea."

"You wouldn't rather be alone?"

Doris shook her head and Rose sat at the kitchen table, her hands cradling the mug of tea that had been passed to her. "Strong enough?"

"You could trot a mouse across it."

They both dutifully smiled at this standard exchange and lapsed into an easy silence. Together they sat in the soft dimmed light, gazing towards the blackness of the night as if their eyes could penetrate it. The occasional car's headlights sliced through the darkness moving the shadows in the quiet room. Their soft breaths and faint familiar comforting creaks of the old house were the only sounds to be heard. Together they listened rapt in their own thoughts as they drank the tea. Finally, Rose asked, "Do you often get up in the middle of the night like this?"

"No, normally if I wake I just lie there but tonight I felt a bit restless, what about you?"

"Me, ah sure, Gareth's always saying he married a shiftworker. Did you ring the hospital?"

"Mrs Tracey is comfortable. That could mean anything, poor creature."

They fell silent again.

"What have I done, Rose? Was it really my crowd who staged the whole thing, everyone seems to think so? It can't have been a coincidence, can it? What a responsibility."

"The detectives certainly seemed to think you had a hand in it. I saw the way he winked at you when you were in the crematorium, and then all those questions when you came back here."

Doris pursed her lips. "You know, Rose, the most shocking thing today...was seeing her so clean. It might sound odd but she looked so...oh I do not know what the word is, sanitised, as if she had been scrubbed clean of all personality and humanity, even her mind seemed to have been taken away from her."

"Ma, at least now she's got a chance, from what I've heard she couldn't have continued as she was, virtually a prisoner, starving and filthy and consumed with fear."

Doris shook her head. "But it was familiar; you know the old saying 'we all choose our own fate'."

"Do we?" The words were out sharp and bitter. Rose's embarrassed smile could not disguise the depth of feeling behind them.

"Shall I make another pot of tea?"

"I think," said Doris gently, "it means we choose how to deal with our fate."

She watched Rose busying herself, filling the kettle, unnecessarily washing the two cups.

"You know, love, I am always here if you ever need to talk anything through. These old ears have heard a thing or two in their time."

"And that's with or without the hearing-aid?" asked Rose, trying to sound light-hearted. "God, Ma, if I don't know by now I'll never know."

"You did say 'yes', didn't you?" Doris looked shrewdly at her daughter-in-law, and thought it did not matter what she said, Rose's thoughts were clearly elsewhere.

"Have you heard from your friend Áine at all lately?" she asked brightly. "What's she up to these days?"

"Oh Áine," said Rose, relief in her voice at the change of subject, "she's great gas. She says she'll have to do something with her life soon, because so far her only claim to fame is that she slept with an astronaut. 'That's my fifteen minutes of fame gone,' says she. There's always someone that asks what it was like. 'Out of this world,' she says and of course everyone cracks up. I'm hoping to catch up with her when I go over, if she's got the time. You've never known a busier woman, what with the job, the opera and all."

"How long will you go to Ireland for? You mother's all right isn't she?" Doris asked, feeling herself grow tense at the thought of Ireland and the search for Siobáin, Prin's mother.

"My mother! Divil a fear of her. She's great. Isn't she like a queen, looked after hand and foot, those Bon Secour nuns are great, really dedicated, selfless women, I don't know how they do it."

"It's a question of faith, I expect," said Doris absently.

Rose stared into her cup. "I rang Mammy the other night and we spoke about Prin. She doesn't think we should try and find his m...mother. You know, even now I have difficulty in saying that. It's one thing to know something but another to feel it in your heart. I am his mother and please God will be grandmother to his baby. Anyway, Mammy thinks we should leave things alone. Things may be a lot different now for unwed pregnant girls but old scandals uncovered could cause immeasurable pain. I don't know. I see Prin going through agonies because he doesn't want to hurt me and I know he has a powerful, almost compulsive urge to find his own. I thought if I supported him he wouldn't feel guilty about me."

"Why now, Rose? Apart from Prin's wishes, I can't help feeling there is another reason. Why this welcome but unexpected visit?" Doris's heart hammered and she hastily replaced her mug on the table lest her trembling hand should give her away.

Rose smiled. "I should have known I couldn't keep anything from you." She paused and looked directly at her mother-in-law. "I've got to have an operation, it's not serious."

"I wondered, I did not know what to think. What is it, love?"

"Hysterectomy, I'm assured it's a doddle these days. It's a cyst, benign they believe. In any case they'll whip it out and I'll be grand. It can't be serious, otherwise they'd have me in straight away wouldn't they?"

Rose spoke matter-of-factly and Doris had no reason to doubt her. "I'm glad you've told me."

"We didn't see any point in worrying you until we had something definite. Gareth and I talked it over. You've been through so much, nursing Pa and then his death and funeral and all. You've had enough on your plate. I miss him." She laughed. "Can you imagine the way he'd grumble now with us up at this hour?" She glanced at her watch.

"My God look at the time, he'd be right. We'll be washed out in the morning." She looked at Doris and saw tears in her eyes. "Oh Ma, I'm sorry."

"No, no, no, love," said Doris waving away Rose's concern. "I am so happy you mentioned Frank, people rarely do."

Chapter Sixty-two

Right now, what are all those things you want us to do together?" Rose sounded tired.

Doris gazed sleepily at her. "Eat ice-cream for breakfast, go to Brixton market, take you on a bus ride to Crystal Palace park, listen to audio books with you, visit Frank's grave, have the young people to tea, go to church, meet Trevor and his mum, and Jyotsna, eat at Jim's, lose ourselves in beautiful music, share TV and Radio 4, natter into the night."

"Mmm, and what shall we do tomorrow?"

"Tomorrow will have to take care of itself." Smiling, they both looked towards the window, which was lightly spattered with raindrops.

Rose yawned. "I'm not sure I'm up to anything today."

Doris turned back the bedclothes and patted the bed beside her. "Get yourself a cushion from the chair there and pop in with me; we needn't budge if we don't want to."

The two women lay propped up with cushions and pillows. Both sighed with contentment. "Do you remember, Ma, we used to do this when the kids were little and we'd plan walks and picnics and things."

"What about the day we set out pushing the pram and walked miles thinking we would catch a bus back?"

"Good Lord, yes, and neither one of us had a penny between us, oh I'll never forget that day."

"We did, I found two shillings in my pocket and we bought…"

"You're right, I remember now, we bought an ice-lolly so the child could have a drink, a few sweets and chewing gum for ourselves to ward off the hunger. Then we trudged back all the long way."

"Happy days."

"But bad for the feet."

Doris switched on the radio. "Delays on the M25 between junctions…" She turned it off again. "Rose."

"Uh hu."

"What you told me last night, is it painful?"

"Yes, it's sporadic. When it hits, it hits."

"I am sorry, if there was…you would tell me."

"Yes, now you know, no more secrets."

They both closed their eyes and dozed, awakening to watery sunshine, Vivaldi and Mrs Evans peering at them.

"If there was room I might join you, you look that cosy. I've made you some soup, it doesn't look like there'll be a hand's turn done here today. That snooty one, the boy with the posh foreign accent rang and said to give you his condolences, I think he means apologies, but he won't be coming this evening. That Trevor's been messing about in your garden all morning, the rain's done his hair no favours. Those teenagers came round and I said tomorrow might be a better day to start clumping around here again. Your daughter said you shouldn't go out, your doctor said you should. You've missed an appointment. I said you'd ring and now your social secretary is going home to a bit of peace and quiet, I'm worn out and it's not what I'm paid to do."

The bedclothes shook with suppressed laughter. Mrs Evans glared at the bedfellows with disapprobation. "Oh, I forgot to tell you the crematorium rang to say you could pick up the ashes on Friday."

Doris could barely gasp thank you, and when the door had closed laughter exploded from herself and Rose. For wonderful moments, they giggled uncontrollably.

"I feel about ten, she's so serious."

"She means well."

Tears of laughter tumbled from their eyes and they wiped them away with their fists and finally the crumpled bedsheets. The paroxysms faded and they lay panting and exhausted.

"I feel like I've run five miles."

"My memory is not that good. I feel as if I have climbed the stairs."

"Oh that was good, I suppose we ought to get up."

"Rose."

"Uh hu."

"Rose, have you ever broken the law?"

"Speed limit's about the height of it. Why?"

"Oh I just wondered." Doris sounded evasive.

Rose didn't press her. "I'm off for my shower, you can be the lay-abed."

Chapter Sixty-three

Rose and Doris ate the soup, listened to *The Archers* and to the afternoon play. Rose read aloud from a book she had been longing to share with Doris. They drank tea and made plans and issued invitations, answered the phone and talked and talked, and then talked some more.

"What's this about a doctor's appointment, Ma?"

"At my age they check you're alive every now and then. I tell you I feel more alive today than I have for many a long day."

"Ma, why did you want to know if I had ever broken the law?"

Doris's smile was a bit sheepish. "You remember I told you about the van and the hash for cash, well I was thinking."

"Yes."

"Ever since Ritzy was here the other day and she said everyone tries it, well, I have been thinking I haven't and…"

Rose's eyes widened. "And you're thinking…" she pointed to herself and walked her fingers in the direction of the dirty white van at the end of the street.

Doris nodded.

Rose grinned. "We couldn't, could we?" They looked at one another.

"We should not but we could if you are game," said Doris. "Of course, I do not want to push you down the slippery slope."

"But I'm halfway there with the speeding, I know."

They laughed and questioned each other with their eyes, excited and girlish.

"Well," asked Doris, "shall we see what it is all about?"

"Let's get this straight. You want me to walk across the road to the van, knock on the side of it or the window and ask for what? We don't even know what it's called."

"Of course we do," said Doris firmly, "we've seen enough films. It's called Mary Jane or the weed or the herb. Look love, he is selling so he will know what you want. Believe me there will not be a problem."

"Are you sure you haven't done this before?"

"Of course not!" Doris sounded shocked.

"OK, so how much do I ask for? I can't just walk up and say enough for two and wrap it please."

"Rose, you're very slow this evening; they call them joints, do they not? Maybe he will have them ready-made."

This idea struck both of them as ludicrous. "Maybe it is in screws of paper like the salt used to be in packets of crisps. Think of it as a fact-finding mission."

"You can't get arrested for having a packet of crisps."

"Where is your sense of adventure?"

"Ma, what makes you think he won't drive off as soon as I approach? I'm hardly in the first flush of youth. I don't exactly look the part."

"Believe me he will not move. He has a routine, I've watched him. I have precious little else to do. The trick is you have to have the money in your hand and you pass it over and take the stuff in one fluid movement. To the casual eye it looks almost as if you are waving a greeting." Doris laughed. "When I first saw it I thought that the man in the car must be very popular, it's a shame the one person he is waiting for never turns up. You can imagine what a fool I felt when I realised what was happening."

"Do you ever see anyone you know? What about the police? Don't they clamp down on it if it's so visible?"

Doris thought for a moment and chose to answer the latter question only. "Every now and then they make a token effort and move him along but he is small beer; they are more interested in the serious stuff that goes on on the estates. They are the ones they really want, the cocaine and heroin dealers, C & H as those of us in the know call them."

Rose smiled but the atmosphere had grown serious. "So what happens with the van, I mean when he's moved on?"

"Well I only know from what I have seen, it's like watching TV with the sound turned down. It seems to me they have a sort of gentlemen's agreement for want of a better explanation. He never returns the evenings the police have had a word, other nights the van goes and then the patrol car comes round. It is all in the timing."

"So you wouldn't like to stroll over yourself and buy the grass?" Rose's eyes were twinkling again.

"I should love to." Doris flushed. "But I could never run if…"

"And I suppose I could. I'm no spring chicken you know."

"Ah but your heart is young."

"And foolish. Shall we do it?" Rose looked like a little girl accepting a dare. "Shall we?"

"I'll give you the money," said Doris standing up to get her purse.

"That's a point, how much shall I take? You'd have to have the right money wouldn't you."

"Take ten," said Doris.

She stood by the window and watched her daughter-in-law walk across the road and enter the newsagents and then with mounting excitement followed her slow progress to and behind the van. What was keeping her? Why was she so long? She couldn't be having a chat, could she? Doris was on tenterhooks. Relief came when Rose reappeared and turned towards the house, almost regaining the pavement when Doris saw her retrace her steps. A hand emerged from the van and proffered something that she took with a laugh. Doris felt a great rush of love. Only Rose could laugh quite like that, a free generous laugh, head thrown back, the sort of laugh that made total strangers stop in their tracks and join in.

Doris felt the corners of her own lips lift as Rose ran for home. She greeted her at the door. "What happened, I want to hear all about it?"

Rose's eyes were shining. "Wait till I tell you," she panted. "It was so funny. I'm puffed out."

"Come in, sit down. Did you get it? I saw you go over to the shop."

"Well I had a brain-wave. I thought that if they're not already made up, we need cigarette papers. Then I wondered if we had matches. Then I thought it might look odd to buy papers without tobacco so I bought that. I think I was more embarrassed buying that than the other stuff." Rose sat in the armchair talking animatedly, leaning forward in her eagerness to impart every detail. "I was heart-scalded, I was that scared when I walked up to the van. You saw me go behind it and my heart was pounding, sure that everyone was watching me. I almost walked past but I suppose he saw it written on my face or something because he wound down the window and muttered something. He had nice eyes, sort of piercing and knowing and looking at you only. I couldn't hear what he'd said, but I presumed it was 'what do you want?' I'd been thinking back as I walked across and I remembered something from a book I'd read so I said, 'Two spliffs please, can you make them up?' It was then I understood quite clearly what he said. Are your ears too delicate to hear this?"

"I want to hear every word," said Doris.

"He said, 'You got to be having a fuckin' laugh. Piss off.' "

"What did you say to him?"

"I didn't, I waved the ten-pound note at him. He sort of eyed me up and down and got the message and closed one eye. You couldn't call it a wink because it was just like he was resting one eye. God, Ma, it was fun feeling part of a conspiracy. Without taking his eye off me, he reached behind him and handed me this tiny package and took the money, just as you said, in one fluid movement." Rose held out the little clear plastic package on the palm of her hand.

"But you went back," said Doris taking it from her and turning it over.

"Oh that was so funny. I couldn't believe it when he shouted after me. You'll never guess what he wanted." Rose went on without waiting for a reply. " 'Fuckin' change,' he said, 'you want to be more careful; I ain't no t'ief.' Dead serious he was. That's when I burst out laughing and ran over here. Let's have a look at it."

Together they peered at the innocuous brown contents of the little packet. "Doesn't look much does it?"

"Could be tea."

"Funny smell though, pungent."

"Shall we?"

For reasons neither of them could define they went into the bedroom and sat on the bed. "Shall I make us one each?" asked Rose. "In the films they pass one from person to person."

"Let's see how we get on with the first one, have you ever rolled a cigarette?"

"No. Have you ever smoked one?"

"Certainly, sixty…seventy years ago. One is not unused to experimentation."

Rose poured the contents of the packet onto a cigarette paper and tried to roll it. It seemed like the easiest thing in the world when you watched others do it. You just packed in the tobacco as tight as you could, rolled up the paper leaving a margin to be licked and stuck down. You then lit up and were on your way to Nirvana.

Rose tried and precious strands developed a life of their own, seeming to leap from the paper to lay scattered on the bedcover. "It's you, you're making me laugh. I can't believe I'm doing this."

"You are not," said Doris. "Give it here."

She did a creditable job "I'm a bit out of practice," she said modestly.

"When...?"

"I learned a lot in the brothel," said Doris. "I taught them French and they were not ungenerous with sharing their skills, but that is for another time. Have you got the matches?"

With backs propped against the headboard and much giggling, they lit up and tentatively sucked. They both coughed and tried again.

"Distinctive smell isn't it?" said Rose and puffed hard.

Doris concentrated on the joint between her fingers. In silence the two pulled furiously while the room became hazy with acrid smoke. "Rose."

"Yes."

"Is anything happening?"

"No. How about you?"

"Me neither."

Rose and Doris burst out laughing. "How do you feel?"

"Absolutely...absolutely...normal."

"This is not an unqualified success is it?"

"Well at least we've had a go. Now we know."

"Rose."

"Yes Ma."

"I'm starving."

"Me too. I'll get us some fish and chips shall I?"

"Now that is what I call a really good idea."

Chapter Sixty-four

The bedroom windows had been thrown wide open, air freshener sprayed to the point where breathing was near impossible. The remains of the experiment had been burned and the ashes wrapped in greasy chip papers, that in turn had been buried deep in the outdoor dustbin.

"Whatever have you been up to?" Mrs Evans sniffed the air when she arrived. "A bit pointless me coming if you do it all yourself."

"Oh no we just aired the place a bit."

"Well if you didn't need me I..."

"I'll always need you, Mrs Evans," said Doris, smiling at Rose who was trying to look innocent.

Mrs Evans looked at both of them with suspicion. "I can't get any sense out of you when you are like this, two grown women giggling and such. There's more maturity in my small grandson." She stamped out of the room.

"She can't know, can she?"

"That's your conscience talking."

"Haven't got one. I'm glad about last night."

"The chips were particularly good. I think we can close the window now, do you not? It is decidedly chilly."

Totally at ease they sat and talked about the day ahead. They touched on Rose's need for an operation and Doris was reassured that it was routine. There was pain and from time to time Rose felt drained and had to take to her bed until her energy returned. Happily, those episodes were rare. She was looking forward to having it all over and done with.

"And in the meantime I'm having a holiday here with you, then I'm off to see the mother. They have a visitors' room at the home where you're treated like royalty. It'll be great to see her. You know she still fusses over all of us."

"And will you search for Prionsias's mother while you are there?" Doris tried to keep the tenseness from her voice.

"I want to but I doubt if I'll have time what with seeing all the relations, sure there'd be war if you missed any of them out." Rose looked shrewdly at her mother-in-law. "You agree with Mammy don't you? You think it's best to leave well alone."

Doris could only nod, not trusting herself to speak.

"You could tell her now," said Frank, "then there'd be no more secrets, no more worries."

Doris with a great effort ignored him. "Do you know what I should love to do, Rose, if it would not be too much for you?"

"What's that, Ma?"

"I should like to go to a supermarket."

"What?!"

"That is what I should like to do, go to one of those enormous supermarkets. I have never been and I am told they are as big as football pitches."

"You could get some bacon, you're right out," said Mrs Evans entering with a huge tray. "Move those books," she said. "I can't hold this all day."

Rose moved swiftly. "That smells only gorgeous. Look Ma, a real breakfast. Mrs Evans you're a marvel."

Mrs Evans snorted. "I obviously wasn't needed for cleaning so I thought I'd do you a bit of bacon and eggs. There's not a sign of you having anything last night and neither of you can live on fresh air." She stomped out, ignoring thanks and the mention of fish and chips. They ate and enjoyed and planned.

Mrs Tracey was "comfortable". Doris could visit her after Rose's departure. Her sojourn in hospital would likely be a protracted affair. Nothing could be rushed. Doris hoped the nurses would now call her Linnie.

Rose went to answer the door and Doris heard her say, "Come in, come in and see us before you troop upstairs. Mrs Roberts is looking forward to seeing you."

They were all there, even Taps, Squirrel and Trunks. "*It's odd how often that phrase keeps coming into my mind,*" thought Doris, as members of Obsidian came in with cautious smiles.

"It is good to have you here again. I have missed hearing you about the place."

"We didn't think ya'd want us in here again."

"You're always welcome. I did try to contact all of you because I owe you an apology. It was wrong of me to take my frustrations out on you. I should not have subjected you to such objurgation."

"Eh? Forgot me effing dictionary didn't I?" muttered Derek.

Ritzy punched him quite viciously. "Shut up," she hissed, "we agreed." He moved away and stood looking bored and sullen.

"Drink, everyone?" said Rose brightly.

Doris looked from face to face as her visitors found places to settle. She saw shyness, embarrassment, pleasure, resentment, relief.

"Now what have you been up to?" and instantly regretted it, silly to put them in a position where they might have to lie.

Rose came in with a laden tray and If rushed forward to help her.

"*How peculiar,*" thought Doris. "*Normally a slight movement of the hand would have one of the others scurrying to do her bidding. Something has happened to the balance of power.*" Aloud she said, "I'm sure you'll be pleased to know that Mrs Tracey is comfortable in the hospital. The circumstances of her departure were…mm…unfortunate but the result commendable."

Almost everyone in the room at that moment found their drinks to be of great interest. Doris said firmly and deliberately, "I don't suppose we shall ever discover exactly what happened. We can only be grateful that she is now being looked after."

Benoit winked at her and she returned his grin. The awkwardness in the room melted away and they were once more a group of people at ease.

Obsidian had a gig so it was great that they had the place to practise in again. Ritzy volunteered the use of her grandmother's wheelchair for the proposed trip to the supermarket. "Ya wouldn't even get down one aisle otherwise."

Nathan with his usual grunt indicated that he would go. He remained a mystery to Doris. "*One day,*" she thought, "*I'll sit down and figure him out.*" If marshalled Taps, Squirrel and Trunks and a reluctant Derek upstairs. They muttered their goodbyes. Ritzy, glaring after her boyfriend, said to no one in particular, "He's seriously pissin' me off," and she went into the kitchen to help Rose clear up, leaving Benoit inserting a tape into the video.

"That's for later," he said, "ya ain't seen it innit."

"Oh it is so lovely to have you back." Doris felt her heart soar. "You're quite right, I fell asleep."

Chapter Sixty-five

Ⅰt is like being on a foreign holiday," said Doris. "It's wonderful. Look at the fish. I want to buy things I have never heard of before and things that I haven't had for years. That is what I miss, Rose, being able to choose and, what is even nicer, being tempted. It is lovely to know that you do not lose the urge to shop."

Rose and Doris slowly passed up and down the aisles of Sainsburys, marvelling at the seasonless fruit and vegetables. They bought papaya from Brazil and physallis and cherimoyas from Columbia. They bought limes and rambutans and apple-bananas.

"Ma, you've got to stop—we'll never eat all that lot."

"It doesn't matter," said Doris airily. "We shall put them in bowls to colour the room and we shall smell the scents of other lands."

Rose bent down and gave her mother-in-law a quick hug. "Ma, there is a look on your face of sheer bliss. You've made me see a visit to a supermarket in quite a different light."

"Oh I'm sorry, Rose, is this very boring for you?"

"No. It's marvellous."

They sped past the pet food and the household tools but lingered by the delicatessen, resisting salamis and unpronounceable cheeses but succumbing to lemon-flavoured olives. They spent a lot of time exploring the makeup shelves. They chose lipstick and nail varnish and with much giggling anti-ageing cream.

"We'll live forever," said Rose.

"Absolutely," said Doris.

They filled their lungs with the smell of newly baked bread and bought cream-filled buns, which, Doris said, in her youth had been called snowballs. They deliberated amongst the wines, threw financial caution to the wind and purchased six bottles of champagne.

Somewhere between speciality foods and stationery, they started to discuss the morning visit. Doris wondered if Rose had noticed anything odd about the group.

"Oh course I wouldn't know them as well as you but there was a sort of undercurrent. Is that what you mean?"

Doris idly dropped a can of palm-hearts in the wheelchair trolley. "I love these. Yes, If seemed subdued, didn't have her usual authority so I suppose that makes the rest feel a bit leaderless."

"Ritzy and Derek won't last long." Rose was passing tins to Doris who was rejecting them.

"Those I can buy any day. I have always felt that they were mismatched, those two. I don't know how it will affect the band." Doris decided to keep the bamboo shoots. "Of course you can see the attraction of Ritzy, bright, pretty, but Derek's merits escape me. He always seems so…I do not know what the word is, resentful perhaps."

Rose pushed the wheelchair to the bakery.

"Benoit was the only one who was his normal cheerful self. Bless him."

Before leaving the store, they just had to have a little box of edible flowers to have with their evening salad.

Mother and daughter-in-law returned to a house that vibrated. Doris smiled as Rose put the key in the lock "I am so pleased that they're back." She meant it. "Darling," she said, "would you have the strength to go upstairs and tell them that they have too much bass?"

Chapter Sixty-six

So that's about it. Prin, what do you think?"

"I think it's a great idea. Elaine wouldn't be up for it though. Throwing up is practically a full-time occupation for her at the moment."

"Poor girl," said Doris. "Give her my love. It'll get better and then she will start to enjoy it. Pregnancy has a lot to commend it."

"Gran, why do I get the feeling you are just paying lip-service? You know very well if my poor suffering wife came in on your little scheme we would have to come in her car. You just want a final ride in the Ferrari."

Doris felt herself blush. "You are right. Well, will it really be the last time?"

"Yep, it's got to go."

Doris was on her fifth phone-call of the day. Rose's visit had left her invigorated and full of plans. She missed her daughter-in-law of course, missed the laughter and the fun and the easy familiarity but the memories of girlie chats and the makeup session and companionable silences left her feeling strong and purposeful. Rose would come through the operation and she would be fine. In the meantime, there were calls to make.

Already she had reassured Joyce that she had not, nor was going to do anything unsuitable. She looked at her fingernails, a delicate shade of blue and wondered what her tweed-wearing daughter would make of such frivolity.

Doris had rung the crematorium and arranged to pick up Rodney's ashes. She had woken up knowing precisely what she would do with them. Andrew had been agreeable as had Mrs Panano and Jim from the cafe. Though the communication was not telephonic, even Frank approved. Now all she had to do was to organise it.

"I wonder whether Harry Cronin would like a ride in the countryside, but then I suppose Lily would have to come along. Oh Lord the world is full of moral dilemmas! I'll have to find out how many Andrew can fit into the parish van."

Ignoring the pain from her hip and the twinges in her shoulders, she made more calls, inviting, explaining, leaving messages. Pamela Bridges, the social research interviewer who had befriended her popped in, "just passing". Doris had her own thoughts on that. Here was a busy woman. She would not be just passing. This was a visit with a purpose, keep an eye on the old woman.

"You look great," she said to Doris, a suggestion of surprise in her voice. She was also invited on the expedition.

"I am so looking forward to seeing the rape glow golden in the fields," said Doris.

Chapter Sixty-seven

"If you had ordered such a day from an illustrated catalogue you would have got yourself a bargain," said Doris.

"That's a bit fanciful isn't it? Easy to see you've been with Mum for a while," said Prionsias, smiling down at his grandmother.

"What do you expect me to say, it is a beautiful day?" Doris looked at the Ferrari gleaming red in the morning sunlight. "Will that thing hold me and the urn? Couldn't take more than a toothbrush, I shouldn't think."

Prin looked at her steadily. "You know the capacity perfectly well but that"—he pointed to the small urn she was carrying—"I suggest we put it on the floor. Sealed OK, isn't it?" He took it gently from her and placed it in the car.

Doris and Prin stood on the Sunday pavement waiting for the others to arrive. "Andrew can't come—obvious really as it is his busy day but it was the only day when nearly everyone could come. He had a word with Rev Mother at the convent and Sister Eucharia who used to know Rodney will drive the minibus. Pamela Bridges couldn't make it either nor Raza but I'm not very surprised about that."

"We're going to look an odd bunch," said Prin, "a nun, a guy with a 'seventies punk hairdo and his mother, an Italian, two black kids, an Asian woman with two children, a middle-aged couple and that girl with piercings and the scary makeup, a gay guy and..."

"That's London for you." Doris looked sharply at Prin. "And I suppose we are the only normal ones."

"Good Lord, no, we're the weirdest of the lot. Normal people would be lazing around on a Sunday morning reading the Sunday papers."

The minibus drew up behind the Ferrari and out stepped a brisk young woman dressed in a blue skirt and white blouse. The silver cross on a chain was the only hint of her calling. She shook Doris vigorously by the hand. "He was a lovely man," she said and tears sprang into Doris's eyes.

The woman's Irish accent had reminded her of Rose but overriding that was the pain of the handshake.

"It's a great day isn't it?" The woman advanced on Prin. "You must be the grandson. I can see the likeness."

Doris and Prin avoided each other's eyes.

Sister Eucharia gave a yell. "They're here, they're all coming now. Sure, none of them will want to come in my old bus when they see your gorgeous vehicle."

Prin neatly side-stepped the slap she aimed at his shoulder. He bounded up the garden path to get the picnic basket prepared by Mrs Evans. "I'll lock up, OK?"

One moment they were a crowd milling about all talking at once, the next they were seated, belted and ready to go, having scarcely had the time to say "good morning". The odd procession set off, the Ferrari, the banger and the bus.

"You'll be there before we've even changed gear. There will be no holding you," Sister Eucharia had said to Prin. She would be right behind Harry Cronin's car in case it didn't make it.

"She's very…capable," said Doris, "a hearty sort of a girl. The convent will be peaceful today. Did you see how meekly Lily Cronin followed her instructions, not a murmur of protest at the Irish Catholic nun and that's three counts against the poor girl."

They drove in silence in traffic no different from other days of the week until they reached the A3. Prin snaked his way into the flow and visibly relaxed. "The others are OK,

298

they're just behind us. You did well Gran, plotting the route."

He put his foot down and Doris doubted that the others were "just behind". She noted that in comparison with the last time they were only slightly above the speed limit. The first sight of fields like golden shimmering seas drew gasps of surprise and awe. The flowers swayed gently as fingers of breeze played amongst them. Doris was entranced. She laughed.

"Tell," said Prin.

"Best not. It was a dark thought."

"But you laughed."

"It was incongruous."

"Mmm?"

"A few years ago a friend of mine, her husband died and I must have asked her something about coping and she said in a very matter-of-fact way 'one thinks of suicide of course'. There was nothing dramatic about it, it was simply an alternative. Frank died and I discovered she was right. One does—think of suicide I mean. It's a fleeting thought because the pull of life is stronger, the pull of children, grandchildren and great-grandchildren not even contemplated. You know, Prin, I think it is curiosity more than anything else that keeps one going, the basic urge to find out what happens next."

"Or sheer bloody-mindedness," said Prin, throwing his grandmother a quick glance.

"Oh, very percipient," she said.

"That too."

She stretched her legs and lost herself in enjoying the passing scenery. The choice to stay had been a very good one indeed.

Chapter Sixty-eight

The convoy took the Petworth road. At a favourite roundabout, Prin swore softly. It was usually a great place to zoom around the traffic but today there was just no co-operation. At Chiddingfold, they stopped for coffee. Emerging from the low-slung Ferrari was painful and Doris leaned stiffly on her stick while trying to find some ease for hip and back. At last, after the rest had arrived and had been shepherded inside, with Prionsias' help she was able to walk into the Crown Inn.

Sister Eucharia beamed. "Isn't this grand? Everything's ordered and we're all here safely."

"Well done," Doris heard herself murmur and thought the girl carried an air of a satisfied sheepdog. As she said her hellos, she was pleased to see that everyone looked quite happy. Lily Cronin dressed in her slightly old-fashioned Sunday best was fussing over the Kumar children. They, being plied with crisps and fizzy drinks, seemed comfortable with the arrangement. Their mother, while keeping a close eye on them, was listening to an earnest Trevor. Mrs Panano, Jim and Trevor's mother were chatting together. Harry Cronin sat with If, Ritzy and Benoit looking vaguely surprised to be in such company.

In the dark-beamed inn, If's appearance was quite startling. Gone were the coloured circles that Doris had thought quite jolly. Now all was black, her eyes deep black pools surrounded by black. Her lips were black, her hair was enclosed in a black snood. Was this in honour of the occasion Doris wondered or was this a new direction? "Fascinating," she murmured to Prin. "I've just realised something, tell you later." To everyone else she said, "Do have anything you like. We shall stay here for about half an hour and you might like to stretch your legs on the green before we press on."

Doris sank gratefully onto a seat. "Just black, please," she said to Prin. "Those teenagers look a bit out of it over there, would you mind jollying them up a bit. I was thinking, love, I'm a bit stiff; maybe I had better have a go in the Cronins' car, I doubt if I could get into the bus. Benoit, I know, is just itching to get into the Ferrari, would you mind?"

"I was going to show you my favourite overtaking spots. There's one where the Ferrari can easily manage 120 to 130 mph in perfect safety. I always call it the Penang straight, you'd love it."

"Be off with you, this is a law-abiding outing."

Harry Cronin looked vastly relieved when Prin joined his table.

Sister Eucharia, unable to find further duties, slipped into a seat alongside Doris, and together they sipped their coffee, looking around at the oldest timber-framed inn in Surrey. For over seven centuries it had slaked the thirst, satisfied the hunger and provided respite for the weary traveller. There did not seem to be a single straight line in the place. "*A bit like me really,*" Doris reflected, "*old and rickety but surviving.*"

Her companion gave a great guffaw. "Haven't ye great friends? They were great fun coming along in the bus."

Doris wondered. "That's nice," she said, hearing rather than listening to the young nun chattering enthusiastically about her lovely passengers who were "great gas". She was tired. The seat she occupied was hard. She had not dared to sink into the body-wrapping settees by the vast fireplace. Her hip ached. Ferrari-riding was perhaps not the wisest thing for a woman of her years, also she was in urgent need of the Ladies but doubtful of her ability to stand. A few trial

301

movements confirmed her suspicions. She looked around. Everyone else had gone out in the sunshine. "Excuse me, dear," Doris interrupted the flow. "I need the loo."

"Right!" Sister Eucharia bounced up. "Come on."

"Sister," said Doris wearily, "at my age you have to plan. I should be very grateful if you would first find out exactly where it is. At the moment I am rather stuck I am afraid." Inwardly she prayed that the good nun would not offer to rub her back.

"It's just through that door and up the stairs."

Doris's heart sank. Stairs. She should have thought of that before. "Oh hell," she said, then, "Sorry dear."

"We'll get you up there," said her companion cheerfully.

"How many stairs?"

"Only about eleven. Up round the bend."

"Bend! Narrow?"

"'Tis."

"Oh Lord."

"We'll have you up there in no time."

Sister Eucharia disappeared and could be heard calling from the entrance. "Lads, lads could ye ever come here, we need a bit of a hand?"

Doris groaned and leaning her forearms on the table tried to raise herself. A slight mist of perspiration on her brow was the only result of her efforts. What could be done?

"You don't half get yourself into a pickle," said Frank.

"And I suppose you think you are being helpful," she snapped.

"Well, we'll try," said a puzzled voice.

Doris looked up to find several pairs of eyes peering at her. Damn, she had spoken out loud again. "I was talking to myself," she said. "I can't move."

The members of her party stood over her and discussed the problem. "We could carry her in the chair."

"But we'd never get it round the bend."

"We could lift her out of the chair that would be easier."

"Whatever you decide, could you make a start?" said Doris. "It's getting rather urgent."

Willing hands supported her elbows but relinquished their hold when she winced with pain.

"Everything all right?" asked the waitress brightly.

Doris nodded, grim-faced and concentrated on trying to move her limbs.

"We'll have to do something."

"Look, move the table out of the way and make some room."

"It can't be that difficult to move one person."

"There's nothing of her."

"That's not the problem—we can't unbend her."

"There must be a knack."

"Let's pick up chair and all, at least as far as the stairs."

Doris closed her eyes as voices she did not recognise added their suggestions. Her whole body felt rigid. Would she stay like this forever?

"Prin," she commanded. "Do something. It is very urgent."

"Right…" doubtfully.

"Right…" More positive. "Heave!"

She felt herself rise into the air still seated. Prin and Benoit carried her in procession while everyone else directed operations. On seeing the stairs, her heart sank; they were narrow, quaintly uneven, though carpet-clad. She did not doubt that her helpers could get her up there, but would she come down with bones and dignity intact? A sudden vision of herself being given a fireman's lift brought on a paroxysm of laughter. The laughter rose in waves too powerful to resist. Smiles broke out. Someone stifled a giggle. The giggle would not be contained. It escaped. It spread; soon everyone was laughing. Strangers entering the inn who had to manoeuvre their way past the diverse group looked puzzled, then found themselves joining in.

Doris clutching her stomach gasped out the words, "It is now extremely urgent."

The manager tactfully suggested that they should move as they were blocking both the entrance to the bar and access to the stairs. For some unknown reason, this plea rendered everyone incapable of coherent speech.

"You are all behaving like children," said Jyotsna Kumar sternly while her children looked on in solemn amazement.

Doris wiped the tears from her eyes and pointed to a door slightly to the left of her vision. "That is where I need to be."

The small crowd looked at the door marked "Gentlemen". Doris sensed hesitation. "Now!" she said with all the force she could muster. As one, the men leapt into action. Benoit took the lead and seconds later escorted a bewildered-looking man from the room.

Doris demanded her stick, slowly straightened up and walked unaided through the narrow guarded door. As it closed behind her, she heard Lily Cronin who had stayed out on the green ask, "Where is the Ladies?"

The drive southward resumed without incident. Benoit roared off with Prionsias. A slightly aggrieved-looking Mrs Cronin mounted the bus. "What was so funny about asking for the lavatory?"

Doris rode with Harry Cronin. He had chosen some pieces specially for the occasion he said, and pushed in a tape. Fields and hedgerows vibrant with shades of gold and green glided by while glorious music soared and surrounded driver and passenger with wondrous sound. Doris slept.

Chapter Sixty-nine

The three vehicles found parking spaces by the side of a small marina. All but Doris climbed out to stretch their legs and to gaze at the boats gently moving on the summer-blue breeze-ruffled water. They watched fascinated while a yacht went through the lock. The children squealed with delight to see the water fall and the lock gates slowly open. As the boat eased into the harbour, the man and woman on board waved cheerily. Tariq and Sunanda waved back until the vessel was out of sight.

"All right, Gran?" Prin asked, peering into the car where she still sat.

"Brahms," she said, gesturing towards the cassette player.

"Us lesser mortals are starving, and scenic as this is, there's no place to picnic."

Doris looked at her grandson with scorn. "Just a little faith and a little patience, that's all you need." She closed her eyes.

Prin closed his too in exasperation. "And you're going to tell that to the hungry masses are you?" he said.

She sighed as the music ended. "Go and get the picnic things from the minibus and I'll tell you where we're going. There's a good lad."

This last had Prin glowering but he went, calling the others to help him. No point in arguing. Doris grinned to herself. Her eyes skimmed over the quiet pool inhabited only by ducks. Harry Cronin had parked facing this stretch of water rather than opposite the forest of masts on the other side of the road. The sleep had restored her and she was in truth a little hungry herself. Looking in the side mirror she could see Ritzy, Sister Eucharia and If standing about and glancing uncertainly at the car. Then Prin was again at her side. He placed the basket on the bonnet. "Time's up," he said, "where's it to be?"

Doris pointed. "There's a path over there through the trees, it more or less follows the water's edge."

Her grandson looked doubtful. "There's just undergrowth, Gran. How long has it been since you were here last?"

"Oh years and years," she said airily. "You go first with everyone and get the food started and then you can come back for me."

They were a curious spectacle winding their way through the trees. Doris watched them out of sight. Shifting her position, she dozed until Prin's shadow roused her. "You were right," he said. "There's a grassy clearing. We're all set up and there's a nice director's chair for you, but listen Gran…um…will you…be all right?"

"If you are referring to the sanitary arrangements there are conveniences by the side of the marina, look you can see them from here. If you are concerned about my walking ability, I certainly can walk the path with your help. The Queen Mother can get about unaided and she's a much older woman."

Chapter Seventy

Shafts of sunlight found their way through the umbrageous canopy of the interlaced trees to touch grass and cheek and limb. Doris raised her face to feel its gentle warmth. She was at peace with the world. Having eaten a picnic of marvellous variety, nearly everyone had wandered off to look at the boats or to explore. Lily Cronin had said, "I'll stay with you, dear," and Doris had tried not to show her feelings. There had been talk and laughter while they had eaten but now she wanted only to hear birdsong, the rustling of leaves and the soft susurration of water on the bank.

Her companion placed a chair alongside hers and there they sat side by side like two people in a dentist's waiting room. The thought had made Doris smile. Then to her surprise Lily bent down and took a book from her bag and without a word began to read.

The old woman closed her eyes and listened to the sounds of summer. There were chirring insects nearby and bees heavy and diligent. She could imagine them, round furry bodies soft and strokeable. "Would it not be nice to stroke a bee?" she said dreamily.

"You can," said a quiet voice.

"Frank?"

"Harry."

Doris saw that he was sitting with his back to a tree a little way away. Without getting up, he shuffled nearer to the bee-laden bush by her side. "You can," he said again. "Look," and stretching forward he gently smoothed a bee with a careful fingertip. "When they are working like that they won't take no notice, it's quite safe."

Her hand trembling a little as she reached out, Doris hesitated, then barely touched the little body, soft and warm with life and sunshine. It was a moment of joy. She smiled at Harry. There was no need for words. Beside them Lily Cronin slept, the pages of her open book fluttering slightly in the breeze.

"It's great," said Ritzy and threw herself noisily on the ground panting. "Came back...to...see...you was all right...and...have we...the time 'cos an old guy said if we were that interested he'd show us his boat. I said I'd go back and tell the others in a mo', OK?"

"I should get your breath back first, dear," said Doris, thinking how pretty the child looked, far too good for that nondescript boyfriend of hers.

As if reading her thoughts Harry asked, "Where's that boyfriend of yours then?"

A shadow crossed Ritzy's face. "Oh him. I'm glad he's not here to spoil things. I'm not black enough for him anyway."

"*What a curious remark,*" thought Doris. She said, "We do not need to go for another half an hour or so; is Prin with you younger ones?"

"Yeah and Sister Eucharia," said Ritzy, grinning again.

"In that case off you go."

"It's a different world," said Harry and Lily sighed in her sleep.

"Perfect day, eh love!" said Frank. "Do you remember the day we came here? It was later in the year and we ate blackberries and watched the swans and tried to remember the Irish legend and swore that we'd return."

"It has been a long time," said Doris.

"Not that long," said Prin cheerfully.

"It has been a long time since I was here last," said Doris and thought, "*I'm getting better at this.*" "Why are you back? Ritzy said an old man was showing you all his boat."

Prin laughed. "The old man must be all of fifty, if that; besides, do you suppose any harm could come to anyone with Eucharia around? No, don't worry Gran, he's a sailing instructor with one of those youth programmes, you know."

Doris did not know but trusted Prin's judgement. She was watching Lily and Harry Cronin stroll arm in arm to the water's edge. He was talking and she was listening. It was a rare sight.

"Is this where…?"

"Oh no, this is just the picnic area, it's too tame and enclosed, pleasant enough for us but Rodney needs open spaces. Shall we get going?"

The picnic things had been returned to the bus and Sister Eucharia was doing a quick head-count to make sure everyone had returned safely from their wanderings. They had walked lanes with hedgerows abuzz with summer life, watched birds swoop and soar over water and crop fields, gazed at becalmed boats and imagined them buffeted by bullying winds. Ritzy, If, Benoit and Sister Eucharia had been given a tour of one of the high-masted sleek vessels. Jyotsna would not allow her children to go on board but Trevor turned their tears to giggles by quoting the Latin names of plants. His mother, strolling by with Mrs Panano, wondered if they were all made up.

"I've always been known as Trevor's mum," she said, pride shining in her eyes. "He could make a broom handle bloom."

Jim had returned to the clearing with wood dust clinging to his clothes, the light of a new-found hobby was in his eyes. He had helped to rub down a small skiff.

"All present? Off we go."

"Are we going to the sea now?"

"No. Rodney was not one for the sea."

"Gran, I think we should have a clue. It has been a long day already."

"I'll know it when I see it. Take the road towards

Brighton, not the main one, the narrower roads by the sea that wind between fields and pass through villages."

Doris was hoisted onto the bus that Jim had volunteered to drive. Sister Eucharia had earned her ride in the Ferrari. Prin revved the engine loudly and unnecessarily just for the fun of seeing the delight on her face.

Chapter Seventy-one

This is getting ridiculous, Gran." Prin was clearly impatient. "This is the third time we've stopped. What the hell's wrong with this place? We've passed the sea, we've passed open fields, pretty villages, everyone's getting restless."

"It's not right."

Prin adopted a gentler tone. "Look, it's perfect here, an open common, trees behind for shelter, a church on the corner, the sea in front, what more?"

"It's not right."

"Oh for God's sake." Prin raised his arms in supplication. "I give up."

"I am sorry but it has got to be…"

"Right, I know."

"I'll know it when I see it."

"Right, I'll tell you what we'll do." Prin warded off interruption with a peremptory hand. "You'll ride with me. If you see the spot, I'll stop. If not, when we get to the A29 to London I'm going to take it. We can't keep wandering around the countryside like this. It's bloody ridiculous. We're going home. Got it?"

In the unbreathing silence, Doris said, "Yes." She was lifted out of the minibus and guided into the Ferrari.

"Prin."

"Yes."

"Prin, now that we are stopped, shall we get ice-creams for everyone? There's a shop over there, it *is* open."

"Why not! Why not stop for a cream tea as well?"

"Prin, you are taking after your father, irritable."

"That's it, then."

"That is what?"

"The nature-nurture debate, it's definitely nurture."

"Could you make mine chocolate, please?"

"What?"

"The ice-cream."

"We can go then, can we? No more diversions or requests."

"Of course, dear." The voice of sweet reason drew a glare from Prin. He got out of the car again and walked across the road, impatience portrayed in every step.

In the side mirror, Doris watched him go and return from the shop and distribute ice-creams to the occupants of the bus and the banger. By the time he was back behind the wheel, there was a smile on his face. "*Just like Gareth,*" Doris thought, "*first the cloud then the sunshine.*" Mostly worth the expenditure of patience. All right for those in the know.

"If it is nurture," she said as he started up, "then why have you not got Rose's temperament? This is my favourite choc ice, by the way. Did I tell you that she got me some for breakfast when she stayed with me?"

"Second childhood."

"Well at least I have been through my first." Doris retorted. "It was one of my ambitions to have ice-cream for breakfast."

Prin took his eyes off the road momentarily. "And you expect me to take after you both, two mad women?"

"So long as we are happy mad and not miserable mad, where is the harm?"

With remarkable restraint, Prin kept more or less to the speed limit through country lanes and pretty villages, past ivy-dressed pubs and solid growing-from-the earth churches, past cricket fields and golf courses, past fields of cows and vibrant gardens with summer flowers ablaze. "A man would be proud to have his ashes scattered anywhere

here," said Prin. "Beautiful English countryside, village commons and all that, wide open spaces, all the space you could wish."

Doris ignored him.

"We're coming up to the A29 and I'm going to take it."

"Yes, dear, you have already said so."

A light rain began to fall only to be whisked away by erratic windscreen wipers.

"They have an unnerving rhythm," said Doris, mirroring the motion with her finger.

"Mmm," said Prin, switching from the intermittent to the slow wipers, concentrated on his driving.

Doris luxuriated in the scenery flashing by, in the fleeting sight of iridescent raindrops jewelling the leaves, in the sun that was newly breaking through the branches arching above them. The Ferrari effortlessly climbed winding hills between dappled trees. Suddenly they were in open sunshine, on a straight stretch of road. To the right and far below lay a patchwork of fields, of muted browns and greens or shining gold edged with the filigree of hedgerows. "That's it. Stop." In her excitement, Doris grabbed Prin's arm.

He checked his rear-view mirror and brought the car safely to a halt. "Don't ever do that to me again."

"But Prin, look, it's perfect. We are high up and the earth slopes down and away as far as the horizon. It's perfect."

Prin gripped the steering wheel and spoke with exaggerated patience. "Gran, this is a main road, even though it's Sunday, look at the traffic, the lorries. There isn't a stopping place, not even a decent verge, certainly not on the other side of the road which is presumably where you want to be."

"Yes, of course. That is absolutely the perfect spot. I knew we should find it."

"Can't be done."

"This is the right spot. I owe it to Rodney."

"Can't be done."

"Stick to your guns, girl," said Frank.

"I am going to stick to my guns," said Doris.

"Please listen to sense; any minute now, Sister Eucharia, with seven adults and two kids and the two Cronins will come and park behind me on a road where there should be no parking. You will then expect us and them to get over there and congregate in a place where any normal pedestrian would fear to tread. Run across shall we, dodging the lorries like in some demented computer game?"

"Don't be silly, dear. When the others arrive we can carry on, do a U-turn and park over there. We can put on our hazard lights, we shall be fine."

"But we…"

There was a rapping on the window. Prin wound it down. "Are we here?" asked Sister Eucharia. "Isn't it gorgeous with the sun out again?"

"Yes, dear," said Doris firmly. "We are going to turn the cars around and park over there."

"That's great, they're getting a bit anxious."

The nun was gone before Prin could say anything. In the mirror, he could see her motioning the Cronin car to follow her.

"I just hope the children will be kept under control. This is madness."

"Don't grumble, dear," said Doris.

They stood by the side of the road, a strange-looking huddled bunch of people surrounding an old woman clutching an urn. The policeman who parked behind their three vehicles walked directly to her. The small throng parted to let him through.

"What are you doing, love?" he asked, settling his hat on his head.

"I am scattering the ashes of my friend, officer."

"Bit of a dangerous spot here with the children and all." His eyes swept over the assembly. "Your friend wouldn't want that, now would she?"

"I doubt whether my friend would have an opinion on the matter. He," she said with great emphasis, "was a man of the road."

"From around here then, was he?"

Doris hesitated. It would be easy to lie and secure a measure of understanding but this was an inappropriate time for dishonesty. "No, or at least nobody knows where Rodney came from."

The policeman appealed to the men in the party. "You must see that this is hazardous. Straight stretch you see, so drivers tend to go flat out." His voice rose as a particularly heavy lorry thundered by.

Both Prin and Harry looked ready to speak. Doris glared them both to silence.

"Officer, I respect your opinion of course and thank you for your concern, but it strikes me that we could just be getting on with it."

"Gran, I do think…"

"Mrs Roberts it might be wiser if…"

"Doris, dear, we could…"

Stronger souls than those present would have quailed before the steely stare that bore into those suggesting retreat.

"This is the right spot."

"Madam, I understand that, but I would strongly advise…"

Doris, feeling her arms tire, handed the urn to Benoit. "Are we breaking the law?"

The policeman cleared his throat. "Um, not technically, but…"

"Right," said Doris, "then we shall not detain you from your duties."

Benoit grinned openly. Some hid smiles. Lily Cronin turned pink. Sister Eucharia who had been mesmerised by the exchange gave a snort and immediately clamped her hand over her mouth. The policeman looked as if he was about to speak, then changed his mind and turned on his heel abruptly.

"Let's do it," said If.

"Is the policeman cross with us, Mamma?" asked one of the children. Both of them clung to their mother's sari.

"No, everything is all right." Jyotsna's anxious face belied her words.

Ritzy tried to distract everyone by asking what the crops were in the field. Nobody seemed to know except for the distinctive rape.

Doris said firmly, "It will not take long but neither will I rush. Rodney deserves more than a few casual moments."

She took the urn from Benoit. The police radio could be heard crackling and the voice of the policeman talking into it briefly, then he was with them again.

"I can see that you are determined and I can't stop you, but I can make sure you are as safe as possible. One of my colleagues will be here presently. I'm going to position the car to warn oncoming traffic. The other police car can be similarly placed on the far side of your party." He saluted.

"Thank you," Doris said. "Officer, just one thing."

"Yes, madam."

"Would you switch on your flashing lights please?"

The policeman nodded and went to take up his sentry duty.

Doris smiled. Rodney would have a police escort after all.

"I think we should start," she said. "First of all I want to thank you all for coming with me today. It means a great deal to be amongst friends, especially when it's time to say goodbye to one of them. As I have grown older, more and more of my friends and acquaintances have died, but Rodney…well I will not dwell on the tragic pointless nature of his death." Doris swallowed, seeing again in her mind's eye the old man's white shoulder. She felt cold. Prin touched her arm protectively and the others drew nearer. Once more, the sun warmly touched her cheek. For a moment she watched birds gyrate and pirouette over the valley.

"You are probably wondering why it was so important to me to find just the right spot. It's very simple. Rodney, as

316

you know, spent years on the streets living rough. We all talk about freedom, about 'being our own man' eschewing possessions, kow-towing to no one, but not many of us would have the strength of mind as he did. He was a brave man on the streets of London, but he told me once that he had a dream of being a 'real man of the road'. He wanted to roam the lanes and fields and woods and sleep beneath the vastness of a sky whose starlight was not obscured by street-lights. He told me he could never bring himself to go, that he lacked the courage." There was a catch in her voice as she almost whispered, "I thought I could give him in death what he could never have in life."

Prin gently took the urn from her, removed the lid and with all eyes on him swung his arm forward so that the urn's contents rose in an arc then spread out and drifted on the summer air towards the earth far below.

"Goodbye and God bless, Rodney," Doris said and her words were echoed by the small crowd.

"May his soul rest in peace," said Sister Eucharia while everyone stood in silence. Then… "Oh we nearly forgot," and she ran to the bus, returning with an armful of flowers. "We forgot these," she said.

Lily Cronin took some and gave them to the children who strewed them by the hedge. As Prin led Doris back to the car, the others threw the remaining blossoms in the air. They fell on the soil leaving behind a faint lingering scent.

Chapter Seventy-two

Amost satisfactory day," said Doris. "I wish you could have been there."

"Me too," said Rose. "I'll just have to rely on your word pictures."

"You're the one for those, love. It was a funny sad day. If has adopted a new makeup, Gothic I believe they call it. All black and foreboding."

"I've seen that on TV. Was she gruesome?"

"If you didn't know there was a lovely girl underneath the black and starch white, you would be forgiven for feeling quite nervous. Ah that reminds me, I suddenly realised what was odd the day the group came to visit me. If had no makeup on and no authority. Yesterday I noticed one raise of an eyebrow, one slight movement of the finger and the others jumped."

"Makeup equals confidence I suppose, an interesting concept. Tell me about the others."

"Ritzy and Benoit were good fun. Trevor had black tips to his hair in honour of the occasion. He and Jyotsna hit it off talking plants. Poor woman, she is a bundle of nerves but I think she managed to relax a bit. She kept covering her face but in truth people were more likely to have been staring at If or Ritzy's intricate hairdo. The children had a lovely time. Lily and Harry paid them a lot of attention and Jim from the cafe and, of course, Mrs Panano were very good with them. I don't think they stopped eating for a single second."

"And you had a lovely time in the Ferrari?"

"Prin turned into Gareth before my very eyes."

"Good and irritable was he?" Rose laughed. "You have to ignore the words, judge the actions."

"The convent sent us a marvellous girl to drive the minibus, but, my God, you would need your full health and strength, heart of gold, boundless enthusiasm. She said she could see the family resemblance between Prin and me."

"Great, isn't it? It used to happen to me all the time. Tell me about the actual scattering, Ma. Was it as you hoped?"

"More so," said Doris, and described finding the right spot, the police escort, the ashes arching towards the sunlit valley.

"Will there be a right spot for you, Ma?"

"Oh I want to be useful. Plant me amongst some vegetables. What about you—burial or cremation?"

"I'm for the ashes but the boys said they want to visit me."

"Well they can. You could have a nice little rose bush. It doesn't have to be in a graveyard."

"Aren't we a morbid lot?"

"I do not believe so, but the question is more immediate to me than to you."

"Not if you use that face cream. I told you you'd live forever."

Doris smiled remembering the supermarket visit.

"Ma, I've got a bit of news. I've got the date for the op. It's in ten days' time, a lot sooner than we imagined, so I'll only manage a few days in Ireland."

"Your mother will be disappointed."

"She will but, sure, I can always go there when it's over. I'll get Gareth to join me, he likes a drop of Guinness, you know."

"You will let me know the exact date, love?"

"Of course. Listen Ma, you sound tired, we'll talk again soon, all right?"

Doris paused. "Yes I am tired after yesterday. I am going to live quietly for a while."

"Joyce will rejoice."

"I love you, Rosaria Roberts."

Chapter Seventy-three

Mrs Evans, grumbling all the while, shielded Doris from what she considered nuisance calls on both phone and doorstep.

Andrew, one of the few to be allowed access, came to tell her of Mrs Tracey's progress and to listen to the tale of the outing, though he had already heard it from several sources. He went away promising to spread the word that Doris needed rest for a few days and would appreciate not being disturbed.

"Time of retreat, eh, girl?"

"Just a pause, Frank, just a pause."

Doris realised that she was enjoying being alone. The need to be quiet would swiftly pass and soon she would resume her active life. She would venture to the church, the hospital, the cafe. She would go to the garden centre where Trevor worked, and see him in action. She would go to the school and suggest ways of expanding their old person scheme. Ideas were rolling round her head like balls in a bingo caller's basket. She smiled as the thought came to her. Odd how the human brain works; she had never been to bingo. The experience could wait, she decided; there was so much else to do, so much living but not just yet awhile. She had to catch up on important things like world news and the Grand Prix and any number of unread books.

Mid-morning, on her way to the front door to pick up the post, she trod on something and painfully jerked her ankle. She gingerly moved her foot, then with her stick pushed the thing away from her and it banged against the skirting-board. Uncomprehending, she peered at it. She watched her hand stretch towards it, while her brain felt befuddled. The walls spun round her. Her heart beat fast, breath was refusing to leave her body. Doris stood transfixed, unable to bend, puzzled, trying to make sense of what she saw, not wanting to understand, not wanting to acknowledge that she did. Her legs would not be willed into moving to her sitting-room to get her "Helping Hand" to pick up the object. Her mind veered away from naming it. Somehow she manoeuvred herself to the hall chair and sank onto it. Her mind was in a trance, her eyes unseeing. There was no way of knowing how long she sat or when at last she moved, moved, touched and grasped what was on the floor. Now she was holding it in her hand. Now her eyes were beginning to focus, awareness returning.

Doris sat and gazed at Frank's pocket watch lying on her open hand. She turned it over. There was no doubt. It was inscribed with his name. She read each letter but there was no variation in spelling. It was Frank's watch. It was the watch that Frank had used to keep in a particular suit. He used to keep it in the suit she had given Rodney. Doris had made a conscious decision to leave it there. Somehow, the suit and watch went together. She had told Rodney so when he had discovered it and had wanted to give it back.

"Humour me," she had said, "maybe one day when you are on your wanderings you will touch it and remember me." Rodney had nodded gravely though they both knew he would never wander nor have need of a time-piece. Every night he would continue to sleep just inside the convent gates as he had done for years. He would sleep there until a murderer would stab him and attempt to burn his body.

Doris curled her fingers around the watch. She did not want to look at it any more. She did not want to think any more. The letterbox clattered and a letter fluttered to the floor. The old woman turned her head with scant curiosity. Her attention returned to the watch. The glass was broken.

She ran her finger across the crack wondering if she had done that when she had stepped on it, wondering how long it had lain hidden in the carpet. How had it got there? Who had dropped it? Her mind was racing now with questions but still it shied away from answers. There were no answers. The watch had been in the suit. The suit had been on Rodney. It had been on Rodney on the night he had died. Rodney had never been inside her house.

Doris glanced at the envelope lying on the floor. It bore a handwritten address. It might be personal, it might be worth reading. It might steer her away from thinking of all the people who came into her home. She would pick it up. Still she sat. In a corner of the ceiling, a spider went about his business, an industrious chap, up and down he went on invisible threads fulfilling his purpose in life. Mrs Evans would not be told. He had a right to peace and solitude.

With a sigh, Doris rose and shuffled stiffly to the door. With difficulty she pushed the bolt across and leaned against the solid wood. "No," she said almost immediately and pulled it back again. "I am not Linnie Tracey." In a gesture of defiance, she opened the door wide and, leaving it open, walked back to her sitting-room. Shaking a little, she picked up the telephone and dialled the police station. Not knowing for whom she should ask, she simply gave her name and said it was about the Thompsett murder. Could she come to the station, asked a bright carefree voice?

"No, dear," said Doris. "I am too old."

Chapter Seventy-four

"Mrs Roberts, I knocked but...your front door was ...er...I'm sorry—did I startle you?" Her detective stood in the doorway.

"No. I was expecting you. Yes, I do know my door is open and what is your name? Sit down."

"Dave Barrett." He looked amused. "What's this about you being too old?" He sat. "How did the scattering...what did you...?"

Doris held out her hand and opened it to reveal the watch.

Dave stood and bent over to exam it without touching. "And this is...?"

"Frank Roberts' watch," said Doris flatly and went on to tell him how it had come back into her possession. "I said to Rodney that it belonged with the suit and he accepted it on that basis."

The detective lifted the watch by inserting a biro into the loop meant to carry a chain and popped it into the clear plastic envelope he took from his pocket. He peered at the inscription. "We'll take a look at this down at the station," he said.

Doris looked doubtful. "I must have rubbed off any finger-prints, there's no knowing how long I..."

"We'll have a look anyway. You are absolutely sure it left the house with the suit? Would Rodney have returned it through the letterbox before he...he...?"

Doris gave the detective an icy stare. "In the intervening weeks do you suppose we haven't hoovered?"

Dave looked suitably chastened. "We have to explore all avenues," he said. "We'll have to check out everyone who comes into this house. Perhaps I could get a list from Mrs Evans."

"Do you suppose I do not know precisely who comes into my house? I am not in my dotage you know. I'll give you a complete list."

"I didn't mean to imply, I just thought…"

"You did not!" snapped Doris. "That is the problem, like a number of people you equate old age with incapability. My body is feeble. My mind is not. I'll start giving you names immediately."

Looking suitably contrite, Detective Barrett took out his notepad and began to write.

"I have to confess," said Doris, softening a little, "the real names of a few people escape me, Squirrel for example, nor do I know Derek's surname."

"We'll work round that," said Dave, hiding a smile.

When he had gone, Doris felt that she had been too hard on him. She had recognised what he had been trying to do, save her from naming trusted friends as possible suspects. It was a pain she had had to face, though her mind sought other explanations. The watch could have been lost or sold or stolen. There were countless ways it could have left Rodney's possession. She was over-dramatising. There was no reason to suppose that the person who brought the watch into the house was a murderer. Drama queen. Frank always said she was a drama queen. But Frank's name was on the watch; if it had been found why not just return it to his widow? Maybe that is what happened, maybe someone had just popped it through the letterbox. That was it, that was the solution.

Thinking of letterboxes, she remembered the letter that had fluttered through while she had been sitting in the hall. Dave Barrett had said he had put it on the hall table. It must be retrieved before becoming submerged in flyers offering pizzas or odd-job work at reasonable rates or take-away curries or Thai food. One of the group usually picked up the junk mail and put it there for Mrs Evans to sift through and dispose of. Doris did not move. All her strength was needed to escape the thought that the watch had been nowhere near the front door and the certainty that she knew that the murderer had entered her home, had climbed her stairs. There was a knock.

"Ah, Benoit," she said her face lighting up, "come in, love."

"Ya lookin' down," he said; "wat'sa matter?"

She hesitated. To voice her fears would give them wings and besides why burden this boy with horrid suspicions? He would be questioned of course along with everyone else but why anticipate that? He was looking around the room as if measuring it for space to do cartwheels if that would cheer her up. She smiled. Just his presence was enough to brighten her world. He brought with him an ease and a rapport that constantly surprised her. They were two no-effort-required friends.

"I am like a lazy dog sitting on a thorn," she said. "I'm hungry but I haven't got the energy to budge."

How could she begin to explain that just a few short hours ago she was happily cocooned in a safe world, now she was battling confusion and betrayal? The horror of the murder had entered her very home. "*For God's sake how the hell did it all come so close?*" For a moment, anger seized her but Benoit was saying something. "What dear?" Doris made a pretence of adjusting her hearing-aid.

"What 'bout a take-away, Mrs R, what d'ya fancy? Pizza, fish an' chips, Thai, rice and peas, patties, burgers, Indian?"

It was a good idea, food might help to distract her from the pall of gloom and apprehension that had settled on her shoulders. "Good idea, love," she said. They laughed about the variety of choice and finally decided that fish and chips were perfect comfort food. He said he always had a hollow stomach so of course he would join her and bring Cokes and mushy peas, and bring her up-to-date with the group's plans, the gigs, his grandmother's activities and…and…and…

He took the money and said, "I'll be back," in a passable Arnold Schwarzenegger accent, planted a kiss on the old woman's cheek and departed.

"Leave the door open," she shouted after him.

Maybe it was an illusion but at least in Doris's eyes the room was darker when he left. Silence hung heavy. She should have asked his help to stir herself before he went away. The struggle to rise from the chair with its back to the door began painfully. They would need plates, vinegar, salt, forks, tomato sauce. She could fetch those before his return.

There was also a more personal, increasingly urgent need for her to move. Where was her stick? Hours seemed to have elapsed since she had made her loathsome discovery. A suggestion of pain hovered about her hip, darting sporadically, disappearing, gripping briefly, fading. At the moment it was a shadow, a wraith that would return full-bodied and cruelly powerful. Yet again, she was trapped. Doris was furious with her defiant limbs, with the murderer, with her present helplessness and furious for being in this "bloody awful situation".

Chapter Seventy-five

Silly bitch, talking to yourself!" Doris froze. Almost immediately, a hand was clamped over her mouth and her head roughly pulled back. Her assailant breathed hard while she herself struggled for breath. Her hands made futile attempts to free her face from the vice-like grip. Something inside her grew still and calm. "*Think, woman*," she told herself, "*think, go limp, do something.*"

"Now listen, listen up." This time the voice, distorted with hatred, was low and menacing. There was something familiar in the tone. This was someone she knew. Her heart leaped. "*He must mean to kill me, he dare not let me turn around and identify him.*"

"Listen!" To emphasise the word, he jerked her head back. A groan escaped her when excruciating pain tore at her shoulders. Her head pounded so that she could scarcely hear what was being said. "Don't make an effing sound. I'm going to take my hand away and you can give me some info, like where the money is." His tone grew lighter, mocking "Let's not forget the jewelry, shall we?"

Doris shuddered. He was enjoying his power. "I want your credit cards and pin numbers and don't even think of lying to me."

The old woman tried to think. When he took his hand away would she be able to scream? Would she make someone hear? She felt the warmth of his face close to hers and his breath on her ear as he bent over to whisper, "You just try something and I'll cut you..." With his free hand he showed her the knife, slowly moving it before her eyes so that she could see its broad body curving acutely to a delicate point. It came to rest flat against her cheek. Instinctively Doris tried to draw back but her head was already pressed hard against the chair and there was no escape from flesh or steel. It surprised her that the knife was warm.

The sweaty hand that held her lower face loosened its grip and she gulped air. The movement jerked the knife, and she felt it prick her nose. Her hand rose to rub away his repugnant sweat and smell from her mouth but it was viciously knocked away. The blow sent ripples of pain up her arm; Doris gasped. The knife lightly traced the contours of her face. "I could give you a facelift," said the man and the ordinariness of his speech was terrifying, 'but, hell, why waste time? Right, old woman, spill."

Doris could feel the blade idly circling her mouth. Her thoughts were frantic, her mouth dry, her throat constricted.

Money, did she have money? Where was her purse?

Pin numbers, did she have pin numbers? She did not have any of those, did she?

She could not think. Her eyes could not focus. She opened her mouth to scream and found she could not do that either. Her body went rigid with fear. No voice, no hope.

"I'm not playing fucking games, where is it?"

A sharp slap stung her cheek. The hand that held the knife disappeared. What was happening? She tried to turn her head, but the hand that had delivered the blow grabbed her chin and fingers dug into her cheek. "I asked you a fucking question, where's your stuff?"

Doris struggled voiceless, terrified. Raising her hands against her unseen tormentor, the action brought a rain of blows on her arms and shoulders and a torrent of ugly words, repetitive, staccato, mindless. The words and blows merged into one storm of hatred. A red mist blinded her eyes. The walls of the room advanced and retreated. Her body felt light and soon, very soon she would just float away.

There was something she had to do first, what was it?

Her brain felt fuzzy. Why could she not go? She only had to close her eyes. Someone was shouting. She blinked away the mist and returned to throbbing pain. The knife was pressed to her neck.

She remembered what she had to do, she had to wait for Benoit.

"You're pissing me off. Who the fuck needs you?"

The knife was drawn across Doris's throat almost gently. It barely stung.

There was a shout from the doorway. Sounds of a scuffle. A thump as of a body crashing against a door. Running footsteps. The man was no longer there but his remembered touch kept her in place. A voice screamed, "Friggin' scumbag shit." Silence. Doris barely breathed. An age later she moved her hand, slowly, achingly, she reached upward to touch her wet blouse. Wonderingly, she looked at her fingers, at the rich carmine glistening blood dripping from them. A red mist pulsed in her eyes.

She escaped into blackness.

Chapter Seventy-six

"Don't try to move, don't try to speak, you're safe now."

Doris stared uncomprehendingly into the eyes of Lily Cronin. Safe! Safe from what?

"You're safe now." The words were reiterated but held no meaning. There was something clammy around her neck. Doris tried to pull it away but it was too heavy and her hands were too weak. Everything was too heavy, eyelids, arms, head. She sighed and closed her eyes. This must be a dream. She was lying on the floor. Lily Cronin was in her room using her telephone, wrapping a blanket around her and all the time saying, "You're safe now," asking her to leave the nasty heavy thing across her neck. "I'll get you a fresh towel. Try to hold it tight against your neck, dear."

"*Oh well, it's a dream so I might as well go along with it.*" But it was not pleasant. She was too tired to work it out.

"I've called the ambulance and the police."

"*There's an odd smell in here,*" thought Doris. "*Blood and fish.*"

"I've got rid of the fish and chips," said Lily, "I stood on them when I came in. I know you're not suppose to remove things from the crime scene, but we don't want an accident, do we, dear?"

Doris did not care. This was a silly dream. Lily removed the wet horrid thing from her neck and replaced it with something soft and dry. Now she was on the floor and cradling Doris's head on her lap, gently holding her shoulders, bringing some warmth to the shivering body.

How peculiar, oddly comforting, how weird that even in a dream you could feel so tired. She must go, have a little sleep before Benoit returned. He must be hungry but Lily had thrown the food away. Why was it so cold?

"Listen, Doris, stay with me, stay with me." Lily repeated the words over and over.

Doris tried to lick her lips but even that was too much of an effort. The thing around her neck was again sticky and weighing her down. The blanket covering her and the floor beneath her were sticky and cold, everything was cold except for the cradling arms of Lily Cronin. "Stay with me you're safe now, they won't be long now."

"*I'll come back later,*" Doris thought she said.

She was enclosed, hemmed in, trapped by walls of huge purple flowers, row upon row of purple flowers with faces that leered and bled. Doris lowered her eyes to look at the purple of her arms. This purple was paler and tinged with yellow. She viewed her purple prison and faded arms with equal disinterest. Beyond the walls was a murmur of voices, low but clear. Different voices, same words.

"No improvement."

"Very withdrawn."

"…was such an active person."

"Physically an improvement but…"

"…her family are very worried."

"I'm worried about my mother."

"Been through a terrible shock."

"Recovery slower than anticipated."

"Time. We'll have to give it time."

Were the voices talking about her? Why? What was their concern? She was perfectly safe. Why were they making such a fuss? Nothing could touch her. People said it was too warm and a fan was brought.

"That's better, eh?"

Was it? She felt neither heat nor cold, nor the softness of lips on cheek or forehead from visitors who came through the purple wall and sat with her. Sometimes they talked, sometimes not. It did not matter. It was their life, their decision. She heard little, listening only to the tone and the rhythm and the flow. There was no need for her words. She just had to be.

"It's that coloured boy, been arrested."

"Dreadful business, used to be in and out of the house all the time."

"You never know, do you?"

"...too trusting."

What colour? Doris wondered why people were not more accurate. What did one never know? And if one never knew how did one know that one did not know? Should people not be precise in their speech? It was a puzzle but not of deep concern. She was in a place where nothing could hurt her. Every now and then a man called her name but it was from a long away and she did not reply. She thought his name was Frank.

"Dem talking him bad." The words vibrated through Doris. She turned her head away while the black woman in the wheelchair shouted, "Dem talking him bad and ya got to say someting and he alway' yer friend. Ya hear me? He's a good bwai, ya know the trut', ya've got to talk."

Doris fumbled for understanding.

While the weeping woman was wheeled away a nurse came and needlessly smoothed the creaseless bed covers. "All right dear, don't you worry."

Doris pondered on that. Why should she worry? She gazed at the bleeding purple faces on the undulating wall and, finding them mildly distasteful, closed her eyes.

Chapter Seventy-seven

We're moving you today, Doris. You'll be able to look out of the window, see a bit of life. You'll like that."

"*Shall I?*"

"Nice little room. You can have all your friends and family in there."

"*All of them, all together in a little room, can that be?*" Doris felt slight annoyance tinged with sadness for words chosen without precision and no thought for literal meaning. Why speak unless it was with total truthfulness?

The purple walls were parted and her bed moved. As she passed them she reached out to touch the nodding, bleeding heads. Flowing material brushed her fingers. Curtains not walls. She herself was guilty of inexactitude. There was no honesty even in one's own senses.

Joyce, Gareth, Robert, Andrew, they and a seeming army of people took turns to sit with a silent Doris. She observed their searching falsely smiling anxious faces and heard their words that bore no correlation to their expressions. They ceased to ask questions, but the questions were in their voices. They left unanswered and said silly incomprehensible things like "she's not herself". "*Who else could I be?*" "If we could only take her out of herself." "*If I am someone else then I must be already be out of myself.*"

Doris found it all a little puzzling. For people whose main concern seemed to be for her safety, they were remarkably blind. Somehow she had found herself living in an invisible bubble and it totally shielded her. Sights, sounds, touch reached her, obliquely filtered of anything sharp or inimical. Nothing could ever harm her again, nothing physical, nothing emotional. Why could they not see that she was safe? For her there was only a vague regret for the wasted worry. Nothing mattered. Everyone was going to die. Just a fact of life, nothing to cause misery.

It was pleasant enough when she was alone. Though it never fully engaged her, the television provided a kaleidoscope of colour and movement. The tragedies, war, murder, crime were easy. There was a logic to them. You could quite see why people who had not yet come to terms with the fact of death might be sad, angry, distraught, weeping. It was futile of course, given the nature of things passing but understandable. A nurse would come into the room and cluck, "You don't want to see such misery. You want something cheerful." With a click, the offending programme would be gone to be replaced by one in which the characters looked no happier but laughter poured from the set with all the incomprehensibility of a foreign language. Comedies were difficulty for Doris, mostly based on a false premise with confusion compounded by lack of revelation. The audience knew the truth but they still laughed. How was the bewilderment funny? Doris thought it was cruel.

It was better then to gaze out of the window. Looking at the sky, some dim memory of forgotten hope stirred within her but her mind would not let her grasp this wisp of elusive contentment. At odd moments, she wondered why she was apparently living in a hospital, why some who might have been expected to visit never came. Perhaps they did not know where she was. They had their own lives to live. It did not matter.

For the most part those who came seemed to be demanding something from her. Maybe she was dreaming— must be. Raza Abolhasan came and, holding her hand, ,spoke, not in French but in English. He told her about his family, how he missed his sisters and his mother, the respect

335

he had for his father who wanted to shield him from the brutal reality of life in Iran. He loved his country he said but he knew what was going on. He knew about the executions that never seem to reach the Western press. It was his duty to continue his education and uphold the honour of the family but sometimes his heart was sad when he remembered his cousin who...Doris did not withdraw her hand.

"She's eating all right," said someone.

"*Oh course I am*," thought Doris, "*it is what one does when one is trapped in existence.*"

"Come on, old girl," said a man called Frank, "they all miss you."

She looked away. It did not matter.

One of the few who did not seem to demand was Lily Cronin who spoke without pause. Doris heard only the sound and the rhythm and oddly it put her at her ease. There were no awkward silences, no pauses that bullied for a reply. There was no expectation of her engagement with the words that she rarely heard.

"I had a child once," she said, "I had a child once."

The repetition reached Doris and she half-listened, her eyes searching the clouds for a glimpse of...

"I had a baby but she died. A lively little thing, always kicking and moving. Sometimes when I'm lying in bed I hold my stomach and I can still feel...I don't know why I'm saying all this when I've never told a living soul, I can feel the little kicks like tickling inside and all you want to do is protect something so small and you can't believe you have had a baby growing inside and that baby will be a person and you'll make sure that nothing harms it, and nothing will be too good for it. That's what we thought back then while I was still young and Harry and me were going to be the best parents in the world. My Harry was ever so proud. He'd say, 'Lily, my girl, he'll be a footballer,' but I knew he only said that to tease, because we both wanted a girl, and...you'd think that in there it would be safe. You'd think it would be the safest place in the world. We had such dreams, especially my Harry.

"Then it stopped, the movement. I used to feel it through the palm of my hand and there was just the two of us in the world, like we was sharing a secret, and I would talk to my baby, make promises. Sometimes I let Harry have a touch.

"Then it stopped, the movement. The doctor said it was getting ready to be born but it didn't feel right. They didn't let Harry in. Well they didn't in them days. I can't remember the birth, not really, just the one light bulb that wasn't working when they told me. "The baby died before it was born, Mrs Cronin." I thought I ought to tell them about the light bulb. I worried about that. 'It's best you don't see the little one,' they said, 'best to try and forget. Best not to know.' We listened to them, well you did in them days, and we never spoke about it again, but it wasn't best really, not for me, not for Harry, not for the baby. I was a mother who had never even seen her baby. We was empty and we both cried. One day I couldn't stand it no more and I went to the hospital and asked. First they wouldn't tell me, but a young nurse whispered, 'It was a girl.'

"It sounds odd but I came home feeling happy. I came home to Harry and when he asked where I had been, something came over me. I couldn't tell him and I never have. I couldn't tell him it was a girl when I knew he wanted a girl so much and I'd let him down.

"I still dream of her. I tried not to think and I've never told anybody, I suppose I wouldn't have told you if you were really here. I don't know what made me think of her today, being in the hospital I suppose. Well, I suppose I'd better get my Harry's tea. He said he'd bring in a tape recorder for you, you'll like that, dear."

"*Shall I?*" The contradiction came automatically to Doris.

She had closed her eyes and was trying to remember something else she had heard about a baby.

Chapter Seventy-eight

She'll have to be told."

"Are you sure, she's been through so much?"

"But we can't risk her hearing it from someone else."

"We don't know how much she understands."

"She hasn't spoken at all?"

"Not a word. The doctors say there's no apparent reason why she shouldn't. That's right, isn't it, nurse?

"She just seems to have given up. The wound was superficial but of course the trauma…"

"Well we can't leave this in abeyance, best to get it done."

Doris thought she detected Joyce's voice amongst the other half-familiar voices. If they had something to say let them say it. They were interrupting her search amongst the clouds. There was music playing on the radio, rich, heavy, syrupy, it weighed her down. It pulled her mind from the sky. Chocolate liqueur music. One could have too much of it. The thought startled her. It was as if it had been voiced by someone else inside her head. How could people talk and play music when she was trying to find the baby? The baby was flying in the clouds. No, that was ridiculous, but there was a baby. Elaine was having a baby. No, not that one. A man called Harry told her about a baby once. No, there was another baby a long time ago.

Doris fingered the bandage on her neck. She must ask someone about that sometime.

"Doing fine," they said cheerfully when changing the dressing.

It did not matter.

"Mother."

Joyce, yes it was Joyce, sat awkwardly by the bed, her hand stroking the frail fingers lying passive on the bed clothes. "Mother...I...we have to tell you something sad."

The older woman sighed. The baby had been almost within in her mind's grasp.

"Mother, I don't know if you can under...but you always preferred the truth and we feel...Rose has died, Mother."

The radio was switched off. Out in the corridor a tea trolley clanked and a voice said, "How many for you, love, or are you sweet enough?" There followed a laugh that rattled the window panes and Doris looked at Joyce and said one word very clearly: "Good."

"She doesn't understand," someone said.

"*I understand perfectly well*," thought Doris. "*Rose is dead. No more worries, no more sadness, no more effort to make and I am glad.*" She closed her eyes and her ears to the quiet tears about her. It would all end. It did not matter. The room's murmur rose and fell like the soft sighing of water over pebbles. Doris let herself drift on the flow and in her mind's eye saw the sparkle and the sunlight dancing on bright newly baptised stones. A light breeze idly stirred the sun-dappled leaves on the trees. She slept.

Doris thought that on the whole she would rather the little red-haired nurse did not adjust her hearing-aid every day or whatever the frequency was. Time did not mean a great deal, light and darkness came unbidden and went. People known and unknown came and went unmourned. She awoke to voices when if she had a choice it would have been music, music as light as air to waft her on the summer breeze to the clouds where...

The voices said, "We think it best...away from London... best solution before...something permanent...wonderful places now...two terrible shocks...safe now...police bail...monstrous...black scum...we won't let...list of

339

visitors...sort out house...choose special things...feel at home..."

Were the voices talking about her or to her? Sometimes there were words like murder, jail, death penalty, GBH, ugly words that did not belong in her sphere.

Were they talking not about her but to her? She saw lips moving in faces relentlessly cheerful with eyes that spoke of hate. Doris wished that they would soon realise that there was no love, no hate, just being.

Chapter Seventy-nine

"What the bloody hell is that?" Prionsias strode into the small ward barely controlling his anger.

An anxious nurse followed in his wake. "Mrs Roberts is not to be disturbed."

Prin threw an open envelope onto the bedcovers and barely polite said, "It's all right, nurse, I'm her grandson."

"Five minutes," said the nurse and, looking meaningfully at the irate man, placed the alarm bell near Doris's fingers.

Prin paced back and forth in agitation. He pointed to the letter. "Explain that to me." His voice was low and electric with suppressed rage. He glared at Doris. The eyes that gazed impassively at him bore no signs of comprehension. "What is it? I'll tell you what it is, lies and betrayal. That's what it is. You, you…" Words failed him and he paced again, curling and uncurling his hands into fists. "You knew all along and you said nothing. How could you do that? You bloody lied to us, what kind of crap is that? You, with all your talk of honesty!" He leant his fists on the bed, his voice rose. "You've got to tell me, you must. Come on, Grandma Roberts, you can't retreat, you can't just lie there. Talk to me, God damn it, I've lost one mother already."

Doris thought her hearing-aid was turned up too high. Prin's voice reverberated through her body, invading her, demanding responses she could not give. How could she when she was in sight but somewhere else? The words he spoke meant nothing to her. She could not begin to make sense of them. She could see that he was desperate to reach her, but there were no echoes of feeling within her.

"You're there somewhere, I know you are." His voice was ugly with frustration. "Look, I'll read it to you and you can explain it." Prin snatched up the envelope and ripped the letter from it. "Listen." He stared into her unblinking eyes and she saw the anguish and anger in his. "Dear Doris," he began, then his voice sank to a whisper, "Love Siobáin." He crumpled the paper in his hand and sank onto the bedside chair. "That's my mother, isn't it? You knew. You didn't say. Blast it, you must have known all these years. For fuck's sake—'Dear Doris', 'Love Siobáin'! That's not something come out of the blue unexpectedly, that's bloody familiarity. '"Thank you for your last…' "

He broke off and began to speak almost conversationally. "It was a good funeral. We gave Mum a good send-off but of course you…you were missed. That's all anyone could talk about, what had happened to you, but it had happened to Mum too. She didn't need all that shit when she was dying."

Prin studied the floor in silence. Doris looked at his bent head and then at her quiet fingers as if expecting them of their own accord to touch it. They made no move. Then the moment was gone because her grandson looked up. "She mentions me and the baby, for Christ's sake, and what the hell is this?" He jabbed his finger at the crumpled paper and his voice growing louder with each word quoted: " '…with the tremendous news I am almost tempted to release you from your promise.' What bloody promise?"

The nurse entered the room to find Prin standing over Doris his body rigid with ineffable fury. "I really must ask you to leave now," she said. "Apart from Mrs Roberts, you are disturbing the other patients."

Prin shook her hand from his arm. "I'll never forgive you," he said to Doris.

Doris turned her head away. There never was such a thing as never. It did not matter.

"Come along now," said the nurse firmly, "think of the other patients."

"Other patients?" asked Prin, allowing himself to be led away.

"You can be heard all along the corridor, come into the office; I'll make you a cup of tea."

Chapter Eighty

Doris was rarely alone. A procession of people came and went in her room, doctors, physiotherapists, tea ladies, cleaners, nurses, visitors. She took the medication, food and flowers they gave her, submitting to the routine of eating, washing, walking, bending her limbs to order. Feeling remote from the activity, she became a watcher. From time to time people with grave hesitant faces came to talk earnestly to her. They spoke of the terrible thing that had happened. She grew tired of that phrase as they never specified what the "terrible thing" might be. Was it Rose's death? Because if that was the case there was no cause for worry. She was safe. Doris fingered her neck. The bandage was gone now and she was left with a thin slightly raised scar. Perhaps she was still dreaming. She must be dreaming because what she thought had happened could not possibly have happened. The flashes she experienced must be from a film she had seen when she lived in the now foreign world of feeling. It was a world to which she had no desire to return.

"You're making very good progress, physically at least. We're very pleased with you."

Doris looked out of the window, her eyes as ever drawn to the clouds.

"Your injuries are healing nicely. With your son's agreement we've arranged for a counsellor, a psychotherapist to come and see you."

"*That will be a peaceful encounter,*" thought Doris and found herself smiling inside. The thought surprised and frightened her. She looked furtively at her visitor and her hand crept to cover her mouth.

"That was not without humour," said Frank.

His widow closed her eyes. Suddenly she felt very tired. She awoke to find Joyce and Gareth standing by the window talking quietly together. They turned and advanced towards the bed. Gareth took her hand in his. "We've...it's been very difficult."

"Mother, we've made a decision, Gareth and I, well all the family really."

"We think it's for the best."

"We've decided that you should come home with us, to Robert and me I mean. We'll look after you, Mother. You like coming to stay with us, don't you?"

Gareth squeezed the hand in his. "Then later perhaps you could come up to me. At the moment...well...Rose..."

"Mother we don't know how much you understand. It was terrible what happened to you and then..." Joyce glanced at her brother, "and then Rose dying and now this thing with Prin."

Gareth cut in. "I don't think we need...the main thing, Mum, is that you're looked after and who better than Joyce and Robert to organise it? You know I would if..."

"Mother, the doctor seems to think you will recover, and please God you will, but in the meantime there is not a lot more the people here can do for you and we'll give you all the care and protection you need."

Joyce searched her mother's face for a sign that her words had been understood. "Mother, I wish you would nod or something."

"*Why?*" Doris understood that she was going to be moved just as they had moved her bed from one room to another telling her she would like it. So too would they move her, to another building, far away to her daughter's house. It did not matter, except...would she find what she was looking for in the clouds before she went?

"We'll leave you now, Mother," said Joyce, "it won't be

345

yet awhile. Your move I mean. We'll have time to make a few changes to the house, make it more comfortable for you."

"Love you, Mum." Gareth brushed his lips against his mother's cheek. Doris closed her eyes.

"Are you going to let that happen?" cried Frank. "You always said that much as you loved her you would never live with Joyce." The voice was hardly audible. "Think, Doris, think. You'll never feel rain or wind again." Alone in her room Doris sighed. It did not matter.

Chapter Eighty-one

Doris was sitting in a high-backed bedside chair. In front of her on a mobile trolley were the remains of lunch. She had eaten until she had grown bored with the food, the effort and the movement. Beside her on the bed were books and magazines meant to tempt her back to pursuits that had previously held her in thrall. The books lay neglected, their covers firmly closed upon the demanding, needy, neglected characters within. There lay traps where one could be surprised by emotion. The magazines had been flicked through desultorily and found wanting. The books and magazines had been placed within reach by an optimistic nurse. "Yer daughter say ya like book readin'."

"Ya got a treat this day, Doris," said the same kindly nurse. "Ya got ice-cream. I know it yer favourite."

The woman took away the discarded lunch plate and ungently placed a dish in its place. "Ya'll like that, ya eat it all up," she said and her laughter echoed from the walls.

Doris looked down at the brown spheres of ice-cream melting and muddily staining the cracked glaze of the white bowl. She began to weep. The tears came silently at first, creeping and seeping surreptitiously from her eyes, then wave upon wave of sobs overwhelmed her body until every fibre of her being shrieked with pain. The shriek broke from her lips, a tortured, irrelative sound. She hugged herself and rocked back and forth but still the low-pitched scream shattered the silence.

The door opened swiftly and she was wrapped in warm arms. A soothing voice crooned, "Stop fret yerself ya're a'right now. Stop fret yerself dahling." The words, the warmth worked their slow magic. The sobs finally subsided, the screams faded away.

"Oh my lovely laughing girl. Oh my lovely laughing girl!" Doris said the words over and over again.

Other people came into the ward and ministered to her while the strong arms continued to hold and the gentle motherly voice to soothe until at last exhausted Doris slept.

She awoke, her mind a jumble of words and images... Rose...head thrown back, laughing in the street...Lily Cronin saying, "I suppose I wouldn't be telling you if you were here...", the warring smells of fish and blood...a woman in a wheelchair saying "dem talking him bad", ...hands...unseen hands...not rough but menacing, pushing, teasing, steering where she did not wish to go...ice cream... She awoke knowing that Rose was dead and knowing at least in part the "terrible thing" that had happened to her. It was too much to take in all at once but she must make an effort to get the story straight.

"We've had a breakthrough," said a voice outside her door, "but we don't want to rush things, it's a delicate stage."

"I'll be careful," said Joyce and entered the room. "Hello, Mother," she said brightly, "how are you, dear?"

"Lonely," whispered Doris.

"That was said with more truth than wisdom," said Frank.

Joyce looked taken aback. "Oh!" she exclaimed with a curious bark-like sound that was meant to be a laugh. "We'll soon cure that. You just wait till you come home to stay."

"How long have I been here?"

"Now, Mother, don't you worry about a thing."

Doris thought, "*I'll ask someone who is not trying to be careful.*" There were so many questions. Great care would have to be taken to ask the right ones of the right people. She remained silent for the remainder of Joyce's visit.

The following days were spent making sense of the world in which she found herself. Sleep claimed her often. Visiting was restricted to immediate family, so for the moment she saw only Joyce who was staying in her mother's house for a while "sorting things out" she said. Gareth could come down to London only at weekends. He had to concentrate on his work and try to get his life back together after his wife's death. Doris asked a nurse to dial his number and when a weary voice answered she said simply, "I am so sorry, Gareth."

He said, "I know, Mum, I know."

The phone was replaced in its cradle and the old woman felt closer to her son than she had for a long while.

Reliving the day when she had found Frank's watch was painful but necessary. She remembered sitting in the armchair with her back to the door waiting for Benoit to come with fish and chips. Closing her eyes she tried to see the hand that had drawn the knife across her throat, tried to catch the intonation of the intruder's sneering voice but they were impossible tasks.

When next her nurse came into the ward, Doris asked if Dave Barrett could be called for. The nurse looked doubtful but before she could say a word Doris added, "Don't tell me not to fret. I must have this whole thing cleared up."

She would do what she could said the nurse, then drew Doris's attention to the cards which hung on strings crossing the room wall to wall. Standing on a chair, she took them all down throwing them in a pile on the bed.

"Aren't you the lucky one?" she said. "It will take you all day to read them. They come all the time."

Reading the cards was a bittersweet task that indeed did take all day. The pretty, garish, funny purposeful cards brought an awakening of emotion and more knowledge about her recent life than she had learned from those determined to shield and protect her. Touched by the good wishes and love expressed, she wept a little as she sorted them into piles. There were cards from the family, from

Andrew and members of the church. One came from Mrs Wilmacott threatening to come and cheer her up. Mrs Evans' card spoke of sorting out mail and keeping the house aired for her return. Doris gazed out of the window. Was there not something about a letter that was important? An enormous card was signed by members of the police station. She studied it but only one of the names was known to her, Dave Barrett. "*How very kind,*" she thought and laid the card upside down. There would be a time to face the reason for police involvement in her life but for now the reminder was too painful.

Some people had sent her several cards and some of them were dated indicating that she had been "away" several weeks. What had happened in the meantime while she had lain remote and silent? Had she not heard of an arrest or had she been dreaming? Why was she not being told how things stood, she had after all come through the experience?

Her hand reached for another card. Her breath caught in her throat and she thought she might faint. "Sorry I can't be there for you," it said, it was signed simply, Rose. The grief was too deep for tears. Dry-eyed, she stared at the signature until the letters leapt and swam and there was no longer any meaning to them.

Doris forced herself to return to the task in hand. The mourning would come later, for now there was something nagging at her brain, a job to be done. There were similarities in the messages on a number of the cards. People spoke of coming to see her when it was all over, what did that mean? They would come and see her when she could have visitors. How long had there been a ban in place? "*Surely only in the last few days since I have come back,*" thought Doris. "*I had visitors before, I know I did.*"

So there had been discrimination. One of those barred was Trevor. Doris smiled to herself. Poor out-of-time Trevor with hair exotic as a tropical bird and kindly heart. She could imagine him being turned away, puzzled but accepting. Perhaps not. She remembered how spiritedly he had run after the stone-throwers. Apart from the love and good wishes in the cards, there was also a great deal of hate written on cards showing flowers and ribbons and cute little animals. People hated what had happened to her and the criminal who had irrevocably changed her life.

"Frank," said Doris, "I don't know what to think. It is all too much."

"You'll get there," said Frank, "you always do."

Chapter Eighty-two

I am so angry," said Doris.

"I'm sorry," said Dave Barrett "I came as soon as I got the word."

"I am not angry with you," said Doris impatiently. "It's this wretched phrase." She stabbed her finger at the pile of cards on her bed. "The 'terrible thing' that happened."

"I see," said Dave, not looking at all enlightened.

"It makes me feel so powerless," said Doris, "a victim. I can accept that I'm a statistic but not a victim."

"I see," said Dave and this time he did. "How are you?"

"Ignorant." Doris peered at her visitor "I need someone to tell me the truth. I am surrounded by people treating me like fresh glazed porcelain. I've been fragile but it's not a condition I mean to maintain. Besides how can you progress unless you interview me?"

"We were told you weren't capable of being interviewed."

"I was not here, my mind had abdicated but…"

"…but now you're back." Dave Barrett grinned.

"Right, where shall we start?"

"We'll stop of course if you feel at all distressed."

"I think it may help if I say things out loud." Doris told the tale of her ordeal without interruption from the detective. The telling was painful and distressing. There were frequent pauses for tears and the search for words that would not wound her recovering spirit.

Doris shied away from "knife" and gestured instead to her neck, which she touched frequently with unbelieving fingers. When she had finished, Dave Barrett switched off the recorder and waited till the old woman spoke again. "I don't think I have taken it in. I doubt…that if I truly believed what I tell myself has happened I would ever be able to sleep again." She paused to look beyond Dave to the window where raindrops trapped a shimmering afternoon sun. "It is, the experience I mean, both vividly real and yet has the hazy quality of a dream." She looked directly at Dave Barrett. "I can talk about the event but I am afraid to think about the person involved."

"You're very brave."

Doris flinched as though she had been struck. "That's a tabloid paper word. I am a coward. I can't even mention the names of those I want most to hear about, will you tell…?"

"If I can. What do you…?"

Doris made a small gesture of helplessness. There was so many things she needed to know. Where could she start? "How long have I been here?" she asked.

"Must be about six weeks now."

"Long enough for how many other attempted murders?"

"Three reported."

"As I am a statistic, I feel I have the right to know," said Doris with grim humour.

Dave Barrett looked at her shrewdly. "If you're not too tired, I would like to ask you a few questions."

"You will do no such thing," said an indignant voice. "I expressly left orders that my mother was not to be disturbed."

The detective stood up. "Good afternoon, I was…"

Joyce swept past him. "Mother, this is intolerable after all you've been through."

"I sent for Mr Barrett," said Doris, suddenly overwhelmed with weariness.

"But there's no reason for you to be involved. They've got the murderer. Oh I can't bear to say his name. Lily Cronin identified him running from your place after…"

Joyce waved her hand as if to ward off the evil of the word she could not use.

Doris said quietly. "I was not murdered."

Dave Barrett slipped the tape recorder into his pocket. "I'll go," he said to Doris. "I can see that you're tired now. I'll come back when you feel up to it."

"There will be no need," said Joyce. "It's all over."

Neither she nor the departing man heard Doris whisper, "Who?" Her chest felt tight and her neck throbbed. She rested her head against the chair back and closed her eyes while Joyce swept the cards from the bed and destroyed the order into which they had been sorted. She spoke of her plans for the future, how wonderful it would be to have her mother at home with her and Robert. They would protect her and she need never even think about this dreadful time again nor be bothered by any of the peculiar people she had surrounded herself with of late.

Joyce with no more to rearrange sat at last and blamed herself for allowing Doris to get into such a situation. "I should have realised how lonely you were when Father died. It made you vulnerable, prey to all sorts. You are so naïve and, of course, you always did have a blind faith in the most unlikely people. We should have insisted then that you come home with us. Well I won't make that mistake again; we'll look after you from now on. We thought we'd do up your bedroom, perhaps a pretty pastel yellow, you'll like that."

"*Shall I?*" queried Doris silently. She felt herself diminishing within the wall of words that grew around her. Perhaps Joyce was right, maybe she had been foolish with unrealistic expectations of life, never attuned to the "still sad music of humanity". Perhaps she would never again have the strength to face reality, perhaps she never had. She would be sheltered in Joyce and Robert's house, loved, cosseted. Only a selfish person would complain about that. Others could make decisions for her. That way nobody would be upset. "Go with the flow." Was that not what If had said all those months before?

"Doris, are you really so feeble that you can't be a witness to your own crime?" Frank's voice was so faint that his widow hardly heard it.

Chapter Eighty-three

O f course you can have visitors, Mother," said Joyce. "Now that the doctors say you are as well as can be expected…"

"*At your age…*" added Doris in her mind.

"…it's just that we don't want anyone to upset you. We were all very angry with Prionsias when he came ranting and raving after he'd found the letter. Apparently you'd known all along about his mother and had kept in touch with her. From what we can make out you were sworn to secrecy and of course that would appeal to your romantic nature."

"*Romantic! Is that how you describe a moral dilemma?*"

"Anyway," Joyce continued, "he's written to her, told her why you can't and about his mother, about Rose I mean. Oh it's all so confusing. We'll just have to wait and see if she replies."

The decorating was coming along wonderfully, she said, moving onto safer ground. Doris wondered how she knew, she never seemed to be away from the hospital. During one of her rare absences, Doris rang David Barrett. "The day that you came here I wanted to show you something."

"Yes." He sounded distant. He was a busy man she had better tell him quickly.

"I wanted to show you a card I received."

"Yes." He sounded even further away.

"It was a card, a collective card from Obsidian. There were two names missing from those one would have expected to sign it."

"And those were?"

Doris took a deep breath. "Derek and Benoit," she said. "When I studied them more closely I noticed that Ritzy had included her brother's name in her greeting. She wrote it for the two of them, I recognised her writing."

The line went silent for a moment. "I'm sorry, Doris, I thought you knew. We arrested the young Johnson lad."

"No—" Doris stifled a sob, "—but he did not...he would not...there was a scuffle, he ran after the assailant. I told you." She fought very hard to keep her voice steady. "Where is he?"

"Out on bail, one of the conditions being that he has no contact with you. Look I was actually on my way out. We need to get a statement from you if possible. Would you feel up to an interview?"

"*Yes*," thought Doris, "*but not to the wrath of my daughter.*" "I am very tired," she said.

"And feeble," said Frank.

"I'm sorry. I'll be in touch." The phone went dead.

"Hello, Mother, how are you today?" Joyce came into the room looking happy. "It's all arranged. We're going to take you home tomorrow, won't that be nice?"

Doris tried to return the smile. "Did you know that Benoit was arrested?" she asked.

"Of course," her daughter replied, sounding surprised. "I told you the other day, don't you remember?"

"You said they got the murderer, it didn't cross my mind that you meant Benoit. It is terrible, how could it have happened? I don't understand. It is all wrong. I should help but..."

"Don't you waste any sympathy on him. He was covered in your blood when they picked him up. He nearly knocked Lily Cronin over as he ran out but...listen, Mother." Joyce sat down and took her mother's hands in hers, looking earnestly into her eyes. "We love you and we want what's best for you. I know how painful this is, you placed your trust in the wrong people and you were horribly betrayed.

It is in the hands of the police now. They interviewed all of us and we told them everything we could. There's nothing you can do but try to put it out of your mind. We'll help you to do that when you come home with us, so you can leave all this ugliness behind." She smiled brightly at her mother. "At your age surely you deserve a bit of peace and not be pestered as you have been, it is an outrage."

Both women turned to the light of the window. Doris felt that she was moving in a fog, everywhere she turned her hand touched something strange and repugnant as it rushed past her in the darkness. Unseen forces were pushing her in a direction of their choosing. No longer did she have any control over her life. Rodney had been murdered and then a man had tried to kill her. Rose was dead. Her friend cruelly used. Her whole life was turned upside down and changed forever. Nothing made sense. Time was needed to get everything straight in her mind, but was there time? "What do you mean 'pestered as you have been?' "

Joyce flushed slightly. "Why, those group members, that wretched boy and that policeman. I told him but he didn't seem to think there was anything he could do."

"What boy, pestered how?"

"The letters, as soon as he was released. It's a disgrace, it must be against the bail conditions, but that detective didn't want to know. We…"

"Bail? You mean Benoit wrote to me?" Doris felt bewildered. "Why did…"

"You've been through enough horror. He'd even got those friends of his to come but we put a stop to that."

Doris kept silent. Benoit had been arrested, jailed, freed and had tried to get in touch her to help prove his innocence. No wonder his grandmother had said, "Dem talking him bad, ya've got to tell dem."

"*Oh Benoit, I am so sorry, I have let you down.*"

Doris said in a voice that trembled, "Where are the letters, Joyce?"

"That's all behind you now, don't worry yourself."

The old woman feigned sleep. *"I am not going to be told anything, not about Benoit nor Rose nor Prin nor anything disturbing. Is she right? Maybe I should not ask questions. Maybe I am just making things awkward for everyone."*

"That's right, Mother, you sleep," said Joyce and kissed Doris before tip-toeing out.

"The pale yellow sounds lovely," whispered Doris.

"That's right, Doris," said Frank, "you just abdicate."

Chapter Eighty-four

Wind rattled the windows and rain drummed upon them as Doris lay sleepless and meditative. At her request, the curtains had been left open so that she could see the demented thrashing of trees black against the impenetrable grey of night. Meagre reflections of light shimmered and danced on the streaming raindrops. There was comfort in the wildness and the dark. She lay in warmth and safety while outside flailing, cracking branches creaked and groaned, driven to a frenzy by an angry wind.

Outside the ward door was another sort of life, a quieter life, still, anticipatory, the dimly lit corridor silent but for a faint thrumming sound, like the breath of a sleeping animal. Doris felt that she was timelessly cocooned between the two states and yet she knew that the dawn would push cold shafts of light through the warm blackness. She only had this night to try to think clearly.

"You'll never feel wind or rain again," Frank had said. Was that so bad? She seemed to have reached yet another turning-point in her life, or had her fate been sealed when the knife had been drawn across her throat? Maybe that was the point from which there was no return. Tomorrow, no, later this morning, she would get into a car with Joyce. "It's all been sorted out, Mother, too painful for you to go back to that room. We'll have all your things sent on."

All her things! All the letters she had kept over the years from Siobáin!

Siobáin, would she understand that the promise had not been broken, at least not deliberately? Doris thought about that promise, easy enough to keep when neither Rose nor Prin showed any need of the truth, but fraught with difficulty once curiosity had been aroused. "I'll never forgive you," Prin had said.

A particularly loud thunderclap caught Doris by surprise and almost immediately lightening momentarily lit the sky and the louring drama of the clouds. A nurse put her head around the door and whispered, "Are you all right, love, are you awake?"

"Yes and yes," said Doris.

"Fancy a cuppa?"

"That would be lovely."

The nurse returned giggling with two steaming mugs and sat on the bed. "I'm not really suppose to do this," she said, "but I had an idea you'd be awake."

"I am going tomorrow," said Doris. "I'm going to live with my daughter." She thought she would try the words out for size.

"Oh that's a shame," said the nurse. "Oh!" She put her hand to her mouth "I'm sorry I didn't mean it like that. I meant it's a shame you're going. Oh that sounds dreadful too. You wouldn't want to stay in hospital."

"It's all right, dear," said Doris. "I think I know what you mean."

They sipped their tea and watched the storm. "Are you afraid?"

"I am confused. I know I have been here for weeks but in my mind it has only been a few days and now I'm leaving. I can't get things straight in my mind. I don't even know how my daughter-in-law died."

"Oh that's terrible, you poor thing."

Sitting in the dark of the early morning it was easy to pour out the fears and doubts and random thoughts that seemed unconnected with anything.

"Do you know what I miss most, Sally?"

"What do you miss?"

"I miss laughing. Doesn't that sound silly? I've always thought of myself as a happy person."

"It's not silly. You'll be fine," said Sally. "If you want to—you're half there. Look I'd better go. Try and get some sleep now, eh!"

Doris looked at the scudding clouds and thought until her eyes closed and at last she slept.

In the morning she awoke, arose, got dressed and asked for the telephone. She made several phone calls, one of them being to Dave Barrett.

"Mr Barrett, Dave," she said without preamble, "you said there were three attempted murders since mine. What was the nature of them? I mean what were the methods?"

"I think I'm ahead of you, Doris, but I don't think the phone…As it happens I'm on my way to the hospital, would it be all right if I popped in?"

"Please do. My daughter will coming to collect me later on this morning."

While she waited, she re-read the cards that Joyce had tidied away. Her nurse in whose arms she had awoken to realisation had retrieved them, along with several that had lain unopened, from the bottom of the locker.

"All right, love." Several nurses looked in on her while she read notes from people who said they did not know what to say, yet in the very act of writing were more than adequately expressing their concern. When she had finished, her eyes as ever were drawn to the sky. Why? She tried hard but no memory came.

"Come in," she said in reply to the knock on the door but Dave Barrett was already in the room.

"Are you sure you're up to this?" he asked before sitting down. "There's been a breakthrough and we're about to make an arrest."

Doris nodded. "Tell me about the attempted murders," she said.

"There was a domestic, a bottling, nasty business. There

was a petrol station hold-up, sawn off shotgun that one and…"

"Yes." Doris bent forward eagerly.

"There was a stabbing."

"Yes."

"I'm sorry, Doris, this may be painful for you."

"Just tell me who was the victim."

"I believe he was a friend of yours, Paul Duggan."

"The *Big Issue* lad, oh I am sorry. What happened, how is he?"

"He's on the mend. Before I go any further, why did you want to know about the attempted murders?"

"I did not sleep last night what with the storm and thoughts of…Oh well I had plenty of time to ponder. Nobody would tell me anything and so I began to think that perhaps I had some of the answers myself. I wondered if anyone else had been hurt with a broad knife." Doris dropped her voice and muttered something.

"I'm sorry," said Dave, "what did you say?"

"You will think I am fanciful but I said a broad knife, warm to the touch except at the tip. Of course the relevance of that would not be apparent to some."

"No, no, carry on. What did you have in mind?"

"Mind is right. I have been seeing it in my mind's eyes, the knife, the hand that held it, where it came from. I think he kept it attached to his arm, in contact with his bare skin except for the tip which was protected by some sort of strap arrangement. All but the end of the blade was warm on my cheek. I remember feeling what I took to be a wristwatch but further up than normal. It touched my face. I did not give it much thought at the time."

Dave looked doubtful.

"Anyway, that's my theory," said Doris. "Tell me about Paul, why was he attacked?"

"We thought at first it was for his takings, poor sod, but now that seems to be secondary to shutting him up."

"Oh."

"We've been waiting to be able to get a statement from him."

"You have had to do a lot of that," Doris said, "waiting."

Dave Barrett grinned. "I usually get them in the end."

"Is he badly injured?"

"Yes, a collapsed lung, but as I say he's on the mend and talking, better late than never."

Doris heard something harsh and unrelenting in his tone. She looked questioningly at him. "He saw someone run from your place and then he saw the Johnson boy run out afterwards. Stupid bastard didn't come forward, wanted to keep his head down. When he heard what had happened, he thought you'd know who had knifed you so there was no need to say anything. Daft bugger."

"Could he identify…?"

"Oh yes," said Dave grimly. "It was a face-to-face encounter. Paul had not kept quiet, he was meant to know who…anyway he's talking now."

"Will he…?"

"Testify, yes?"

Doris's eyes strayed to the window. "It was drugs was it not, the need for money?"

There was a long pause before Dave answered, "Yes. You knew?"

"Yes, I used to see him go to the van but I had no idea…No, no excuses. Yes, I knew."

They both sat with their own thoughts, then, "Will you be a witness?"

"Yes…and Dave."

"Yes."

"When you pick up Derek, put my theory to the test. You will search him of course. Look on his arms. You know, I've watched a lot of television over the years. Anyone who is searched, up go the hands virtually ignored, (not in all cases of course) and the body and legs are…frisked, is that the word?"

"Right. Doris, you should know he is also being linked to Rodney's murder."

"Yes I thought so, and Benoit?"

"Just a few formalities and he'll be able to visit you."

"Please God he will want to."

Chapter Eighty-five

Dave Barrett departed and Doris prepared for Joyce's arrival. Her nurse had propped open the door and there was great to-ing and fro-ing as people popped in to say their farewells. Her things were packed. She sat in her outdoor clothes in a wheelchair waiting to be pushed to the hospital entrance. She smiled and said her thanks and ached because now that some of the living were sorted out she could begin to mourn the dead. It was odd that she should feel so sad when the picture of Rose she carried in her head was one of laughter and joyous life. She was looking towards the window when she heard footsteps come into the room. "*Maybe I look to the sky because it so vast and mysterious, both open and secretive hiding behind clouds.*"

"All set then, Mother?" said Joyce.

Doris turned in the wheelchair and said very clearly, "No."

A spider in the far corner could be heard spinning a web.

"What do you mean? Are you not well?"

"I am not going to live with you, Joyce."

"You mean you're not coming home today."

"I am going home, but I am going to my own home."

"You can't." Joyce sat on the bed. "You can't go back there. It's all arranged. Your room has been done up especially, I told you."

"And it will not go to waste because I'll come to visit, often, if I may, but not now."

"But how can you, how can you think of going back there, where it happened?"

"Do you not see, love, that is precisely why I must, even if it is just for a short while and alone. It was a 'terrible thing' and it changed my life entirely for as long as I let it. Now I am saying Stop, I will take it from here. I feel, what is the modern word, empowered. That poor boy nearly took my life, I am not going to give the rest of it to him on a plate. I am going to go back to my books and my music and my little nips of gin and, the biggest of all, I am going to learn to trust people again. Without that I might as well be dead."

"But…"

"I am sorry, Joyce, I really am sorry, knowing what efforts you have made, but I can't fit neatly into your plan. Old and arthritic and more feeble than I was I'll need a great deal of help, I know that and one day I dare say I'll have to go into an old people's home. Is it too much to ask that that day should be, while I am capable, a day of my own choosing?" Doris searched her daughter's flushed face and felt a great rush of love for her. "Please try to understand, love. I have to do this. I have to go home. I have a great many fences, or should that be bridges, to mend, explanations to give, apologies to make, and please God, friendships and relationships to re-establish. It has dawned on me that, if I have the courage to take it, I have one more chance to make things right. I need to face my fears or be destroyed by them. I'll go to court and bear witness and if one of those tabloid newspapers calls me brave, I'll sue."

"Bravo," said Frank. "Bravo."

At that moment, a deep-throated engine rent the air. Doris turned towards the window to see Concorde soaring majestically across the sky. Her heart gave a leap of recognition. She smiled at her daughter.

Joyce struggled to keep her voice steady. "And I suppose you've already sorted it all out? The nurse said you had been on the phone since dawn."

"Yes I have rung Mrs Evans and Andrew, I hope there will be some friends awaiting me at home. Darling, I know it is asking a lot—will you take me there?"

The question hung in the air while the two women gazed at one another. Joyce at last lowered her eyes and reached out to cover Doris's hand with hers. "Welcome back," she said with an odd sideways smile. She stood decisively and took hold of the wheelchair. "Come along, Mum, let's get you to your home." She bent and briefly rested her cheek against her mother's.

"Then when I've settled down a bit," Doris's voice could be heard as they moved along the corridor towards the lift, "I feel that I should get out more. I have been too engrossed in my own small world. There is so much to be done and to see, parks, entertainments, galleries. I've been reading too about the Dome and I want to judge that for myself. The one thing I really want to do is go up in the London Eye in the Sky. There is no time to lose because, like me, I'm told it is temporary.

THE END